She never expected her morning jog to turn into running for her life...

Kate jumped behind a tree as soon as she realized what she was watching. But one of the men spotted her. He said something to the other man and his hand went to his waist. Kate couldn't see if he had a gun, but she didn't wait to find out. As she turned and started to run, she heard one door slam then another as the trucks' engines roared to life. Along the edge of the ridge, Kate paused to look back. A billowing trail of dust enveloped the blue pickup as it raced away. The other truck, the four-wheel-drive, pulled off the road, onto the trail, and headed for Kate.

Running for exercise and running when a drug dealer's truck was after you required the same leg movements, but that was the only similarity. Kate ran for her life. Her feet pounded the desert floor as she sprinted along the Jeep trail. It took her at a right angle from the truck's path. She wanted to cut though the brush to where the trail narrowed and headed directly toward civilization. But jumping around the thick vegetation—that included prickly pear—would slow her progress too much. She thought her long legs would carry her to safety when she heard the whine of the engine and saw the truck's cab appear over the ridge. A black steel framework—some sort of extra bumper—protected the front of the truck and added to its menace.

The truck hit the top of the rise and crashed down the slope, kicking up dirt as it picked up speed. The roar of its engine grew louder, but Kate couldn't waste the seconds it would take to look back again. She heard a grinding noise as the pickup jostled over rocks. No cell phone, no way to protect herself, except speed, Kate pushed into high gear as if she were racing down the basketball court on a fast break with ten seconds to go.

Metallic thunder from the truck's gears and screaming exhaust echoed right behind her.

Nostalgia City executive Kate Sorensen finds the body of a mechanic crushed under an automobile hoist in the theme park's garage. Accident or murder? Will it impact Kate's decision to become advisor for one of two competing statewide campaigns to legalize marijuana in Arizona?

When the death is ruled a homicide and the DEA stages a surprise raid, park cab driver Lyle Deming is recruited to help solve the murder and find out if the park's garage is being used to smuggle drugs. The sometimes erratic ex-cop is soon poking around a Mexican border town, looking for a park contractor who might be a drug mule. Or he might be dead.

Meanwhile, Kate is dragged into a dangerous, high-stakes race to control the legal pot market in Arizona. Amid setbacks and threats, she and Lyle must sort through a tangle of complex evidence and shifty suspects.

Then there's another murder.

The Marijuana Murders is the third novel in this mystery series set in Nostalgia City, a theme park that re-creates—in every detail—a small town as it would have appeared in the 1970s.

Praise for Mark S. Bacon

The Marijuana Murders

"Bacon deftly blends nostalgia and crime. If you're looking for a mystery that touches on today's issues while harking back to earlier eras, *The Marijuana Mysteries* does so in a fast pace with humor and style." ~ Debbi Mack, New York Times bestselling author of the Sam McRae Mystery Series

"Visit the Nostalgia City theme park, where the 1970s are alive and well, and the murders are dope. Suspects are as plentiful as bell bottoms at the disco, and the mystery as twisty as a vintage roller coaster." ~ Becky Clark, author of the Mystery Writer's Mysteries

Desert Kill Switch

"This is the kind of book where you keep saying 'just one more chapter." ~ Anne Saller, owner, Book Carnival Mystery Bookstore, Orange, Calif.

"…straight out of classical detective fiction…told at a fun, engine-revving pace." ~ *Ellery Queen Mystery Magazine*

"Bacon's prose is slick, his dialogue taut, and he makes great use of short chapters to tempt the reader to keep turning those pages. His creation of Nostalgia City, a retro theme park in which nothing older than 1975 is allowed, is a stroke of genius." ~ Mark Campbell, *Promoting Crime (UK)*

Death in Nostalgia City

"The book pulled me in from the very beginning and never let me go." ~ Open Book Society

"Bacon is an excellent storyteller...readers won't be able to put this book down." ~ Karen Hancock, Bella Online's Suspense/Thriller Books Editor

"Off-beat ex-cop Lyle Deming pursues suspects with an intensity bordering on obsession. He frustrates his younger partner with his questionable logic and his puzzling references to '60s and '70s trivia he knows well. Reading this theme park thriller is more fun than winning a trivia contest and riding your favorite wooden coaster on the same day!" ~ Wilson Casey, syndicated columnist, author, and Guinness World Record trivia guy

"'Accidents' are intentional and the incidents are piling up. Bad press is adding to the pressure of keeping the park afloat. There is danger, murder, secrecy, a bit of romance, and down-to-the-wire, hold-your-breath anticipation. I truly do wish there existed, a Nostalgia City." ~ Linda Marsheells, LibraryThing top 1% reviewer

"A rollicking good read! That's how I would describe Mark S. Bacon's novel, *Death in Nostalgia City*. It's a page turner, a fast-paced mystery....Bacon plots well, characterizes well, and writes well. In addition, "Nostalgia City" turns Disneyland into Magic Mountain into Dollywood into Wall Street into the mean streets of New York City, a winning collage of baby boomer fantasies and reminiscences." ~ Ann Ronald, Bookin' with Sunny Reviews

The Marijuana Murders

A Nostalgia City Mystery #3

Mark S. Bacon

A Black Opal Books Publication

GENRE: MYSTERY/THRILLER

This is a work of fiction. Names, places, characters and incidents are either the product of the author's imagination or are used fictitiously, and any resemblance to any actual persons, living or dead, businesses, organizations, events or locales is entirely coincidental. All trademarks, service marks, registered trademarks, and registered service marks are the property of their respective owners and are used herein for identification purposes only. The publisher does not have any control over or assume any responsibility for author or third-party websites or their contents.

THE MARIJUANA MURDERS
Copyright © 2019 by Mark S. Bacon
Cover Design by Jacci Larsen
All cover art copyright © 2019
All Rights Reserved
Print ISBN: 9781644371091

First Publication: MARCH 2019

All rights reserved under the International and Pan-American Copyright Conventions. No part of this book may be reproduced or transmitted in any form or by any means, electronic or mechanical, including photocopying, recording, or by any information storage and retrieval system, without permission in writing from the publisher.

WARNING: The unauthorized reproduction or distribution of this copyrighted work is illegal. Criminal copyright infringement, including infringement without monetary gain, is investigated by the FBI and is punishable by up to 5 years in federal prison and a fine of $250,000. Anyone pirating our ebooks will be prosecuted to the fullest extent of the law and may be liable for each individual download resulting therefrom.

ABOUT THE PRINT VERSION: If you purchased a print version of this book without a cover, you should be aware that the book is stolen property. It was reported as "unsold and destroyed" to the publisher, and neither the author nor the publisher has received any payment for this "stripped book."

IF YOU FIND AN EBOOK OR PRINT VERSION OF THIS BOOK BEING SOLD OR SHARED ILLEGALLY, PLEASE REPORT IT TO: lpn@blackopalbooks.com

Published by Black Opal Books **http://www.blackopalbooks.com**

The Marijuana Murders

A Nostalgia City Mystery #3

Chapter 1

That can't be blood, there's too much of it. Kate Sorensen watched the automobile hoist lift the 1975 sedan off the garage floor. As the car rose, inch by inch, she peered under it looking at a damp, red area three feet wide. Seconds later, the lift operator on the other side of the car staggered backward, gagging. Kate moved toward him.

"No," the mechanic sputtered as he held up a hand. "*Esta muerto.* Dead."

Kate still took tentative steps toward the car suspended four feet off the ground. She peered around the left rear fender then took in a breath as if there were no oxygen left in the building. Beneath the car, a leg and arm squashed into pulp, lay on the concrete. Kate looked away before she saw more.

"We've got to call for help," she said. She forced her legs to carry her to a counter where she'd left her purse—and cell phone. Her footfalls echoed through the cavernous auto repair facility, nearly deserted this early in the morning. She dialed 9-1-1.

"There's been an accident. The Nostalgia City garage. Someone's dead." She paused for a moment to breathe and steady herself. "My name is Kate Sorensen. Yes, Nostalgia City, the theme park. I'm in the garage complex. No, it doesn't have an address that I know of. The thing's as big as an aircraft hangar. The sheriff knows where it is. They can get access through the park's emergency entrance."

When Kate hung up, she knew she should also call security, but there was no time. She looked at her watch. Five fifty-one a.m. The TV crew she arranged would be there any minute. Too late to cancel. They were coming more than 100 miles up from Phoenix. The show must go on. And what would the show broadcast about the park? A bloody corpse, a ghastly accident that crushed an employee?

Kate could do nothing for the victim, but she had to keep the TV cameras out of this area. She knew well the TV news maxim, *if it bleeds, it leads.* She stared at the wide-open metal roll-up door and the parking lot outside. She could imagine the TV van appearing any second.

The mechanic walked toward her on unsteady legs, his face pale. She thought he'd thrown up. She didn't have the luxury.

"Can we close this door?" she asked.

The mechanic seemed to have trouble swallowing. He stared without expression.

"I know, horrible. But the sheriff won't be here for a few minutes and I need help. I'm expecting a TV crew almost any time. Can we close this door and let them in at the other end of the garage? You can come back and open the door for the sheriff."

The man blinked, trying to regain his composure. He looked up at Kate. Her Nostalgia City name badge identified her as vice president of public relations.

"*Si*, okay…yeah." With trembling hands, he pushed a button and the wide metal door clanked as it descended. "This way. Follow me. We open the west entrance."

The mechanic, dressed in blue work clothes, had the name *Luis* written on a patch over his breast pocket. At first, Kate followed him, but then her long legs and nervous energy propelled her past him. A head shorter than Kate, he hustled to keep up.

They passed rows of service bays occupied by cars from the '60s and '70s, nearly all built before Kate was born. Maintaining a fleet of forty- and fifty-year-old curiosities—most used as rental cars—was a key to the success of Nostalgia City, the elaborate retro theme park. She'd planned to feature the classic cars and the park's vast automobile restoration facility when she invited Tamara Cox, a host of *Rise 'n' Shine, Phoenix*, to broadcast a portion of her morning show from the park.

Prepared for her on-air appearance in an emerald dress with her long blonde hair gathered behind her head, Kate reached the west entrance several steps ahead of Luis. She paced as she watched the mechanical door roll up. She wasn't being heartless. The man was already dead. She couldn't help him. She had her job to do.

Kate stood at the end of the restoration garage, hundreds of feet away and around a corner from the accident scene. Luis finished raising the door then turned and headed back.

Kate's cell phone rang. The camera van was rolling down a back street in Nostalgia City. She managed to direct them to the west end of the garage. As Kate watched a few employees arrive early for work, she saw the red and gold Channel 9 TV truck. She considered it a PR coup, persuading Cox to broadcast part of her show from Nostalgia City. Cox had a solid following in Arizona, and Kate hoped her credibility and charm would rub off on the park, *provided no one stumbles over a flattened corpse.*

When the truck stopped just outside the garage, Cox got out. She wore a dress and blazer and walked up to Kate extending a hand. "Good to see you, Kate," she said. "Looking good this morning. You don't even need much makeup. I'm envious. You look stunning."

Stunned is more like it.

"May we pull the truck inside?" Cox asked.

"Sure," Kate said.

She stepped back, and the camera truck rolled forward. Two crew members got out and started setting up a camera and sound equipment. Kate turned around, glancing up and down the service bays searching for an interesting background. Unfortunately, most of the cars at this end of the building were new arrivals, beat-up refugees from who-knows-where. Kate would have to shift gears. She and Tamara would focus on the "before" aspect of the automobile restoring process. Kate told herself to concentrate on just what she had to do, nothing else.

She looked to her left and spotted a bright, two-toned convertible, probably a rental in for a tune-up. The aged vehicle looked brand new.

"You could get lost in here," Cox said looking around, "and they'd never find you."

Kate put on a smile she didn't feel. "Welcome to the center of Nostalgia City's car culture. We could start the interview in front of that convertible over there."

Cox nodded and asked her camera person to check out the lighting near the new-looking rag-top sedan.

"Since you opened," Cox said, "lots of stories have already covered your mid-1970s town, and your Fun Zone with the movie-themed rides. A behind-the-scenes view of the world largest theme park is a good idea. It is the world's largest, right?"

"In terms of square miles, Disney World is slightly bigger. We like to say it's the living history theme park and resort. Or just one-of-a-kind."

"Or the most expensive?"

Kate knew her talking points as well as a seasoned politician. It helped her extoll the virtues of the park, even though her mind kept traveling back to the dried blood and the lifeless limbs. "We're not *in*expensive," she said, "but we do have special school days and discounts for service members and vets. What I'd like to talk about today is our accuracy and authenticity. Everything here is as close as possible to 1975."

"And you have authentic examples to show on camera."

"Right," Kate said, and she froze.

A siren wailed from a distance then reverberated throughout the building making talking impossible.

"What's going on?" Cox asked as the siren faded.

"An accident this morning," Kate said.

"What kind of accident? Anyone hurt? The news director is always pestering me to jump on breaking stories. Can we go see?"

Chapter 2

"Is that a joint?" Lyle asked.

"Shhh, man. I'm on the air."

"Now?"

"Not this second."

"Then give me a hit."

"Wait a minute," the other man said. He flipped a switch on the console and spoke into the microphone hanging in front of his face. "This is Big Earl Williams on K-B-O-P, oh-fficial radio station of No-stalgia City. You just heard 'Black Water,' the new hit from the Doobie Brothers. I like that *name*." Earl winked at Lyle "Next up, somethin' from the Temptations, right after these messages."

Earl hit a couple of buttons then turned in his swivel chair and pulled his earphones down around his neck. "Lyle Deming, my man. You can't have a hit now. Aren't you supposed to be driving your taxi around the park this a.m.?"

"I was kidding." Lyle leaned back in his chair, trying to find legroom in the cramped broadcasting booth and wondering why the park didn't give their star DJ a bigger studio. "I've got to drive a four-hour, fill-in shift for someone today. Anyway, it's kinda early to toke up, don't you think?"

"I ain't *tokin' up*, as you put it. Just a couple of puffs so Big Earl can mellow out for his morning countdown show. Just two. Late night last night."

Earl took his second puff and held his breath as he extinguished the tapered cigarette and put it in a small metal box that originally held breath mints.

"Here, hand me that spray," Earl said pointing to a can of air freshener. He grabbed the can and waved it over his head, spraying imaginary shapes in the air above his radio console. A sweet pine scent replaced the faint smell of marijuana. "Can't be too careful."

"Expecting anyone?"

"The station manager drops in sometimes." Earl tucked his metal box into a pocket of his battered canvass jacket.

"Didn't you know, marijuana's illegal?" Lyle said. "Aren't you afraid I'll bust you?"

"Yeah, sure. How long's it been since you were on the Phoenix PD?"

"Not long enough. But I could have a badge tucked away. Maybe I can still arrest your ass."

"A badge? You crazy? The way you got booted from the department, I bet they don't even let you into doughnut shops anymore."

Lyle was ready with a return insult, but Earl held up a hand, pulled on his earphones, and slid in front of the mike. Every time Lyle had a snappy—or rude—comeback, Earl had to say something on the air. But Lyle always came back for more. Visiting with his old friend from Phoenix was one of the benefits of working at Nostalgia City. They first met at a radio station when Earl was the top-rated oldies DJ in the city and Lyle was a homicide detective who had volunteered to record a public service announcement.

Lyle left the police department when two senior officers conspired to force him out of the department amid allegations of mental illness when he wouldn't cooperate in manufacturing evidence in a case. He refused to fight his termination because he ached for a stress-free job. Driving a taxi in a theme park seemed the perfect escape from forever worrying about the broken lives of murder victim's families. Earl left Phoenix shortly after Lyle did when Nostalgia City offered him more money. A lot more money.

"Remember," Earl intoned into the microphone, "The Xanadu Boutique. Unique gifts, clothing, and *other* items. If you remember it from the seventies, you'll find it here in Nostalgia City at the Xanadu Boutique."

"Xanadu is advertising?" Lyle asked when Earl turned off his mike.

"Concessionaires get a few freebees, but Xanadu bought a whole *flight* of commercials. *They* like my program."

"It's a popular place. Guests are always asking me to take them to the head shop. Do you play pot songs before their commercials?"

Earl shrugged. He reminded Lyle of Mean Joe Greene and weighed in about the same as the football player did in his prime, although Earl was probably a little past his prime. But then, what *was* your prime? Being on the other side of fifty, Lyle was still waiting for his.

"I don't have to pick anything special, y'know," Earl said. "Plenty o' pot songs to choose from."

"Like 'Puff the Magic Dragon,'" Lyle said.

"Hey, Peter Yarrow always said that song wasn't about grass."

"Yeah, and 'Along Comes Mary' was about Mary Poppins."

"Mary Poppins smoked dope?"

"You're the dope, Williams. You don't know 'Along Comes Mary'?"

"The Association." Earl said. "Nineteen sixty-six."

"Yeah, that's an easy one. I wasn't trying to stump you."

"Stump me? You? Never."

Lyle took off his yellow cabbie hat and ran his fingers through his dark brown hair. He loved their favorite pastime, challenging each other with rock trivia. He rubbed his chin and made a show of thinking. "'Judy Mae,'" Lyle said.

Earl stared at him.

"How about Rod Stewart?" Lyle asked.

"Are you messin' with me? Rod Stewart did '*Maggie May*.'"

"Okay, who is it?"

"You hadda look that one up, bro. *No one* remembers that. But Big Earl knows the business. This *sort-of* hit was from Boomer Castleman, nineteen hundred and seventy-nine."

"Big Earl, when are you going on *Jeopardy*?"

Earl smiled and flipped him off.

"Is there anything you *don't* know?" Lyle said.

Earl pointed to a notice he'd stuck to the wall with tape. "I don't know what *this* means."

Printed on Nostalgia City letterhead, the notice said, "The Transition is coming. Ask your supervisor."

"Everybody knows what the transition is," Lyle said.

"No, they don't. I hear people talkin' about it. Maybe no big deal for some. Right? Except for *me*."

"So does that mean you're going to play—"

Earl interrupted with a wave of his hand. "Don't even start. I gotta feeling—" He paused when a light on his console flashed, telling him he had a phone call. He answered then handed the phone to Lyle. "It's for you."

"Yeah, Rey," Lyle said. "Sure. I know Don Perez. What do you mean, *was* he a friend of mine?"

Chapter 3

"Tamara," Kate said when the TV host answered the phone, "I can't thank you enough for not mentioning the accident on the program this morning."

"No need to thank me. *Rise 'n' Shine, Phoenix,* is not tabloid television. I'm just so sorry for that poor man and his family."

"Yes, an accident with the car lift. They're working on it this afternoon." Kate stopped short. "Oh, my God. Tamara, can you hang on?"

Eager to talk to the TV host, Kate forgot Nostalgia City's number one employee directive: *no cell phones in the park.* Walking down a side street in Centerville, the park's retro town, Kate had pulled out her phone and called the TV station. When she realized what she was doing, she held her phone at her side and looked for a place to hide. Fortunately, no one saw her twenty-first-century technology. Kate ducked into a souvenir shop.

"May I use a back room for a minute?" Kate flashed her Nostalgia City employee badge at the store clerk. The clerk pointed to an open doorway.

"Tamara, you still there? Sorry."

"I was hoping there wasn't *another* accident," Cox said.

"Nothing like that." Kate explained her faux pas. "Your focusing on the interviews in the garage—right after the accident—took poise. The segments turned out well. We're indebted to you." Kate sighed. "But a sad story."

"You have a small city there. Accidents happen," Cox said. "This might be a story on the evening news but without footage, it'll be short."

Kate thanked her again then silenced her phone and hid it at the bottom of her purse. She walked out of the stock room and continued on her way to a meeting.

Arthur Poole had offered to come to her office, but Kate wanted exercise. Although it was almost a mile from her office along Centerville's retro streets to Poole's store, Kate considered it a short walk in comfortable flats. After the morning's shock, striding outside in the sun, even amid the bustle of tourists, helped to renew her spirit. Still wearing her emerald dress from her TV appearance, she passed the Centerville Cinema where the marquee advertised *The Towering Inferno* and *Young Frankenstein.* Next door, a record store sold real vinyl records, 33s and 45s. Baby boomer tourists stood in front of the window looking at posters of Elvis, Paul McCartney, and Joni Mitchell.

Although situated on the outskirts of town, opposite a new plaza, Poole's Xanadu Boutique nevertheless drew more visitors than just about any concessionaire or Nostalgia City-run retailer. Poole's attention to detail, plus his emphasis on customer service helped, but Kate thought the major reason for his success lay in the nature of his business. Everyone who came to the park to visit the 1960s and '70s expected to find a store like Xanadu.

As she opened the door, Kate smelled incense. Sandalwood? Inside, sitar music formed a counterpoint to the hum of customers' voices. Black light pictures on one wall highlighted the display of posters for sale. Part of the store featured clothing, another area offered officially licensed merchandise such as lapel pins and beer glasses bearing Nostalgia City's NC logo. But the display in the center of the store drew the most attention. Counters and shelves were lined with colored cigarette papers, pipes, bongs, and hookahs.

The water pipes ranged from tiny, one-person numbers to ornate models with multiple hoses coiled in circles like snakes. Above the metallic echoing of the sitar, Kate could hear the sound of cash registers chiming.

Eager shoppers packed the store aisles, but Kate had no trouble spotting Arthur standing by a display of books. At six foot two and a half, Kate could almost always see over a crowd. Poole grinned when he saw Kate and directed her down a hallway and into his office at the rear of the store. He settled his thin frame into a wooden swivel chair in front of a roll-top desk pushed up against a wall. Kate pulled up a wooden chair.

Poole looked at Kate through round, John Lennon glasses that sat on his beak-like nose. His uncombed hair hung over his forehead. "Kate, thanks for coming down here."

Kate looked at his relaxed, crinkled cotton shirt and light olive vest. She didn't know if his outfit—complete with sandals—helped him play a part in his head shop or whether it represented his normal wardrobe. Regardless, it suited him. He looked comfortable. The loose-fitting clothes reminded Kate of the scrubs he'd worn when she first met him.

"Tell me what's new, Kate, and how's Trixie?"

Asking about her life—and even her cat—and then making eye contact and focusing his attention as she spoke was typical Arthur. You knew he really listened. A rare trait. After a few minutes, Kate turned the conversation to him.

"You *look* at home here," she said. "But you don't remember the years of hippiedom."

"No, not really. I was born in the eighties, but everyone knows about the sixties and seventies counter culture."

"And your new cause fits right in." Kate looked at the wall behind Poole. Next to a framed Bob Marley photograph, a red, white, and blue campaign poster said, *Safe Weed Project ~ We Need Your Signature.*

"That's what I wanted to talk to you about," Poole said. "You're familiar with our initiative, aren't you?"

"Yes, legalizing recreational marijuana. From the polls I've seen on TV, people are starting to look at it favorably."

"That's only half the story. Basically, there's *two* pot initiatives. Ours is the Safe Weed Project. We want to make marijuana widely available and let people cultivate it at home if they want."

"And the other ballot measure is like Colorado?"

"Not really. The Legal Marijuana Control initiative is being promoted by Consumer Cannabis, Inc., a big corporation that already controls most of the medical marijuana in Arizona. They want to restrict the sale of *recreational* marijuana. It'd be like letting one organization run most of the bars or liquor stores in the state. It means big money; a limited, regulated amount of pot available; and high prices. It's unconscionable."

Pot peddlers competing for the moral high ground? "Is that the difference? I haven't followed it closely."

"There's more. The Consumer Cannabis initiative—" Poole held up two fingers of each hand making air quotes. "—*says* it would set up a state agency to regulate pot sales. But you know what it really does?" Poole tapped a finger on the arm of his chair, his words tumbling out at a rapid pace. "It basically establishes a system for corporate control of everything. Only a small number of marijuana licenses would be available, with existing medical dispensaries getting first choice. They not only get the store licenses but they'll have a big say in how marijuana is grown and distributed. Most people wouldn't even be able to grow their own plants at home."

"The initiative would do this?"

"Yes, and it's not just Arizona," he said, his voice rising. Kate remembered his penchant for ramping up his discourse when he was excited. "Consumer Cannabis is trying to get control of marijuana growing and sales in others states, too," he added, pausing to push his glasses back on his nose. "It's just money, money, money."

Kate shifted in her chair. "Are you asking for my opinion, or..."

"You know the value of *medical* marijuana and how ignorant it is to withhold it."

"Of course."

"And I'm assuming you're on board with legalization."

Kate paused then made a tentative nod.

"Okay," Poole pressed on, "I was hoping that you would agree to join the Safe Weed Project advisory board."

"Arthur, I—"

"Marijuana's going to be legalized. It's inevitable. It's like ending prohibition." Poole leaned forward. "Won't you help us make the marijuana marketplace free and competitive?"

His last line sounded like a telemarketing spiel, but he'd probably been pitching his ballot measure for a long time, using the same words. Kate didn't know what to say. She couldn't imagine telling her boss, park founder Archibald "Max" Maxwell, that she was on a pot committee. "Even if I joined as a private citizen, this would still reflect on the park. I can see the headlines: '"Nostalgia City Exec. Endorses Marijuana.'"

Poole drew his eyebrows together and stared at the floor. Kate hated to disappoint him, but hadn't she repaid her debt? And getting corporate approval was something—well, she didn't even want to think about it.

"I'd have to clear this with my boss, Arthur. And you know who that is. I just don't know."

"Please think about it," Poole said as Kate got up. "It wouldn't take much time, and your ingenuity and common sense would be an asset to the board."

Kate opened the office door, and the smell of incense persuaded her that Max would never agree.

Chapter 4

Yellow police tape ran around the NC garage service bay. Lyle looked past the tape to an expanse of dried blood. "So it was murder?" he asked.

"Could be," said Rey Martinez, undersheriff for San Navarro County. "We need to test this equipment *and* see what the autopsy shows. An expert from the automobile lift company is coming out this afternoon."

Outside the taped-off area, dozens of mechanics worked on, in, and under a diversity of decades-old automobiles that filled the vast facility.

"Everyone told me it was an accident," Lyle said

"That's what people want to think. Even the mechanics who know better."

"What happened?"

With most other law enforcement officers, Lyle's question would have been off limits. But Lyle and Rey knew each other well, a result of working together at times when the park, and Rey himself, was at risk. He knew Lyle was an experienced homicide detective. They shared stories and a cynicism common to cops. Yet, when necessary, they tried to bolster each other's faith in humankind.

Martinez stood tall and slender in a tan uniform and gun belt, his dark hair and eyes a hint of his Hispanic heritage. He glanced around before he spoke. "Perez got crushed by this car lift and the old Lincoln it was supporting."

"Take a look?" Lyle asked.

"Yeah, the guys have already gone over everything. Prints don't look promising. Body's in transit." He lifted the police tape and he and Lyle stepped under.

Rey walked over to one of two wide metal columns about ten feet tall. Attached to each column, hinged steel arms, designed to lift an automobile, extended toward each other across the floor. "You press this and the lift goes up or down," Rey said. "But it's not automatic. You have to hold it. If you let go, the lift stops. We tested it several times. It's working okay."

Lyle stepped around the dried blood and looked at the simple controls. He slid his cabbie hat to the back of his head then crossed his arms on his chest. "So someone would have had to hold the lift until it came all the way down."

Rey nodded. "There ya go."

"But anyone could just jump out of the way. So he'd have to be tied up or—"

"Unconscious when the lift came down. No sign of ligature marks."

"Maybe someone hit him over the head. Or drugged him."

"Drugs should be easier to find out." Rey said. "Head bruises, not so much."

It was Lyle's turn to look around to see that no garage employees were within ear shot. "Was he in that bad a shape?"

Rey grimaced. "Crushed the chest and head, nearly pinched off an arm and a leg. Not something you'd want to see, especially if you knew him."

"Autopsy may help," Lyle ventured.

"Possibly."

"So your main evidence will be the lift. If it's not broken some way—"

"Then I'll have to treat this as a homicide."

"When was he killed?"

"Looks like he'd been dead for some time. Late last night. TV news crew was here this morning. Don't know how they found out about it so soon, if it was a tip or what."

"So it was on TV already?"

"I haven't heard. Someone in the garage called it in about six."

As Lyle and the undersheriff walked back under the tape, Lyle knew who he'd have to talk with as soon as he left the garage. They strolled toward a wide door to the outside.

"We've been interviewing employees," Rey said. "So, you knew him. What kind of a guy was he?"

"Didn't know him well. He worked on my cab. We went out for beer after work a couple of times. I went to a barbecue at his house once and met his wife. When I think about it," Lyle continued, "Don just talked about sports. That's all."

"You and I talk sports."

"Yeah, but we talk about real things, too. Life."

They walked away from the garage, through the parking lot to Rey's cruiser.

Rey held up a hand to shade his eyes from the sun. "Didn't Perez ever say *anything* about work? You know, if he got along with people here?"

"Once in a while but only car stuff not about people. He gave me a raft of shit about not taking care of my taxi. That was it. I have no idea whether he liked his job or not. What'd the people you talked with say?"

"Perez didn't seem to have any close friends in here, though everyone said they liked him. He worked here for over two years, back to when the park was under construction. Two guys who worked with him tuning up the rental cars said they didn't know him except for small talk. You'd think—"

"Maybe he was a loner. Didn't exactly seem like it, though. Did you talk to his wife?"

"They live in Polk. I just came from there. She was upset of course, but maybe not surprised. Sounded reserved. Hard to judge. I haven't had to talk to many murder-victim widows." Rey paused and looked across the parking lot. Then he made eye contact with Lyle. "Maybe she was holding something back," he said. "One of the guys in the garage said he thought they might be getting a divorce, but she said everything was fine. I don't know. You've got the experience at this."

Lyle wondered where this was going.

Rey took a step in front of him and lowered his voice. "It's tough. You know how small the department is. We've had to grow quickly since the park was built. I've been *trying* to get more experienced personnel. We used to have about one homicide a year—and that was usually domestic violence, nothing to solve."

"Uh huh."

"You know more about this than anyone in the sheriff's department."

"Yeah, I talked to lots of victims and survivors, but I never had time to help them. You know that. It's why I let them kick me out. I never had time." As if out of his control, Lyle's thoughts drifted to the wives, husbands, and children of murder victims he'd known. He forced himself to focus on the present. He looked away for a few moments. He knew Rey respected his experience, his opinion. *Oh hell.* "Rey," he said, "would you like me to talk to Mrs. Perez?"

"That's an idea. It could be a big help, especially since you know her."

"You don't mind a civilian nosing around your murder?"

"Just talk to Lydia Perez. See what you think."

Lyle hadn't needed a Valium in weeks. Now he wondered how his supply was holding out. But by helping Rey, he'd be helping the park, too. Maybe he could even offer some comfort to Mrs. Perez, but he doubted it. "Will do," he mumbled.

Chapter 5

"Lyle honey?"
As soon as he walked back into the shade of the garage, Lyle heard his name.

"Lyle honey," repeated the bulky woman holding some sort of mechanism in her hand. She motioned with her other hand for Lyle to come over.

"Yes, Gayle."

Gayle LeBlanc, the garage manager, stood at a counter near what Lyle called her command center. Her desk, situated on a platform, afforded her a view down the length of the garage. As he got closer, Lyle saw Gayle held a two-barreled carburetor.

"You still use those?" Lyle asked.

"Yeah, they're still reliable," she said, "'cept this particular Holley. It's used up." She set the carburetor on the counter. "Guess you heard about Don Perez. I saw you talking to the sheriff."

"Yes, Rey Martinez just told me. I knew Don." Lyle looked away.

"Lyle honey, I dunno know what they told you, but jus' 'tween you and me, warn't no accident. Thought you should know."

Gayle's Louisiana drawl and her Tammy Faye Baker makeup tended to disguise the fact she had an engineering degree and knew more about operating an auto shop than most managers in the business. She wasn't a bad judge of people, either.

"No accident?"

"Those lifts don't come down by themselves. 'Sides, they're slow. Anyone could get outta the way."

Lyle nodded. "But if it's broken."

Gayle shook her head. "Ya know, it's kinda scary, thinking we had a murder in here. But I can't see anyone wanting t' kill Don."

"Sheriff Martinez," Lyle said, abbreviating Rey's title, "says Don got along with everyone but didn't have any close friends. We hung out together a couple of times after work, but I didn't know him well, either."

"Quiet guy. Scroopalous with his work. Sure's hell knew how to repair these old V-eights. Did you hear 'bout the fight?"

"Fight?"

"Yeah, he and two other mechanics got into it right after work. This is maybe three, four months ago. Nobody hit anybody. I was too far away to tell who they were, except for Don. I saw him walk back from the body and frame shop area." She motioned down the long building. "Way down there where they inspect the cars when they first come in for restoration."

"Did you tell Rey?"

"Uh huh."

"You think there was a grudge, maybe someone got back at him for something?"

"Don't see how. I talked to Don the next day. He said it was just a little disagreement over the way the other guys handled one of the cars. I said Don was scroopalous. And everything went quiet after the little set-to. Dutch might of settled them down."

"Dutch?"

"Niles DeGroot. Everybody calls him Dutch. He's my body shop supervisor. The guys know not to get out of line."

Gayle picked up the carburetor from the counter and dropped it into a metal trash can with a resounding crash. "You think someone from outside killed Don?"

Lyle shrugged. "You have security cameras in here?"

"Not inside. We have some in the parking lots outside, but the building cameras are on the entryways, facing out at the regular doors and the roll-ups. That Sheriff Martinez said a deputy would come by and go through the video from last night. I got it set aside."

"When will that be?"

"I dunno. You want me to let you know? Say, Lyle honey, you gonna let the sheriff handle this one or *you* gonna get involved again?"

Chapter 6

Damn. Less than an hour before the next transition meeting. Not enough time in the day. Kate wondered why Max insisted she take part in so many transition sessions. Department heads could handle it. Kate's job was to dream up ways to announce it to the public. And she knew how they would do it. The transition represented a beautiful opportunity to grab publicity in advance of the coming season. She'd need to coordinate with Drenda. It could be big.

Riding the elevator to her office in the Maxwell Building, Kate's thinking switched to pot. Yes, a bunch of states, mostly in the west, had legalized recreational use—a euphemism for *getting high*—but would Arizona voters go for it? She'd smoked marijuana in college—who didn't? But adding her name and title to a list of pot promoters? She pushed it out of her head as she pushed open the door to the PR department and walked around the cubicles toward her office.

Her secretary, Joann Nye, caught her attention. "Do you want me to see about sending condolences to Don Perez's family?"

"Good idea," Kate said. "But it should come from someone higher up in administration. Maybe you can call Max's assistant with a gentle reminder."

Since Kate started at Nostalgia City, she'd noticed a positive change in Joann's dress and hair. More executive suite than PTA meeting now. Kate had never said anything. She tried to lead by example. Professional, efficient, and circumspect, Joann's performance could not have been better, especially since she'd been hired by Kate's predecessor who Max fired after six months on the job.

Kate turned toward the door to her office then stopped. "We better check with the garage first, find out how the accident happened. Was it equipment failure? I promised Channel Nine I'd give them details, but if there might be a lawsuit..."

"I can check with legal," Joann said.

"Good job. And see if you can get just a little personal information about Mr. Perez, how long he worked here, what he did. That sort of thing. We're bound to get media calls—if we haven't already."

"I'll check."

"Thanks, Joann. And would you do a little research for me? See if you can find and print out the state laws in Oregon and Colorado that legalized marijuana."

"Marijuana?"

Kate just nodded, adding a small smile as she went into her office. Her furniture reflected the past with its brushed aluminum finish and rounded corners. A ficus tree struggled to survive near a window.

When she sat at her desk and put a finger on her computer's touchpad, her list of incoming emails sprang to life. Arthur Poole's name topped the list. In fact, he'd sent three emails in the last half hour, all with attachments. *Well,* she thought, *I told him I needed to research this in depth. Here's the background.*

The first email contained a text of Poole's marijuana proposition and a link to the Safe Weed website. The home page looked like cross between a corporate annual report and a political advertisement—with a little hippie flavor thrown in. Kate recognized the Safe Weed logo at the top

Let's see who else is on the advisory board. Kate clicked on the menu and scrolled down the list. Her mouth opened in surprise. The board included a lawyer, a police captain, the president of a large Arizona corporation, a well-known physician, a state senator, and a news broadcaster. The list read like the board of the Boy Scouts or the Red Cross, not a pot party. *Why didn't Arthur tell me this? He wanted me to find out on my own. A prestigious group. But still.*

Kate knew, in order to be on the board, she'd have to persuade Max. And before she could do that, she'd have to persuade herself. Marijuana and a theme park. Hmm. How would their visitors react? Baby boomers and seniors—well-heeled seniors—made up a big chunk of NC's market. And millions of boomers smoked pot in college in the '60s and '70s. Would they object if the park were linked—even remotely—to the marijuana campaign?

Arthur's next email answered her questions. It contained links to public opinion surveys showing the demographics of legalization supporters. A mixed bag. Older people, i.e. NC patrons, didn't favor legalization as much as younger Americans. On the other hand, the latest poll showed 51.5 percent of Arizonans favored legalization—or *ending prohibition* as Arthur had called it.

Kate had almost finished Poole's improvised prospectus when a trim, athletic looking man with dark brown eyes and firm jaw walked into her office. He was tall, two inches shorter than Kate, but tall enough. She looked up at Lyle Deming with a smile reserved for him. Some people might not see beyond his NC-issued bow tie, cabbie hat, and his banter with tourists, but Kate did. He was handsome in an older-wiser-yet-still-vulnerable kind of way.

"What do you think of pot?" Kate asked.

About to sit in one of Kate's guest chairs, Lyle paused halfway down. "How'd you know? I didn't have any." He lowered himself into the chair. "Wait a minute—"

"What are you talking about? I want to know what you think about marijuana."

"Pot, huh? Well…"

"You don't have to be defensive," Kate said. "I smoked it in college. You too?" She explained Poole's marijuana initiative. "He wants me to be on his advisory board. At first I was skeptical, but looking at the big picture…"

"And you're worried about how Max will react."

"Exactly."

Kate's relationship with Lyle had progressed beyond business colleagues, a fact she hoped had not become common knowledge at the park.

"Legalization's a good idea," Lyle said. "Not what you might expect to hear from an ex-cop, but I think you can guess how successful our war on drugs has been. That's one reason. But listen, I need to tell you what happened. It's why I came over. At the garage last night—"

"I know all about the accident, Lyle. I was there this morning when someone found the body. Then Channel Nine arrived and—"

"It was no accident. At least that's pretty much what Rey Martinez thinks."

Kate's eyes grew large. "Crap. *What* then?"

"Murder. As soon as I found out, I knew you'd need to know."

"Murder?" Kate remembered the garage scene that morning and felt a shiver. She would not soon forget the gruesome image. She leaned back in her chair. "It was awful. Horrible. And now…" She imagined getting a flood of excited media calls as soon as the word *murder* got out. "Who knows about it? Is the sheriff going to announce something? Does security know it was murder? Who killed him?"

When Lyle opened his mouth to speak, Kate interrupted.

"Sorry. One question at a time, right?"

After a year of working with Lyle, off and on, Kate knew the solid, professional side of their relationship. She trusted his judgment—most of the time. He did wear a rubber band on his wrist for his anxiety issues. But she could always rely on his support and counsel, particularly in situations like this when the priorities of law enforcement and park security might differ from Kate's responsibility to maintain NC's public image. Personally, she and Lyle were also close, but their nascent relationship moved ahead slowly—as a result of reticence on both sides, for a collection of reasons.

"It's not official yet," Lyle said. "All I know is, the lift holding the car came down and crushed the guy. I guess you knew that," he said more softly. "These things have controls that shut off if you let go. It won't move without someone's hand on it. But Rey says an inspector from the hoist company is going to check it out today, just to be sure. So I guess—"

"I could say the death is being investigated. The media are going to bug me about this as soon as it gets out, but I don't want to say any more than we know for sure. *Never speculate* is the first rule of PR."

"The autopsy will take a while, and I suspect the guy from the lift company will have to file a report with his headquarters. So it may be a day or two before the sheriff's office confirms it."

"Max is not going to like this." Kate leaned forward. "So we're not going to tell him yet."

Chapter 7

Lyle couldn't remember exactly where Don Perez lived, but his GPS app did. He found the modest frame house on an uneven, patched asphalt street on the west side of Polk, the town nearest Nostalgia City. Many NC employees lived in the small community, the seat of San Navarro County, northeast of Phoenix. As Lyle approached, he saw a new, silver Acura in the driveway. Lydia must have visitors, probably family. He would not stay long.

The attractive, dark-haired woman who met him at the door wore an expression Lyle had seen before, someone going through the motions of life without solid comprehension.

Lyle started to introduce himself, but Lydia Perez stopped him.

"I know, you work at the park. Friend of Don's."

"I was here for your barbeque a few months ago."

"Yes, I remember." She spoke with an Hispanic accent. "You have someone drive you home."

Shit. That's how she remembers me? I wasn't tanked that time, just trying to be responsible. "Don made some delicious margaritas," Lyle said, looking around and hoping to change the subject. "Am I intruding? I saw the car outside."

"Car? Oh, that's Don's car. Someone from the park drive it over this morning. I don't know why."

Lyle recalled Don driving an old Nissan. The Acura was a current model.

Lydia Perez invited Lyle into the living room. He remembered the gray and brown overstuffed sofa and chairs. He sat down and expressed his condolences and asked if she had any immediate needs. When Lyle had talked to widows and other surviving relatives in Phoenix, it had been after a murder, only occasionally after an accident. Presumably Mrs. Perez didn't know it was murder.

"Rey Martinez called me this morning," Lyle said, "and told me about Don."

"Is he the sheriff? He came here today." Mrs. Perez looked at Lyle through puffy eyes. He guessed her age in the early forties. "But he didn't tell me why it happened."

"A car hoist, it came down. They don't know why. It was very quick. They're investigating the equipment now." Lyle didn't want to provide any more details than Rey had told her. Not his place. And he wouldn't mention the word *murder*. But he wouldn't be helping Rey if he didn't probe just a little, and perhaps it would prepare Don's widow for the expected conclusion that her husband was intentionally killed.

"I guess you were worried when he didn't come home."

"No. I feel bad 'cuz I didn't know he not home. I should have known. Should have done something." She started to tear up. "I work at Desert Manor nursing home. Eleven to seven o'clock in the morning." She stopped talking and stared off across the room. She reached for a coffee cup on the table in front of her. Her hand trembled as she lifted the cup. She took a sip then started again. "Since Don, he started moonlighting, we don't see each other a lot. During the week, I mean. I'm at work when he gets home."

"Moonlighting?"

"Yes, he works in an auto shop downtown."

"Which shop?"

"I don't know. He told me, but I forget."

"He goes there right after work at the park?"

Lydia Perez looked blankly over Lyle's shoulder. She nodded.

"How long has he been doing this?"

"A few months ago," she said looking as if she were trying to focus. She turned back to Lyle. "That's how we get that new car, and that." She motioned to a TV set not quite the size of a jumbotron.

Lyle bit his lip as he did some mental figuring. He realized, too late, that doubt was written on his face. "We're paying everything on time," Mrs. Perez said. "Don say this is the best way. And we can afford it now."

Although it sounded as if denial was part of Mrs. Perez's reaction, she seemed to be defending her dead husband. Not surprising. Lyle's stomach knotted up. He knew he'd have to continue.

"So, do you think he worked last night?"

"He didn't come home. The bed wasn't slept in."

Lyle knew the reason. Last night at the NC garage Perez laid under four thousand pounds of automobile. "He was a good man, providing for the two of you by working so much. You don't have any kids, do you?"

Mrs. Perez started to cry softly. When she recovered, she started relating how she and Don had met, struggled for some years, then moved into the house. Lyle listened. She needed to talk. After a few minutes, she looked at him with a sad smile.

"Did Don have any arguments recently at work?" Lyle asked.

She shook her head.

"Were there people there who didn't like him? Maybe someone mad at him for something? A disagreement?"

Lydia Perez shook her head again briefly. "No."

"No enemies?"

"No."

Someone violently murdered *had* enemies—at least one. Lyle plunged on to another subject. "Mrs. Perez, Lydia, Don was my friend. And I don't like it when people say stuff about him." Lyle hated himself for what he had to say next. "Someone told me you were thinking about a divorce."

Mrs. Perez didn't respond right away. Lyle couldn't read her face. She was in shock—the first stages—and he had just poked a nerve. Lyle sat watching her blank stare, waiting for a response.

Her mouth became rigid. She looked around the room. Was she searching for something to throw at Lyle? "Why you asking questions? Didn't Don say you used to be a cop? Are you a friend?" Her voice rose on the last words.

"I'm just a cab driver at the park." His stock response to questions about his police past.

"You're investigating Don? Investigating me? We have a lovely marriage. I don't understand." She began to grasp and rearrange the pillows on the couch next to her.

"Sorry. I didn't mean to upset you. Don was a good guy."

Mrs. Perez put her head in her hands then looked up when two people opened the front door and walked into the room. "Madre, Padre." She started to cry and the couple—in their sixties—both rushed over and hugged her.

Back in his car, Lyle felt the same regret that attended all such visits. He started the car. He wanted to get out of the woman's life. His Mustang fired up, and he steered down the road, but halfway in the block, the car shuddered as the automatic transmission shifted gears. Lyle's way-out-of-warranty Mustang GT had been acting up. The transmission shifted at unexpected times, accompanied with a clunking sound. Now it refused to shift up at all. "Damn. C'mon car. Move." He turned the car off then restarted it.

Moving ahead normally, Lyle stopped talking to himself and held his breath. Focusing on his car problem actually brought relief. He lamented the fact he couldn't have his personal car fixed at the NC garage. Perez had kept his Dodge cab running so smoothly.

Chapter 8

"Marijuana? Are you kidding? First we have a fatal accident in the garage and now you want to talk about pot? We have better things—"

"Max, hear me out."

Kate sat opposite her boss, Max Maxwell, Nostalgia City CEO, in his top-floor office in the Maxwell building. His broad sixties-style Danish modern desk kept them five feet apart but Kate leaned forward to narrow the gap. She spread out her report on the desk's edge facing Max, and set her blue eyes on him.

The founder of the theme park feigned indifference as he often did when Kate presented an unconventional proposal or something the wiry, and wary, septuagenarian *thought* was unconventional. He tilted back in his chair. "Okay, tell me why you want to be advisor to this pot proposition. Reflects on the park."

"Yes, but not directly. I don't plan to give any speeches or send out news releases with my name on them."

"What are you going to do?"

"Just advise Arthur Poole and his people about media relations."

"Your name will go on their letterhead or website."

"Possibly, but here's the company I'll have." She pointed to the list of other Safe Weed proposition board members. Max leaned forward.

"Bryan Odom is on this, too? He's a damn fool. He thinks *this*'ll help him get reelected to the state senate?"

"Did you know that a majority of Arizona voters favor legalization?"

"What? Who says?"

"It's slim now, but it may grow." Kate passed him a sheet of survey results.

Light glistened off his bald head and his eyes held their usual intensity as he looked at the paper.

"People want to smoke pot. Okay. Doesn't have anything to do with the park. You'd have to do this on your own time."

"It wouldn't take time away from my work." Kate paused and looked up, matching Max's stare. "But it *could* have to do with the park."

Maxwell waved a dismissive hand in the air. "Nah."

"I was skeptical about this whole thing at first," Kate said, telling Max her honest, initial reaction. But online research and little critical thinking the night before had persuaded her marijuana could be a game changer in the tourism and theme park world. She thought Max might resist. The best way to energize him, to encourage him to allocate park resources, would be to give him the facts and let him draw his own bottom-line conclusions—with a little prodding.

"Take a look at this," Kate said. She held up a map of the United States.

She pointed to the states highlighted in dark green. "All these states have legalized recreational marijuana. Of course, Colorado and Washington were first. And these states," she pointed to states in yellow, "are in some way considering it. They have ballot measures or legislation pending. And more than *half* of the states, the ones colored in light green, have *medical* marijuana now. That includes Arizona."

Max scowled, then looked quizzically at Kate. "This is spreading, isn't it?"

She watched him in silent thought for a minute then said, "Have you ever read about marijuana tourism in Colorado?"

"Yeah, lots of idiots go there to get stoned."

"They have tours, marijuana tasting, and pot friendly hotels. Visitors like it."

"Never did have time for that. Knew lots of people at college who smoked it." Max paused and looked away. "So if these other states have it and we don't…"

Kate listened.

"How many people smoke pot?"

"You can eat it, too," she said. "Cookies, candy, snack food, drinks."

"Whatever. It's getting popular, isn't it? Look at your damn map."

Max got up and paced the wall of windows along the east side of his office. He circled around past a row of paintings by artists famous in the 1970s. As he walked, he put his hands on his waist, behind his back—a sign Kate recognized. Thinking, weighing. "Sounds like we need to legalize it here. The more states that legalize it—and we don't—the worse off we'll be." He looked down his hawk nose at Kate. "How come nobody has mentioned this before? What the hell happened to our planning committee?"

Max sat back at his desk, took out a pen, and started jotting notes as he spoke. "Say you live in Chicago and you're looking for a vacation. Why not go somewhere with pot *and* theme parks? Then you look at Nostalgia City in Arizona and wonder why it's not legal here." Max was getting into the topic. More than she'd expected.

"So," Kate said, "once all of our competitors and big markets have pot and we don't—"

"People will stay home. Or go somewhere else. But we're going to legalize it, right? You said it was going to pass."

"I said legalizing pot here has just a slight majority now."

"Then get busy."

"Okay. If it passes here in Arizona, do you think the park should—"

"Sell pot? Damn good question. Natural tie-in with the seventies."

Kate didn't say anything. She could see Max's dollars-and-cents brain going to work.

"Makes sense. Maybe we could have a pot bar. You know, like one of those places they have in Amsterdam."

"I think they're called coffee shops. But I get your idea. I'll see what they're doing there and find out what's happening in some big US cities."

"Why in hell didn't someone talk to me about this before now?"

"We all kinda missed it, I guess. Everybody's been focused on the transition."

"That's history and culture. Why don't *you* start a pot committee? Talk to division heads. Get some input. Tell 'em we need to move on this."

"There's one other issue. Did you know there could be *two* marijuana propositions on the ballot?"

Kate summarized the advantages of Poole's initiative.

"Sounds like a good way to go, especially if we want to sell pot in the park. But try not to piss off the other guys, in case they win. We may have to deal with 'em."

Kate nodded.

"Okay, get a committee together. Give me a report in two weeks. No, make that one week."

Chapter 9

"Stop. What was that?" Rey asked.

He stood behind a deputy who sat at a desktop computer. They both watched the screen as the deputy operating the video playback hit *reverse*. The recording of two men walking together stopped, then the men moved backward in a herky-jerky motion, like a bizarre dance. When the deputy hit play again, the men sauntered across the computer screen at normal speed as they came out of the Nostalgia City garage entrance.

"It's nothing I guess," Rey said. "Keep going."

Lyle watched as he walked into the NC garage office stockroom where Rey directed the deputy operating the computer's video controls. "Reruns again?" Lyle said.

Intent on the screen, Rey flinched then glanced over his shoulder to see Lyle. "We're looking at the surveillance video from the other night, trying to see who was coming and going when Perez was killed."

"Are you calling it murder now?"

"Not officially, yet. But I'm not waiting for reports. Deputy Collins has been going over this video for hours, but it's not telling us much. We've got recordings here from cameras at seven different doors to the garage over a period of hours. People coming and going, mostly leaving for the day."

"Your office said you were here," Lyle said. "I have to

go on duty in a few minutes. I'm running kinda late. Thought I'd tell you about Mrs. Perez."

"Oh, yeah. Good. Keep at it deputy," Rey said. "I'll be right back. And remember, we need to make a complete copy of all this." He motioned for Lyle to follow him down the hall and out into the main auto service area. Two technicians were pushing a 1978 Chevy Nova toward a service stall.

"Damn near had to push *my* car today," Lyle said. "The transmission's acting up. I need to take it into the shop. That's why I'm running late."

"You don't exactly baby that Mustang."

"It was made to run. But now I'm afraid it's a lame pony."

"How'd it go with Mrs. Perez?"

"Not great," Lyle said. "She's teetering between denial and shock. Probably moving toward guilt. She works night shifts at a nursing home so she didn't know Don didn't come home."

"Yeah, that's what I got from her. We're going to check on her employment."

"I don't think she's involved."

"But—"

"It's usually husbands, not wives. And I'd be surprised if she's tied up in his murder. She hasn't fully accepted it yet. She talked about him in the present tense. What surprised me though, was when I asked her if Perez had any enemies or recent arguments. Often family members, spouses, say no one would want to hurt the victim. Or they say it couldn't be *murder*. She just gave one-syllable answers."

"Yeah?"

"And she didn't wonder why anyone would want to kill her husband."

"What about the divorce rumors?" Rey asked as they watched the technicians push the old Chevy onto a hoist and raise it up six feet.

"That's what got to her. I asked about that and she got

upset. Said they had a great marriage. So I don't think there's anything to that angle. What would be more interesting to find out is why someone *said* they were splitting up."

"Thanks for doing this, Lyle."

"Did you know Perez was moonlighting?"

"His wife said something about it. Obviously he wasn't doing it the other night."

"She said he worked at some repair shop in Polk. Didn't remember the name."

"Isn't that funny," Rey said, "not knowing where he worked?"

"I dunno. She was upset. You could check. Gayle might know. I don't know if she keeps track of her employees who moonlight. I never heard him mention working somewhere else. When I went out for beer with him it was right after work, but Mrs. Perez said he went to the other job directly from here."

"We'll check repair shops in Polk."

"They have a new car. Lydia Perez said Don's moonlighting helped them finance it."

The sound of an air wrench reverberated nearby. Lyle glanced over then said, "The garage is pretty busy these days. They're working on cars like that Nova, getting ready for the transition."

"What's that? Oh yes, I saw your commercials. So you're busy."

"Yeah, they've been working on new cars for weeks now. I wonder if overtime is available. Maybe Don could have picked up some extra hours here."

"Even if he worked someplace else, the murder was probably done by another employee here. Someone with access, who hung around after work."

"See anything on the video?"

"No mucho. Not a lot. At least two hundred people work here. The hours are staggered so we've got scenes of guys leaving over a long period of time. And it's mostly the back of people's heads as they leave. The cameras face outward to keep people from breaking in."

"See anyone coming in about the time you think Don was killed?"

"Can't be sure. Lemme show you."

Back in the stockroom, Rey asked the deputy to cue up a scene. Rey pointed to the screen. "This is the west entrance, a long ways from where we found Perez. About six o'clock, a truck came in with a delivery. See? They parked it right there, blocking the camera."

Lyle watched a bobtail delivery truck back into the wide entry door and stop so that all the camera showed was the name of an auto parts supplier. "So people could have gone into the garage on the other side of the truck and you wouldn't see them."

"Yes. And the truck sat there for more than a half hour."

"You want to look at the guy with the hat again?" the deputy asked.

"Sure, bring that one up," Rey said. "Watch this guy," he said to Lyle. "This is taken from the main entrance. It's close to the place they found Perez."

Lyle watched as a man wearing blue NC garage work clothes and a ball cap walked out the door. After a couple of steps he stopped and started to glance to his side, then looked straight ahead again."

"See him glance over like that?" Rey said. "Like he was looking to see if anyone saw him. Then he turns away quickly, away from the camera. Now look, he's walking away pretty fast. Not running, but making good time. You can't see his face, but look at the back of his cap. Is that a logo or a design? We can't quite make it out."

"Could be a baseball team logo, but not one I've ever seen. Or it could be a smear of grease or oil," Lyle said.

"I'm going to have photos made from this. Might help."

"So as soon as you officially call this murder, you can start looking for that guy."

"Officially?" Rey said. He reached in a manila folder on

the computer desk and pulled out a newspaper clipping. "You tell me what you think. Someone stuck this under the windshield wiper on one of our patrol cars in Polk."

The clipping contained a newspaper news brief. The headline read, *Mechanic killed in Nostalgia City accident*. Someone had circled the headline in red and next to it scrawled the words, *This was no accident!*

Chapter 10

"I'm certain Earl Williams wants to kill me."

Kate laughed. "It can't be that serious. Earl's a big sweetheart."

"Big, yes," Dr. Drenda Adair said. "Big and…well, you should have seen his face at the meeting."

They sat opposite each other at a work table in Drenda's memorabilia-cluttered NC office.

"Was this a KBOP station meeting?" Kate asked.

"Correct. We were in the conference room and I presented an abstract of the park's transition and how music is so important to the post-sixties milieu. Arguably *the* touchstone of the era."

Kate made eye contact and waited.

"Then Earl stood up and said, 'I ain't playin' no disco.'"

"Earl's usually smoother than that. Maybe he just did it for effect."

"I reported this up the chain of command to you-know-who," Drenda said, making a soft noise between a grunt and a snort. "And now I have to rethink the musical interpretations of our transitional perspective. Big Earl, it seems, is one of our top-rated attractions so I'm expected to be accommodating."

Kate liked Drenda, another young, female executive—younger than Kate—in a generally male-dominated field. The petite former academic wrote a research paper proposing a mock retro town as a socio-historical experiment. Unintentionally, it became the blueprint for Nostalgia City, the massive theme park founded by her uncle, billionaire Max Maxwell. Drenda became senior vice president of history and culture.

"You'll think of something," Kate said. "Unfortunately, this is one of many challenges of the transition."

Tucked away in one of the behind-the-scenes areas of the park, the Office of History and Culture combined business offices with a research library and a 1960s and '70s archive. Dr. Drenda Adair, PhD, history, University of Wisconsin, filled her office with academic journals, architectural blueprints, and a variety of artifacts from the period.

"Ah, the transition." Drenda pulled out a printed report. To make room on the table she pushed aside a heavy stone model of a Rubik's Cube. "We're getting complaints from a variety of concessionaires," she said, "and even some park employees, in addition to Mr. Big Earl." Delicate features and short auburn hair made Drenda look even younger and more fragile than she was. Drenda had become a formidable corporate ally of Kate's.

"Believe me, we have tried our best to make it clear to everyone," Kate said. "My staff has been pumping out stories about the transition for the employee website and newsletter. We have explanations, tips, and have tried to get people into the spirit of it."

"I know you have. But we're dealing with change and change can be threatening, even if it is of the ultra-minor variation."

"It certainly makes sense from a marketing standpoint. No question." Kate leaned back and glanced around the room at some of Drenda's artifacts, including an Etch A Sketch, a row of Pez dispensers, an egg-shaped plastic chair that enveloped its occupant, and a recent addition, a framed portrait of President Jimmy Carter.

"I wish we didn't call it *transition*," Drenda said.

"That was advertising's fault."

"Yes, and the new commercials don't exactly spoil the surprise, but they make it sound as if we're going to have an entirely new theme park."

"That's one issue," Kate said, looking across the room to where an eight-inch statue of Elvis guarded a corner of Drenda's desk. "I just talked to Max, and we have another assignment."

"Marijuana."

"How'd you know?"

"Actually I just read an article about the influence of marijuana prohibition in the *Journal of Popular Culture*."

"I've agreed to be on the advisory board of Arthur Poole's marijuana ballot campaign."

"And Uncle Max thinks marijuana could be a big money-maker for Nostalgia City, correct?"

"You're way ahead of me, as usual," Kate said.

"It's becoming more popular as more states consider legalizing non-medicinal use of cannabis. It would be logical for Max to see the bottom-line advantages."

"Max wants a pot committee. We need to consider the security and legal ramifications, marketing and, of course, how we could integrate it into the park."

"That last part won't be difficult. From an historical perspective, pot's popularity in the '60s and '70s is well documented."

"I'm going to ask each division head to attend our first meeting—or send a senior representative. We'll need you, of course. I bet pot was still common when you were in college."

Drenda pinched her index finger and thumb together and brought them up to her mouth. She breathed in noisily. "Pot, at *my* university?"

Chapter 11

Glass exploded through the air. A sledgehammer crashed into the corroded car body and the side window shattered raining safety glass fragments, like jigsaw puzzle pieces, on the half dozen onlookers. Lyle brushed the glass chips off his sport coat. A man with a shaved head and a blue windbreaker with DEA emblazoned on the back lifted the sledgehammer again and drove it into the fender.

The two TV news crews, filming from behind a chain link gate forty feet away, focused on the explosions of glass and metal.

"They're wrecking our car," Gayle LeBlanc said to Lyle as they stood in the parking lot next to the NC garage and watched the demolition. She raised her voice, directing it at the agent with the sledgehammer. "You're destroying the car. We can take the body apart for you. Y'all hear me?"

The agent responded by slamming his hammer into the car again. The fender separated itself from the body and crashed to the ground.

"They already had it on the rack," LeBlanc said. "Before you got here they took off the gas tank, mufflers, oil pan. Didn't find anything."

"Did they look for fingerprints?"

"I dunno. They jest wanted to take this car apart."

While the sledge-wielding agent continued his work,

now using a crowbar to remove various parts of the car, another agent used a razor knife to slash around the base of the car's seats, which had already been removed and placed on the pavement. A third agent used a stubby pry bar to remove the upholstered panel from the inside of the right front door. It came off with a pop as the door handle and window crank flew through the air.

Lyle turned to Rey who stood on his left. "When did this start?"

"DEA came in without advance notice." Rey grumbled. "They called our office, but only after they were entering the park. This car just arrived in a shipment for restoration."

"Looks like it's beyond restoration now."

Lyle glanced over at the man standing on the other side of Rey. He too wore a DEA windbreaker. "What do you think you're going to find?" Lyle asked, raising his voice.

"Could be a big load o' smack or possibly a couple hundred pounds o' pot all bricked up."

"*Could be*, heroin, *possibly* marijuana?" Lyle said. "And you got a warrant on that basis? But that's not exactly what you told the judge, was it?"

The DEA agent looked at Rey. "Is this guy with you?"

"Lyle works for the park," Rey said after a moment. "And he's an ex—"

"I drive a cab," Lyle said.

The agent stared at him with cold blue eyes.

One of the agents went to work on the engine. He removed the air cleaner and took off the valve covers, dropping them on the pavement with a metallic bang. Lyle spotted Howard Chaffee, NC's chief of security, standing a few yards away on the other side of the soon-to-be-totaled classic car. Howard made eye contact and Lyle wandered over.

"Did you know this was coming?" Lyle asked.

"No idea. Rey called me when he heard from the feds."

"I'm off duty. I happened to be walking by when I heard the racket."

"Fortunately their warrant targeted only the one car from

Mexico," Howard said. "They were looking for this specific model." Howard wore a gray suit and a serious expression.

"I saw TV vans outside," Lyle said. "They must have called the media."

"This is not like the DEA I knew when I worked in San Francisco," said the former police commander. "We had a task force, a good relationship. Frankly, I never expected to be dealing with them here. That agent giving orders over there is a group supervisor, likes to throw his weight around. Tried to tell our mechanics what to do. Then he trotted over and made a quick statement to the cameras and came back."

"I worked with them a little," Lyle said. "Never saw this guy, though."

"He told the garage staff to keep the gates closed. He told the reporters it was to protect them from flying metal and glass. Then they started tearing the car apart."

"Uh huh."

"I was going to tell him to stop ordering our guys around, but I don't know what Rey's relationship is with them."

"I don't know if he has one. He's not happy."

"Take out the radiator," the DEA supervisor shouted to the bald-headed agent wielding a crowbar. Sweat dripped off the man's shiny head. After another twenty minutes, the car became an empty shell surrounded by parts, many hammered into oblivion. The DEA obviously didn't find what it was looking for. Lyle wandered back to the other side of the car.

"Guess you had wrong information," Lyle said conversationally.

The supervisor ignored him. "That's it," he said to the other agents. "Pack it in."

A black SUV pulled up next to the demolished car, blocking the TV cameras. As the DEA agents started collecting their tools, Lyle walked into the garage, found the first telephone he could, and called Kate. Her secretary said she was out of the office.

"Does she know about the media here and the DEA?"

"Oh, yes," Joann said. "She's probably talking to the media now."

Lyle hung up and walked outside through a side door of the garage.

Reporters and camera people stood beside two TV station news trucks parked next to the curb. Kate stood by herself next to one of the trucks.

When Lyle reached her, they both looked up to see two dark SUVs speed past the cameras without stopping.

"What th' hell?" said a reporter who waved his microphone at the rear of the trucks as they went by. "Pride said he'd have a statement about drugs," the reporter said to no one in particular. "This was supposed to be a big bust."

"I like big busts," Lyle whispered to Kate.

She smiled momentarily but whispered back, "What happened? DEA was looking for drugs, right?"

"Yes, but they found nada, just tore up a nice old Buick that came in for restoration."

With nothing to show for their trek to Nostalgia City from Phoenix, the two reporters turned to Kate.

"We don't know anything about this," she said. "The agents rushed in here without notice, tore up one of our cars that was being restored and then…well, you saw them."

Lyle let Kate handle the media, and he headed back to the garage, looking for Rey or Howard. An excited Gayle LeBlanc found him.

"Lyle, honey," she said, waving her hands in front of her for emphasis, "those horrid agents really dismangled our car. It's useless. What are we supposed to do? That head agent told me I'd have to make a claim with the government for the damage. Then he said they weren't liable so don't waste my time."

"Did you get his name?"

"Shore did. Justin Pride. That bastard said I had to tell

him next time we're gonna get a shipment of cars. Do I have to? We got another load a cars comin' in soon."

Chapter 12

"So it's homicide," Lyle said.

"'Fraid so," Rey said. "The automotive lift company said the equipment was functioning normally." His chair squeaked as he leaned toward his desk.

"But they'd have a special interest in not finding a problem."

"Yes, but an insurance investigator and the most experienced guy at your shop also tested the equipment. It wasn't broken. Someone had to be there to hold the controls."

Martinez's wall clock read five-fourteen p.m. Worn blinds kept the late afternoon sun from streaming into his office. Rows of cardboard storage boxes lined two walls. The undersheriff wore his tan uniform, his collar open, his appearance solemn. He motioned to a report on his desk. "This is the preliminary autopsy."

"That was quick."

"I told the sheriff this was probably murder so he persuaded the ME to put in some overtime."

"What's it say?" Lyle asked.

"I'm getting to that. We told the ME to look for signs of a head wound. And she found one. Likely didn't come from the lift, but it could have if Perez was trying to get away, and the lift knocked his head to the concrete. More likely a blunt object."

"And that garage is full of blunt objects."

"There ya go." Rey nodded his head. "The ME is not one hundred percent positive, but it fits our hypothesis."

"Okay, I have another hypothesis for you. Has to do with drugs."

Rey's phone buzzed. He nodded at Lyle as he answered. "Yeah, send him on back."

A moment later, Howard Chaffee walked in. He wore a shirt and tie. He'd left his suit coat behind. He didn't seem surprised to see Lyle.

"I dropped by to see if you got the reports back on Perez," Howard said.

"That's why I came over, too," Lyle said. "Rey thinks, well..." He gestured to Martinez.

"Let's go into the conference room." Rey said. "It's too crowded in here. We're remodeling some of the offices. The department's growing." He picked up his files, stood, and led them down a hallway.

"Why don't we adjourn for a drink to talk it over," Lyle said. "You guys get paid for this."

"You don't have to stay," Rey said.

"You don't think I'm indispensable?"

Rey managed a slim smile. "Let me think about that one."

"Ask my ex-wife. She said I was completely dispensable. Or was that insensible?"

Lyle decided to stay. He followed Rey and Howard into a meeting room. The oval conference table seated ten. Howard sat down in one of the tired swivel chairs opposite Lyle with Rey between them. Howard's close-cropped gray hair and bland, Midwestern face contributed to his cop-like image, yet his not-quite rigid bearing and relaxed smile belied the stereotype. He rested his hands on the table. "What have we got?"

Rey explained autopsy and mechanical report findings.

"But you haven't announced anything yet." Howard said.

Rey shook his head.

"So DEA doesn't know we had a murder in the garage."

"And we're all thinking this could be drug-related," Rey said.

"Sure. I thought about it," Howard said. "I looked up all the drug reports we have in our files. All in all, there wasn't much. We've only been around for less than two years." He looked at Rey. "You make many drug arrests at the park?"

"Nothing big. Mostly possession. Nothing like what the DEA was looking for."

Lyle could see the case expanding in several directions, getting complicated. Why was he sitting here? Because Rey asked for his help? Because Rey and Howard were good, honest guys to work with? Because he was crazy and should otherwise be back in his nice, quiet cab?

"I can tell you," Howard said, "my boss is hot to know why the DEA was out there."

"And he doesn't know the Perez killing wasn't an accident," Lyle added. "If you think Max is agitated now, Howard, wait 'til he finds out Perez was murdered."

Howard frowned, turned to Rey. "So, you're going to start a murder investigation."

"Already have. Now it's official. We'll have to come out and re-interview some of the garage employees."

"Did you talk to that Dutch guy about the argument Don had?" Lyle asked. Before Rey could answer, Lyle turned to Howard and explained what Gayle had told him.

Rey opened one of the file folders he'd brought with him and tapped the top of a page with a pen. "Dutch was tight-lipped. Like a lot of 'em. We asked him about the fight. He said it was a long time ago and that he didn't witness it, just heard loud voices and investigated. He says he talked to Perez, and Perez told him it was nothing so he dropped it. Says Perez was a perfectionist and he respected him for that. Sounds like a load of crap. We've been getting a lot of that from the mechanics. 'Don was a great guy,' they say, but no one saw anything."

"What did the guy who found the body say?" Lyle asked.

"Not much," Rey said. "One of our guys had to go to his

house to interview him. He was so shaken up he went home for the day."

"Was he a close friend?" Lyle asked.

"A friend. I don't know about *close*. He said it was mainly finding the body in that condition that freaked him out. Have to admit," Rey said, "it was one of the worst I've seen. Like a bad car crash, only more so."

Howard pulled out a small pad and started taking notes. "You knew Perez, didn't you?" he asked Lyle.

Lyle turned in his chair and untied his cabbie outfit bow tie. "A little bit. He used to work on my cab."

"We never had a clue that someone might be using your imported junk cars to smuggle drugs," Rey said. "*My* boss is pissed that the DEA bypassed us."

Lyle saw Rey glance at the conference room door. Making sure it was closed?

"But then Sheriff Wisniewski has never been too excited about DEA task forces," Rey said. "And luckily we've had very little drug activity in the county. A little pot, and we busted a meth lab three years ago, but that's pretty much the extent of it."

"There's really no *evidence* of drugs, is there?" Lyle said. "DEA didn't find anything. And most of the cars don't come from Mexico."

"As I understand it," Howard said, "the park has two guys who travel around looking for cars we can restore and put on the streets."

"Yeah," Lyle said. "One of them is Tony something. Don't know the other guy. They find cars stashed in sheds, junkers from car lots, anywhere. If a car's in even halfway good shape, our garage can resurrect it, so to speak. They don't go to car shows to buy restored vehicles. Too expensive."

"But some cars do come from Mexico?" Howard asked.

"Some of them, yes," Rey said. "Obviously, they'd be checked at the border." He looked at Lyle.

"Probably. I've never been involved in it. Most of the

cars come from Arizona, and surrounding states."

"How do they get here?" Howard asked.

"A private transport company," Lyle said. "That's what Gayle LeBlanc told me."

"So you're going to be talking to these car buyers?" Howard asked Rey. "And maybe the transport people?"

Lyle hoped Howard wasn't going to do a here's-how-we-did-it-in-California routine. Rey looked young, but he had a state college degree and served in patrol and investigation divisions for years before becoming undersheriff. He didn't have lots of experience in murder cases, but he had good instincts.

"If there's a drug connection, yes," Rey said.

"I'd like to know," Howard said, "what kind of information the DEA had and where it came from."

"And is this related to Don Perez's death," Lyle said.

"I knew the sheriff would want to know—*yesterday*—why this happened," Rey said, "so I called a guy I know at the DEA. Not the guy who was out here yesterday. He said they got a tip. No surprise there. He said this Agent Pride didn't want to tell anyone in advance because he was afraid it might leak out."

"They thought you'd tell someone?" Howard asked.

Rey shrugged. "I don't know, but this guy I talked to kind of apologized for not calling us earlier. Wouldn't tell me where they got the tip, though. I got the idea this guy Pride likes publicity."

"No shit," Lyle said. "He called the media before he called the local sheriff."

"Maybe cooperation depends on the office," Howard said. "The DEA crew we worked with in San Francisco—"

"The chief is part Native American," Rey said, "and he doesn't like helping the DEA look for peyote. Immigration's been an issue with the feds, too."

"And they probably think San Navarro is a hick county," Lyle added.

Rey turned and glared at Lyle.

"Regardless," Howard said, "the park and the sheriff's department may have to work with them."

"We'll have a day or so before my report gets out. Maybe we can get on top of the murder before the DEA wants in."

Howard looked at his watch. "Thanks for the briefing. Let me know what I can do out there. Seasonal crowds are building so we'll be busy, but I can check records or assign guys to the garage. Whatever you want." He got up to leave but paused at the doorway. "I'm going to see Max first thing in the morning. I'll have to tell him the Perez death was murder, but it will stay with us. We don't want it to get out any sooner than you do. The DEA might like headlines, but, in security, we don't."

When Howard left, Lyle leaned back in his chair and stretched. "Calling it a day?"

"Not quite. As you said, I get paid for this. I have to assign one or two people to go over to the garage with me tomorrow."

"Find out anything about Perez's moonlighting?"

"Nothing yet. We're still contacting the garages in town."

"You like Howard?"

Rey moved his shoulders. "His office calls us whenever there's anything serious we don't know about. We work okay."

"Better than his predecessor."

"Yeah."

"You didn't tell Howard about the anonymous note you got saying it wasn't an accident."

"Guess I forgot."

Chapter 13

When Kate woke up, she didn't know where she was. Then she remembered and smiled. Turning over, she saw the empty space in the bed next to her. Lyle was probably in the kitchen. Soon, he stuck his head in the bedroom door.

"Ready for coffee?" he said.

"Yes, please."

"Be right back."

Kate got up and reached over to the nearby chair where her clothes were draped on the arm. She pulled on her blouse and got back in bed. She sat up against her pillow and the headboard and looked for her phone.

"Here, Kate," Lyle said, setting a brimming cup on the nightstand. He wore running shorts and a T-shirt.

"How long have you been up?"

"Just time enough to make coffee and bring in the paper." He leaned over and put his mouth on Kate's.

After a long moment, he stood beside the bed and massaged her neck and shoulders. She leaned back and felt her muscles relax.

"I'm glad you called last night," she said. "Today's going to be rugged. The second round of media calls about the DEA raid, I'm sure. But I feel up to it." She looked into his brown eyes then admired his thin nose and firm lips.

"Don't forget," Lyle said, "this morning Howard is going to tell Max that Don Perez's death was murder."

"Don't remind me. I can hear Max's voice now."

Lyle leaned over and kissed her again.

"Mmm, that helps," she said. She reached for her coffee. "So does this." Momentarily lost in thought, she looked into her cup then took a sip. "The TV stations and papers will go nuts when they hear about the murder. And they'll want to know if it's connected to the drug raid. That's what I'd ask."

Lyle gently moved Kate's legs over so he had more room to sit on the edge of the bed. "That's the sixty-four thousand dollar question. Rey and his guys are going to go over the evidence again today, talk to witnesses. Maybe we'll know something."

"The less *I* know, the better. When I tell the media I don't know, it will be the truth."

"Do you find honesty to be a hindrance in public relations?"

"I considered time-share sales, but I went to journalism school instead."

"So far, there's no evidence of drugs, so you really *don't* know anything more. All we know is, the DEA got wrong information from somewhere. That's what you can tell 'em."

"And who are they going to believe, now that I joined Arthur Poole's pot board."

"Can you quit?"

"It's already posted on the campaign website. And I'm not sure what kind of message it would send if I quit right now."

"Sort of damned if you do or don't situation?"

"That's optimistic," Kate said. "What time is it?"

"Six thirty."

"Really? Why didn't you tell me? I have to go."

Kate got out of bed and took her clothes into the bathroom where she ran a brush through her long hair. She didn't have fresh clothes, cosmetics—or anything else for that matter—in Lyle's condo. Their relationship, and the number of times they slept together, had not advanced to the point where convenience might indicate a higher level of commitment. Neither Lyle's condo nor Kate's apartment showed any signs of the other's presence. Thus, Kate threw on her clothes, smacked Lyle on the lips, then dashed out to her car. She'd have a little more than an hour to shower, do her hair and make-up, and be at work before Max started fuming.

Conveniently, Lyle and Kate both lived in Timeless Village, a collection of homes, condos, and apartments, mostly for NC employees, located just outside the park. She beat her own personal best time getting ready and walked into the PR office wearing a new Banana Republic suit when she remembered she'd promised to give Lyle a ride to work after he dropped off his car to be repaired. No time now.

"The AP wants to know if there's evidence of drug trafficking at the park," media coordinator Amanda Updike asked Kate a few minutes after she sat down at her desk.

"Of course not, Amanda. We've never had a problem. Try to keep it in context. The DEA came out here and demolished one of our cars, but that's all we know. And obviously they made a mistake."

Amanda leaned against the frame of Kate's office door. "Should I call the security chief and see if they know more about the raid?"

"Howard Chaffee doesn't know any more about the DEA raid than we do." Kate's pillow talk was useful at work. Of course, she wasn't about to discuss her source. "Give them the usual about how secure the park is, how we screen visitors. You know the rest."

When Amanda left, Kate stared at the two ceramic cats on her desk. The smaller one looked sleepy, curled up with her head on her paws. The other, slightly larger, was Kate's favorite, a whimsical cross between a house cat and a mountain lion. Reaching for her second cup of coffee of the day, Kate could almost hear Max Maxwell telling his assistant to get Kate Sorensen on the line. Or maybe he was dialing her cell phone himself. She was off by thirty seconds.

"Hello, Max," she said. "I know. It was murder. What am I doing about it? What do you want me to do?"

"Don't tell the media anything," Maxwell said. "Let the sheriff and Chaffee figure this out. I called Sheriff Wisniewski. He's coming to see me."

"The official crime report will probably hit the media tomorrow. Then all we can say is, it's being investigated."

No sooner had she assuaged Max's anxieties—for the moment—when Joann ducked into her office carrying with her a sense of alarm.

"Arthur Poole is on TV talking about marijuana."

"God, now what?"

"It's a morning interview show. You want me to turn it on?"

Kate nodded, and Joann picked up the remote control off a table and clicked on the TV. Arthur Poole appeared. "Yes, Nostalgia City," he said. "And Kate's going to help us explain that we're just putting an end to a prohibition that's never worked."

He mentioned her. *What else had he said?* The live broadcast didn't permit Kate to back up. Poole wore a light-colored cotton shirt and knit tie, his concession to dressing up for TV. But it was a casual show, Kate rationalized. He looked comfortable. He and a young female interviewer sat on a low couch. What's he going to say *now*?

"Lots of parents are worried about their kids getting access to marijuana if the proposition passes," said the interviewer, an earnest young woman seated next to Arthur.

"That won't happen," Poole said, taking an awkward sideways glance at the camera. "According to *our* proposition, marijuana licenses will not be dominated by one company. Many will be locally-run stores. They'll be small business people, people interested in families and their neighborhoods. It won't be an industry controlled by a faceless corporation that doesn't care."

"Surveys show that twenty five to thirty percent of high school seniors have used pot." The host adopted a more confrontational tone. "Do you really think legalizing it won't just give kids more opportunities to smoke it?"

"Basically, there already *is* a marijuana market in Arizona—a black market. But ending prohibition will cut the flow of illegal, untested, marijuana into the US." Poole leaned forward on the couch. He could be persuasive, but he was talking too fast. "Since marijuana prohibition ended in Colorado and other states," he said, "the amount of illegal marijuana seized by the Border Patrol dropped twenty-four percent. And Mexican authorities report an even greater drop in illegal marijuana smuggling."

Kate hadn't seen those figures. She grabbed a pen and made a note to research it. And, she'd definitely talk to Poole to find out what else he'd said about her and the park.

"So," the TV host said, "you're trying to tell us that legalizing marijuana production would mean *less* illegal marijuana for sale?"

"It makes sense. If adults can legally buy safe recreational marijuana, they won't patronize street-corner sellers. If prohibition is ended across the county, we could shut down marijuana smuggling completely. And it would be a bigger blow to the Mexican cartels than the war on drugs."

Chapter 14

The sign read, *Hooper's Auto Repair and Towing*. Lyle pulled into the parking lot. "Why are you doing this now, huh?" he asked his car. "Why did you have to start acting up?" He put the gearshift in park and got out.

Lyle walked into the small office at the front of the industrial style building. Faded oil company posters adorned one wall above a table with a dented coffee maker, an irregular stack of Styrofoam cups, and a surface speckled with powdered coffee creamer. Lumpy wood and fabric chairs sat on either side of the table, daring you to sit down. Opposite stood the oil-stained counter and behind it a row of shelves filled with stacks of paper and dusty mechanic's manuals. Lyle walked to the counter where a man in gray work clothes and a pencil behind his ear stared into a computer screen and hit one key several times. He looked up at Lyle but was obviously still thinking about whatever was on the screen when he spoke. "Yeah?"

"I'm Lyle Deming. I called yesterday for an appointment."

"Deming." The man looked back at the screen, tapped again on the dirty keyboard, then he looked back at Lyle with more interest. The man's round face, wide mouth, and week's growth of beard made him look like a seedy John Denver. "Oh, you got the Mustang with the tranny problem."

"That's me."

Lyle explained what his car had been doing, jumping gears erratically. The man entered Lyle's complaints and personal information into the computer then waited while a gray printer whirred on a shelf behind him. Lyle looked at the form.

"So it's going to cost one hundred fifty dollars?"

"That's just to flush the transmission—change the fluid. If it needs anything else, we'll call you."

Lyle grunted, signed the form, and dropped his car key on the counter. "It will be difficult to get a hold of me during the day. I work at the park. But leave a message at my office and I can call you back."

"We'll let you know. Thanks for coming in." It sounded perfunctory.

Lyle had a hand on the office door handle when he stopped and turned around. "Are you open in the evening?"

"Some nights, but not—"

"It's not about my car. I'm just wondering if Don Perez works here part time."

The man looked at Lyle then down at the service contract. "No. No Don Perez here."

"He would have started just a few months ago."

"This is a small shop. I know everyone that works here. I run the place." He shook his head.

"Sorry to bother," Lyle said and he stepped outside. "Well, this is one more place the sheriff doesn't have to check," he mumbled as he walked up to Earl Williams' car idling in the parking lot.

"What's that, bro?" Earl asked as Lyle got in the new Camaro.

"Nothing. Just talking to myself."

"Still?"

"Gimme a break, Earl. I'm thinking about another damn murder case and why I'm getting dragged into it."

Earl wore a gold and olive Hawaiian shirt and enough jewelry to fill a store display. He maintained his retro DJ character with gusto. "You working on another case? For someone who's retired from the PD business, you shore busy."

"Tell me."

Earl dropped his bright yellow Camaro into gear and crept out of the gravel parking lot before he put pressure on the gas pedal. "This murder. That wouldn't be that guy from the garage?"

"Don Perez."

"You knew him, right?"

"A little." As they left Polk, heading for the park, Lyle said, "So, are you staying out of the disco music scene?"

"Yeah, I made that real clear at our *transition* meeting. Maybe too clear. I think I scared that Drenda person."

"Drenda Adair, the senior VP of history and culture?"

"Yeah, the nostalgia Nazi."

"What did you do?"

"I kinda yelled."

"Oh?"

"She kinda jumped."

"You're about as subtle as an earthquake."

"Maybe I'll call her and apologize."

"Yes?"

"Sorta."

When they reached Nostalgia City, Lyle slapped Earl on the shoulder, thanked him for the lift, and headed to his taxi. A big V-8 powered his 1973 Dodge Polara cab. Not too maneuverable on corners, but the car could haul ass if necessary. Nearly all the time, however, Lyle's trips were at twenty-five miles per hour or less as tourists gawked at the historical scenery and Lyle entertained them, noting points of interest as if the past four decades had not yet happened.

At noon, Lyle parked his cab near the taxi office to retrieve messages. How much more would the Mustang cost him? The taxi dispatcher handed him a message from Hooper's repair shop. Lyle didn't have his cell phone with him, following the letter of the law in the park, so he used the taxi office phone to call Hooper's. Surprise.

"Car's ready," he was told. "We flushed the tranny. All set."

Dodged a bullet, Lyle thought. Next, he called Rey.

"You busy? I just wondered if there's anything new. Could I—"

"Can't really talk now, Lyle. I'm in the NC garage lunchroom with a bunch of employees. We can talk later."

"I'm on lunch break. I'll come over."

༺༻

Rey addressed more than a dozen people as Lyle walked into the lunchroom. Mechanics and others sat on plastic and metal chairs around Formica-topped tables glistening under bright LED lighting. Most of the employees wore blue work clothes. Oil stains spotted sleeves and pant legs. Rey wore a suit instead of his tan sheriff's uniform. Less intimidating.

"So that's where the investigation stands now," Rey said to the group. "We're talking to a number of employees individually, people who worked in Perez's department. But I want to hear from anyone who might have seen or heard anything unusual on Monday afternoon. Did any of you know Mr. Perez?"

A few hands went up.

"Don was an okay guy," said one young man with an armful of tattoos. "He knew engines, 'specially."

"Did you know if he was upset about anything or if he had an argument with anyone recently?"

The man shook his head.

Lyle took a seat at the rear.

"Same question to any of you who knew Mr. Perez."

People looked at each other, glanced back at Rey, but no one spoke.

A thickset guy with a full head of black hair spoke up.

"You think this was someone who snuck in and killed him?"

"We don't know at this point. That's why we're talking to as many people as possible."

Not a good idea to tell everyone he thinks the murderer is a garage employee. Rey wasn't going to share any details he didn't have to. But then, *could* it have been an outsider? Lyle couldn't see the questioner's face. The man shrugged his shoulders in response.

"Once again," Martinez said, "did any of you notice anything out of the ordinary Monday afternoon? Even if you don't think it's relevant, it could be helpful to us."

A few people shook their heads; no one spoke.

When Rey had finished, the employees filed out of the room. As Lyle walked up from the back, one mechanic stopped to talk to Rey.

"Do you think this has somethin' t' do with the drug raid the other day?" The man sounded concerned.

Rey gave him a noncommittal answer. In truth, no one knew.

"Picking up anything useful?" Lyle asked when they were alone in the lunchroom.

"You know how it is. A little here and there. Mostly nothing."

"Same old shit. Nobody saw anything."

"Something happened last night, though. Someone burglarized the Perez home."

Chapter 15

"You're an asshole, you know that?"

The woman's shrill voice carried down the hallway as Kate approached Arthur Poole's office.

"Calm down, Perse." Poole spoke with a soft, measured voice. "Sit. Take a deep breath."

"Whaddaya mean *sit*? Like a fuckin' dog?" The female voice rose an octave. "Tell me, will you, why'd you lie to me? Why'd you leave me hanging?"

Kate didn't want to interrupt the argument, while her curiosity made her linger within earshot.

"I spent over four hours on the road this morning driving to Mesa," Poole said. "I'm tired. Please don't yell."

"You're tired? You're tired, and I'm broke."

"I never said I'd co-sign that loan for you. I said we'd talk about it. It's just too much liability. Don't you see?"

"What, you don't think I'm worth it?"

"Court-ordered alimony ended months ago. You know that. I didn't have to send you anything else. I tried but, Perse, you've got to help yourself."

"Think I'm going to beg you for charity?"

"You told me flat out that you would go back to rehab," Poole said. "That's what I was counting on."

"You just wanted t' control me. Like always. I can handle myself. I tole you before." The woman's voice now varied in pitch and speed.

"Look, I wish you'd think about it."

"About what?"

"You know."

"Rehab? Hell no. You tried this controlling shit when we were married. I shoulda listened to my folks. They said I never shoulda married you. My dad always said you're—"

"A devil," Poole said, his voice level.

"Yeah, a devil. A drug-dealin' devil. You ruined my life. That's what my dad says."

"Are you still with Nick?"

"Don't you say anything against him. He's just had bad luck. That last arrest was bogus, totally bogus. The other guy hit him first."

"What does your father think of Nick?"

"My father? He's a pompous prick, but at least he tries to help. More 'n you. He was right about you all along."

"You still living in Phoenix?"

"Yeah. I never shoulda followed you to Arizona. I should move back."

"Maybe that would be best."

"What d' you care?"

"That's not fair," Poole said. "There's nothing more I can do. Please, give some thought to rehab. You tried it before and you liked yourself better for a while."

"Here's what you can do, *Ar*-thur."

Kate could hear by her voice and footsteps the woman was moving to the office door. Kate ducked back into the shop just as a thin woman with brown hair streaked with blonde backed out of the office, gesturing at Poole as she went.

Kate watched her go. She wore shorts and a light cotton blouse and walked with unsteady strides on flip flops. Kate waited in the shop for a minute before she walked down the hall and into Poole's office.

Poole sat at his desk with his back to the door when Kate walked in. She knocked on the door frame and he turned around. "Hi, Kate. Did you hear any of that?"

"Just a little. Sounds like someone was upset with you."

"My ex-wife. Just a disagreement about money."

"Her name is Perse?"

"That's short for Persis. It's Biblical."

"She didn't sound reverent."

"Perse is having a tough go. Basically, she has some addiction issues. I've tried to help."

"Addiction?"

"She was in rehab for alcohol, but it didn't take. I tried. Her family blamed me."

"I can't imagine you didn't do everything you could."

Poole sighed and looked at the wall beyond Kate. After a moment, he made eye contact. "Oh," he said. "Did you want to talk about your internal marijuana group?"

"You mean my pot committee? Not really. It's next week. You're going to send me more background on marijuana legalization in the west, right?"

"Yes."

"What I wanted to ask you about is the TV program today."

Before Poole could answer, a man in his thirties with flowing dark hair, and eyes that made him look like a romantic soap star, walked into the office. "Oh, sorry," he said in a whiney voice that didn't quite match his sultry looks.

"Remo," Poole said, "this is Kate Sorensen. She's director of PR for the park, and she's joining our Safe Weed board. Kate, this is Remo Bellard. He's one of the assistant shop managers."

Bellard looked down at Kate, smiled, and raised his eyebrows enough to let Kate know he was just as interested in her as a woman as a park exec.

"What do you need, Remo?" Poole said.

"I wanted to talk to you about the grow supplies."

"Does it look promising?"

"Yes."

"Okay. We can talk about it later."

Bellard nodded, gave Kate the once-over, and left.

"The TV program?" Kate said.

"Yes, did you see it?" Poole said. "I hope it helps us get more signatures."

"You definitely know your stuff," Kate said, "but—"

"I should have put more emphasis on the signature drive. We need lots more signatures."

"I think you did okay, but I didn't expect you to talk about me and the park."

"I should have told you I was going to be on, shouldn't I?" He sounded like an embarrassed child carried away by emotion.

"If I'm going to advise you on public affairs, it would help."

"Paige got a call from the station the other day, and I wanted to take advantage of the opportunity."

"Paige?"

"Oh, she runs the office in Phoenix. She's coordinating the signature campaign. You should meet her some time. Paige's...well, she's a special person. Dedicated to this."

From the look on Poole's face, Kate wondered how special Paige was *to him*. "I missed the first part of your program," she said. "What else did you say about the park?"

"Nothing else, I don't think, why?"

"Arthur, don't you know what's going on around here?"

"Something about the DEA?"

"Yeah, something about the DEA. The TV host didn't ask you about that, did she?"

"No. And all I said about you and the park was that you just joined the advisory board. And they introduced me saying I was owner of Xanadu in the park. That's what they always say."

How could Kate be mad at Arthur? She'd often wondered if he really was as guileless as he appeared. She leaned over toward him. "Arthur," she said, squeezing his right hand in both of hers, "you're a piece of work. But I love you."

Chapter 16

One of the most popular bars in Polk, Pete's Grill, unlike many local establishments, revealed no hint of the 1960s or '70s. It featured no pictures of Farrah Fawcett or Bill Bixby, no Route 66 signs, and no drinks named after Jan and Dean or The Supremes. The jukebox carried nothing older than Taylor Swift. Thus, Pete's Grill attracted droves of Nostalgia City employees eager to leave the past behind, if only for a couple of hours.

Among people dressed in a variety of NC outfits, Lyle spotted a cluster of garage employees at the far end of the restaurant's crowded bar wearing their mechanic's blues. The hum of voices clashed with contemporary music and the crack of plastic from people playing air hockey off in a corner. Lyle had been to Pete's before, and he wasn't exactly sure what he might gain now by visiting the employees' favorite watering hole. Yeah, he'd been thinking about Don Perez, mostly trying to figure out what someone had been looking for when he or she tossed the Perez residence. Rey had told him Mrs. Perez said nothing was stolen.

Lyle found an empty stool at the bar between two garage workers. The beefy guy to his right, with light red hair and thick neck, watched the baseball game on the big screen behind the bar. The more slightly built man seated to his left leaned on the bar, holding his smart phone in one hand, thumbing the screen as he hoisted a tall beer with his other hand. Lyle ordered a drink.

"Damn," said the guy to Lyle's right as his fist hit the bar.

Lyle looked up to see a Los Angeles Dodger circling the bases as a stunned Arizona Diamondbacks pitcher looked skyward, for inspiration or perhaps intervention.

"Pitching. We need more pitching," Lyle said.

"At least today," said the man. "Where'd this lad come from?"

"Up from the minors," Lyle said, "or in some trade. D-backs are always trading away good players."

"Another," the man said to the bartender. "Yeah, scotch."

The next batter struck out and the inning ended. Lyle's drink arrived.

"You work at the park?" asked the scotch drinker.

"Now, would I wear this bow tie if I didn't?"

The other man smiled. "I don't believe you would."

"Do you have an English accent?" Lyle asked.

"Yeah, but I've been here twenty years, long enough to appreciate baseball."

Lyle glanced at the name embroidered on the man's work shirt. "Your name is Dutch? You don't sound like you're from Holland."

"Me dad was born in Rotterdam. He met me mum in England. We lived in the UK while I was growing up."

"So the nickname just stuck," Lyle said. He introduced himself and watched to see if "Dutch" recognized him. If he did, his light blue eyes didn't show it. "I drive a taxi in the park. What do you do?"

"Body and frame shop supervisor," he said reaching for the fresh drink the bartender delivered."

Lyle took a relaxed sip of his gin and tonic. "How long have you been at the park?"

"About six months. Came up from Tucson."

"I'm in the garage every so often getting my cab serviced. In fact, Don Perez used to work on it."

Dutch's jaw tightened and he switched his attention back to the TV.

"Did you know him?"

"Yeah, but he didn't work in my department."

"Horrible thing. I guess everyone misses him."

The man grunted.

"You think someone crept in after work and got him?" Lyle said glancing at the game and trying to sound natural.

"Who knows?"

Lyle looked at the blond-haired man to his left, short but muscular, in his late twenties. Still focused on his cell phone, he twitched rather than waved his thumb across the screen. His stitched-on name badge said *Blake*.

"Did you know Don Perez?" Lyle asked.

"The guy who got killed? No." The man made brief eye contact. His look changed in about a second from inquisitive to ominous. "Why you asking?"

"No reason." Lyle said sipping his drink, "I knew him. Just sorry it happened. Do you think someone had it in for him?"

"None o' my business." Blake picked up his beer, slid off his bar stool, and walked away. He settled at a table with others in shop uniforms.

Lyle wasn't sure if Dutch had heard his question. He soon found out.

"This ain't a great thing to be asking people," Dutch said, still looking at the ballgame.

"What?" Lyle said. "Just something to talk about."

"Bollocks. We already got asked questions by the cops. They're hinting someone in the shop killed him. Okay?"

"Sorry. I guess that's kind of tough for you."

"Think so? We don't talk about it."

"Okay, okay. Don seemed like such a nice guy. Quiet. Never bothered anyone."

"Like I said, he didn't work for me." Dutch finished his drink and started looking for the bartender. He glanced up and pointed at the TV screen.

Lyle looked up to see an Arizona player dive into second base, just ahead of a throw. "We still have a chance," Lyle said. Picking up his drink, he stood and turned to Dutch. "Sorry to upset you. Take care."

Dutch only grunted.

Lyle approached the table where Blake sat with three other NC employees. Not intending to sit, Lyle put a knee on an empty chair, held his drink in his hand. "Hey, I guess everybody's stressed over this," he said to Blake. "Didn't mean to bring up a sore subject."

"No problem," Blake said. He glanced at Lyle then turned away.

"You talking about Don?" asked a young man across the table. A scraggly moustache sat above his upper lip and he wore plastic-framed glasses.

Before Lyle could respond, Blake put a hand with spread fingers on the table as if demonstrating some authority. "We're done talking about it." The two other men at the table became interested in the ballgame.

Lyle glanced at the man who had mentioned Don. He too, turned away. Lyle stood and wandered off a few steps. He looked over at the air hockey tables. Maybe he could strike up a conversation with the players, two of whom wore NC garage work clothes. Out of the corner of his eye he saw the young man with the moustache get up from the table and look in his direction. In a smooth motion, Blake stood and stepped close to the man, saying something Lyle couldn't hear. He grasped the man's arm. The young man froze. Blake chuckled as if he were sharing a joke then sat down. The young man stood for a moment, as if trying to regain his equilibrium, then sat down.

Lyle continued toward the air hockey players. He stood a distance from the game pretending to watch, but kept an eye on Blake's table. After a few minutes, the young man with the moustache said something to the two other men then got up. He walked a slow and irregular path to the door. Lyle followed him, careful not to be visible from Blake's table. Outside, he caught up with the man as he moved toward a parked car.

"Did you want to tell me something, something about Don Perez?"

The man looked up, startled. As he turned to face Lyle, his name patch showed him to be Austin. "Nothin' to say."

"I saw what Blake did. Why didn't he want you talking?"

"Are you a cop or somethin'?"

Damn, *sounding* like a detective again. Lyle fretted that he still *looked* like a cop too, even with his retro sideburns. "I just work at the park. I was a friend of Don's."

"Somethin' got him killed. Blake's just nervous...he...everybody is."

"Were you a friend of Don's?"

"I didn't know him." Austin opened his car door. "I gotta get home."

Chapter 17

"What do you plan to do about it?" said the first news media caller of what Kate expected to be a long, taxing day.

Kate cradled the phone on her shoulder while she prepared to scribble notes.

"The San Navarro County Sheriff's Department says the death of Don Perez was *murder*." The reporter from a Phoenix all-news radio station had an annoying sing-song voice. Kate wondered how she got a job in broadcasting. "Is the murder affecting your operations?"

Kate stared out her fourth floor office window. The low morning sun cast square, heavy shadows of buildings across the street below like a cityscape in an Edward Hopper painting. "Sheriff Wisniewski has met with our president, and we're doing everything we can to cooperate with the investigation. It doesn't affect our guests. It's a beautiful day in Nostalgia City. People are enjoying themselves."

"What about the DEA raid you had Wednesday? Is the sheriff looking for drugs, too?"

Kate had been answering the drug question for two days and had the answer memorized, but she modulated her voice and tried not to sound *too* serious. "As you know, there were no drugs found at the park. Our security screening keeps this a safe, happy place."

When Kate got off the phone, thankful the reporter didn't directly ask about a drug connection for the murder, she grabbed her empty coffee cup, and walked to the PR department's small coffee room, actually an alcove. Kate wore a gray pants suit and an off-white blouse. She probably wouldn't have to talk on camera today, but murder at a theme park sounded like a classic "film at eleven" story, so you never knew.

"Calls this morning?" Kate asked when media coordinator Amanda walked in.

"Yes, I just talked to someone from the *Flagstaff Bulletin*," said the usually upbeat young woman. "He asked about the murder, then about the DEA. I told him no drugs were ever found, then he goes, 'aren't you guys promoting marijuana?'"

Kate *knew* her connection with Arthur's pot initiative would be a problem. "What did you tell him?"

Before Amanda could answer, Kate's secretary, Joann, crowded into the coffee corner. "Do you want to talk to Brandon from KWTQ news? He wants to know about park security."

"Would you tell him someone will call him back soon," Kate said. "Ask about his deadline." She turned her attention back to Amanda.

"I told the *Bulletin* we weren't promoting pot," Amanda said. "I said you were on an advisory board for the proposition but that the park had no position on legalizing marijuana."

"That's great," Kate said.

As Amanda went back to her desk, Joann lingered. "There's something else," she said. "Last night there was some sort of bar fight in the park. It involved a woman named Poole and security had to respond."

"Poole?"

"Uh huh."

"What happened?"

"I don't know the details. A friend of mine who's dating a security guard told me about it this morning."

"Thanks, Joann, you're a gem. Now I have two reasons to go see Howard Chaffee."

Twenty minutes later Kate sat in an almost comfortable office chair facing the security chief across his wooden desk. With two banks of drawers, sharp corners, pedestal legs, and a wide overhanging top, the desk looked like it would have been ultramodern fifty years ago. Howard had plenty of work space.

"Thanks for taking the time, Howard."

"Sure," he said, "what's up?"

Kate knew Howard from executive meetings, but mainly as a result of his help with a previous scrape. By comparison, what Kate planned to ask was easy.

"We're getting lots of calls from the news media about the murder—and the drug raid, if you can call it that. Reporters are asking what we're doing about it, if we have increased security. The media love this stuff."

Howard nodded. "In San Francisco, the press was all over us sometimes. It's challenging. I know how it is."

"I thought you would." Kate glanced around Howard's office. It wasn't filled with police memorabilia as might be expected. He had a few certificates and diplomas, but no sign of medals, plaques, or framed grip-and-grin photos. Framed posters of 1960s San Francisco police cars hung on one wall. "I was wondering if you would be willing to field a few news media calls and talk with reporters."

Howard grinned. He wore a white, button-down collar shirt and a paisley tie in subdued colors. Short gray hair, not quite a military cut, receded from his forehead.

"You did a little of that in San Francisco, didn't you?" she said. Howard's impressive law enforcement pedigree, his deep, authoritative voice, and his killer smile, made him perfect for the assignment. Kate told him so, leaving out the smile, but saying he'd look good on camera. "You would really be doing a big service for the park and a favor for me." Kate heard Howard sigh, but she continued. "I'm not asking you to tell the media any secrets. You'd just be saying what I've been telling them, that we're cooperating with the sheriff, etcetera, etcetera. But the big difference is, you're the voice of our security. You can tell them about how we screen guests and patrol the streets."

"Okay, you can halt the sales pitch," Howard said. "I'll do it."

"I'll screen the calls so you won't have to do too many."

"Is anyone going to come out here to film?"

"I don't know. If you want to stay off camera, you can."

Howard raised a hand. "I can do that too, if you need it, but I don't have a lot of extra time."

"I'm grateful for whatever time you can spare. You're more authoritative about this than I am, and I don't really want to talk much about the drug hunt."

"Because of your connection to the marijuana ballot thing?"

Kate nodded. "I agreed to advise Arthur Poole on his ballot measure campaign."

"You're frowning. Are you not happy about it?"

"Probably bad timing, but if marijuana *is* legalized, we—the park—need to be prepared. And speaking of Poole, I heard about someone—probably *Mrs.* Poole—getting in trouble last night. Could you fill me in a little? Is this something that's going to hit the media?

"Last night we had an incident at the Centerville Tavern. But you won't have to worry about it getting in the news. Two individuals were intoxicated and started a disturbance approximately one a.m. A bar employee put in a call and two of our security personnel responded." Howard paused, tapped his keyboard, then glanced at the computer screen on his desk. "According to the report, the people in question, Nick Rafferty and Persis Poole, both had been drinking. They were unsteady and they spoke with slurred speech. The security officer said the tavern manager asked them to leave and they refused. There was pushing and some profanity." He looked up at Kate. "The individuals, Rafferty and Poole, were broke. They stated they couldn't pay for their last drinks and had no way of getting home."

"What did they do?"

"We try to solve problems with guests whenever we can, before bringing in law enforcement. The tavern manager understood. The Poole woman apparently phoned Arthur Poole. Is she his ex-wife?"

"That's right."

"Subsequently, Poole came over to the park and settled up the individuals' bar tab. Then he gave her some money and called a Polk city taxi to take them back to wherever they were staying. All in all, simple. No need to call the sheriff. Problem was resolved by two a.m."

"Wow."

"What kind of a guy does that for an ex-wife?" Chaffe asked.

"A guy like Arthur Poole."

Chapter 18

"It still doesn't work, the transmission. Jumps in and out of gear."

Lyle stood in a service stall at Hooper's Auto Repair and Towing next to a Chevy sedan with the hood up. Cody Hooper leaned against a fender and shook his head. "You do a lot of fast acceleration?"

"Hey, it's a Mustang. But I'm not abusing it." Lyle moved his head and shoulders forward and back, mimicking the erratic motion of his car. "The car shifts when you least expect it."

Hooper wiped his hands on a greasy rag and glanced around at Lyle's car. He shook his head again. "Okay, I'll take another look it. Can you leave it? We'll call you."

"Yes, I'll leave it. It stopped working about twenty minutes after I picked it up last night."

Hooper scowled. "We'll call you."

"There's my ride," Lyle said and he saw Hooper look up at the sheriff's car. Lyle waved to Rey then gave Hooper a look that said, *big consequences if you don't get it right this time.* At least that's what he hoped it said.

As Lyle walked around toward the passenger side of the sheriff's car, Rey smiled and nodded at Hooper.

"Don't look so friendly, Rey," Lyle said as he got in. "I paid him a lot already and my car still shifts like shit. I want him to think he'll be in the back of this car if he screws up."

"Clutch problem?"

"It's an automatic, remember? I only took it here because one of the other cab drivers told me Hooper did good work. Yeah, after how many tries?" Lyle spoke a bit louder than he intended.

"Okay. I get it." Rey pulled out of the lot and headed for Nostalgia City.

"Sorry to be a crab this morning. I appreciate the ride."

They rode in silence for a minute.

"This is like old times," Lyle said. "I haven't been in a black and white in years."

"I should have taken an unmarked car."

"You want me to duck down?" Lyle tugged at his shoulder harness and slide down in the seat.

"Very funny. This is official department business anyway. You're going to fill me in on your recent *unofficial* investigation."

"Yes. I spent last evening at Pete's Grill."

Rey grinned.

"Hey, this was work."

"Sure. Go ahead."

Lyle filled him in on his conversation with Dutch. "He's in charge of the body and frame shop. I guess you know."

"Yes. He say anything new?"

"He just told me they don't talk about the murder and said he only knew Perez in passing. Hard to figure him, but not so hard to peg a little guy named Blake."

Lyle explained his encounter with Blake and Austin. "When I left their table, Austin got up, maybe to talk with me, but Blake just put a hand on him and he turned pale. Later I tried to get the kid to talk, but he was obviously too scared."

"Of Blake."

"Of something."

"Something's going on out there. We couldn't get anyone to tell us anything useful about Perez. Even people in his department. Maybe we should talk to Blake and Austin again. The name Blake sounds familiar."

Rey drove out of Polk and turned onto the new four-lane highway that approached Nostalgia City. A modern version of a Burma-Shave sign stretched along the road: *Don't go fast / visit the past / be sittin' pretty / in Nostalgia City.* Too young to have seen the originals, Lyle remembered his parents talking about Burma-Shave signs. Quaint and more appealing than LED billboards that flooded out the stars at night.

Lyle looked back inside the car. "Any luck finding where Perez moonlighted?"

"None. We contacted every repair shop and garage in the county. No one had heard of him. We could try Flagstaff or Prescott, but do you think he'd drive that far every night?"

"Not likely."

"And Lydia Perez said he worked in Polk," Rey said. "So if he wasn't moonlighting in a garage, where did he get the new car?"

"Drugs."

"There ya go."

"Let's assume we have a drug trade somewhere in the park and Perez was involved."

"So how does he get himself killed?"

"Keeping something for himself."

"Think he was doing drugs?" Rey asked.

"An addict? No."

"Then he was skimming and got caught."

"Or, maybe it was hush money. He found out something and they paid him to keep quiet."

"Usually they'd just eliminate him."

"What do you call having a car dropped on you?" Lyle said. "That would send a message."

"And no one at the garage is talking."

Rey turned into one of the employee parking lots, on the edge of Nostalgia City. Long rows of cantilevered solar panels formed canopies to shade parking spaces. Martinez parked in a shady spot and he and Lyle got out.

Lyle pulled off his dark glasses and glanced toward the horizon. Rabbitbrush, greasebush, cholla, and other greenery he couldn't name punctuated the tan and brown desert that stretched to the base of distance hills. Did only natives of the southwest appreciate the subtleties of this arid land?

"I've been thinking, Rey."

"Oh, that's dangerous."

"I know. But listen." Lyle held his dark glasses in his hand and turned to Rey. "Whoever broke into the Perez residence. I think they were looking for something that would connect back to drug smuggling."

"To keep a lid on it? Or were they looking for drugs?"

"No, not drugs. Something else. Information on deliveries, maybe something with people's names."

"Would he keep something like that?"

"Someone thought he had *something* valuable."

"We need to talk to Lydia Perez again," Rey said.

"We?"

"The sheriff's department. I want to look through Don Perez's things."

"The guy who broke in either didn't find anything, or he took it."

"Thanks for the advice, Mr. Deming."

"Thanks for the ride, Undersheriff Martinez."

Chapter 19

Out jogging near her home Saturday morning, Kate stopped along a ridge when she saw two pickup trucks pull up on the dirt road below. She watched the drivers get out and walk toward each other. One carried a brown package. Something about the way the two men looked up and down the road made her freeze.

Less than an hour earlier, Kate had started off on a routine run. While Lyle ran to reduce stress, Kate ran out of habit. Even though it'd been twenty years since she played college basketball, she still worked out regularly. No, not just habit. Running kept her slim, her reflexes sharp, and her mind clear. Summer and its overpowering heat had not arrived, and the network of desert trails beyond NC's Timeless Village called to her for a late morning jog.

Suited up in spandex shorts, a bright green Xanadu Boutique T-shirt and running shoes, Kate dashed through scrub brush and Pinion pines, over the dusty trail that led away from her apartment building. Three miles from any paved street, she hit her stride. Ahead, the narrow path intersected an overgrown Jeep trail that ran up and over a low ridge. She jogged along the trail to the top of the ridge where she stopped.

She'd never seen a car on the unpaved road about 75 or 100 yards away, but now the trucks and the drivers riveted her attention. The trucks parked side-by-side, facing in opposite directions, a tall, four-wheel-drive pickup with a camper shell and behind it a dark pickup. One of the two men—he appeared to be dressed in jeans and a long-sleeve shirt—held the package, either a full grocery bag or a beat-up cardboard box. He offered it to the second man who examined it, then handed it back. The second man, wearing a red baseball cap, then turned and walked to the passenger side of the four-wheel-drive truck. He paused and looked up and down the road again. Then he pulled a sports bag out of his truck and the two men exchanged packages.

Kate jumped behind a tree as soon as she realized what she was watching. But one of the men spotted her. He said something to the other man and his hand went to his waist. Kate couldn't see if he had a gun, but she didn't wait to find out. As she turned and started to run, she heard one door slam then another as the trucks' engines roared to life. Along the edge of the ridge, Kate paused to look back. A billowing trail of dust enveloped the blue pickup as it raced away. The other truck, the four-wheel-drive, pulled off the road, onto the trail, and headed for Kate.

Running for exercise and running when a drug dealer's truck is after you require the same leg movements, but that's the only similarity. Kate ran for her life. Her feet pounded the desert floor as she sprinted along the Jeep trail. It took her at a right angle from the truck's path. She wanted to cut though the brush to where the trail narrowed and headed directly toward civilization. But jumping around the thick vegetation—that included prickly pear—would slow her progress too much. She thought her long legs would carry her to safety when she heard the whine of the engine and saw the truck's cab appear over the ridge. A black steel framework—some sort of extra bumper—protected the front of the truck and added to its menace.

The truck hit the top of the rise and crashed down the slope kicking up dirt as it picked up speed. The roar of its engine grew louder, but Kate couldn't waste the seconds it would take to look back again. She heard a grinding noise as the pickup jostled over rocks. No cell phone, no way to protect herself, except speed, Kate pushed into high gear as if she were racing down the basketball court on a fast break with ten seconds to go.

Metallic thunder from the truck's gears and screaming exhaust echoed right behind her. The Jeep trail flattened out giving her pursuer unobstructed running room. As Kate dashed forward, a ditch appeared next to the trail. She saw the narrow running path on the opposite side. Adrenalin pushed her waning stamina to the limit. She leaped from the Jeep trail but didn't clear the ravine. She landed on the upslope and fell. With the truck just yards behind her, she dug her feet into the rocky soil and pushed herself up to the path above. Driven by muscle memory and fear, she jumped ahead with mad strides.

The noise behind her changed pitch. She heard the engine rev coupled with a rushing, whirring sound. She looked back. The driver had followed Kate off the trail. The truck angled nose down in the ravine, its wheels slipping and spinning.

She didn't stop. She pushed herself for two miles until she reached the first streets and homes of Timeless Village. Kate planned to run into the first home she saw, but she didn't have to. A Nostalgia City security car was just turning a corner when Kate hurried by.

She took a few deep breaths before she started to tell her story to the surprised security officer. She identified herself and explained, as cogently as she could, that a crazy man in a pickup truck had chased her through the desert.

"I think I saw a drug deal. That's why they chased me. You need to call the sheriff right away."

The officer thought for a moment. "I should call my dispatcher first."

The security officer described the situation briefly over the radio and the dispatcher responded immediately.

"Where did this happen?" the dispatcher's voice crackled. "We gotta call the sheriff."

Kate snatched the radio mike from the young man. She identified herself and explained as accurately as she could what the truck looked like and where deputies would find it, stuck in a ravine.

She apologized to the security guard then felt a wave of exhaustion sweep over her. She'd done what she could. It was up to the sheriff's deputies now.

Suddenly she felt undressed. She knew she'd be the center of an investigation—maybe for hours—so she excused herself from security and dashed the block and a half to her apartment building.

She threw on a fresh blouse and shorts, putting her running shoes back on. Then she grabbed her cell phone and jogged back to where she'd left the NC security car. By then, a sheriff's car had joined it. Kate introduced herself to the deputy then stepped back for a moment to call Lyle. She reached him in a hardware store in Polk. She gave him a synopsis and he said he'd be there in twenty minutes.

Kate didn't want to wait for reports from deputies on the scene. "Let's go out there," she said to the deputy who stood next to his car talking to the security officer. "I can show you exactly where it is."

"Units should be there by now," the deputy told her.

"Let's be sure," Kate said in her most commanding voice. "The sheriff will want to get this guy."

Kate was already sitting in the sheriff's car before the deputy had time to get in. Kate directed him out and around the housing tract and straight to a street she knew connected with the dirt road where the trucks had been.

When they got there, a County Sheriff's SUV, lights flashing, sat on top of the rise where Kate had stood when she witnessed the suspicious exchange. A deputy with several stripes running down the arms of his uniform walked down from the ridge.

"I'm Sergeant Galton," he said, "are you the victim? Did you report this?"

"I'm the person that lunatic tried to run down, yes."

"You said it was a beige pickup with big wheels, camper shell, and some kind of aftermarket bumper?"

"That's right."

"We found the place he got stuck. Ripped up a lot of brush, but he got out. We put it on the air. He's had a little time to get away. Report said you didn't get a license number, right?"

Chapter 20

Lyle's Mustang barreled down the dirt road. It slipped out of gear, started coasting, then lurched forward. Lyle swore, smacked his hand on the dashboard, and urged the car on. It responded with a burst of speed before Lyle skidded to a stop next to the sheriff's car, forgetting the cloud of desert dust following him.

Kate and the two deputy sheriffs looked away and tried to shield their faces from the cloud. As the airborne powder subsided, Lyle got out. He wore jeans and a Hawaiian shirt. He hugged Kate then apologized to her and the deputies for his cavalry-style arrival. He put a hand on Kate's arm and squeezed as he listened to her give an account of her ordeal. Dusty and windblown, thanks partially to Lyle, she looked frazzled around the edges but sounded determined. *Thank God she's okay. If I only could have been there.*

Kate explained to deputies that she'd been too far away to identify the men, but she recounted everything she saw, up until the terrifying pickup stalled in the ditch.

"I don't *know* if it was a drug deal," she said. "I was up on that ridge. It just looked like it to me."

"We'd like you to come into the station when you can to make a full report," the sergeant said.

Kate agreed.

Lyle took a deep breath. *If we weren't sure about a drug connection before this...*

Simultaneously, all four people looked up as a siren's wail cut through the air. A half mile down the dirt road, a brown cloud followed a racing vehicle. As it got closer, Lyle saw the hulking blue Ford Crown Victoria, unmarked but lit up a like a carnival ride with red and blue lights pulsating through the grill and windshield.

When the car came to a sliding stop, smothering everyone again, San Navarro County Sheriff Jeb Wisniewski lumbered out. Wearing a uniform shirt, badge, and gun belt over jeans, Wisniewski planted his cowboy boots into the ground as he plodded over.

"You two again, huh?" he said scowling at Lyle and Kate. "You kinda attract trouble, don'tcha?" The sheriff stood with his hands on his gun belt, head lowered as he glared at Kate and Lyle through bushy eyebrows. The two deputies gave each other questioning looks. Then the sheriff smiled. "Don't look so glum there, Deming," he said, slapping Lyle's upper left arm. "Are you okay, Ms. Sorensen?"

"I think so. Thanks, Sheriff." She brushed fine grit off her shoulders.

Kate put up a good front, but Lyle watched her closely.

"Keith," the sheriff said, looking at the sergeant, "these two are Nostalgia City's hotshot amateur detectives. Well, *he* didn't used to be an amateur. You may have heard of 'em."

Sergeant Galton looked from Lyle to Kate and back to Lyle, a sign of recognition lighting his eyes.

Lyle looked at the overweight, often truculent law enforcement boss of the county. The sheriff had to get in a *dig,* but that was his nature. Wisniewski's long black hair, combed straight back, shone in the sun. Lyle could see his Native American heritage, no matter how many generations removed. "Pleasure to see you too, Sheriff," he said. "Glad to see you're on top of this."

"Top o' what? That's the question. A drug deal? Then someone tries to run you over," he said, looking at Kate, "and we arrive too late."

"We broadcast the description of the truck as soon as we got it," the sergeant said.

"Yeah, a light colored pickup," Wisniewski said. "That'll narrow it down. Every other goddamn vehicle in the county is a pickup. I got one myself."

"We think it might have been a Chevy or GMC," Sergeant Galton said.

"We?"

"Sorry I couldn't be more specific," Kate said. "It was chasing after me about thirty miles an hour. I didn't have much time."

"Of course you didn't. Not a fault o' yours," Wisniewski said. "I'd just like to get the bastard." The sheriff stalked back and forth for a few moments staring at the ground. "This may be tied into that crap we got going in the park's garage. We gotta get a handle on it. In the meantime, we don't want this incident—aggravated assault, attempted murder—to get in the media. It'd cause another shit storm for the park and the county. And the damn DEA started it." He turned to Sergeant Galton. "We're gonna sit on the report for a while or maybe treat it as some kind of random assault. Not too many details. Nothing the reporters can get a hold of." He looked at Kate. "You okay with that?"

She shrugged. "I wouldn't want to explain this to TV reporters right now. They've been on us enough since the murder."

"So," the sheriff said turning to Lyle, "you gonna figure out what's goin' on here?"

"I don't know. It's a tough one. Rey is working hard on it."

"Guarandamntee you he is. He knows the Perez murder and all this supposed drug crap is *numero uno*."

The sheriff walked toward his cruiser but paused when he saw a cloud heading down the road. Long before the car reached the gathering, it slowed down and covered the last hundred yards at a crawl. When the car stopped, Howard

Chaffee got out. Dressed in slacks and sport shirt, he walked toward the sheriff's car.

"You're kinda late to the party," Wisniewski said.

"I was at home. The office called. Everyone okay?"

The sheriff chuckled. "Deming here can bring you up to speed. We got other things to do." He turned to the sergeant. "Okay, Keith, let's take a look at the scene." The two men headed up the slope.

"Why were you going so slowly, Howard?" Lyle asked.

"Didn't want to kick up too much dust," Howard said.

Kate looked at the deputy and they both laughed. "We appreciate that," she said.

"Must be an *in* joke," Lyle said, smiling, walking over to Howard. "Kate needs to get back. If you follow me, I'll drop her off and then fill you in."

Kate walked with Lyle back to his car, his arm around her waist. "Are you really okay?"

"Surprisingly calm. Tired, and I need a bath."

"Scared hell out of me when you called."

"By then I was safe."

When Kate got in, Lyle dropped his car into gear, monetarily forgetting his recalcitrant transmission. He glanced in his rearview to see that Howard was following. His car accelerated slowly then jerked forward with a loud clank.

"Still doesn't work?" Kate said.

Lyle just grumbled.

The day before, he'd paid Hooper an additional $750. "Needed a new solenoid," Hooper had told him. "Now it runs like new." *Bullshit*. Before Lyle got home that evening, the transmission clunked, clattered, and almost refused to move. He called Hooper's. Voicemail told him the garage was closed, would reopen on Monday, and that his call was very important to them.

"Are you going to take it back in?" Kate said.

"Hell no. He's not touching the car. I'm taking it to the dealer. See if they can figure out what that crook Hooper did to it."

Lyle felt Kate's hand on his shoulder. Here she almost got killed by a madman in a truck, and he was complaining about car repairs. Maybe he *was* nuts. Taking his anger out on Hooper was some sort of release. He couldn't punch out the truck driver who chased Kate. He couldn't, it seemed, do anything. He started to wonder if the pursuer in the truck would be able to identify Kate, figure out who she was. From the distance, they probably couldn't recognize her face, but inconspicuous Kate was not.

❡❡❡

"She used to be an athlete, so she just ran away from him," Lyle told Howard as they sat at Lyle's kitchen table after Kate was safely back at her apartment. An array of cooking tools sat on the counter along with a mini food processor. Conventional tools—plyers, screwdriver, and a saw—lay on the table.

"I was looking for parts to build a kitchen shelf when Kate called me. She's tough," he told Howard with a touch of pride.

"Are you and she…"

"We work together," Lyle said.

"I remember."

Lyle went to the refrigerator and pulled out two beers. He opened the bottles and handed one to Howard.

"So, you think it was drugs?" Howard said.

"Two guys on a deserted road looking over their shoulders as they exchanged packages? They weren't swapping recipes."

"I agree. It's becoming a serious problem." Howard had the gift of understatement. "Has Rey got any leads?"

"No." Lyle explained his night at the bar with garage mechanics and said Rey would be checking out specific employees.

"You think Rey is up to this?" Howard asked.

"You've worked with him."

"Yes, but not on anything like this."

"He's a good detective, keeps his department running well, sometimes has to run interference for his boss and—"

"Okay, but—"

"And I've seen him trade point blank shots with two of the meanest guys you've ever met. So yes, I think he's up to it."

Howard silently processed the information. "Gayle LeBlanc says she expects a new shipment of cars soon."

"Then we'll probably have to deal with the DEA again."

"Not so sure," Howard said. "They made a mistake coming out here, and I don't think we'll see them again soon."

Chapter 21

"Are you all right?" Joann asked when Kate walked into the PR department Monday morning.

Nostalgia City, like a small town, didn't keep secrets. Kate had wondered if Saturday's run for her life would get around. It hadn't taken long. One of the things Kate liked about her secretary was her connections throughout the park. It helped keep Kate informed of rumors and trouble spots that might require public affairs intervention. Kate also valued Joann's discretion. Therefore, Kate's lowered eyebrows and barely perceptible nod of her head as she walked by told Joann all she needed to know.

Max would no doubt be informed. In some parks, security reports went through channels to the top. Owing to past difficulties, and the CEO's personality, at Nostalgia City it was the chief of security's job to keep Maxwell informed of crimes and disturbances. Still recovering from her ordeal, even after a quiet weekend, Kate focused on Max and keeping him from overreacting. When she placed her purse and sunglasses on her retro desk, she decided she'd go right up to his office to reassure him. She'd say she was fine, even though she occasionally imagined she could hear the pickup's engine. She'd tell Max that the incident was best forgotten or at least put aside for now.

The elevator let Kate off on the top floor of the Maxwell Building. She started to rush through the op-art decorated reception area and straight to Maxwell's office when the clerk at the desk stopped her.

"Ms. Sorensen, are you looking for Mr. Maxwell?"

"Yes, is he busy?"

"He's not here today. But Marion needs to speak to you."

"I need help," said Maxwell's fiftyish administrative assistant when Kate plopped down in the chair next to her desk. "I hate to bother you. I know what you've been through." Marion Keegan had her own office, appropriately appointed with a Jasper Johns print and a photo mural of Jim Morrison. "Do you know Daniel Fapp?" she asked Kate.

"With a name like that, I should," Kate said. "But I don't."

"He's the owner…well, the lessee/concessionaire, of the Bohemian Coffee House."

"The coffee shop next to Xanadu."

"That's right. And Mr. Fapp has been complaining about our famous headshop. He's got a long list of grievances."

"Why has this come to you?"

"Mr. Fapp has not been satisfied with results from the Concessionaires Support Department and has been constantly calling Mr. Maxwell. He's kind of rude."

"I can imagine the reception Max would give him, especially if he's already worn out his welcome elsewhere."

"Yes, well, Mr. Maxwell—"

"Wants me to handle it. Give him the PR treatment." *I almost get run over by a drug dealer and now I have to coddle some recalcitrant concessionaire?* Kate had worked for Max for years in Las Vegas before he recruited her to the park, and he knew she had a way of consoling, petitioning, threatening—when necessary—or even charming pesky malcontents into line.

"Has Fapp talked to Arthur Poole? I can't imagine that Arthur wouldn't be willing to solve a little disagreement quickly."

Maxwell's administrative assistant wrinkled her forehead and leaned back in her chair. "Mr. Fapp used some vulgar language to describe Mr. Poole."

"Mr. Fapp sounds delightful," Kate said.

༺༻

"Sending PR out here now, huh?" Daniel Fapp said. "You here to help or just pacify me?"

Kate sat outside under an umbrella in the Bohemian Coffee House patio looking at Daniel Fapp. "Mr. Maxwell wanted me to talk with you about your concerns."

Fapp wore a wide-collar shirt in keeping with the NC look, but his thin moustache and abbreviated goatee did not fit '70s retro. His dark hair was moussed in place. He obviously spent time on his appearance and Kate couldn't tell if he was thirty or forty or somewhere in between. "Well, my *concerns* are that Xanadu is ruining my business."

When Kate had picked up a coffee inside, the coffee bar was far from deserted, and most of the tables outside were filled. But Kate wasn't there to argue. Often just letting someone gripe in detail, in this case to a vice president, was half the battle. She smiled, professionally, and nodded for him to continue.

"Look at those signs," he said, pointing with a thin finger to two low, A-frame signs on the sidewalk between Xanadu and the coffee house. "They block access. Then there's the parking lot in back."

Kate started to say something, but Fapp interrupted. "Yeah, I know lots of tourists just walk, but when people want to come here and park their NC rental cars—there's no room. Xanadu has taken them all."

"Have you talked to Arthur Poole?"

"Poole?" The corners of Fapp's mouth, and his moustache, turned down. "Huh." It was a cross between a snort and a growl. "He's a useless jerk."

Kate looked at a customer at the next table over. On the seat next to her sat a Xanadu shopping bag. Kate brought her gaze back to Fapp and made eye contact.

"Yes, we do get some Xanadu customers here, but most of them have to go outside. It's the smell."

"The smell?"

"That's what's really unbearable. You know when people come to the Bohemian they want to smell our rich coffee aroma. The ambience, that's what sells us. Xanadu stinks up the place. That guy Poole, he comes over here and says he can't smell anything but coffee. What an idiot. Thinks it's my imagination. He's obviously the problem, but no one in the park has the balls to do anything."

Kate looked at him as he took a breath. She remembered the incense at Xanadu. Part of the image. She said, "How could it be getting into your shop?"

"I don't know. Through the walls, through the vents. No one will fix it. Is that stupid?"

Kate listened for ten minutes more, nodding or making a brief comment, hoping that Fapp would run out of steam. Eventually, he did.

"You'd better do something," he said. "That Poole doesn't give a shit. I need to get his attention." With that, he pushed his chair back noisily and marched into his shop.

Kate could see he'd attracted the attention of customers sitting on the patio. She just smiled and walked next door into Xanadu where she found Poole rearranging a display in an uncrowded part of the store.

"Arthur, I have a question about your neighbor."

"Mr. Fapp?"

"The very one. Have you talked to him about settling some of his problems?"

"Yes, I met with him more than once. I thought we settled the incense issue."

"He says he wants someone from maintenance to come out and check the A/C vents. Maybe some of your—" Kate waved a hand in the air. "—*atmosphere* is bleeding over next door."

"It's already been checked. Maintenance guys tested the seals on all the vents, but Mr. Fapp had a problem with it. He wanted tests on the air quality in the coffee house. I don't know what happened after that. All you can smell in there is coffee."

"Fapp was pretty insistent. He said you're being—" Kate smiled to herself. "—*uncooperative*. He thinks you're...well, let's say unfriendly."

"Oh, Daniel's okay. Maybe just a little forgetful."

Chapter 22

Lyle coaxed his Mustang into the nearest Ford dealership first thing in the morning. The young service writer looked at him sympathetically as Lyle explained the car's symptoms and what allegedly had been done by Hooper. The man gave Lyle no indication of what he thought the problem might be, but his expression made Lyle feel as if his beloved pony was headed for the glue factory. The fact they gave him a free loaner car cinched it.

Modern cars, Lyle knew, were controlled by an internal computer network. The network told sparkplugs when to fire, monitored manifold air pressure, stabilized the ride, performed self-checks, *and* shifted gears. Unlike today's cars, however, his 1973 Dodge taxi had few, if any, automated systems. He tinkered with a few parts under the hood and made the big V-8 sound like it was gasping for breath. He didn't sabotage Nostalgia City equipment out of malice or frustration with his Mustang. He wanted an excuse to hang around the NC garage and talk to mechanics.

Rey had told him that additional interviews with garage employees Blake, Austin, Dutch, and a few others had yielded little, although deputies were checking alibis. Austin, in particular, showed reluctance to talk at all. Deputies were careful to make the repeat interrogations appear random to cover Lyle as their source of information.

When Lyle chugged his wheezing taxi into the NC garage east entrance Monday morning, a mechanic waited for him. Lyle had phoned Gayle LeBlanc ahead of time and asked for her help in arranging the service appointment. Dressed in his cabbie outfit of white shirt, bow tie, and yellow hat, he drove the Dodge into a service bay near where Perez was found. At this east end of the sprawling facility, Lyle was not likely to encounter the mechanics he'd talked to in the bar, but even if he did, he reminded himself, he had a believable reason for being there.

Thanks to Gayle's tinkering with the work schedule, the mechanic assigned to Lyle's taxi was Luis Nieto, the man who found Perez's body.

"You can get an idea of the problem," Lyle told Nieto, "just by starting it up. These old buggies just don't stay in tune. Maybe it's the fact we're always idling or crawling along Main Street."

Slightly built, Nieto moved with quick, short motions. His hands were used to work. He opened the taxi's hood and spread a protective canvas cover over the car's left fender. He started the car then leaned under the hood.

"Don used to keep this running smoothly," Lyle said over the noise of the engine. He didn't acknowledge he knew Nieto had found the body.

"Sounds like timing," Nieto said. He turned off the car and walked to a tool chest.

"I was really shocked about Don," Lyle said. "You too? I mean do they really think it was murder?"

"That's what the news said. Deputies were asking questions."

"Everybody liked Don, don't you think?"

The mechanic didn't reply. He leaned back under the Dodge's hood.

Lyle stood on the opposite side of the car, looking at Nieto as he worked. "You knew he was moonlighting, right? That's where he got his extra money."

The mechanic dropped his screwdriver, and it clattered noisily through the engine compartment and landed on the floor below the car. He looked up at Lyle and covered a surprised expression with a show of anger. "Look," he said, standing up straight. "You're not supposed t' be here. Rules say you stay out."

Lyle held up a hand. "Okay, sorry." He stepped back from the car as the mechanic knelt down and reached under the taxi to retrieve his dropped tool.

Before Lyle could offer another "casual" question, he saw Gayle LeBlanc walk over and motion to him when Luis had his head down. Gayle wore a plus-size white shop coat and looked like a parody of a TV doctor selling a remedy for an embarrassing personal problem.

"Lyle honey, sorry to distract you," she said as they walked into her office, "but I just got a call from Tony Guerra, our car scrounger. He says we can expect another shipment of cars tomorrow. Do I have to call the DEA you think?"

"Why don't we call the sheriff and let him handle it. May I use your phone?"

Lyle stood next to LeBlanc's desk. The garage manager had two desks, one a mass of papers, computer screens, and random tools at her command center overlooking the shop and this second one topped by a broad glass work surface in her commodious, quiet office. Lyle punched in the phone number and asked for Martinez, figuring Rey would want to tell Wisniewski the news.

Lyle waited in Gayle's office until Rey and Howard arrived. All three sat in front of her desk.

"So one of the cars you're expecting is from Mexico?" Howard asked.

"Yes," Gayle said. "One of three. A 1974 Monte Carlo. Doesn't run but we'll fix that. Might need a new engine."

Lyle tried to picture Chevrolet's '70s version of a two-door luxury car. Big by present standards, with plenty of places to stash drugs.

"Only three cars?" Lyle asked.

"Yes, they're coming in on one of those fifth wheel pickup trailers. Be here tomorrow morning." Gayle turned to Rey. "Did the sheriff call the feds? Y'know, the DEA?"

"The sheriff doesn't want to waste the DEA's time," Rey said. "When a car arrives, he wants to be sure there are illegal drugs involved before he calls them. A courtesy."

Lyle wondered how Rey could keep a straight face.

"Ms. LeBlanc," Rey continued, "we're going to need your cooperation. I'd like to put two deputies in the garage tomorrow. Dress them up like technicians or something so they can watch the Mexico car being off-loaded and worked on."

"They're going to kinda stand out, Rey," Howard said. "It's a big place, but if two new guys show up when the shipment does, they'll look suspicious.

Rey shot Howard a look punctuated with pursed lips.

"Why don't we use cameras?" Howard said. "Set them up in the appropriate places. We could have the feed coming right back in here." He looked at Gayle.

Gayle looked from Howard to Rey.

"Set them up *tonight*?" Rey said.

"Sure. They're small and wireless. I have a tech who could install them in a couple of hours."

Rey didn't respond right away. Was he pissed that Howard criticized his strategy *and* in front of a civilian. Lyle traded glances with Gayle, who seized the initiative.

"If you're fixin' to insinuate deputies in here," she said, "why don't y'all dress 'em up like the A/C repair crew. Our air conditioning system has been on and off for days. They been workin' on the blowers and crawling around the vents in the ceiling. Your guys could be hanging in the rafters watching everything."

֎֍֎

"How is Kate doing?" Rey asked Lyle when the meeting

broke up. "Everybody's looking for that truck."

"She's a little rattled—I would be. But I think she's settling down."

"That's good. Maybe this new load of cars will give us clues we need." Rey pulled out his cell phone and called his office to recruit deputies for A/C duty. Howard headed to his car saying he wanted to get started on his CCTV plan. Lyle followed him out to the parking lot.

"Sheriff Wisniewski would love to bust drug dealers here," Lyle said. "Call the media, *then* call DEA. Maybe."

"I hope we don't find anything," Howard said.

"Yeah, I know, bad for the park. But something's going on. We all know it. I'm surprised DEA didn't come back. After the Perez death became murder, I thought the place would be lousy with feds."

Howard stopped next to his NC security patrol car. "I'm not surprised."

"Why not?"

"I think the feds have an agent in the garage. They made a mistake when they came charging in here. Maybe that media-hound Pride wasn't on the same page. All in all, they're going to stay away until their agent has proof in his hands."

"But they already put everyone on notice with that raid."

"As I said, a mistake. But they won't do it again."

"Any ideas who the agent might be?"

"None at all."

"Probably someone who has only worked here a short time," Lyle said.

Howard agreed then unlocked his car door and sat in the driver's seat. He turned over the engine and rolled down the window.

Lyle said, "Why didn't you tell Rey?"

Chapter 23

Kate saw the big pickup truck with a camper shell in her rearview mirror. It turned onto the main street in Polk right behind her car. Kate's shoulders and legs tensed up. She accelerated, but the truck stayed close. Then she punched the phone button on her SUV's dashboard. Should she just dial 9-1-1? She approached a traffic signal and hoped it would stay green. It turned red.

She braked and looked in the mirror. The truck made a sudden right turn into a parking lot. The camper shell looked different. And it was the wrong color. This wasn't *the* pickup.

Kate took a deep breath and looked at herself in the mirror. *Relax girl. Time for meditation when you get to the office.* She smiled at herself and headed back toward Nostalgia City.

After an early-morning trip to Polk, Kate had an appointment with Arthur at an unusual place. She arrived first and looked around inside the empty warehouse. Situated on one of the spoke roads that linked the '70s town, Centerville, with the park's amusement area, the Fun Zone, the storage building had been built for a food distribution company but never occupied. Light filtered in through a few narrow, vertical windows forming bright rectangles on the bare concrete floor. She wondered why Arthur had asked her to meet him here. Kate assumed it had to do with Xanadu merchandising, but why did he need to see *her*? She walked from the warehouse back into the building's outer office and saw Arthur Poole and another man come through the open door.

"Thanks for coming over here, Kate. You remember Remo Bellard?"

Kate nodded at the young man she'd met at Arthur's office the week before. She remembered his mysterious dark eyes. Bellard carried a portfolio case. He set it down on a makeshift table fashioned from saw horses and a slab of unfinished plywood. Poole wore his usual hippie Xanadu costume, but Bellard wore a shirt, tie, and a come-on look—or maybe that was Kate's imagination.

"Sorry for making it so early in the morning, but we have things to do at the store before we open," Poole said. "And I know you're busy, so let me explain what we have in mind. Basically, this building is unused and available for lease. We have an idea of how we can use this, and I wanted to get your opinion."

"You need a storehouse for your goods? I know Xanadu is doing well, but—"

"Nothing like that, exactly," Bellard said with a smile. He looked at Poole.

"Yes, please, go ahead," his boss said.

"We're pretty certain that recreational marijuana will finally be legalized this year. And when that happens, there will be an increased market opportunity for cannabis products. And our Safe Weed initiative says, independent growers will be encouraged."

"At your marijuana committee meeting this week," Poole said, "I wondered if you think it would be—" He made air quotes with his fingers. "—*appropriate* to put this on your agenda."

"Put *what* on the agenda?"

"We can show you the plan," Poole said.

Kate had told Poole about her pot committee so he could give her background information. But now it sounded like he, or his tall, dark, and handsome assistant manager, was launching another proposal at her. "Go ahead," she said with a sigh.

"If the park decides to sell marijuana," Bellard said, "it would be beneficial to have a local supplier of bud. We think it could be a top growth profit center here." He opened his case and spread out a set of drawings and sheets with columns of numbers. "The Colorado experience—and other states—has demonstrated that marijuana can be grown and harvested efficiently indoors with the right equipment." He brushed a long sweep of hair from his forehead and pointed to one of the drawings. It showed rows of planter beds.

"Are you talking about growing marijuana, *here*?"

"Yes," Poole said. "Remo has figured out how we could cultivate a good quantity here in this building."

Kate glowered as she looked over the drawings.

"Take a look," Bellard said as he led Kate into the warehouse. He waved his arms up and down, showing where the rows of growing tables would be located. "Then over there—" He pointed into a corner. "—we'd have the drying room. Then curing in a vault before packaging."

"Of course, special lighting for growing," Poole said. "Basically this would be a complete marijuana plant." He smiled at his pun.

"It sounds complex," Kate said, crossing her arms. "How would you even get started with something like this? Provided it was legal. Provided you received authorization. Provided we all didn't lose our jobs."

"It might be easier than it sounds," Poole continued, oblivious to Kate's sharp tone. "Remo found a company in Washington that's going out of business and is selling all its equipment."

"Oh, it would be a turnkey operation," Bellard said, his voice rising. "Completely turnkey."

"We would likely set up a separate company," Poole said. "I haven't quite worked it all out, but we'd have a new company to provide recreational marijuana—and medical, too."

"Yes," Bellard said. "Nostalgia City would be the primary customer. We think this would be a win-win situation, for all the participants."

Bellard sounded more enthusiastic than Arthur. Arthur could get wound up, but calm remained his default demeanor.

"Could you let Arthur and I talk about this for a minute?" Kate asked.

"Sure, sure." Bellard walked back into the office and started stacking up his papers. Kate and Poole wandered toward the back of the warehouse. They stepped around an irregular stack of metal wall studs and empty wire spools.

"Did you ask me to be on your advisory board so I would help you start this pot farm?"

"No of course not." Poole looked hurt.

"Sorry, but don't you think this is just a *little* premature. We haven't even decided *if* the park is going to sell marijuana."

Poole held up a hand. "Yes, I know. But ending prohibition looks likely. And I'm sure the park would want to accommodate its customers."

"But at this point, it's all speculation. I know the medical side of this is as important to you as anything. In *theory*, this sounds plausible. But oh my God, we haven't even had one committee meeting yet."

Poole looked up at Kate. "I understand."

"And how were you going to pay for this?"

Poole looked away.

"Arthur, you don't think the park is going to lend you the money for this, do you?"

"Remo thinks there are other financing options, too. We would start small."

"How small do you mean? You're probably growing some at home now, right?"

Chapter 24

Lyle endured a restless night. He had a day off, but sleeping-in apparently wasn't on the agenda. He'd made Gayle promise to call him when the old cars arrived in the garage, and he spent part of the night fretting about what kind of upheaval a load of drugs would bring to the park and his usually anxiety-free job driving his cab. But that wasn't the main reason he was in the middle of the case now. The attack on Kate, whether or not connected to the Perez killing, made it personal. Kate had told him yesterday she was fine and knew deputies were looking for the truck. She appeared to be more distracted over the marijuana proposition being pushed by the guy who ran Xanadu. But still, Lyle worried. Even his failing Mustang figured in his distress. And so the rotating concerns kept his mind turning over.

Giving up on sleep, he decided running would be a good idea. Serious sweating instead of serious—and useless—thinking. After a quick jog, in the early morning light, Lyle showered and almost had his clothes on when Gayle called.

"Did the cars arrive?"

"Yes and no. The truck got here, but the Monte Carlo didn't."

"What?"

"That's what happened. The car's gone missing. They took the truck driver to the park security office. I guess they're going to grill him or something. He didn't look too good, know what I mean?"

◊◊◊

Lyle walked up to the security office door when he saw a black and white come to a sudden stop in front of the building. It parked in a space marked "emergency vehicles only" and Rey Martinez got out. He wore a suit and tie and carried a small zippered leather case.

"I thought you might be here," Rey said. "You want to know what happened this morning when the cars arrived."

"I couldn't sleep."

"Uh huh. How'd you find out?"

"I asked Gayle to call me." Lyle put a hand on the security office door. "So the car from Mexico didn't make it."

"No. They've got the driver inside. I didn't want to attract attention by detaining him in the garage. One of Howard's guys asked him to come over here to file a report."

Lyle pushed open the door and they walked in.

The NC security office looked like a small-town police station transported from the 1970s. A mahogany railing with a swinging gate separated the entryway from the central part of the office. A map of the park occupied a portion of one wall. Next to it, Lyle saw a polished wood frame containing a large formal portrait of an older man. In a real police station this would have been the mayor or the governor. In this case, it was a portrait of Archibald "Max" Maxwell.

Lyle and Rey stepped up to the counter. At the far corner of the office, a deputy seated at a desk, talked to a man sitting with his back to them. Howard Chaffee stood near the desk. When he noticed Rey and Lyle, Howard walked to the front of the office.

"That's the driver," Howard said, looking at Rey and pointing to the back of the office. "His name's Derek Sharp.

He arrived short one red Chevy Monte Carlo. Your deputy there has been talking to him."

When the sheriff's deputy interviewing the driver saw his boss, he got up and headed for Rey. "He sounds flaky," the deputy said. "He says he doesn't know anything about the car. Says he reported the theft as soon as he saw it was missing this morning."

"Did he fill out the park's stolen property report?"

"He's working on it now. Not too cooperative."

Rey thanked the deputy and asked him to call the garage to find out what was happening with the two cars that did arrive.

"Thanks for getting him in here quietly," Rey said to Howard.

"I don't think he's deeply involved," Howard said. "He's...well, you'll see."

Rey walked down the row of desks and sat facing Sharp. Lyle wandered over.

"I'm Undersheriff Rey Martinez," he said, showing the man his ID. "You're not arrested. We just need to ask you a few questions and have you fill out the report. You need anything? Want some water?"

The man shook his head and rubbed one of his hands on his thigh. He wore light-colored slacks and a sweat-stained denim shirt. Lyle guessed Rey bathed regularly so the bouquet belonged to Sharp.

"I need to get going," Sharp said. "I got another delivery."

"I understand," Rey said, glancing up at Lyle who stood against the wall in front of the desk. "Mr. Sharp, this is Lyle Deming. He works for the park."

Sharp barely glanced up.

"I know you've been over this before," Rey said in a soothing voice Lyle admired, "but I just need you to tell me what happened. Then you can finish the report and you're on your way."

"Okay, look, can I smoke in here?" Sharp looked at Rey, then Lyle, through bloodshot eyes.

Lyle knew the park's strict rules against smoking, but Sharp looked desperate. Lyle spotted an empty office across the room. He looked at Rey. "We could go in there."

Rey picked up his leather case, Sharp carried the forms he was filling out, and Lyle led the way to the sparsely furnished small office or interrogation room. When Sharp sat at a table opposite Rey, Lyle opened a sliding window then looked around for something that could double as an ashtray. A paper coffee cup with dregs in the bottom would have to do. Sharp fished out a crumpled cigarette pack from a shirt pocket. Lyle walked over and closed the office door.

"Thanks," Sharp said, lighting up. "Now whatcha wanna know?"

From a distance, Sharp could pass for forty. Up close, it was a forty after a long, hard night. Maybe a long, hard life.

"Just start from when you first noticed the car was stolen," Rey said.

"Okay, I was staying overnight at a friend's house, outside o' Camp Verde. I got up this morning to drive in here and I saw the car was gone."

"What time was this?" Rey asked.

"I dunno. Seven, eight maybe."

"What kind of condition was that Monte Carlo in?" asked Lyle who again leaned against a wall.

"Damn thing didn't run. Front axle maybe bent, too. Hard to steer it. Had to push it on the trailer. It was on the back."

"So it would be easiest to remove," Rey said.

"But whoever took it," Lyle said, "didn't drive it away."

"No way," Sharp said.

He took a deep drag on his cigarette. Lyle pointed to the window and the truck driver exhaled in that direction.

"So you didn't see or hear anything last night when someone hauled a big Chevy off your trailer," Rey said.

"I called the cops, though." Sharp looked up, showing Rey and Lyle a glassy, puzzled expression.

Rey pulled papers out of his case. "You told the Yavapai County deputies that you were at a party at this house—a mobile home I think it was. Isn't that right?"

"Yeah."

"And you were drinking and you passed out."

"Naw. I was tired. I drove up from Bisbee. Long way."

"You picked up the three cars from Bisbee?" Rey asked.

"That's right. Sometimes I get Nostalgia City cars in Sierra Vista, but Bisbee this time."

"So who was at this party?" Lyle asked.

"I dunno. Bunch of guys, women."

"You told deputies you didn't know anyone," Rey said, "anyone except a woman named Vanessa who lives there."

Sharp took another puff on his cigarette. "Vanessa, yeah. Nice lady."

"Is she your girlfriend?"

Sharp shook his head.

"The Yavapai sheriff's report says you told them her name was Vanessa Meyers."

"Meyers, Mayer, something like that."

Lyle took a step behind Rey and looked over his shoulder at the Yavapai sheriff's report. "You really can't tell us *anything* about the other people at the party?" he asked.

"You don't remember a lot of it, do you?" Rey said softly.

Sharp screwed up his mouth like he'd eaten something he shouldn't have. He looked at his cigarette then took a drag.

Rey pushed the papers into his case and leaned back. "What did you do with the drugs?"

"What drugs? No drugs at the party. Just whiskey. 'N beer."

"Drugs in the Monte Carlo," Rey said.

Sharp's stare told it all. He took a routine transport trip, stopped off, got drunk, and remembered little else.

"How do you know Vanessa," Lyle said.

"Tony, he introduced us, sorta. He told me I should look up Vanessa on the way up. Said it could be a lot of fun. You didn't expect the delivery until this morning. Tony gave me her number, and I called her. She told me how to find the place."

"So this was the first time you saw her?"

"Yeah, they said she has a party goin' all the time. It was fun."

"Except," Rey said.

"Yeah, except someone stole the car." Sharp took a final puff of his cigarette and dropped it in the paper cup where it sizzled and died.

"What's Tony's last name?" Lyle asked.

"You know. Guerra. Tony Guerra. He works for you."

Rey stood up. "Just finish filling out the report and write down where we can get in touch with you. We appreciate your help."

Howard waited for them at the security department entrance.

"Guess you figured him out," Rey said to Howard. "Guy was drunk. Doesn't remember much."

"He was set up," Lyle said. "Tony Guerra buys the derelict cars for us."

"So he's the drug connection," Rey said.

Howard leaned back against the front counter. "So maybe this guy Sharp is a mule."

"I don't think so," Lyle said. "He didn't drive across the border. He picked up the cars in Bisbee. He's just a dumb driver for the transportation company."

Rey held his leather case in front of him with both hands. "I wonder where the car is now. And what's inside it."

"All in all, the two other cars will probably be clean," Howard said.

"I agree," Rey said. "Since you have those cameras still rolling, we can monitor what happens. I'll let my deputies go for now."

"That guy Dutch you told me about showed up last night," Howard said, "when we were installing the cameras."

Lyle looked up. "Did he see anything?"

"No. We were careful, but there's not too many employees around at eleven o'clock at night. He said he needed to do something to prepare for the salvaged cars to arrive."

"What'd he do?" Rey asked.

"Moved some big tools around. Dragged a portable lift halfway across the building."

"I'd say he's on the watch list," Rey said. He thanked Howard, and Rey and Lyle left the office.

When they were outside, Rey said, "Sharp might be lucky."

"They could have just killed him and taken the car," Lyle said, finishing the thought. "But with Vanessa getting him drunk, the drug cartel—or whoever they are—judged him to be harmless."

"This does not bode well, *mi amigo*."

Chapter 25

*I*s *that really Remo Bellard trying to get it on with someone in the Safe Weed office?* Walking along the side of the building, Kate had the sun behind her and it illuminated a small room with open blinds. An attractive young brunette leaned over a table looking at papers. Bellard stood close to her and put a hand on her back. She stayed in the same position as Remo slid his hand down past her waist and momentarily stroked her buttocks. She stood up and took a half step away from him, putting her hands on her hips in what looked like mock reproach.

That afternoon, Kate had driven south to Phoenix in search of good news. She put the pickup truck scare behind her. Taping an interview with an NPR station would be a great opportunity to talk about NC's exciting transition and their plans for the year. With surprisingly little traffic on the interstate, Kate arrived early so she decided to check out the Safe Weed Project headquarters on Bell Road in the northern part of town. She didn't expect to see Bellard there groping someone.

Kate walked around to the front of the office and opened the door. It looked like a typical campaign headquarters with tables, chairs, telephones, two laptop computers, campaign posters, literature and, on the back wall, a large, green drawing of a marijuana leaf. She couldn't see anyone, but soon she heard a noise coming from the back. The young woman she'd just seen came through a doorway. Her blue knit dress rode up in the back, but the woman showed no signs that she'd been interrupted.

"Hi, welcome to Safe Weed headquarters," the woman said. "Would you like to volunteer? Help us get signatures?"

"I'm Kate Sorensen. I was in Phoenix today so I thought I'd just stop by to see the office."

The young woman recognized Kate's name because she immediately smoothed down her dress and stepped forward to shake hands, adopting a more formal air. "Hi, Ms. Sorensen, I'm Paige Ellerbe. I'm in charge of the office."

Kate wandered over to a table spread with clipboards and stacks of petitions. "How is the signature drive going?"

"Oh, fine. More to go, of course."

"Not too many weeks left."

Ellerbe walked over to a bulletin board. "It's on our calendar here. It shows the number of signatures we get in every day."

Kate heard footsteps and turned around to see the person she'd just seen through the back window. "Mr. Bellard, what a surprise," she said.

"Please call me Remo. Arthur sent me on a trip for supplies." He smiled then touched the corner of his mouth as if wiping something away. "I stopped to see if Paige—the office—needed anything. And we were just going over some figures."

Ellerbe looked from Kate to Bellard. "Yes," she said, "we have a tight budget."

"I was just asking about the signature drive," Kate said.

"It's a...challenge," Bellard said, pausing and looking at Ellerbe. "The other guys, Consumer Cannabis, pay people to gather signatures, and we have mostly volunteers."

A telephone rang and Ellerbe walked to the back of the office to answer it.

"Ms. Sorensen," Bellard said. "Okay to call you Kate?"

"Uh huh."

"Can I talk to you a minute?" Bellard's voice lost the uncertainty it had when he entered. He switched to business mode. "This grow plant at Nostalgia City is really essential. We didn't get a chance to discuss this too much this morning, but right now in Arizona, marijuana is limited to medical purposes, medical dispensaries. When it's made legal for everyone, the whole supply and demand curve changes."

"Presumably, people will want to try it."

"Uh huh, and if Nostalgia City decides it wants to get into it, it would be months before adequate supplies might be available—maybe a year or more. And costs. We're looking at maybe four, five dollars a gram. Or more. Who knows? And this is wholesale."

As he talked, Bellard moved closer to Kate. She sat on the edge of a table, sticking her legs out in front of her as a way of keeping distance between them. "I understand your position, Remo. But we don't know if it's going to pass and *if* Nostalgia City will want to permit pot at the park, let alone sell it to our visitors. I think Arthur is aware of these possibilities."

"Now, Kate." Bellard lowered his voice and his dark eyes flashed. "Arthur has these great ideas about medical marijuana, but does he see the big picture? I want you to know where I'm coming from." He stepped around Kate's outstretched legs. "We're all on the same team. Think of it. Wholesale to retail under the same roof. With the grow farm and the park's marketing we'd have the whole package. If we had our own—"

Kate stood up in the middle of Bellard's pitch just as Ellerbe walked up from the back of the office. "There's no real point in going on with this," Kate said. "I got the message this morning." *What's wrong with this guy? A pot factory, right in the middle of Nostalgia City? He's gorgeous, but really.*

"Talking about the grow farm?" Ellerbe asked.

"Enough for now," Kate said.

"Okay," Bellard said raising an arm, "But—"

"So," Kate interrupted, "what happens with this pot factory if the Safe Weed Project fails? Are we sure we're going to get enough signatures? And what happens if *both* pot measures are on the ballot?"

"Why, uh—" Bellard's gaze moved from Kate to the marijuana poster on the wall. "We have the best program. We'll step up. You'll see."

Kate glanced at her watch. "I have to go. I'm doing a radio interview. Nice to meet you, Paige." She looked at Bellard. "Where are you off to?"

"Oh, yeah. I have to see glass artists in Paradise Valley."

Kate turned toward the door. She paused to see if Bellard would linger.

Chapter 26

Lyle brought a gun with him but just for insurance. He probably wouldn't need it. "So what the hell are you going to say if you do see Vanessa?" he asked himself aloud as he drove along Spirea Trail Lane, a dirt and gravel road in the village of Camp Verde. The road led him through a stretch of open high desert punctuated with trailer homes and manufactured houses in various states of repair. "Am I looking for a trailer or a mobile home, and what the hell's the difference?"

Soon he found the address he was looking for. The home appeared to be a double-wide construction, angled toward the street. It backed up to a stand of trees and scrub brush. An empty carport was attached to one end of the house and a broad aluminum awning sheltered the front door on the other end. Metal skirting ran around the base of the house and a swamp cooler sat on the roof. The front yard consisted of gravel dotted with a few dry-looking ocotillos.

"No cars. No surprise," he said.

Lyle drove slowly by, turned right, and following the irregular pattern of streets, he circled back and parked 200 yards away from the mobile home. He got out and walked slowly toward the property. It was more than warm. No clouds shaded the sun. Lyle couldn't see any sign of movement in or around the house. He walked up to the carport. No windows faced this side of the home so Lyle decided he'd peek around back, see if there was any activity, then knock on the front door.

A jumble of broken lawn chairs, sage brush, and trash covered the back yard. This was no luxurious vacation home. Lyle looked in a plastic trash can and saw pizza boxes and lumps of rotting food. When he turned to walk around to the front, he heard a noise. Someone was walking on the gravel front yard and the sound came closer. Lyle decided his best move would be to play dumb and make a lot of noise walking through the carport so he didn't startle whoever came around the side of the house.

"What are you doing here?" Rey said when Lyle walked around the corner. He looked like he'd been reaching inside his coat.

"Probably the same thing you are."

"How did you—oh, you saw this address on the crime report this morning. How'd you get here? I didn't see your car."

Lyle pointed to the white Ford Fiesta down the street. "It's a loaner. My car's back in the shop. Transmission's shot."

"The place looks deserted," Rey said.

"No one out back."

"I'm going to see if anyone's inside." Rey motioned toward the front door. "You coming?"

They walked on a soft dirt path that didn't make noise.

"Aren't you taking a chance coming out here alone?" Lyle said.

"I told you we were shorthanded. I called the Yavapai detectives and told them I was going to be in the area. I don't see your backup, either. Are you here because you think I need help?"

"No. Not at all."

"Part of you is still a cop."

"I moved to Nostalgia City to avoid murder cases. But stuff happens."

"I didn't think this trip would be dangerous," Rey said as they approached the door, "since whoever lives here allowed Sharp to report the car theft."

"Or likely they're long gone," Lyle said.

"Yeah." Rey knocked on the door. A heavy steel screen door covered the beige wooden one. Through the thousands of tiny perforations in the security door, Lyle could see the regular door closed up tight.

Rey banged again. "County sheriff." he said, "We have some follow up questions about the car theft."

They waited and Rey tried a second time, then a third. "Guess they took off."

Lyle and Rey walked around the house, shading their eyes with their hands as they peered in the windows. In one living area Lyle saw a collection of cheap furniture sitting on a worn Navajo style rug, probably from China. Beer cans, no doubt empties, crowded together on a coffee table also littered with plates, scraps of food, and a liquor bottle. "Hey, Rey, your kind of cuisine in here. Except I don't see any kidney pie."

"I think I'm going to regret ever telling you my grandmother was Irish."

"O'Martinez?"

Rey scowled.

"Hey something to be proud of. My grandmother *drank* Irish whiskey. Does that count?"

"You're sick, Deming. What were you going to ask if someone *was* here?"

"I dunno. I didn't really expect anyone."

"What if they were? What if it's a Mexican cartel?"

Lyle lifted his Hawaiian shirt exposing his holstered 9mm.

"Did you tell Sheriff Wisniewski the other day that you were going to solve this case?"

"Heck no. He razzed me after that truck chased Kate. But I sure as hell would like to find out what's going on.

And see if it's connected to the guy who tried to run her down."

"Well, if we don't get *something* soon, I'm in trouble."

"The sheriff on your case?" Lyle asked.

"Yes, and everybody else is too. Maybe I'll get a rubber band like yours."

"It works, sometimes." Lyle snapped it against his wrist. "One snap and it jerks you back to reality from wherever your mind went. But I don't wear it all the time."

"You've had it on every time I've seen you the past week."

"Hey, you want to try the neighbors? C'mon."

The next home sat a hundred yards away. "No one here likes their neighbors close, do they?" Rey said as the two walked along the dusty road.

"Did you ever check alibis for that guy Blake and the others I talked to at the bar?"

"We didn't get anything helpful. We checked a few others' alibis, too. No luck. Some of the guys alibied each other. Out partying on a Monday night."

"Probably more than one person is involved in this. And no one wants to talk."

"We talked to Mrs. Perez again about the break in. She let us look around. If Don Perez had a secret, he didn't leave any evidence of it behind."

"What about the auto transport company? Wonder what they say about Sharp."

"I got a new detective working on it. The transportation company's worked with the park since it opened. Sharp is one of several drivers, and he hasn't made many deliveries to the park. Tiff says your guy Guerra has used this company exclusively for Nostalgia City deliveries."

"Tiff?"

"Tiffany Smith. She's a new detective. Young, but has several years in patrol. I thought I'd give her a chance. We need help."

"When did the sheriff call the DEA about this morning's car delivery?" Lyle looked at his watch. "Five minutes ago?"

"Funny. Yeah, he waited until we detained the driver. Strange they haven't shown up at the park. You suppose the DEA has dropped their idea of a drug connection?"

"Howard thinks DEA has an agent working in the garage."

"Really? Who does he think it is?"

"He doesn't know. Just a hunch. He thinks they're going to keep a low profile and let their inside guy catch somebody with drugs in hand."

"That could explain why they haven't been back," Rey said as they approached the next mobile home. They paused in the street. "I wonder if that could be the person who gave us the anonymous note about Perez's death."

"Yeah," Lyle said. "Did you ever mention that to Howard?"

When Martinez didn't respond, Lyle said, "He's doing a good job for the park. He knows police work, and he's not trying to tell you what to do."

"Always reminds you he's from the SFPD."

"Yeah, and he can be a little abrupt too, but what do you want? He *is* an ex-Frisco cop. Occasionally, he has a good idea. Like me."

"You have good ideas?"

When they started up the walkway to the neighbor's house, a double-wide trailer home, they heard a dog growl somewhere within. A large dog. When they stepped up on the home's wooden deck, a middle-aged woman in jeans and a western blouse cracked the front door open. "What do ya want?"

The growling got louder.

Rey pulled out his badge and identified himself. "I wanted to ask you a few questions about your neighbors."

"Okay, come on in." She pulled the door open wide.

A rottweiler slightly smaller than a Bengal tiger sat on the floor near the door. His growl rumbled like a low-rider car stereo.

"Oh, don't worry about him," the woman said. She motioned to the dog. "Benji, quiet. Stay."

Lyle and Rey stepped into the living room. "We're following up on the car theft next door. Do you know your neighbors to the west very well?"

"Them? Hell no. They come and go. Sometimes late at night. Vanessa, I think that's the woman what owns it. She says she has a big family that mooches off her. I ain't stupid. Somethin's going on over there. Cops were here this morning asking about that car theft."

Lyle stole a glance at the massive K-9. "Did Benji bark last night?" *Benji?*

"He did, about two, three o'clock. That's what I told the other cops. I heard some noises, but I mind my own business."

"How long has Vanessa lived there?" Rey asked.

"Maybe six months. The Carlsons moved out."

"You know where she came from?"

"Said Tucson."

"You ever talk to any of Vanessa's family," Lyle asked, "visitors?"

"No, sir. They don't come 'round wantin' to talk. 'Course I usually leave Benji out on the porch."

Chapter 27

"We haven't had a media call about the murder since last week," Kate said as she prepared dinner in her apartment kitchen. She'd changed from a business suit into a short dress and leggings, something she hoped would be comfortable *and* attractive. She opened a bag of fresh green beans, cut them up, and put them in water on the stove.

"That's good news for the park," Lyle said as he sat on the living room couch, petting Kate's cat Trixie. "But Rey isn't any closer to finding who killed Don Perez or who tried to run you down with the truck."

Kate walked around the counter that separated the kitchen from the sitting area. She sat on the couch next to Lyle. "You know there're connected?"

"Pretty sure. I told you about the stolen salvage car."

"And the trailer house in the desert near Camp Verde."

"Right. Rey finally got into the house with help from deputies in that county. Looked like the residents had left town. Deputies found heroin residue in plastic wrappers stuffed in the trash. The first concrete evidence of drugs we've found."

Kate stared at the floor while she absently stroked Trixie. She looked up at Lyle. "What I saw *looked* like a drug buy." For a split second she had a flash of the loud pickup truck bearing down on her. She reached for Lyle's hand.

Lyle took her hand in his and squeezed. "You okay?"

"Yes. I just wish we could get this over with. Get the drug smugglers out of the park."

Trixie jumped off the couch and Lyle held Kate close. She could feel the reassuring warmth of his body.

"Rey's doing everything he can," Lyle said, "but everyone in the garage is scared to talk. They've got hidden cameras in there now—don't tell anyone—but I doubt they'll be sending any more drugs though the garage. After the DEA raid and us tracking down the trailer house, they must know they're being watched, one way or another."

Camera surveillance is reassuring, I guess. Kate got up and walked back to the kitchen. Brushed nickel hardware and expensive granite countertops overshadowed the ordinary white painted cabinets. Her upscale company housing would do for a while more. She peered in the oven to see how the salmon filets were doing. Almost ready. Turning to Lyle she was about to say something when, for a reason known only to Trixie, the cat jumped up and ran across the room then dashed down the hall. "She does that occasionally," Kate said. "I think she can sense tension."

Lyle must have heard Kate unscrew the cap from the sauvignon blanc because he got up and leaned on the counter, looking expectantly at her. She handed him a glass. "You can put mine on the table, too. Here you go."

"You sound like Rey. He's started saying, 'there ya go' all the time." He took a long sip and topped off his glass. "I wish I had better news," he said when they faced each other over the dinner table. "They lifted fingerprints at the trailer. One belonged to a drug trade fugitive named Carlos Guzman. None of the prints could be linked to NC employees. Rey's still trying to get a line on the people who rented the home. He's getting a lot of pressure from the sheriff to do something. But he's got no new leads and, with the park's tourist traffic filling up the county, his department is stretched thin. Wish I could do something constructive. Maybe I could help find Tony."

"Tony?" Kate mumbled, putting a forkful of green beans in her mouth.

Lyle explained that Tony Guerra hunted for old cars for the park and that he was suspected of being the middle man in the NC drug trade. "Deputies have tried to contact him, but he doesn't answer his cell phone or email. Howard Chaffee's been calling around trying to find him. He's telling people the park's looking for more cars. The theory is that Tony might respond to someone from the park, rather than the sheriff."

Lyle stopped to wash down a chunk of baked salmon with a swallow of wine.

"Where does Tony live?" Kate asked.

"His home address is Bisbee, but he travels all over looking for cars." Lyle stopped talking and looked down. "Oops. Sorry." He scooped up bits of rice from the tablecloth with his fork. "Sloppy eater. Well, what's happening with your marijuana initiative? You still planning an NC marijuana committee?"

"Committee? Oh yes, we meet tomorrow. But now Arthur Poole wants to start a pot farm in the park. Can you imagine?"

"Don't we have to wait to see if it's legalized?"

"That's just what I told Arthur."

"He runs Xanadu?"

"Yes, He really means well but, I don't know, he's naïve about some things."

"I don't see any naiveté at Xanadu. The incense, the music. He's got the perfect atmosphere. Tourists love to spend money there."

"It's not that." Kate paused and sipped her wine. *With Arthur it's more about people and motives.* "I haven't ever told you about Arthur, have I?"

"No, but the way you say his name, maybe you should."

Where to begin about Arthur? Her meal finished, Kate pushed her plate aside and focused on her wine. She tried to read Lyle's expression, gave up, and dived into her story.

"You know my mother died of cancer four years ago. Well, Arthur was her nurse. I worked in Vegas, but I flew up to Portland to see her as often as I could, especially after she went into the hospital—for the last time."

"Arthur was a *nurse*?"

"A very caring one. He would sit and talk with her, hold her hand. My dad was there, of course, but Arthur was there for twelve hours at a time. I got to know him over those last weeks and months. We'd talk when my mom was asleep. He'd ask me about my mom's background, about my job in Vegas. He's a great listener. Rarely talks about himself."

Kate finished her wine. Lyle got up and retrieved the bottle from the fridge. He poured her another glass, refilled his own, then sat looking at Kate.

Kate held her wine glass in front of her with both hands. *I haven't thought about mom recently. Is that bad?* "Mom had a lot of pain," she said. "Lower back, stomach, on her side. They gave her heavy pain meds, but it made her dopy. At this point, we knew her cancer was incurable." She paused, took a breath, and slowed down. "She didn't want to be in a fog or drug-induced sleep. My mom was a smart woman. She wanted to talk about things, the family, her life. Arthur gave her marijuana. It was legal in Oregon but her doctor was against it. Arthur did it anyway. Marijuana doesn't work for everyone, but it did for Mom. They were able to reduce her pain meds significantly. With the marijuana, she didn't need as much. And she felt better. She brightened up, and we were able to have some great conversations. She even joked about being a pothead."

"I bet the doctor didn't think it was funny."

"No, he didn't. He didn't find out until later. Arthur saw Mother much more than the doctor did, and he arranged for other people—nurses, probably—to administer the marijuana when he was off shift. The doctor found out after Mother died. He went ballistic. Arthur was also giving marijuana to two other patients. The hospital fired him, and because he refused to expose anyone else who helped him, the doctor made it a crusade to be sure that Arthur never practiced nursing again."

"Wow," was all Lyle said.

"I kept in touch with him after he lost his job. He moved to San Diego for a while. He'd heard of a health center that might hire him, but it's hard to hide from your past today. Eventually, he and another guy started a book and crafts store. Just when the store started to make money, he got divorced. That's another story. Arthur was down for a long time. Guess he didn't know what to do with his life. Last year, when the park decided to contract out the new headshop, I called Arthur, on the chance he might be interested. I thought it had potential. Arthur's partner in the San Diego store agreed to buy him out, and Arthur Poole became our local headshop concessionaire."

"Is that why you agreed to help him with the ballot initiative?"

"I suppose. I thought he needed my help. He makes a great case for his way of distributing marijuana, and he has the support of many prominent Arizonans."

"And now he wants you to help him start a pot farm?"

"Not exactly. He didn't ask me to support it. He just showed me what he wanted to do. He's got an assistant in the store who is really pushing it."

"Getting approval for a pot farm here is a stretch, even if we assume it will be legal. Arthur's asking a lot."

But he's not taking advantage of me. Lyle doesn't know him, and Lyle can be a touch cynical. "Nothing's going to happen for a while. I'm not even mentioning this at the committee meeting. I need to see how other execs, other departments feel about permitting pot at the park. But if voters legalize it, we'll have to decide whether to offer it here—or tell our customers it's off limits."

Chapter 28

When Lyle and Howard Chaffee rolled into Bisbee, Arizona, Wednesday, the sun tickled the western horizon as evening set in. Howard drove cautiously. Had Lyle been behind the wheel, they might have shaved off a half hour or more. But since Lyle's Mustang still lacked a functioning transmission, Howard drove an unmarked NC Chevy sedan.

Earlier, Lyle had talked to Rey about finding Tony Guerra. The undersheriff had sent a detective to Bisbee the day before. He'd come back empty handed. Guerra did not answer his phone and was not at his apartment. The San Navarro County detective talked to a neighbor who told him that Tony was always traveling and hard to keep track of. The detective had contacted local Cochise County deputies. They promised to keep an eye on Guerra's apartment as manpower permitted.

Lyle decided he'd see if he could do something. Howard volunteered to help.

A morning meeting in Gayle LeBlanc's office sent Lyle and Howard on their way south. Howard explained that he had finally reached Guerra on the phone. Guerra sounded evasive and uncertain, but finally agreed to meet with him. Howard told him the park desperately needed more cars—which they did—and wanted to talk with him about specific automobile models the park was looking for—more or less the truth. The NC chief of security neglected to tell Guerra his official job title.

"Tony is a good guy," Gayle told Lyle and Howard. "Had those carne asada tacos and margaritas with him last time he was up. He's got a wife and kids. Told me all about 'em. Hell, I had more margaritas than he did. He's a quiet, family guy. The way he talked about his kids, I don't think he'd do anything with drugs."

"We'll find out," Howard said, writing down the Bisbee address Gayle gave him. "Maybe we can persuade him to come up to Polk. If he's not involved in this, and comes up voluntarily, it'll be a lot easier on him."

"Do you know," Lyle asked, "does he drive or haul the vehicles across the border himself?"

"Not sure," Gayle said. "The local transportation company we use just picks up the cars this side o' the border. The company's not licensed in Mexico. That I know."

Guerra had told Howard he would meet him at his car storage lot in Bisbee Thursday morning and he gave him the address. He said they could have breakfast at a nearby café. When Howard and Lyle reached Bisbee, Howard called Guerra to tell him they'd arrived and to confirm the meeting time. Guerra didn't answer. Howard left a message and he and Lyle checked into Bisbee's Copper Queen Hotel. They had dinner and kept their fingers crossed.

జుడు

Next morning, having failed again to get Guerra on the phone, Lyle and Howard headed to the address of the car trader's storage lot. In order to reach the lot, the two ex-cops had to drive past the Lavender Pit, an abandoned copper mine that gaped between Bisbee and smaller communities to the south. As they drove by, Howard slowed down and stared at the wide excavation. Rocks of reds and yellows stair-stepped hundreds of feet down making the open mine look like a smaller version of the Grand Canyon. The bottom wasn't visible from the road.

"I don't see any lavender or purple," Howard said.

"It's named after some mine executive named Lavender," Lyle said. "The mine's been closed for more than thirty years. Sort of a tourist attraction now." He wondered if they'd ever found a body at the bottom.

In a few minutes, they drove through a commercial and light industrial area and pulled up in front of a blacktop lot surrounded by a high chain-link fence and a locked gate. The only sign said, *Private Property ~ Keep Out* in both English and Spanish. Heavy chains and an imposing padlock secured the wide gate on wheels. Most of the cars in the lot were post-2000 vintage, many with crumpled fenders, bashed-in doors, or other signs of a collision. Over in a corner, near a small, weathered wooden shed, sat a dirty 1978 Mercury. That year, many Mercs had decorative flipdown doors covering the headlights. On this car, only one of the doors was open so it looked as if the car was winking at them.

They waited for an hour.

"Dammit," Lyle said. "I wonder where the coffee shop he mentioned is."

Two blocks away they found the Roadrunner Café and sat silently as they made quick work of breakfast. After Lyle's last bite of huevos con chorizo, they drove back to the lot. No Tony. His phone repeatedly went to voice mail. They called Gayle LeBlanc. She hadn't heard from him.

They drove northwest, back through Bisbee, to the small apartment building where Guerra lived and walked to unit seven. They knocked several times.

"You guys looking for Tony?" said a voice behind them.

Lyle turned to see a man in his thirties in jeans and a T-shirt. His light brown hair stuck out in all directions. Maybe he'd just gotten up. He stood a few steps from the open door to the next apartment.

"The other cops were here the other day looking for him,

too" the man said. "Someone from out of town and the local sheriff."

Other cops? Lyle knew Howard, with his short gray hair and conservative dress, still looked like a cop. But him? *Maybe I should wear bell-bottoms, get a tattoo.*

"Have you seen him?" Howard said.

"I think he went in and out of his apartment late yesterday," he said putting his hands in his jean's pockets, "but I haven't seen him since."

"He wasn't here last night?" Lyle asked.

The man shook his head.

Lyle looked at Howard with a sigh.

"What's this all this about?" the neighbor said. "No one told me anything. Just said they wanted to speak with him."

"How well do you know Guerra?"

"Not too much. He's a car trader, something like that. Travels a lot. Goes to Mexico. I already told the other cops this."

Lyle thanked the man for his time and they got back in Howard's company car. "This is not looking good for Guerra," he said. "If he *is* connected to the drug trade, he could be on the run."

"Let's wait and see," Howard said. "We'll try his storage lot again."

Lyle told himself not to keep expecting the worst.

When they returned to the lot, the gate was rolled open. They pulled in, parked, and got out.

As they walked toward the shed, a man in work clothes approached them from the other side of the lot. He was dark skinned and although slightly built, looked wiry and strong. "This is a private lot, amigos. Are you looking for your car?"

"We're looking for Tony Guerra."

"Oh, *si*. He is not here."

Lyle introduced himself and Howard and explained they worked for Nostalgia City and that Guerra had a steady contract with them for old cars. "Do you work with him?" Lyle asked.

"No. I work at Desert Springs Auto Body. Our repair shop is down the block. Tony shares this lot with us." He pointed to the old Mercury. "That's one of his cars there."

"We were supposed to meet with him this morning, and he didn't show up," Howard said.

"We're a little worried about him," Lyle said. "Howard is chief of security for the park. We hope he hasn't disappeared. Have you seen him recently?"

"Late yesterday afternoon." He gestured toward the shed. "In the office. He said he had to pick up another car in Agua Prieta."

Lyle looked at Howard.

"He knew we were coming," Howard said.

"Do you know where he was going in Agua Prieta?" Lyle asked.

The auto body man shook his head. "I didn't talk to him very long. There was another man with him."

"What'd he look like?"

The man described the person with Guerra as Hispanic, casually dressed, and in his thirties. "I had to move a car into the shop so I just waved and said '*adios*.'"

"Agua Prieta is just across the border," Lyle told Howard. "Take a half hour, forty-five minutes to get there."

"Does he have a desk here?" Howard asked the shop man, gesturing toward the shed. "It might give us some idea of exactly where he went."

The man looked from Howard to Lyle for a moment then pointed to the office. He unlocked the door.

Inside, they found the shed more organized and neat that Lyle expected from the dilapidated exterior. Two metal desks occupied opposite corners of the small room. One had a cheesy auto parts calendar on the wall above it and contained only a coffee cup, pencils, and a small metal storage box. The other desk had a phone, blotter, appointment book, stapler, pens, and a computer printer. A picture frame sat face down at the edge of the desk as if it had been knocked over. When Lyle picked it up, an Hispanic woman and three dark-haired children smiled out at him from a snapshot.

Howard reached for the appointment book. Lyle turned to the auto body employee to keep him busy in case he might take exception to their snooping. "Did Tony say anything else to you yesterday? Anything out of the ordinary."

"He drops off cars all the time," the man said, leaning on the opposite desk. "I know most of them are for you. That amusement park. You have 1970s cars, right?"

"Sixties and seventies, yes."

"I hear Tony say he gonna pick up a 1977 Oldsmobile."

"There's nothing on his calendar for today," Howard said. "He's got addresses here that look like they may be car lots or something. How's your Spanish?"

Lyle looked at Guerra's book and saw three addresses in Agua Prieta under the simple heading, *Vendedores*—dealers. He pulled out his cell phone and took a picture of the page.

"Want to go look for him in Mexico?" Howard said, as they walked back to their car.

"Okay," Lyle said. "I have a picture of his list of dealers—presumably *car* dealers."

Howard started the car and headed for the road south. "Guerra could be picking up a car for some other client."

"But we have so many cars on order, I don't see how he'd have time for anything else."

They'd traveled only a few miles toward the border when Howard's cell phone rang.

"Yes, yes sir, I understand. But they're mostly senior citizens, professional people. Okay. Yes, I will. That's right, Bisbee. Airport? Okay, we'll find it." Howard glanced over at Lyle. "That was Max. He wants me back at the park. There's a convention of bikers this weekend, and he's worried. And we have some other security issues, apparently. He's sending the company plane. It's going to land at

Bisbee-Douglas Airport in half an hour. You can take my car. Sorry to bail out."

"Not a problem."

"How many bosses send a *plane* after you?" Howard said.

"Only one I know of."

Chapter 29

*A*gua Prieta, "brown water" in English. Welcome to Mexico.

To get to Agua Prieta, Lyle had to pass through Douglas, Arizona. On the map, both towns appeared to be part of the same small metro area, with the majority of the population on the Mexican side of the border. Luckily, the GPS in Howard's car included Mexico so Lyle plotted a course for the first of the three contact points they'd picked up at Guerra's office. Before he crossed the border, Lyle pulled his 9mm out of his suitcase in the trunk and stuck it under the seat of the car. He'd be getting into drug cartel territory, so it was best to be safe. He tried Guerra's cell phone one last time. No answer.

Once across, he drove down a sunbaked commercial street passing a variety of worn storefronts: *Pelqueria, Gran Mercado, Restaurant de Girasol, Zapatos, Funeraria Garcia:* Hairdresser, Grand Market, Sunflower Restaurant, Shoes, Garcia Mortuary. Lyle looked for what he hoped was a used car lot on Calle Nueve. When he saw the sign *coches usados*—used cars—he pulled over to the right.

A strange assortment of vehicles rested on the uneven blacktop, from near-new Japanese cars, several in bright colors, to beat-up sedans that, with hundreds of hours' work, might suit the streets of Nostalgia City. Although he'd been running the A/C, when Lyle got out of the car, his shirt stuck to his back with sweat. He pealed the shirt away from his skin as he walked toward the car lot's office. With his hair askew and his clothes bearing wrinkles from too much time in the car, Lyle hoped he didn't have that cop look. A stucco rectangle, the large office offered windows mostly covered with posters touting the lowest prices in the area.

Inside, the air was no cooler. Two men sat at a wooden desk, one behind it, the other partially sitting on top. They talked rapidly as if they wanted to finish before Lyle approached.

The man sitting on the desk stood up. Short, he wore a white shirt with the collar open and the sleeves rolled up. His thin face featured a vertical scar on his cheek, a long, slender nose that hooked slightly at the end above an uneven moustache, and wraparound sunglasses.

"What can we do for you, *señor*," the man said in English.

"I work for Nostalgia City, in Arizona."

The man gave him a puzzled look.

"It's the old-time theme park. Rock and roll and old cars."

"Ah, *si*," the man said slowly.

"We work with Tony Guerra," Lyle said. "He sells us old cars from the sixties and seventies. I'm trying to get in touch with him. I was supposed to meet him today in Bisbee."

The man just stared at Lyle, his glasses making eye contact impossible.

"You do business with Tony, right?" Lyle asked.

"Once in a while we sell him a car, but we haven't seen him in, what?" He looked at the man behind the desk. "At least two weeks, huh?"

The other man grunted.

"Do you have any cars for him now? Do you expect to see him?"

The man pulled off his sunglasses and stared at Lyle. "We have not heard from him. No, we have nothing for him now."

Lyle glanced around the room not knowing what he was looking for. The floor needed to be swept and two of the desks were piled with papers. "Well, if you see him, if he calls, would you have him call Nostalgia City? He'll know who to talk to."

"*Si*. If we see him."

The second address on Lyle's list took him outside of town to an auto junk yard. A gray corrugated metal building sat in front of a dirt field filled with hundreds of half-demolished cars, many stacked four or five high. As Lyle walked up, he watched a tractor drag an old Plymouth down an aisle. The car lacked rear wheels and it shed parts as it scraped nosily along the ground.

The metal building had a garage-style door standing open and beyond the door, Lyle saw a man working on a corroded four-cylinder engine.

"*Buenas tardes*," Lyle said.

"Hello, what can we do for you?" the man said in Spanish. He put down a socket wrench and turned to Lyle.

Lyle started to explain who he was in English and quickly switched to Spanish when he realized the man didn't understand him. Lyle's conversational Spanish was as rusty as the engine the man was working on. He spoke slowly, deliberately.

The man smiled, showing a row of irregular teeth. He wore work clothes and appeared to be in his sixties. Deep lines crisscrossed his face.

After Lyle explained who he was looking for, the man introduced himself as the owner of the wrecking yard. Yes, he said, he had traded with Tony for some years. Tony was honest and easy to work with, not like some of the con artists he had to deal with.

"Have you seen Tony recently?" Lyle asked.

"A week, maybe ten days ago. You guys are really running him around looking for more and more cars," the man said. He said Tony told him he'd discovered another source that has a lot of cars to sell him.

Lyle asked him to slow down a bit so he could follow his Spanish.

"Okay, I talk a little slower," the man said. "Tony looking for lots of 1970s cars these days."

"Does he travel back and forth across the border often?"

"Yes, sometimes I help him get Mexican trucking companies—ones that are okay to do business in the US. They haul small loads of cars. Much of the time, he takes cars across himself. He never has to wait. All the American border guards know him and wave him through."

Lyle asked about Guerra's family.

The lot owner told him he thought Guerra's wife and children lived somewhere near Nogales, Mexico and that Tony had been working to bring them to the US.

Legally? Lyle wanted to know.

Yes, but any way he could, the man said.

Lyle thanked him and asked him to tell Guerra to call the park.

Lyle's last address was a car lot on the other side of town. As Lyle followed the GPS instructions, he noticed that a silver Honda with two men inside had shadowed him through the last two turns. Lyle had been to Agua Prieta only once before and had only the vaguest notion of its layout, but he knew the direction of downtown. Ignoring the GPS route, Lyle hit the gas and took a sharp turn west at a liquor store. The Honda followed.

Lyle kept the pedal down as he approached fifty miles per hour, then sixty. Ahead he saw an equipment rental facility and houses scattered across the arid landscape. Was the Honda accelerating to keep up? Lyle braked hard, turned the wheel, and put Howard's Chevy into a skidding slide onto a dirt road. The car fishtailed as Lyle buried the gas pedal, and he fought for control. When a car started to back out of a gravel driveway ahead of him, Lyle hit the brakes and swerved around it. Two more quick turns on dirt roads put him back on a paved business street. He didn't see the silver car behind him. He slowed down. Aside from whoever was in the Honda, Lyle didn't want to face a Mexican speed cop, either.

Lyle found his last address close to the border on a mixed commercial street with restaurants, bars, shops, and a car lot. Nothing similar to the silver Honda had appeared in his mirror. Maybe he overreacted. He parked on a side street, down from the lot. He looked over his shoulder as he got out and saw nothing but an empty street. He walked to the sales lot decorated with strings of banners and balloons in the colors of the Mexican flag: green, white, and red.

When he explained himself to a salesman, the man shook his head and suggested Lyle talk to the manager who was having a late lunch down the street. The salesman pointed to a bar in the next block.

Lyle walked into the bar and paused for his eyes to adjust to the darkness. Several patrons sat on stools spaced out the length of the bar, and a row of high-back booths lined the opposite wall A heavyset man in a shirt and tie washed down a plate of machaca with beer from a bottle. Lyle sat next to him, introduced himself, and ordered a beer. Although he focused on the meal in front of him, the auto sales manager welcomed Lyle's conversation.

Lyle spoke to him using a mixture of English and Spanish. When Lyle mentioned Guerra's name, the man smiled.

"Yes, I know him," the man said in Spanish. "He's always looking for cars almost as old as I am. Which means from the seventies." He smiled again and sipped his beer.

Lyle's beer arrived and he saluted by tipping his bottle toward the man.

"I was supposed to meet Tony in Bisbee, but I was told he came down here to pick up a car."

As he spoke, Lyle glanced in the back-bar mirror and watched two men enter from the street. In the dim light he couldn't be sure, but one of the two looked like the man with the dark glasses and scar from the first car lot. The men took one of the unoccupied booths.

"If Tony's wanting more old cars, he should talk to me again," the sales manager said to Lyle. "I can tell him where he can find a couple of old crates he can get for almost nothing out in the country. I could buy them myself and re-sell them, but it's a lot of hassle. Tony appreciates a good deal."

Lyle got another look at the man in dark glasses behind him. The man turned to talk to the other newcomer. Lyle recognized the profile.

"Do you think Tony could be into drugs?" Lyle asked the sales manager. "Taking drugs across the border?"

The man shook his head. "Not Tony. He'd never."

Lyle glanced in the mirror again. The man in dark glasses gestured toward Lyle and his partner picked up a cell phone and dialed.

"Excuse me for a minute," Lyle said in Spanish to his buddy at the bar. "I have to pee. Make room for more beer."

A back door, if there was one, had to be at the rear of the room, behind saloon-style swinging doors. Lyle looked straight ahead and went through. In the short hallway, one open doorway led to the kitchen, another to a toilet. A screen door covered the third doorway. Lyle pushed it open and peered down an alley. His car sat less than a block away.

He stepped into the alley, and someone knocked him to the pavement. The bulky Mexican looked down at Lyle with dead eyes, one clenched fist held chest high. "What kinda cop are you? DEA?" the man said in Spanish. "You ain't going back north."

Lyle held the side of his head where the six-footer had hit him. He groaned, took a deep breath—then kicked the man's ankles as hard as he could. The man fell backward and Lyle heard something clatter to the ground. He stood up quickly and kicked the man's gun down the alley. Then he kicked the man in the ribs for good measure and sprinted off in the direction of his car. By the time Lyle reached the end of the alley, a bullet ricocheted off a concrete wall next to him.

The Mexican thug had gotten to his feet quickly. Before he had a chance to fire again, Lyle rounded the corner of the alley and dashed up the street to his car. He climbed in and was more interested in getting out of there than in groping under the seat for his gun. He started the car and dropped it into gear. The man with the scar and wraparound dark glasses appeared down the street in front of him. Lyle spun the wheel, turned the car 180 degrees, and accelerated. Watching the scar-faced man in his rearview, Lyle didn't see the other thug emerge from the alley. He leveled his gun at Lyle.

Chapter 30

Kate never knew what the vice president of communications for a theme park would be called on to handle next. This morning it had been a flock of irate Gold Wing motorcycle owners who didn't know why they couldn't drive their big bikes into the park. Something that should have been settled by guest relations or security, it fell to Kate to mollify the president of the large—and prosperous—seniors motorcycle club.

That issue settled, Kate sat in the passenger seat of Arthur Poole's Prius as they drove toward Scottsdale, the upscale Phoenix suburb, on the way to face another surprise she could not have anticipated, even a few weeks before. Creston Dealey, vice president of Consumer Cannabis, invited Poole to meet and discuss common issues. Kate had agreed to accompany Poole, ostensibly to check out Dealey and offer advice later about whatever the corporate pot exec had in mind. Kate thought another purpose might be to represent the power and influence of her corporation, Nostalgia City.

"Before the meeting, Kate," Poole said as they drove south on Interstate 17. "I want to apologize."

"What for?"

"For bothering you with the grow factory. I wasn't trying to pressure you or anything. It's mainly Remo's idea."

"It's okay. I know you're enthusiastic about getting marijuana legalized, but we need to take it one step at a time."

"You're right. I told Remo to put all this on hold and work on our ballot measure. So, how did your committee meeting go?"

"Good," she said. "Some of the department heads had already thought about it and they had good suggestions. Drenda, a friend of mine, reminded us that pot may have been popular in the 1970s, but it wasn't sold in stores. We'll have to dream up some appropriate way to sell it. Maybe street-corner vendors. We'll work on it."

"Remo may have some ideas about that."

Remo again? "Tell me about Dealey."

"He's hard to figure out. I heard he was on Wall Street. Don't know why he got out." Poole turned onto another freeway headed to Scottsdale. "I don't think he's from Arizona. New York, Connecticut, someplace back east."

"Does he think marijuana is the next big money maker? Is it more lucrative than the market?"

"Consumer Cannabis is making lots of money in the states where they run the medical dispensaries, and their complete legalization campaigns are gaining ground in several of those states. They want to be the *Budweiser* of marijuana," he said taking his hands off the steering wheel to add air quotes.

"Have you met Dealey before?"

"Basically just once at a marijuana symposium. That was before our campaigns got started, but he acted like the Consumer Cannabis program was the gold standard."

Just as they arrived at the office, Kate remembered something. "I met Paige the other day."

"Yes, she told me."

"Are you seeing her?"

Poole glanced at her with raised eyebrows then shrugged. "We've gone out a few times, why?"

"Well, if you're serious about her, you might want to talk. Find out how she feels."

He smiled. "Are you giving me dating advice?"

"Maybe."

Consumer Cannabis occupied a ground floor office in a small, two-story building. Lush by desert standards, the landscaping throughout the office park featured white, red, and yellow wildflowers encircling diminutive hedgehog cactus in beds of tan decomposed granite. A row of saguaro stood along the walkway.

As they walked to the entrance, Poole pointed out a low, powerful-looking sports car sitting in a spot marked, "Reserved for Mr. Dealey."

"Is that his car?" Poole said. "Looks expensive."

Kate bent over the silver and blue bullet. "It's a McLaren," she said reading the insignia. "Looks like a race car. I've never heard of it. Even has a radar detector."

Stepping into the reception area, Kate took note of the Indian rugs, stone floors, oak furniture, and oil-rubbed bronze fixtures. Apparently, Dealey liked to show off his money. At least he had good taste. She'd decided to dress executive for the meeting with a stylish mid-length dress and a Neiman-Marcus blazer.

A well-dressed, middle-aged woman greeted them from behind a counter and directed them to a conference room just off the reception area. "Mr. Dealey is expecting you," she said.

Kate walked in and was surprised to see Remo Bellard sitting at the end of a conference table next to the man she assumed was Dealey.

"Remo," Poole said, "I didn't think you could make it."

Bellard and Dealey stood. "I called Abbi and she agreed to come in this morning and take over for me," Bellard said. "I just got here."

Dealey walked around Bellard's side of the table to greet them. He wore an expensive suit and a bolo tie. If he wasn't from Arizona, at least he looked the part. Combed straight forward, his salt and pepper hair was cut short. He introduced himself with a thin-lipped smile. He clearly knew who Kate was and shook her hand firmly.

"Would you like coffee?" he asked, indicating the coffee service on a counter.

Poole helped himself then took a seat opposite Bellard. Before she followed Arthur, Kate glanced at the coffee mug in front of Bellard. Almost empty. Dealey took his seat at the head of the shiny glass table supported by a tangle of metal legs designed to look like cactus skeletons.

"It's a pleasure to meet you. May I call you Kate?" Dealey said, turning to his right when they had all taken seats. "I haven't been to Nostalgia City yet," he said, "but from all the reviews, I know it's marvelous. You probably have all the envy of the people who run the Disney parks."

"Not quite," Kate said, "but our artists and engineers are good at what they do."

"Arthur," Dealey said smiling again, "how is your campaign going? Polls show voters still favor recreational marijuana, but it's close."

"We're doing okay," Poole said slowly. "Still working on signatures, as I know you are."

"You're wondering why I wanted to get together," Dealey said looking around the table. He presented an unusual countenance. His wide-set gray-green eyes and dark eyebrows contrasted with a narrow chin. And his teeth were almost too much for his lips to cover. When he smiled, his canines overlapped his lower lip. "As I was explaining to Remo," he continued, "even though we may have different interpretations of how marijuana should be marketed, we're both facing the same opposition. And candidly, they're developing considerable resources. There's a so-called citizens committee that's collected more than a million dollars already. They're going to run anti-pot TV ads."

"We've heard rumors about that," Poole said, glancing at Bellard.

"The committee has been holding hush-hush fund raisers in Phoenix. As well, there's been a rise in local anti-pot community groups. And I've heard that some TV preacher might join the anti-pot campaign."

"Arthur is going to speak at a public forum this weekend," Kate said. "Not all local organizations are against marijuana, are they?"

"Maybe not. But at the end of the day, there are still big campaigns and lots of money at odds with both of us." Dealey paused and looked from Poole to Bellard and back to Poole and Kate. "Moving forward, I thought we could share some ideas to blunt the opposition."

"Our campaign, "Poole said, "emphasizes the use of marijuana exclusively for adults."

"That's a good starting point," Dealey said, "but we need more outside involvement." Elbows on the table, he rubbed his hands together. Kate wasn't a poker player but she recognized a *tell* when she saw one. Dealey proved her right.

"Candidly," he continued, "it will take allies to help us get the message across. I can tell you, I've been talking with the Arizona Taxpayers Alliance. They're interested because marijuana tax could offset tax increases elsewhere. We could develop some meaningful synergy with that group."

Generous to mention that, Kate thought. She wondered if Dealey had already sewn up an endorsement from the group, and if so, why tell Arthur before it becomes public?

Dealey answered the question. "Now, Arthur, State Senator Bryan Odom is on your board. It would benefit us both if you encouraged him to float the idea of a state senate resolution. I think you should do that. Something about how tax on recreational marijuana could create a windfall for education in the state. Maybe we don't care if the resolution passes. We want people talking about it. Our goal would be to shift the media focus to education funding rather than on *evil weed*."

An effective public opinion strategy. Dealey is sharp. Kate waited to see how Arthur would respond.

"That could really help," Bellard ventured. "I've talked to Senator Odom before."

"Think about it," Dealey said to Poole. "Talk with

Odom. See what he has to say. We're trying to put a lot of street smarts into this campaign."

The meeting continued for another half hour with Dealey asking questions and Poole answering mostly in single syllables. Kate watched.

"You know, Arthur, Consumer Cannabis has the resources and the momentum for this long battle. And we could use your experience and expertise."

"What?" Poole said.

Dealey clasped his hands in front of him. "Arthur, does it make sense to have two propositions, both with the same purpose? Why don't you consider joining us?"

"Safe Weed is different."

"Yes, a little. But the voters don't know that. They'll just be confused. I'm sure we can modify our operations in ways you'd approve once the election is over." Dealey's smile did little to reinforce his sincerity.

"Our culture is just different," Poole said.

Dealey paused and Kate could see he was not out of inducements.

"As you know, Consumer Cannabis is strong in the medical marijuana field. If you decided to join us, I would see to it that you had a medical marijuana license. Think about it. You could provide necessary marijuana to hundreds of patients."

When Poole didn't respond, Kate wondered where the conversation would go. Dealey was obviously used to getting his way.

"We have two hundred twenty thousand signatures already. I expect we'll get three hundred thousand well before the deadline." His smile now forced, he continued. "If you have trouble with signatures—you know the deadline is approaching—you can still come onboard. And the medical dispensary license will still be available for you."

Bellard raised his eyebrows and looked at Poole, but Poole frowned and stood up, signaling Bellard to join him.

As the two of them walked to the front door, Dealey asked Kate to stay behind. "You understand how public campaigns work," he said. "Arthur is no businessman. Frankly, we see him as an obstruction. He's out of his league here." He chuckled. "Maybe he's smoking some of that pot."

Dealey smiled. Kate didn't.

Undaunted, he pressed on. "I don't know how you're planning to take advantage of the pot business, but a dispensary in Nostalgia City could take you to the next level. I think you understand that. Your target customers would eat it up."

"What are you saying?"

"Max Maxwell would see the bottom-line benefits. I'm sure of it. *You* know the business side of this. Our ballot measure has a real chance to pass. But we need a unified campaign. After an election like this, there's months of delays, but we could see to it that Nostalgia City was a premier location for early sales of recreational marijuana. We're willing to work with you. Let us know what we can do."

೧೨೦

On the drive back to Nostalgia City, Poole appeared absorbed in his thoughts.

"Arthur?" Kate said after many minutes of silence.

"He's worried," Poole said. "If our measure passes, it would sidetrack his attempt to take over the marijuana business. There's no way I'm going in with him."

Kate tried to imagine what it would be like working with—or more likely *for*—Creston Dealey. "How many more signatures do we need?"

"A lot. We've barely reached the minimum of one hundred fifty thousand. And you need double the minimum because so many signatures are disqualified.

"What happens if we don't qualify? Would you support Consumer Cannabis?"

Chapter 31

Lyle woke up, staring at green and pink floral wallpaper. He shoved off the covers and sat on the edge of the bed. It wasn't the hours spent with various law enforcement agencies the night before that made his mouth feel dry and sticky. It was the gin and tonics he'd consumed before returning to his period-decorated room at the Copper Queen in Bisbee.

The day before, in Agua Prieta, Lyle had looked up in time to see the man from the alley pointing a gun at him. Survival instinct—or suicidal tendency—made Lyle swerve his car right at his assailant. The man lunged for the sidewalk and fell over the curb as Lyle raced by. A few minutes later, Lyle waited in the relative safety of the US border check point queue.

Once back in the USA, he stopped at the Border Patrol office and identified himself. He reluctantly included his law enforcement history—to bolster the believability of the story he was about to tell—and explained what had happened to him and who he was looking for. The station's watch commander listened with interest. Lyle told him he'd formed the opinion that Guerra didn't know he had been transporting drugs. When the San Navarro authorities investigated the last car shipment, Lyle explained, deputies discovered a trailer home headquarters for the drug smugglers in Camp Verde. This, he said, blew the cover for the drug transit scheme and ended Guerra's usefulness. Lyle theorized that the drug smugglers kidnapped or blackmailed Guerra and forced him to make one last border crossing. After checking with others, the watch commander told Lyle that Tony Guerra had indeed crossed earlier that day. He drove his pickup with an old Oldsmobile on a trailer. The Olds had been given only a cursory search.

A DEA agent appeared before Lyle left the Border Patrol office, and he repeated his tale. Almost immediately, the agent called his superior to mobilize a search for Guerra, the old car, and its contents. It didn't take profound thinking for Lyle to figure the drug gang had already retrieved the contraband and packed it away in different vehicles for delivery farther north. With Guerra's fate not much more difficult to imagine, Lyle found himself in a familiar situation: virtually powerless to help someone in trouble. The helpless feeling that drove him out of his backlogged police detective work—and almost out of his mind—came over him again.

Although he provided the Border Patrol and DEA agents all the information he had about Guerra, including his storage lot, his desk, and his calendar book, Lyle called the Cochise County Sheriff's Department and met an investigator at Guerra's apartment building in Bisbee. Cochise County deputies had a file on Guerra now and were the cops most likely to find him—if he wasn't in the ground. The apartment manager let the sheriff's detective and Lyle into Guerra's unit.

If Guerra *was* sharing drug profits, he certainly wasn't spending it on furniture or amenities. The main room and adjoining kitchen were bare bones. More like skid row than Martha Stewart. Nothing looked otherwise amiss until they walked into the bedroom. A wooden chair lay on its side along with the broken parts of a small lamp. Two faded brownish-red spots on the bedspread and one on the floor told how Guerra had likely been persuaded to make another border crossing.

When a crime scene tech and other deputies arrived at

the apartment, Lyle gave them his official statement then called Rey Martinez to say he couldn't find Guerra. His next stop was the Copper Queen Hotel's restaurant and bar. The Cochise deputies and the DEA would do whatever could be done to find Nostalgia City's classic car scrounger. Lyle was not optimistic. Before he'd even looked at the menu, he'd ordered his second G and T.

✧✧✧

Kate's arms around him when he walked into her apartment Friday evening wiped the Mexican cartel from his mind—at least temporarily. On the long drive home, he'd wondered whether or not to tell Kate everything—especially that he'd been shot at. He decided to come clean, so he got the worst of it out right away. When he told her about the fight in the alley, she hugged him tighter, running her hand up and down his back.

"I think I'll tell you I've been shot at all the time," Lyle said, feeling the pressure of her body against his. Forty-five minutes later, they pulled their clothes back on and shared the work of preparing dinner.

"Are you a little more relaxed now?" Kate said, unwrapping a package of frozen tilapia.

"Mexico was scary for just a few seconds," Lyle said. "But what happened to me proved my theory about Guerra, the car trader. He didn't know he was helping them smuggle drugs into Nostalgia City, and when he found out, it was too late. The cartel already had a hold on him—somehow."

"So when you went looking for Guerra—"

"They made sure I didn't find him. And they tried to make sure no one ever found me, either."

Kate gave him another hug. "Thankfully they didn't." She looked deep into his eyes for a second—then handed him a package of noodles. "Drop that in the boiling pot, please. Do you think all the stuff in Mexico is connected to the drugs in the NC garage, Don Perez's death, and the guy who tried to run me down?"

"I think so," Lyle said, reaching for a bottle of wine in the fridge. "Are you still getting media calls about it?"

"Not many recently, but Max thinks the murder and the DEA raid are the reason attendance has dipped. Maybe the transition will help."

Lyle set placemats on the kitchen bar and pulled out two wine glasses.

"But I'm afraid the marijuana proposition isn't going to help attendance," Kate said. "Arthur and I met with a guy named Creston Dealey at Consumer Cannabis this morning. He's head of the competing marijuana ballot measure. He says a citizens group has already raised a million dollars to oppose both marijuana propositions with TV ads."

"And that campaign could rub off on the park if people see us as pro-pot," Lyle said.

"Now you see how *easy* PR is. And that's only part of it. Dealey is a predator. He wants Arthur to give up his campaign and join him. But he made it clear he'd love to give NC some special favors if I can get Arthur to throw in with him—or drop out and endorse him. But if it suited him, he'd also drop Arthur like a hot cliché and make a deal for our support."

"Is there a lot of anti-pot sentiment out there?"

"Ask me tomorrow. Arthur is speaking at a meeting at the Polk Library."

Chapter 32

"Have you heard from Dealey?"

"No, why?" Poole said.

"I had the impression," Kate said, "he might try some other way to persuade you to go in with him."

"If he calls, I'm telling him flat out no."

Kate and Poole sat waiting in the front row of the Polk Public Library community room where Poole had been invited to speak at a forum on marijuana legalization. Kate's curiosity about what anti-pot citizens might say brought her out to the Saturday morning program. She turned in her seat when she realized the noise level in the long, narrow room had risen considerably. People filled all the seats, and standing room at the back became scarce.

"I found out some interesting information about Dealey yesterday," she said. "It answers a few questions. But my friend in New York said he has to get more details to be sure."

"What did you find out?"

Before Kate could answer, a middle-aged woman with a long nose and wide, square-framed glasses walked over. "Mr. Poole, I think we'll get the meeting underway. You'll be speaking first." The woman wore a flowery halter-neck dress, a little too formal for the community meeting.

Although the host's brief introduction sounded half-hearted, Poole nevertheless stepped confidently to the front of the room. Rather than stand behind the lectern, he rested an elbow on it and spoke without notes. "Marijuana prohibition in the United States has a shameful history founded, in part, on racism. It began in the 1930s with Harry Anslinger the first director of the Federal Bureau of Narcotics. African Americans and Hispanics were primary users of marijuana at the time," Poole asserted, "so Anslinger demonized marijuana by demonizing those who smoked it. He said smoking marijuana made black Americans think they were as good as whites. Anslinger told everyone that cannabis made people crazy and made women want to have inter-racial sex," Poole said.

"We've come a long way as a society since then, but legally and rationally, marijuana policy is filled with contradictions, basically based on myths and old prejudices. Look at the facts. Today, thirty states recognize the value of medical marijuana. It can be legally sold to patients. Yet federally it remains illegal, a schedule-one drug along with heroin. Cocaine is only a schedule *two* drug."

As Kate watched Arthur, today dressed in a sport coat and tie, she heard the beginnings of rude mutterings behind her.

"Marijuana is legal, and even encouraged in some states," Poole continued, "but it can put you in jail for years here in Arizona. Does that make sense? Marijuana prohibition has encouraged the drug cartels just like alcohol prohibition empowered crime syndicates in the 1920s." He segued into a description of his Safe Weed ballot initiative and how it encouraged local, independent sellers and growers. He finished up with a pitch for members of the audience to sign his petition.

"Questions?" said the moderator.

"Do *you* smoke pot?" asked a man in the third row, his tone revealing his thoughts on the subject.

"Recreational pot is presently illegal in Arizona. I have smoked it out of state where it's legal."

The man snorted and sat down.

"If you're in favor of marijuana," asked a woman with a high-pitched voice, "then do you approve of cocaine, heroin, all the rest?"

"No, of course not. Heroin and cocaine are dangerous drugs," Poole said, eliciting a small chorus of laughs from the audience. "No, they are. They're *not* like marijuana. If marijuana prohibition ends, law enforcement can concentrate on the hard drugs and not waste time arresting people for having a joint."

Kate sensed a foul mood in the room. No one would have to worry about a waiting line to sign Arthur's petition. *He should thank people and sit down.*

"How can you promote pot smoking when teenagers are dying of overdoses?" Kate didn't like the hard edge on the woman's voice.

Poole looked down and shook his head slowly. "Ma'am, no one, to my knowledge, has ever died of an overdose of marijuana. You can't say that about everyone's drug of choice, alcohol."

"*That's* not true," shouted an angry voice from the back of the room.

Finally, Poole got the message. He thanked the host and sat down next to Kate.

"Sorry," she whispered. "Obviously not a receptive group."

"No kidding," Poole said softly.

Kate knew he wanted to swear, but he rarely did.

"I'm out of here," he said.

And before Kate could say anything, Arthur got up to leave. A low hum of jeers followed him. Kate turned to watch as a man at the back of the room who had shouted stood up and looked as if he was going to follow Poole out of the room. A woman sitting next to him grabbed the man's arm to stop him.

Kate wanted to get up and console Arthur, but he'd likely faced the similar questions before and built up a tolerance. The atmosphere in the room, however, worried her. If marijuana were legalized and sold at the park, would it create a local backlash in Polk or elsewhere?

Kate waited for the opposing speaker who turned out to be a PTA officer. A practiced speaker, the woman talked for a half hour focusing on the dangers marijuana posed for children and teens. She asserted—as Kate knew—that cannabis can affect teenagers' developing brains and can hinder problem solving, memory, and have other long-lasting effects. *Keeping pot out of the hands of kids would* have *to be a priority.*

As the moderator thanked the speaker, hushed voices rose in the back of the room. Kate turned around.

Chapter 33

"Ah, we have a special surprise for you," the overdressed host said as the PTA speaker sat down. "I know some of you heard the rumor about our special guest being here today, this most illustrious, distinguished member of the clergy. But we couldn't confirm it until just now. This is a special honor for us in Polk," she gushed, "to have such a strong champion of family values here. I'm so excited to introduce him. He's ah—" The woman stammered and shuffled papers behind the podium, then started reading. "Reverend Nathaniel Jameson is pastor of the Skylight Cathedral in Los Angeles, where he has been preaching the word of God for about five years. Prior to following his call to California, he served as associate minister and a director of Green Empire Ministries of the Pacific Northwest. He is also presently executive director of Skylight Television."

The speaker stopped reading and looked up for a moment. "I'm sure you've all seen him on TV. Reverend Jameson recently received the lifetime achievement award," she said, returning to the script, "from the American United Religious Crusade Association, and he is vice president of the Religious Broadcasters League."

As she listened to the introduction, Kate turned and saw a silver-haired man in a dark, shiny suit striding up the aisle. He walked up next to the moderator and put a hand on her trembling shoulder. "Thank you for your kindness," he said, interrupting her as she listed the universities he attended and the honorary degrees he'd received. "Thank you. All those titles and degrees don't mean as much to me," he said, "as my chance to talk with good folks like you. I'm really just a hometown preacher."

More than just polite applause greeted the reverend, and eventually nearly everyone in the room stood as they clapped. Kate didn't know how to react. When she finally decided to stand, too, the speaker held up his hands palms out and the applause faded away.

"Thank you so much for having me here today. It is an honor and a blessing to see all of you and tell you about the terrible threat of this—this drug culture that is sweeping the west." He swept an arm across in front of him.

Kate noticed manicured nails and French cuffs.

Powerfully built, the reverend spoke with a modulated voice that filled the room. He stood relaxed, but appeared to look into everyone's eyes with a sense of urgency. Fluffed and combed straight back, his hair flowed over his collar. "I brought my crusade here to Arizona, bringing the word to one and all. In the coming days, I will be conducting services in Phoenix, Mesa, Tucson, Chandler, and yes, even Sun City. Dangerous drugs threaten our senior citizens, too. They start on pot and end up, well…" He spread his arms wide. "…who knows where? I want to thank your lovely chairwoman for inviting me. I'm so pleased I'm able to visit you at the beginning of my crusade."

Kate tried to recall if she'd ever seen Reverend Jameson before. His name was vaguely familiar, but she doubted she'd seen him on TV. She guessed his age to be somewhere past fifty.

"Now this marijuana proposition, and there are two of them, would put the evil weed out on the streets of your town. They say it's safe. They say it's regulated. They say it's not harmful." He spoke with an up-and-down rhythm, his voice echoing in the hall. He had a habit of nodding his head forward and back as he spoke. With broad, sturdy shoulders and a large, square head, he reminded Kate of a bobble-head doll. "Safe, not harmful, regulated. Can we believe the drug dealers?"

"No," shouted a handful of people from different parts of the audience.

"How can this be regulated, friends, when the government in Washington says that marijuana is a *dangerous* drug." He emphasized the word by raising his voice and raising his hands in the air, then he gripped the corners of the podium and continued. "Tell me this, how can you just approve a proposition, and *presto,* the dangerous drug is not dangerous any more. How? With magic? *Black* magic? I have read both of these pot initiatives. They have paragraphs of legalese about dispensaries and marketing and inspections and what have you. It's all bunkum designed to make you think it's safe, make you think it's a good idea. I'm not going to speak to any of that. All you need to know is the word *addiction.* All you need to know is what this drug can do to young people, to mothers and fathers. I can tell you from personal experience, in my very own family, about the evils of addiction. It ruins lives."

The hushed air in the room gave weight to everything the speaker said. Seated in the front row, Kate grew increasingly alarmed. She imagined what the reverend's words and his campaign could do to Arthur's proposition and to her position. An NC executive and spokesperson first, she'd quickly become associated with the movement to legalize pot.

As the speaker paused momentarily, Kate noticed him look at her with an appraising eye. Was she mistaken? A reverend?

"You know that your body is a temple," the reverend intoned. "First Corinthians tells us this." Was he eyeing her again? "And you can't glorify God in your body if it's polluted with immoral weed." His voice softened. "You notice how they call it *weed*? And what is a weed, but an invasive species, crabgrass, something we root out." He took a breath then raised his voice. "We root it out and throw it away. We don't keep weeds in the garden of our lives. We want it clean, fresh, pure. This *weed* as they call it, weakens our very society. So what should we do?" he said, raising a hand. "We need to find some *strong* weed killer."

Murmurs in the audience rose and fell with the cadence of Jameson's voice.

"Is there anyone here who has had this drug invade their family?" He paused and scanned the audience.

"I have, Reverend," said a woman's voice from the center of the room. "My brother became a pothead and it destroyed him, totally destroyed him."

Kate clasped her hands. *What have I gotten myself into? What have I gotten* the park *into? First we were just fighting Consumer Cannabis. Now we're fighting God?*

Chapter 34

"So, you got yourself shot at again," Rey said.

"Spoiled my day," Lyle said without irony.

"And you gave a description of the guys to the Border Patrol and the DEA."

"Uh huh."

With no new breaks in the Don Perez murder case and the attack on Kate, Lyle's mood had tanked. He went into the park to check in with the taxicab office and rearrange his schedule, yet again. Maxwell, and ultimately Lyle's transportation boss, had given him whatever time off he needed to try to help get rid of the garage drug problem and resolve the Perez killing. As Lyle had made little progress, he thought maybe some time back in his cab would trigger a flash of insight. When his taxi shifts had been adjusted, he called Rey. He offered to fill him in on his ill-fated trip to Mexico and hoped the undersheriff had something new and encouraging. Working on a Saturday, Rey stopped to see Lyle on his way to a meeting about park security. They met for afternoon coffee at the Bohemian Coffee House in NC's Centerville. They sat outside with the temperature at eighty-five degrees, Rey in his uniform and Lyle his cabbie outfit.

"You plan any follow-up from Agua Prieta?" Rey asked.

"None. I have no interest in getting involved with Mexican law enforcement or DEA. The cartel guns missed their chance on me in Mexico. Now my only interest is the connection to Guerra and how it can help us find the guys who went after Kate with the truck *and* killed Perez."

"You couldn't find Guerra."

"Nope," Lyle said, pulling the brim of his hat down to shade his eyes. "I don't think he disappeared voluntarily. I think he was naive and they probably killed him."

"Or he was dirty and just disappeared."

"No, I don't think so. I think the cartel hid drugs in the old cars, then sold them to Tony because they knew those kind of cars would be shipped here. Tony had a clean reputation, so the drug-filled cars sailed through the border. Eventually, Tony must have found out and then he became expendable. They knew they couldn't use him anymore, *and* he knew what they looked like.

"When he agreed to see us, he must have known what was happening," Lyle continued. "Maybe he wanted to tell us about it, or tell someone."

Rey shifted in his chair and leaned toward the table. "If Guerra was innocent, why didn't he just leave and call the feds?"

"I don't think he could. The cartel wanted him to make one last trip across the border, and I think they had a hold over him. Maybe they kidnapped his wife and kids. He had a picture of them on his desk. Or maybe they promised to get the family into the US. I told you about finding the blood in his apartment. I don't think Tony did this willingly."

Martinez seemed to think about what Lyle had said. He popped the lid off his coffee drink and peered inside.

"What's the matter, not enough whipped cream in that outrageous drink," Lyle said.

"It's not outrageous."

"Pumpkin spice?"

"Just a caramel latte, Lyle. For a change."

"I would razz you about the calories in that thing, but you could have one every day of the year and not gain a pound."

"Okay, so look," Rey said, "if Guerra just got sucked into this, what about him telling that driver, Sharp, to go look up Vanessa. She could be one of the top drug people in this area. Who knows? Guerra might have known the load would be hijacked."

"But we didn't ask Sharp if there were other people with Tony at the time. Maybe they were already extorting him. Or maybe one of the gang posing as a car trader just recommended it to Tony, and he passed it on. You could ask Sharp, but I doubt it would help find Tony."

"Maybe the feds will find him. That's their territory. But regardless, San Navarro County is my territory and that's what I need to concentrate on. I think the guy who tried to run Kate down lives here. May be the same person who murdered Perez."

"Yeah?"

"I've got two strong reasons for this. First," Rey said, "we don't have the budget or manpower to chase all over the state or into Mexico looking for these people."

"And second?"

"Sheriff Wisniewski says we concentrate on the county. He's stubborn and wants us to solve this ourselves, here."

"Definitely two good reasons."

"There ya go. And," Rey said, "it makes sense. So now I could use one of those good ideas of yours."

"Good ideas? Oh, yes. Actually I have one idea. But I need to talk to Earl."

෴

"So, you were supposed to get your wheels back," Earl Williams said, just before putting a thick, deep-fried onion ring in his mouth. He sat opposite Lyle at a table in the empty KBOB employee lounge. The room featured the usual chairs and Formica tables, a counter with a sink and microwave. A row of vending machines lined up along the side wall. Lyle couldn't peg the machines as retro. Electronic, rather than mechanical, they didn't have the vertical row of pop bottles behind a tall, narrow glass door.

"You going to eat all those by yourself?" Lyle said, referring to the large paper plate of rings next to the burger Earl doctored with little tubes of mustard and ketchup.

"Hey, this is my breakfast," Earl said, pulling the plate of onions rings closer to him."

"Breakfast?"

"Well, lunch, dinner, whatever you wanna call it. I usually don't get up the same time you do, cab driver. I go on in fifteen minutes."

Lyle made a show of slumping in his seat.

"Oh-kay." Earl waved a big hand toward the plate. "Help yourself, if you can stand the cholesterol." He wore a loose, silky shirt with a wide collar and a peace sign pendant the size of a Olympic medal. "So, *did* you get your car back?"

"This morning. It's back to normal. Running great. Now my big issue is the..." He paused to help himself to a long, thin ring.

"Can't understand you, bro, with your mouth full."

"Sorry, these are great." Lyle got up and bought a soda out of one of the vending machines. After he'd washed down the onion ring—and one more—he wiped the grease from his mouth and continued. "When I picked up the car, I drove over to Hooper's garage. I didn't know if the shop was open on Saturday, but I found him in the office. You know he worked on my transmission *twice* and nothing happened."

"Except you be out some cash."

"No shit. That's what I tried to explain to the guy. I told him the dealer had to replace the whole damn transmission. Everything *he* did was a waste of money."

Lyle started to reach for another onion ring then stopped. "Guy at the Ford dealer said Hooper should have known a solenoid couldn't solve the problem. The bands were worn out. The transmission all ground up inside. That's what I told him." As he replayed his conversation at the garage, Lyle started to get stressed all over again.

"So Hooper asks me if I have the old parts," Lyle said. "What'd he think, that I'd carry the old transmission around in my trunk?"

"Hey, slow down," Earl said. "Chill. Eat another ring."

"You're right." Lyle took a breath. "Hooper said he'd have to get back to me. He better. That car is costing me a fortune. Good thing the park has a credit union." After he'd relaxed and stolen a small onion ring, Lyle forced himself to get to the reason he'd come to see Earl. "Who is your supplier?"

"Say what?"

"You know, I mean where do you get your, um…"

"You mean where do I buy my weed?"

"Yeah," Lyle said, looking around, although he knew they were alone in the room.

"What, you want a joint? Probably what you need. Mellow you out. Here—" Earl started to reach into his pocket.

"No, I don't want a joint. I want to know where you get it. We're trying to solve the murder and drug ring at the NC garage. I thought if you have a local source, we might be able to—" Lyle stopped when he saw Earl's expression. "No, that's not what I mean. Please, I don't want to turn in your supplier. I'd just like to know what kind of network there may be here. Any thread of an idea might help. These guys tried to kill Kate with a truck. We need to find them."

Earl leaned back from the table. "Okay. It's cool. Wish I could help, but I don't think there's much traffic in Polk. Sounds stupid, I know. But since I live in Flagstaff I'm not tuned in here. I have friends back in the old 'hood in Phoenix. That's where I mostly get my stuff. 'Sides, I 'spect your guys ain't jus' smuggling weed. Know what I mean?"

"Yeah, likely coke, heroin—"

"You know I don't do that bad shit. Can't help you."

Chapter 35

A heavy veil hung over the park—and Kate's office—this Monday morning. The murder of Don Perez and rampant rumors about drug trafficking touched everyone. Kate's memories of a truck's grinding, angry sound had not completely vanished. She stared blankly at her computer screen until she noticed Amanda Updike standing in her office doorway.

"Amanda, you startled me. I'm just thinking about,...well, lots of things."

"Sorry to interrupt but I've got a call from the *Phoenix Standard*. A reporter says a Reverend Nathaniel gave speech yesterday in Sun City. He criticized the marijuana ballot measures and mentioned Arthur Poole and Nostalgia City. The reporter said the reverend called marijuana an 'evil weed' and said it—quote—'tainted all who were associated with it.'"

"Crap," Kate muttered.

Amanda must have heard her because she pursed her lips. Suppressing a smile? "So what should I tell him?"

"Tell the *Standard* that we have the greatest respect for Reverend Jameson and that he represents *one* side of the marijuana debate. The issue will be decided by voters."

Amanda scribbled notes. "Got it. Good response."

Kate's cell phone rang. *Now what?* When she realized who it was, she welcomed the distraction. Astoria Gulliver, quirky writer from a Phoenix alternative newspaper, was one of the reporters who had Kate's cell number. She had written idiosyncratic, unconventional stories about the park, sometimes chiding NC, but—Kate understood—the stories helped them appeal to a younger audience than their traditional seniors-heavy crowd.

"Astoria, what can I do for you? I suppose you're calling about pot."

"Sorta yes and no. I've been trying to get a hold of Arthur Poole. It's like he's not at his store or answering his cell. I talked to someone at the store, Remo-something, but he just gave me the runaround."

"What did you want to know?"

"I'm doing a story on the marijuana propositions. Creston Dealey claims they have enough signatures to pass the state's review, even if thousands of signatures are thrown out." She hesitated for a moment. "I get it that this is like, private information, but I just wondered if you have enough signatures yet."

"We're getting close," Kate said with her fingers crossed. It was the truth, but any assurance they'd meet the deadline with enough valid names was another story.

"So could you tell me the number?"

"I don't know it exactly. Tell you what, Astoria, I'll talk to Arthur today and call you back."

Kate tried, without luck, to contact Poole throughout the day. The store said he was out, but he didn't pick up his cell phone.

As she packed up her purse and laptop and prepared to leave work that afternoon, she called Lyle. "Sorry to be a bother, but I'm concerned about Arthur."

An abbreviated taxi shift over, Lyle answered from his condo. "What's up? Is there a problem?"

"It's probably just my dark mood today, but he doesn't answer his phone, and people at Xanadu said they haven't seen him since this morning."

"Is he away from the park on business? Didn't you say he had a campaign office in Phoenix?"

"I tried that. He wasn't there. I'm going over to his apartment in Polk. Would you mind meeting me there?" She gave him the address. "It's probably nothing, but—"

⁕⁕⁕

Lyle waited outside when Kate pulled up in front of Arthur's corner, ground-floor apartment. Kate didn't like the expression on his face.

He put his hands on Kate's shoulders. "I knocked. The door was unlocked." He didn't have to tell her. She'd known before she pulled up.

"The sheriff is on the way," Lyle said. "There's nothing we could have done for him."

"Oh, Arthur." Her legs felt weak. Lyle held her firmly.

Sirens announced the arrival of Rey Martinez in a black and white and a second, unmarked car, with flashing lights.

Kate stood trembling. She let Lyle hold her for a moment as they stood in the parking lot in front of the apartment. As Rey approached, she turned and looked at the apartment door standing ajar.

"You sure it's homicide?" Rey spoke to Lyle.

"Take a look." Lyle motioned his head toward the door. He held on to Kate as Rey walked by. Kate noticed a young blonde woman in a suit get out of the other sheriff's car and walk toward them. She started to say something to Kate when Rey called to Lyle from inside the apartment.

"You going to be okay for a minute?" Lyle asked.

"Uh huh."

"I'll be right back," Lyle said.

The young woman followed him into the apartment.

Kate stood facing the blinking red and blue lights on the cars but barely seeing them. *The drug business, trafficking, murder, and now poor Arthur.* Tears filled her eyes. Did

Arthur get involved in a business for which he was completely unsuited? Pushing recreational marijuana was a far cry from looking after patients in a cancer ward. How could she explain he just wanted to help people? The drug scene was eating up the park and now her dear friend.

She dabbed at her eyes with a tissue and then noticed Rey standing next to her. How long had he been there?

"Kate, we found his wallet and ID. It's Arthur Poole. Lyle said you were a good friend. If you could, it would help us if you could just identify him. To be sure."

As she walked toward the apartment, she hoped it had been a mistake. They found someone else in Arthur's apartment. A tragic accident. When she entered and turned toward the kitchen eating area, she saw Arthur on the floor. He looked like he was sleeping, except for the blood. China and silverware lay on the floor next to him. An upended chair sat across the kitchen. She nodded to Rey then backed slowly into the small living room. She could hear Lyle and Rey talking.

"Looks like a fight," Lyle said.

"Yeah, but a short one. Two coffee mugs, a pot. Probably just one other person."

"Didn't last long. He got hit in the head with something."

"I think his head hit the table," Rey said. "Look on the edge there."

"Did you feel him? He's been dead a long time. That blood's dried."

As Kate listened, the young woman in a suit appeared next to her.

"I'm Detective Smith," she said. "We need to move outside so the techs can get in here."

Outside, Kate saw a small sheriff's van pull into the lot. She clasped her hands in front of her and looked around…for what, she didn't know. She felt Lyle's arm around her again and she leaned into him.

"Looks like he got in a fight with someone," Rey said. He stood next to Lyle.

"Or someone just hauled off and smashed him while they were having coffee," Lyle said.

"He ran the Xanadu shop at the park, right?" Rey asked.

"Yes, he did," Kate said.

Detective Smith stood in the group taking notes.

"Was he married?"

"Divorced. More than a year ago. Maybe two years." Kate took a deep breath.

"Is this okay?" Rey said. "Do you mind?"

"Go ahead."

"Did he have a girlfriend?"

"I'm not sure." Kate explained what Poole had said about Paige Ellerbe.

"Any family in town?"

"Just the ex, as far as I know. Somewhere in Phoenix. His parents were older. They both died before I met him. I think he mentioned an aunt or cousin living back east."

"We have his phone and an address book so we should be able to find out about friends and maybe relatives," Rey said. "When did you last see him?"

"Saturday afternoon. He spoke at a public forum at the library."

"Do you know who might have done this?"

"Drug people."

Two uniformed deputies walked up to Rey and he stepped away to speak to them.

Kate noticed Lyle's frown. "What?"

"This could be related to drugs," Lyle said, "but more likely he was killed by someone he knew."

"Well, he didn't know any drug pushers."

Kate heard Rey order the deputies to canvass the apartment building, then he stepped back. "You said drugs. Do you have anyone in mind?"

"He was campaigning for legal marijuana," Kate said. "He told everyone that legal marijuana would put the pot dealers out of business."

"Could be," he said. Was Rey humoring her?

"I know," she said, "It couldn't be a mob hit. They just put a bullet in the back of your head, don't they? But Arthur wanted to stop the illegal marijuana trade. He was a nurse for God's sake."

Kate described Poole's medical background and his kind-heartedness, as if that meant anything to anyone else. She told Rey about his Xanadu business and his interest in medical marijuana. Detective Smith wrote quickly to keep up.

"What about the other marijuana initiative?" Rey asked. "I've read the two proposals. They're in competition, right?"

"Yes. I'm not really sure what would happen if both propositions were on the ballot." Kate told him about meeting with Creston Dealey. "Oh, and Arthur had an argument with his ex a week ago."

Rey and Lyle stared at Kate.

"But Arthur went way out of his way to help this woman. He even kept her out of jail when she and her boyfriend got drunk at the park one night. Why would she kill him?"

Rey asked for details as Smith wrote.

"With no relatives that we know of in the area," Rey said, "we should talk to his employees. Is the store still open?"

Chapter 36

Later, Kate sat on a couch in Lyle's condo. He put a glass of wine in front of her. She didn't want it. Yes, she was sad, upset. She needed to mourn the loss of Arthur. But she didn't need a drink, she needed a clear head. Her mind raced. She couldn't separate Arthur's murder—it gave her the chills to think of his passing in that way—from the drug trafficking that threatened to define Nostalgia City.

She leaned forward, bracing her forearms on her knees. She'd taken off the jacket to her pants suit and rolled up the sleeves of her peach blouse. "Remember several years ago, all those people in Ohio who were murdered," she said. "They were marijuana farmers and a Mexican cartel wiped them out."

"I don't think they proved it was a cartel killing," Lyle said from across the room where he stood by a window. "But they *were* shot execution style with a pistol."

"They represented competition for the traffickers, just like Arthur."

"You mentioned an argument with his ex."

"She was yelling about money. I overheard them in his store. I'd never met her, and Arthur rarely mentioned her. But don't you think—"

"Kate, Rey and his people will work on this systematically. You gave him a lot to go on."

She stood up. "Remo."

"What's a Remo?"

"Let's go. I'll explain in the car."

As they sped around the edge of the park from Lyle's home in Timeless Village, Kate told him about Remo and his pot farm scheme. The more she talked, the more her grief morphed into anger. "That smooth bastard pushed Arthur's buttons, taking advantage of his zeal to get the Safe Weed proposition on the ballot—and maybe two-timing him as well."

"Two-timing him?"

"Well, messing with his girlfriend."

"What's his motive for murder?"

"Motive? I don't know. Something to do with the business. C'mon, Lyle. Let's go talk to him."

They sailed into the south employee parking lot, commandeered a '70s-style electric cart, and a few minutes later, walked into the Xanadu Boutique.

Kate led Lyle through the store as she searched for Remo. The usual crush of customers wandered the aisles. When they reached the back of the store, still no Remo. *Did he bail out? Is he on the run?* She saw Detective Smith come out of a back room along with a store clerk. The clerk made her way back to a check-out register.

"What's happening?" Kate asked the detective. She looked much too young to be carrying a badge and, presumably, a gun.

"Undersheriff Martinez and I are interviewing staff in the break room."

"Who's back there now?"

Detective Smith hesitated.

"We think we have some additional information," Lyle said.

"Oh, I'm sure Martinez will want to hear it. Just now I need to bring back another employee." Detective Smith walked over and talked to a male clerk stocking shelves. He accompanied her back to the breakroom.

"I don't see Remo anywhere," Kate said. "There's only one more place to look. I have to find him." She turned, took a step, then looked back at Lyle.

"Go ahead," he said. "I'll keep busy."

Kate opened Arthur's office door without knocking. Bellard sat at the desk, staring at the computer screen and banging away on the keys. When he turned and saw Kate, he got up.

"Did you hear?"

"Yes."

"Oh, it's terrible, isn't it?" he said rushing up to her. "So terrible."

When he put his arms around her, she froze. His touch felt rehearsed and repellent. Obviously he felt—or didn't feel—her response, but he carried on unperturbed. "Kate, it's so awful. No one knows what to do."

Kate stepped back. Bellard leaned against the desk. "So what are you doing?" she said. "What are you going to do?"

"I don't know. What do you mean?"

"I mean, who is going to run the Safe Weed campaign?"

"Paige maybe. I'm working on it, too."

"Where have you been all day? All morning? Did you go to see Arthur?" Kate wanted to shake some answers out of him. Did she ever think he was attractive? His dark hair and smoldering expression now gave him a sinister mien. *Why wasn't he answering?* "Well, Remo?"

"I've been here all day working, like everyone else. I didn't see Arthur. Abbi told me he called and said he'd be in later. What's going on, Kate?"

"You've been here all day?" Kate sat down in one of the side chairs. "When did you get here?"

"About eleven. I worked late hours yesterday. Kate, I know you're upset. I am too." He tried lowering his voice, injecting a little more feeling. He sat in the desk chair. "So tell me, what's happening?"

"What's happening? Arthur was murdered, that's what's happening. So you say you got here at eleven o'clock?"

"Yeah, about that, maybe a little later. But the police—the sheriff—already asked me these questions."

Kate didn't take her eyes off him. Maybe he felt the glare.

"What, me?" He left his mouth open for a moment without saying anything. "You think *I'm* responsible for his death? Even the police know I loved him."

Wrong. "Loved him? Really? Is that why you were fooling around with Paige? And what have you got going with Creston Dealey?"

"Paige, what? Nothing. And Dealey? What's going on with you, Kate?" He held his hands out. "You were there. Arthur knew what Dealey wanted. He wanted us to cooperate. He's a little pushy, but he's a businessman. Legalizing marijuana's what we all want. It was driving Arthur...and me. We had no secrets."

Remo babbled, trying to catch up to the truth, some truth. "Is this your story?" Kate said. "You and Arthur were working together for the same thing? Sorry he's gone. Now you're taking over? The store, too?"

"Kate, you're upset. I understand. I'm upset, too," he said, slowing his speech. "We don't know *what's* going to happen."

"I know what's going to happen. They're going to find your fingerprints at Arthur's apartment and then you're going to be answering more questions—in jail."

Bellard leaned over in his chair, reaching out for Kate with both hands. "I thought we were friends." When Kate didn't respond, he stood and took a step toward her. His mouth turned down, the corners of his eyes crinkled. "Please."

Kate rose and held up a hand as if in self-defense. Anger boiled inside her. So mad she dared not say anything, Kate left, slamming the door behind her. She hurried down the hall and through the store. Lyle caught up with her at the entrance.

"Let's go," she said.

They stepped outside and settled into the electric cart. "Rey has interviewed most of the staff here," Lyle said.

Kate turned to him as he released the cart's parking brake. "Wait. We've got to talk to Rey. Remo is in there working on Arthur's computer. Rey has to confiscate it. Hold it as evidence. Something's going on with Remo. Something about the ballot measure, about marijuana."

She started to get up.

"I'll go talk to him. Be right back."

Kate sat in the cart, staring straight ahead. She put her hands on the dashboard, her mind clicking back to things Arthur had said, clicking ahead into the unknowable. She didn't notice the tourists who passed by looking at her, but reality broke through when a vintage sheriff's car, lights flashing, pulled up in front of the store.

Kate recognized the 1974 Ford police car. Nostalgia City had restored the vehicle and presented it to Sheriff Wisniewski to keep him in character when responded to a call in the park. The sheriff got out and walked over just as Lyle came out of the store.

"Evening Ms. Sorensen. Sorry to hear about your friend," the sheriff said.

"We're *in* this, Sheriff. I know Rey Martinez is—"

"Sure, okay," he said, glancing briefly at Lyle then back to Kate. "But I think you may have your hands full with the news media. Some reporter apparently saw all the commotion there in Polk and started asking questions."

"Where was he from?" Kate asked.

"Don't know. Doesn't matter now. This is probably gonna be in the news tomorrow. And 'course they'll link it to the park and the pot and the damn drug raid. I hope t' hell you can keep this from becoming a bigger media shit storm."

He lowered his eyebrows and glared at Kate before making his way into the Xanadu Boutique.

"Okay," Kate said when Lyle sat down in the cart. "We're in this."

"What about the publicity?"

"I'll deal with it. What did Rey say?"

"He said he would check out Remo and the computer."

"Did you tell him Remo was a lying sleaze?"

"He got the picture when I said you didn't think Remo should be diddling with Arthur's laptop."

"Remo has a lot to hide."

Lyle got in the cart and they took a back street to the parking lot.

"Rey talked to the medical examiner and she says the time ah, time of ah. I mean..."

"It's okay, Lyle. I appreciate your feelings, my feelings. What did he say?"

"The murder took place sometime between nine and eleven this morning. This is based on body temperature. The examiner may have something more later."

They got in Lyle's car and headed back toward Timeless Village.

"Rey said his deputies couldn't find anyone in Arthur's apartment building who heard or saw anything. Most everyone was at work at the time."

Kate leaned back against her seat's headrest. She tingled, yet she felt her energy draining. This had to do with pot, somehow. Marijuana *did* kill.

Chapter 37

"Wiped clean," Rey said. "One of the coffee mugs, the table and chair, and the inside of the front door at Arthur Poole's apartment were wiped clean. No prints. And they used soap. Looks like he used the dish rag we found in the sink. Was the killer also trying to wipe away his DNA?"

"Probably just grabbed the rag as the first thing he saw," Lyle said.

As they drove to the Phoenix suburb of Glendale, where Arthur's ex-wife lived, Rey and Lyle discussed the evidence gathered the night before.

"So, as usual," Lyle said, "the evidence leads in several directions."

"Or no directions," Rey said.

Lyle had been reluctant to ask Rey about tagging along with him, but he knew what it meant to Kate.

Rey surprised him by not arguing. "You'd probably drive there yourself anyway, wouldn't you?" he said. "And I wouldn't know when you'd show up. This way I can keep an eye on you."

Before they reached Glendale, Lyle told Rey what Kate had told him about Arthur's argument with his ex-wife. "She had a shouting match with Poole last week. Arguing over money. Lots of 'fuck this,' and 'fuck that.' Then there was the altercation at an NC bar. I wonder if the ex-Mrs.

Poole will be too distraught when you give her the bad news. Regardless, her reaction should tell us something."

"I've got Tiff—Detective Smith—checking this woman's background. I didn't have time. I was at Xanadu until it closed last night, then I went back to the scene. Tiff's also going to see what we can do about Poole's computer. And that guy Bellard is a little too solicitous."

"Solicitous?"

"Hey, I went to college, too. I wasn't a lit major like you, Shakespeare, but I can talk good Inglés."

"*Muy bien.*"

Persis Poole lived in a small tan house a block from a major commercial street. Fronted by a porch, its roof made of corrugated fiberglass panels, the house sat back from the street, surrounded by a low, white picket fence. The fence looked new, the home as old as Mick Jagger. A woman in her thirties with light streaks in her brown hair answered the door. Lyle couldn't tell if she was wearing a dress or a bathrobe that buttoned down the front. The pattern on it looked like fleur de lis. Or maybe butterflies.

Rey, dressed in a suit, identified himself and asked if she was Persis Poole. He said they had some bad news and could they speak with her. The woman let them in without comment.

They stepped into a living room with worn carpeting where they stood waiting for Poole to ask them to sit. The sound of a TV sitcom drifted into the room from what appeared to be the kitchen. The woman just stood with a hand on a hip. "Yes?"

"I'm sorry to tell you," Rey began, "but your ex-husband, Arthur Poole, died yesterday."

"Uh huh." The woman showed almost no reaction.

Lyle watched her for a moment when a tall, lanky man in cut-offs and a baseball jersey, shirttail hanging out, walked in from a back room. He buttoned up the jersey as he walked.

"These are cops from Polk," Ms. Poole said, turning to

the man. "Somebody murdered Arthur yesterday."

Lyle and Rey exchanged looks. Rey spoke. "We didn't say he was murdered. What makes you think that?"

She waved a hand at them. "Aw, I heard it on the news this morning. I didn't catch a name, but they said some guy who ran a headshop at Nostalgia City was murdered. It happened in a Polk apartment. I figured it was Arthur."

"You weren't surprised?" Rey said.

"Oh, sure. Who'd want to kill poor, sweet Arthur?" Persis Poole's face clouded over. She looked at if she regretted the sarcastic remark.

The man in the baseball jersey walked over and put his arm around Poole.

"I'm sorry," she said. "I didn't like him, but it's too bad. Somebody killed him, huh?" Poole looked at her companion. "Oh, this is Nick."

"Nick…" Rey said.

"Nick Rafferty. You're police?" His expression reflected curiosity more than anxiety.

"I'm San Navarro County Undersheriff Rey Martinez. This is Lyle Deming." He turned to Poole. "Your ex-husband was killed between nine and eleven yesterday morning. Where were you at that time?"

"I said I didn't like him," Poole said. "In fact, I never should of married him. Everybody knows that. But that doesn't mean I wanted t' kill him."

"She was here with me yesterday morning," Rafferty said.

"Yesterday morning," Poole said. "Yeah, I was here. Except, remember—" She looked at Rafferty. "I ran out to the store for a little while."

"The store?" Rey said.

"Safeway down the street."

"You didn't meet Mr. Poole yesterday to discuss something, did you?" Lyle said.

"No, I told you I was at Safeway."

"When did you see him last?" Rey asked."

"Last week," the woman said. "You may as well sit down."

Lyle had been trying not to stare at a blindingly bright fuchsia couch.

"Everybody notices that," Poole said. "It's not ours. We're just renting the place."

Rey chose a wooden rocker. Lyle settled into an overstuffed chair while Poole and Rafferty sat on the fuchsia couch.

"You live here, too?" Rey asked Rafferty.

"Yeah. What's that got to do with anything?"

Poole patted Rafferty's arm. "What would you like to know?"

"Where did you see Mr. Poole last week?"

"At his store in the park."

"Why did you go to see him?"

Poole paused and looked at Rafferty for a moment.

Lyle studied her. Kate had told him that Arthur Poole said his ex-wife had addiction problems. Her bathrobe—or dress—didn't hide her skinny frame.

Her exceptionally pale skin seemed an anomaly for someone living in Phoenix, a city with more sunshine than the planet Mercury. He looked at her teeth when she spoke. Small, even, and whiter than her skin, they showed no signs of a meth addiction.

"Were you looking for money?" Rey said.

"We talked about it," Poole said.

"Did you have a disagreement over alimony? Did you argue?"

"No. Just a discussion. He stonewalled me. Are *you* married, Sheriff? Ever been dumped, divorced? We had some rough times. I wanted to work it out. I needed some help. But he just left me." She paused for a moment and looked at the carpet. "It hurts, y'know."

"Do you have any children?"

"No."

"How long have you been divorced?"

She looked at Rafferty again. "Divorced official? Less than two years or so."

"Did you have a problem paying a bill at Nostalgia City when you were there last week?" Rey asked.

"Why? Did someone tell you that?"

Rafferty placed a hand on her knee.

"We didn't need his help," Poole said. "We were fine. Just had a little disagreement at that bar. You're supposed to have fun at Nostalgia City, aren't you? But it's mostly for rich old folks, isn't it? They kinda frown on us. We upset the seniors."

"So he settled your bill?" Rey said.

"See, that's what he does. Always trying to be a goody-goody. It's just for show. Like he only cares about others. Those are the kind of people who get killed sometimes, don't they?"

"You mean deserved to be killed?"

"No, it's like he's so perfect what would ever happen to him?"

She definitely had a grudge, but how bad? Her thin face and long hair only hinted at what she might look like dressed up—and filled in with a few added pounds.

"So, you know where he lived in Polk?" Lyle asked, suddenly remembering a question they'd missed.

She paused a little too long. "Been there once or twice."

Trying to get back together or just begging for money? Lyle didn't need to ask.

"I saw him last month and he said he'd help me get a loan. But when I talked to him last week, he goes, 'Sorry, Persis, nothing I can do for you.' Yeah, that's the way he was with me. But I'm sorry he's gone and I hope you find who did it." She leaned back on the couch as if to say she'd told them her whole story.

"Do either of you know of anyone who would want to murder Mr. Poole?" Rey asked.

"Have anything to do with pot?" Persis asked.

"Why do you say that?"

"He made a lot of people mad."

"You mean people against drugs?"

"Maybe, but don't you think the people selling now are going to be a little pissed if Arthur's proposition passes? Pot'd be legal and you could buy it anywheres."

"Do you use pot?" Rey asked.

"You gonna bust us?" Rafferty said.

"I was just wondering if you knew of any of these pot sellers who might be angry at Arthur Poole."

"Don't know any of 'em in Polk," Poole said. "You gotta just ask around."

"Know of anyone else who might want to do him harm?" Rey asked."

Poole swallowed before she spoke. "Not that I can think of."

Rey ascertained that neither Poole nor Rafferty had steady jobs. "Nick just got laid off," Poole said, "but he's looking hard for something new."

When Rey asked about relatives, Poole told him what he and Lyle already knew, that Arthur Poole's parents were both dead. After a few more questions, and Rey's suggestion that leaving the state would not be a good idea, Lyle and he got up.

As Lyle opened the front door and prepared to leave, he heard Poole and Rafferty murmuring in the living room.

"Excuse me, Sheriff," Poole said. "You wouldn't know if Arthur left a will, would you?"

Rey shook his head.

"Where could I find out?"

"You'd have to ask at the county hall of records in Polk."

Chapter 38

Sheriff Wisniewski was right. Kate had just parked her car in an employee lot Tuesday morning when the media calls began.

"Kate, this is John Kellogg with the *Standard*. We have the story about the Arthur Poole murder. I'd like to know how this is going to affect the park. Is Maxwell going to have a statement?"

Kellogg was another of the reporters Kate trusted with her personal cell number. She sat in her car and tried to respond. "John, in terms of our operations, it won't alter what goes on at the park." *Just what happens in my head.* "We all mourn the loss of Arthur Poole. He was a friend who was well liked by park employees and he was a favorite of our guests."

"How does Maxwell feel about this?"

"I've spoken to President Maxwell and he has confidence in the county sheriff's department's efforts to find whoever did it."

She sighed—as silently as she could—and took deep breaths as she talked about her poor friend. What she said sounded trite. As the morning progressed she was able to put together a more complete statement that did justice to Arthur. His popularity around the park was no hyperbole. But would anyone outside of NC care what a gracious person Arthur was? During the next hour in her office, she fielded more calls, dodging speculation about a relationship between the murder and Poole's Safe Weed Project.

"What's the connection between Arthur Poole's murder and the murder of the mechanic in your garage," asked a sharp news blogger. "Are these related?"

Kate *wanted* to say he was probably correct, that drug trafficking and legalizing marijuana were the cause of these deaths. "You really need to talk to the sheriff's department about the investigation," she said.

The Perez murder and DEA raid had taken the shine off the world's most elaborate theme park. Now Arthur's murder threatened to tarnish it like a forgotten silver tea tray. Kate's to-do list about the upcoming debut of the park's *transition* could keep her busy for days, but she ignored it and focused on ways they could find the person who killed Arthur. When Lyle called her, Kate brightened up, momentarily.

"We just talked to Poole's ex-wife and her boyfriend," Lyle said. "We're on our way back. She wasn't surprised when we told her. In fact, she already knew. Has this been on the news?"

"You could say that. I've been answering calls all morning. The AP moved the story at five or six o'clock."

Lyle asked her to hold on while he shared the information with Rey.

"Not a lot of help from the forensics at Poole's apartment," Lyle said after a pause. "Rey says fingerprints were wiped off the coffee mug and chair. And they didn't find a weapon in the apartment or outside in the neighborhood. It could have been anything."

Kate had heard the technical terms, the cop talk related to a murder, before, but hearing it in relation to Arthur made it difficult to take.

"You still there, Kate? Do we have a bad connection?"

"I'm here. Sorry. I wish we knew what Arthur was doing yesterday morning. Who came over to his apartment."

"Here's a start. One of the Xanadu employees told Tiffany—Detective Smith—that Arthur called the store early yesterday morning about eight thirty. He said he would not be in until later because he was meeting someone. The employee said Arthur told her he needed to *finally resolve* something."

Kate was about to speak, when she looked up and saw her secretary standing in front of her desk, an expectant look on her face. "Okay, Lyle. I gotta go. Let's talk when you get back. Maybe lunch? Oh, wait. You didn't say. Is Persis Poole—"

"I don't think she did it. As you said, we'll talk."

"Sorry to interrupt," Joann said when Kate hung up, "but I just got a call. Paige Ellerbe is on her way over from Xanadu."

Ellerbe had been second on Kate's list of people she wanted to talk to and she'd learned Ellerbe would be in the park that morning. Did she come to the park to find out what would happen to the signature campaign? Maybe she was mourning. Kate didn't figure Ellerbe as the murderer—though you never knew—but she was eager to ask the Safe Weed office manager about Remo and the crap he'd rattled off the night before in Arthur's office.

She wanted to pump her immediately, but when Ellerbe walked into the office, something told Kate that talking across her desk wouldn't work. Paige slouched into a chair, made brief eye contact, then looked down. She wore jeans, a long-sleeved blouse, and little makeup. Her expression looked defeated.

Kate stood up almost as soon as Ellerbe had sat down. "There's just a few things we need to talk about. Let's go get some coffee." She walked around her desk. "There's a little place down the street. It's a bakery and has great coffee."

The pastry shop occupied a narrow storefront next to a bookstore featuring best sellers by James Michener, Sidney Sheldon, and Kurt Vonnegut. The bakery's pink and white awning shaded a window filled with goodies Kate had eyed many times, especially the variety of fresh berry scones. Few customers sat inside. Kate ordered their coffees and bought a cranberry scone for them to split. As they sat down in a quiet booth by the window, Kate noticed Ellerbe's slender waist and thin legs squeezed into tight jeans. She looked small and vulnerable. Although wanting to pelt Ellerbe with questions, Kate leaned forward and smiled while she used a plastic knife to cut the scone in half. Ellerbe's first words touched her.

"I know how much Arthur meant to you," Ellerbe said. "And he was like in awe of you. I could tell when he talked about you. When you joined the advisory board, he thought we really had a chance." She paused and put both hands around her coffee cup. "He was kind and straight with me. I owed him a lot."

Then why were you fooling around with Bellard? But Kate took it slow. She pushed half the scone in front of Ellerbe. "Arthur was a great guy. How long did you know him?"

"Less than a year. I answered an ad for someone to run the Safe Weed office. He hired me even before we had a place to work. I took poly sci and psychology classes at Phoenix College. I thought that background might help. It sounded like an interesting job working on a ballot proposition."

"I got the impression you and he were going out."

Ellerbe looked up at Kate with a sad smile. "I think he wanted to. We had lunch a few times and dinner once, but we mostly talked about the campaign."

"What about Bellard—Remo?"

Ellerbe's expression changed. "What about him?"

"Were you going out with him?"

"Why do you want to know? I thought you wanted to talk about the campaign."

"I do, but the most important thing is to find out what happened to Arthur. Who did it."

"I don't know why anyone would want to hurt him. He

was awesome. He said I could work on my college homework if I didn't have anything else to do at the office. Of course I could anyway, he wasn't there very often, but…" Her voice trailed off and she looked down again. She continued without looking up. "Remo has lots of ideas about making money with legalized weed. He told me Arthur was too conservative." She picked at a corner of her scone, tasted it, then picked up her napkin. "One day he's like, 'you know Paige, you could be an important part of our marijuana company.' Remo's always like that. Big ideas."

"Did you go out with him, sleep with him?"

Ellerbe shook her head and her voice cracked. "Why do I have to talk about this?"

"The sheriff will be asking you the same questions."

Ellerbe looked over her shoulder momentarily toward two customers standing at the counter. "They're going to ask me if I slept with Remo?"

"I don't know. Did you?"

"No, I didn't. I know he's not my boss, but it's like he's running things. He put his hands on me three times. I hated it. I didn't know what to do." A slight sheen of tears covered Ellerbe's eyes. "I need this job, Ms. Sorensen. I'm helping support my mom and my kid brother. I'm close to getting my associate's degree."

Kate put a hand on Ellerbe's arm. "Paige, call me Kate. If Bellard is harassing you, we'll stop it right now." She regretted misinterpreting Bellard's harassment and Paige's defensive actions in the back room of the Safe Weed office. *That bastard was groping her, and I thought they were getting it on.* "I can make him stop and wish he never touched you." She squeezed Ellerbe's arm. "I mean it. Men can't get away with abuse. Not today. Things have changed, although not everyone got the message." She knew about sexual harassment—she'd been a victim herself. She wished she had her hands around Bellard's neck. "Did he call you last night?"

"Yes. Very late. That's how I found out about Arthur."

Ellerbe ignored her half of the scone, but Kate's anger made her hungry. She took bites between questions. "Tell me what Bellard planned to do," she said. "I know he wanted to start a pot farm here."

Ellerbe sniffled and took a deep breath. "He talked about finding investors to help build the pot farm, but Arthur shot him down. Remo said Arthur was all about *medical* marijuana. He said Arthur needed to get going, but *he* could make things work if Arthur didn't."

"What do you think he meant by that?"

"Just that he could run the pot factory and make lots of money."

"You mean even if the other marijuana proposition won?"

"I dunno. Remo just said we could totally make money but he said Arthur was—"

"In the way?"

"He didn't say it like that, but maybe that was the idea. He said Arthur was fooling himself thinking Safe Weed would make it to the ballot."

"Is that right? Are we behind schedule?"

Ellerbe slowly shredded her napkin as she talked. "I'm afraid so."

"Did Arthur know?"

"I tried to tell him, but he was like, 'we'll make it, Paige, you just have to have faith.'"

"Is there a chance?"

"Only if we can afford to hire some people to collect signatures. The volunteers are cool, but they're not enough."

"Did Bellard ever mention Creston Dealey?"

"He's the head of the Consumer Cannabis campaign, isn't he? No, Remo never mentioned him, why?"

"Well, if Safe Weed doesn't make it, then the Legal Marijuana Control Initiative from Consumer Cannabis will be the only one on the ballot."

Ellerbe twisted the last portions of her napkin. "What's going to happen to me?"

Kate had harbored grave suspicions about Bellard before. Now, she wanted to choke the life out of him. "First, you won't have to put up with Remo's sexual harassment any more. Guaranteed. Second, I'm going to contact all the advisory board members to decide what our next move is. As far as I'm concerned, for now you're in charge of Safe Weed."

Chapter 39

Lyle stared at the truck parked in the lot next to the NC garage. The sign on the truck's door read: *Hooper's Auto Repair*.

Rey had just dropped him off at the park after they'd questioned Persis Poole. Lyle wanted to see if Gayle LeBlanc had heard from Guerra—a longshot—and ask her if she'd known Poole—another longshot. Was there a connection between the garage, drug trafficking, and Poole's murder? These questions, however, evaporated from Lyle's head when he saw Hooper's name.

He walked inside directly to Gayle's command center. "What's going on, Gayle?" he said. "Do you call Hooper's garage when you need to get a car fixed? I thought you did that yourself."

"What're you talkin' about?"

"I see Hooper's tow truck outside. D'you call him for help?"

Gayle laughed. "Heck no. He works here. Part time."

"So that's why he doesn't return my calls. Can you tell me where he's working?"

"What's in your head today, Lyle honey?"

"I just need to talk to him."

Gayle pointed toward the end of the building. "You'll find Mr. Hooper way down yonder. He's replacing wheel bearings or somethin' like that today."

Lyle tossed a "thanks" over his shoulder and headed toward the wheel shop. The cacophony of power tools, electronic sounds, and car doors and hoods being opened and closed accompanied him as he hiked purposefully down the main garage aisle. He walked fast and was breathing a little heavy when he spotted Hooper standing beneath a car on a lift, looking up at a wheel housing. "Mr. Hooper, could I talk with you for a minute?"

Either Cody Hooper didn't recognize Lyle wearing street clothes instead of his cabbie get-up, or he knew exactly what Lyle wanted and just bought time by twisting a bolt with a wrench. Lyle couldn't imagine why he thought Hooper looked like John Denver. More like Timothy McVeigh.

"I've been calling you. You did all that work on my Mustang's transmission. Remember? And the transmission really needed to be replaced?" Lyle stood just inside the service bay, beyond the old Pontiac that was raised up to eye level.

Hooper took a few steps toward Lyle. "Yeah, I remember." He shook his head, holding his heavy wrench waist high. "Look, we did a lot of work on that tranny. Put in a lot of parts. I can't give you your money back."

"But none of the work was necessary. Or, I mean useful. It needed a whole new transmission."

"It was okay when it left the shop. I checked the records. I can't be responsible for what you do to it."

"What I do—" Lyle had raised his voice just shy of a shout, only partially to be heard above the garage noise. On the edge of a panic attack—or a fight—he took a breath and looked around. Several other mechanics had stopped work to glance over. Lyle tried to relax. "I talked with you last week," he said, trying to restrain his tone. "Then you never returned my calls."

"I been busy. S'all I can tell you." He turned to go. Lyle reached out for his shoulder. As soon as he did, he felt someone's hand on his arm.

"You don't wanna do this," said a man in a blue mechanics uniform. "Let it be."

Lyle turned to see Blake, the guy he'd talked to in the bar, the same guy who scared the other mechanic from talking to him that night. Lyle was angry that Blake touched him, but the mechanic probably stopped him from doing something he would have regretted.

Coupled with the car on the lift, the sight of Blake pushed the Perez murder back into Lyle's head. "Hey, did the sheriff's deputies question you, Hooper?" Lyle said to Hooper's back. "Well, they will," Lyle said almost to himself as he walked back toward the other end of the building.

Somewhere, an engine overheated, burning off oil and filling the area with its unmistakable fragrance. "Shut it down," someone shouted.

Lyle snapped the rubber band on his wrist.

Halfway to Gayle LeBlanc's command center, Lyle saw someone else he recognized: Luis Nieto, the mechanic who found Perez's body. Nieto saw Lyle then turned back under the hood of an old Gremlin. *He recognized me. And I think he knows something more about Perez—about what got him killed. Got to follow up on this shit.*

"Didja find him," Gayle said when Lyle approached. "Find Hooper?"

"Yeah," Lyle grunted.

She got up from her desk and stepped off her platform with the poise of someone a hundred pounds lighter. She walked over so she could talk to Lyle face to face. "S'matter?"

"How long's he worked here?"

"I dunno. Maybe eight months. I'd have to check. Is it important?"

"I don't know. I don't like him. He did a thousand dollars' worth of work on my Mustang that it didn't need." Lyle explained his repair problems.

"You should be able to tell pretty quick if a tranny is chewed up inside," LeBlanc said. "You do any racing?"

"Gayle, not you too? No, I don't race. I drive hard sometimes, that's it. It's a Mustang, not a minivan."

"All right, honey. That's too bad about those expensive repairs." Gayle's outfit of the day consisted of olive slacks, a matching short suit coat, and a yellow sort of tent blouse with frills that hung down six inches below the jacket. "I guess I can see why you don't like Mr. Hooper. He seems to get along, though. I've never heard a complaint about him. Lots of guys grouse about other workers but not a word about Hooper."

"How often does he work here?" Lyle said. "Certainly not every day."

"He jus' works part time when it's slow at his shop and we need help, which we almost always do. You know, these ol' sixties and seventies jalopies were always in the shop. Still are, 'cept we do a better job on 'em these days. This guy Hooper's got a lot of experience so he can work in all departments, tune-ups to tires."

"Slow at his shop, huh?" *Maybe that explains why he charged me for useless work.* "But what I want to know is, was he working here the day Perez got killed?"

"I'm not following you 't all. What's your Mustang gotta do with poor Don Perez?"

"Humor me. I know. I'm crazy. I talk to myself. We got two murders here and—" Lyle paused to collect his thoughts. "I got up too early this morning. We drove to Phoenix. Just—" He smacked his hand down on the counter. "—just look that up for me, will ya?"

"Lyle honey, these are bad days 'round here, f'sho. You okay? I can find that for you. I gotta look at the computer in my office. You're off duty today. Got your phone? Can I text you?"

Chapter 40

Lyle found a drinking fountain in the lobby of the Maxwell Building and took a Valium. About twenty minutes too late, but still welcome. Since music from NC's KBOP radio station flowed into every corner of the park, it included the elevators up to the executive offices. As Lyle punched the button for Kate's floor, he heard The Eagles doing "Take It to the Limit."

When the door opened, his secret girlfriend stood facing the elevator. She wore a tailored navy dress with red piping. That was what you called the colored border, wasn't it? Anyway, it made her look professional *and* delicious, but not to everybody, Lyle hoped. "I just got out of a meeting with Max," she said. "Let's get out of here. How about the Tiki Kai."

Lyle made a face.

"C'mon. It'll be quiet, and we can talk."

They found the Tiki Kai, a throw-back Polynesian restaurant, located in the Harvey Plaza Hotel, on NC grounds but two miles away in the hotel-restaurant cluster. It afforded them quiet and privacy.

Apparently, the Polynesian trend of the 1960s and '70s didn't hold as much appeal today as the restaurant stood nearly empty. They sat at a table for four looking out over a Koi pond.

"I could use a glass of wine," Kate said, "but right after

we eat, I'm going to grill Remo Bellard. Well, maybe just one."

Since he'd just downed an anxiety pill, Lyle opted for tonic and lime. It arrived in a glass shaped like a tiki god.

"I talked to Paige Ellerbe this morning," Kate said after they ordered lunch. "She's the manager of the Safe Weed office in Phoenix. I thought she might have been Arthur's girlfriend. She liked him, but apparently Arthur was too shy or too distracted by the signature campaign."

She explained what she'd seen through the blinds at the Safe Weed office the week before.

"Feeling her up at work?"

Kate nodded.

"Did she complain?"

Lyle felt Kate's admonishing look. "Actors and politicians get caught and they can lose their jobs due to public pressure. At lower levels, this crap continues. Paige was afraid to say anything because of her job."

"Sexual harassment doesn't make Bellard a murderer."

"I don't trust him. I'm going after him this afternoon. He was supposed to be working for Arthur, but Paige made it sound like he was ready jump ship if necessary to cash in by harvesting marijuana."

"The pot farm was Bellard's idea?"

"He was the real promoter, yes."

"What does he gain by killing Arthur? He's just an employee."

"I'm not sure, dammit. Paige said he told her he had some sort of agreement with Arthur, but I think that was just BS."

"So without more evidence—"

"Yes. I know. I'm left with just disliking the bastard."

As Kate said the last word, lunch arrived. Her heated words didn't faze the server. She just smiled and set down plates of Szechuan beef and sweet and sour chicken.

Lyle held up chop sticks then did a drum roll on the table. He set the chop sticks aside and picked up a fork. After he'd taken a few bites, he reached inside his tan corduroy sport coat and pulled out a narrow notebook. "I started taking notes."

"No yellow pad?"

"It's at home. This is mobile. I used a pad like this when I was a detective." Lyle flipped to the first page. "I'm surprised you haven't mentioned what I told you about Arthur's last words to that employee."

"I remember," she said in monotone. "I haven't stopped thinking about it. He met with someone at his apartment and that someone killed him."

"To finally resolve something," Lyle read from his notebook. "Bellard?"

"It could fit. They could be resolving issues about the pot farm or maybe something about the signature campaign."

Kate poked at her food with her chopsticks then took a sip of wine. "Arthur was having coffee with someone. So we can assume this was not premeditated."

"That's what it looks like. Or that's what we're supposed to think." Lyle flipped a page in his notebook and a breeze ruffled the paper. The restaurant kept air moving with large, fabric-covered fans shaped like giant window shutter slats that swung back and forth in the ceiling. At times, the wind sent small ripples across the koi pond. He glanced up at the fans, frowned, and continued. "Here's something else. Arthur had several phone conversations on his cell yesterday and Sunday. The Safe Weed campaign office, Xanadu, Consumer Cannabis, and a number Rey said they can't trace. Could be a burner phone."

"We know he called the store early yesterday morning. What time were the other calls?"

"The Safe Weed office that morning. Consumer Cannabis the evening before. That's that guy Dealey, right?"

"Yes, the marijuana competition. I mentioned this to Rey last night."

"So what would Dealey gain by Arthur's death?"

"That depends on a lot of things. First of all, if the Safe Weed Project fails—and without Arthur, that's a good possibility—then Dealey's the only game in town."

"Are the ballot measures very different?"

"Yes. Dealey's favors corporate control with strict regulations on growing. Arthur's is more mom and pop and grow your own."

"Mutually exclusive?"

"Almost," Kate said, pointing her chop sticks at Lyle. "But here's the deal on Dealey. At the meeting he asked Arthur to quit the campaign entirely and work for him. However, I think—no, I *know*—that Arthur was going to turn him down, completely."

"So yesterday morning Dealey could have been giving it one more try to persuade Arthur. The phone call could have set up a meeting at Poole's apartment."

"And Arthur was going to turn him down, regardless," Kate said.

"Did Dealey know that?"

Kate shook her head.

"Then that puts him at the top of my suspect list," Lyle said. "His motive, at least, is getting rid of the competition. Maybe he had it in for Poole personally, too. We can ask him where he was yesterday morning. Maybe I'll go with Rey or deputies and talk to him."

"Why don't you leave him to me. Obviously, Rey or someone will want to talk with him, but I was at that meeting. I have an idea how Dealey operates, and I know some of his secrets."

"Okay, you can handle Dealey, but stay in touch—"

"I know, if it turns dangerous."

"Or if you just want a ride in my overhauled Mustang."

"We did that last night, remember."

"Well, I could put the top down." Lyle's remark barely registered a smirk from Kate. "Okay," he said, "we've got Dealey because he's competition. And Remo, because he's a sleazebag."

Kate took a small bite of sweet and sour. "And what about Persis Poole?"

"She obviously hated him. She made no excuses there. But she's kind of skinny. Doesn't look like she's strong enough to overpower him, but the boyfriend could."

"Do they have an alibi?"

"They're alibiing each other, so you know how solid that is."

"They argued over money. Arthur wasn't going to give her anything more. Aside from revenge, she didn't have anything to gain."

"She asked us about Arthur's will."

Kate picked up a bite of Szechuan beef, but it slipped between her chopsticks. "His will? She thinks she's going to inherit something?"

"Pretty strange. She asks Rey about inheritance after he lets her know she's a suspect in his murder."

"Doesn't surprise me. She sounded wacked out when I overheard their argument."

Just then Lyle's cell phone played Chuck Mangione's flugelhorn solo from "Feels So Good," telling him he had a message. He pulled out the phone and shielded it with his hands, an unnecessary gesture as no customers or staff were close enough to see. The text message said:

> *Cody Hooper started work here five and a half months ago. He did not work the day D. Perez killed. Or the day before that. This help?*
> *Gayle*

"Sorry, Kate. That's was from Gayle at the garage." He stopped talking as he put his phone away and tried to decide what or how to tell Kate. "You see—"

"What's going on?"

"Well," Lyle began. "Keep in mind *your* gut feeling that Bellard was behind Arthur's death."

"Okay. Let's have it," she said with a half-smile.

Lyle explained his suspicions about Hooper and the botched repairs on his Mustang. "I found out he works part time at the garage. I saw him there today, and he refused to give me any money back."

"He overcharged you on car repairs so you think he could have murdered Don Perez."

"Not exactly like that."

"Exactly like what then?"

He almost told Kate about Blake grabbing his arm, but he didn't want her to think he was any more reckless or crazy than she already did. He wasn't going to hit Hooper. That *would* have been crazy. He just wanted to ask another question. "Just a hunch. No one is talking in the garage so we don't have much to go on."

"A hunch is okay."

"As long as it stays this side of an obsession, right?"

Kate patted his hand.

"I'll just ask Rey to run a background check on him. Just to be sure." Lyle winked.

Kate frowned.

"Rey told me Sheriff Wisniewski wants him to interview many of the garage mechanics again to try and break the code of silence. But now with Arthur Poole's murder, the sheriff's department has its hands full." He looked at his notebook. "And we have a list of suspects."

Kate looked at her watch. "I keep wondering what the connection could be between the two murders."

"Me, too. I need to diagram it out or something."

Chapter 41

As Kate walked toward a showdown with Remo, she admired the colorful Xanadu sign. A marijuana leaf formed part of the elaborate, colorful design along with sunflowers, a peace sign, birds, the moon, stars, and a parade of smiling cartoon characters. Kate wondered, as she had occasionally since she started at Nostalgia City, what it would have been like to grow up in the 1960s and '70s. She always suspected her mother had been a hippie. When her mother died, Kate's father let her look through an old photo album. The young men and women in Mrs. Sorensen's pictures looked just like NC employees. They wore bell bottoms, tie-dyed shirts, beads, Nehru jackets. Along with the pictures, her mother had pasted in concert ticket stubs. Mrs. Sorensen had seen The Animals in person. And The Monkees and The Who.

The spell of Kate's reminiscences broke when she almost tripped over a low A-frame sign advertising the cappuccino of the day at the Bohemian Coffee House. She complained out loud—as Lyle might—and stepped around the impediment. Then she stopped and looked back at it. The sign sat on the sidewalk in front of a portion of the Xanadu storefront.

A round, three-foot wide wrought iron table with a Bohemian menu and two small matching chairs also sat on the sidewalk. So Arthur was barely gone and what's-his-name already paid back the presumed slights against his establishment. Fapp, that was his name, Daniel Fapp. *How could she forget?*

Did Arthur arrange to meet *him* yesterday morning to *finally resolve* their disagreement? Kate remembered Fapp as a grouchy malcontent, but a murderer? His relatively mundane argument with Arthur, however, was just the kind of dispute you read about in the news when one party couldn't take it anymore and pulled out a shotgun—or slammed someone into a table. Remo could wait a few minutes.

Fapp stood at the end of the service counter where three employees prepared drinks. A rich roasted coffee aroma filled the café. Fapp looked up at Kate as soon as she walked in.

"I'd like to talk to you for a few minutes, Mr. Fapp," Kate said. "Is there another place where we could talk? Or we could go outside on the patio."

"This is about Poole, isn't it?" Fapp said in a voice loud enough to be heard ten feet away. "What are you women trying to do, anyway?"

Kate decided to take a conciliatory tone. "Women? Trying to do? I don't know—"

"Hell, you don't. Is this good cop, bad cop, or what?"

"Mr. Fapp—"

"That little girl cop with an attitude was just here questioning me. What do *you* want?"

Detective Tiffany Smith. "Remember, I work in park administration. We talked about your store's problems," Kate said calmly. "I just need to find out a few things." *Like why you're the one with an attitude when your neighbor is killed.*

"You're the PR person. Want me to help you put a good spin on this?" Fapp said when they had walked outside. His voice dropped with his last words and something like embarrassment colored his face. He rubbed his thin moustache with his fingers and looked away for a moment.

They found seats under one of the big umbrellas. Although customers filled most of the patio, they found a quiet spot. Fapp sat down, his shoulders sagging. "Look, I'm sorry. I'm very sorry. This is upsetting, very upsetting." His voice dropped even lower. "Murders in the park. Customers ask about it. They want to know if it's safe."

"You shouldn't be surprised the sheriff is talking to you," Kate said. "You made some angry accusations around the park about Arthur Poole."

Fapp held his lips together tightly then looked down as he spoke. "I get it. I was pissed off, okay? But it was just business. God, I wouldn't kill him. Everybody's making a big deal out of this. No. I didn't mean that. It *is* a big deal."

"Daniel," Kate said in a soft tone, careful not to sound patronizing, "no one knows why he was killed. Every possibility has to be explored."

"I know, it's on me. I get a little excited at times."

A little?

"I can tell you," he continued, "there's no way I would want to kill him." He raised his shoulders. "God, it's horrible."

"When did you find out about the murder?"

"Last night. One of the Xanadu employees came over for a coffee and told us."

"So, you were in the store—"

"Lemme cut to the chase, okay? I mean, it's terrible." He raised his shoulders again with a shiver. "Okay, we open early. Six a.m. every day. I got in about five thirty to get things going. I didn't take a break until after ten o'clock. My employees will tell you. Then I took off at noon for lunch and took a break for a few hours. I came back and worked until late."

"Did Detective Smith tell you when the murder took place?"

"She just wanted to know where I was yesterday. I guessed that's what you wanted, too."

"When did you last see Arthur Poole?"

"I dunno, maybe four days. He works long hours, too. Sometimes comes in for coffee or a bun."

So Fapp carried on about Arthur, but Arthur still patronized The Bohemian. "Did you settle your feud with him?"

"Wasn't a feud. But yeah, some people finally checked out the air circulation in here. It's been better now."

"Did any of your employees share your animus toward Xanadu?"

"Share my—oh, were they pissed, too? Not really. Jennifer, my assistant manager, thinks I over reacted."

Smart woman.

Fapp looked wrung out. "No, I don't know anyone who would have wanted to do it."

"Okay, thanks for your help."

"Does this have something to do with that mechanic who got killed? It is drugs?"

Sadly, Fapp's questions echoed conversations throughout the park. "We don't know. The sheriff is working on it. I wouldn't be worried." Kate stood up ready to go. "Oh, your sign and table out front. It's kind of…encroaching."

"One of my new employees must have done that. I'll fix it. You want a coffee or a cappuccino on the house?"

Kate declined and headed down the sidewalk toward Xanadu. Before she got to the door, Tiffany Smith walked out.

"Ms. Sorensen. Good afternoon."

Probably just under average height for a woman, Smith looked up at Kate. She adopted a serious demeanor when she spoke, more serious, than she needed to. But Smith looked young enough that strangers might ask her what grade she was in, so she might need the compensation.

"I guess you just talked to Daniel Fapp," Kate said.

"Yes, some of the Xanadu employees mentioned he had a running battle with Mr. Poole."

"I just came from there. He thought we were a tag team. He got upset at first, then he realized yelling at me was pointless and…well, a tad insensitive. He's picked up a reputation around the park as a crank, but I don't think he killed Arthur. What did you think?"

"Undersheriff Martinez has a great deal of respect for you and Mr. Deming."

But you're still a little reluctant to share much police information. Kate smiled. "We've been through scrapes together. We feel the same way about him."

"I agree Mr. Fapp doesn't seem like a promising suspect. And he has a fair accounting of his whereabouts yesterday morning." The detective wore a pastel blouse and gray suit that matched her gray eyes. Her eyes seemed large, or did her thin nose make them appear so?

"I was just going in to see Remo Bellard. Is he there?"

"He hasn't come back from a late lunch break."

"Oh, are you…"

"I'm headed back to the office for now."

"You parked in the employee lot? I'll walk with you."

Carrying on a conversation while walking with someone almost a head shorter could challenge Kate. She tried to look forward as much as down and to walk slowly. Her long legs sometimes gave her an unintended speed advantage.

"I talked to Paige Ellerbe this morning," Kate said. "You saw her, too?"

"I was second on the tag team this time. Was she Poole's girlfriend?"

"Not really. I think she could have been, but Arthur was too distracted by his proposition—and the store. Did she tell you about Bellard, his wild dreams about making money growing and selling pot?"

"She mentioned Mr. Bellard."

"He's a sleazebag and he sexually harassed her. I know because I saw him playing grab ass once when they couldn't see me."

"She didn't mention this."

"I knew to ask the question. I doubt she'll want to report it and, sadly, she may be out of her job pretty soon."

"How's that, Ms. Sorensen?"

Tiffany didn't look like a cop, but she sounded like one. "Please, call me Kate. If the Safe Weed proposition doesn't get on the ballot, there will be no work for her."

"She seems credible."

"That's what I thought. She's a sweet young woman, and I don't think she's mixed up in the murder."

"Uh huh," Smith said.

"Did you manage to keep Remo away from Arthur's computer?" Kate asked.

"We got permission from assistant manager Abbi Tucker." She paused for a moment. "I think Undersheriff Martinez said it was okay to share this. We downloaded the contents and I'm going to have a look at it."

When they reached Smith's unmarked sheriff's unit, the detective unlocked the car. "Good talking to you Ms.—Kate."

"There's someone else you need to know about. I told you and Rey yesterday about Consumer Cannabis. But I need to fill you in on Creston Dealey."

Chapter 42

Lyle didn't know whether to ask Rey or Howard. Either one might think he was crazy. Especially if he told the truth. Maybe he could make up some story about why he wanted them to check Cody Hooper's background. Hooper, however, *had* to clear a background check to work at the park. So he was probably clean. But still...

Lyle decided to buy Howard a beer at Pete's Grill so Howard might get a look at some of the garage employees kicking back after work. At some point in the evening, he'd subtly slip in the suggestion that a quick peek at Hooper's personnel file might just clear up a few things in the NC garage.

When Lyle reached the security office, most of the day shift employees had left. He found Howard at his desk, his suit coat on the back of his chair and his face pressed toward his computer screen. Lyle lounged in a chair opposite him.

"Just a couple more minutes and I'll be finished," Howard said. "I can't believe the park's been around less than two years and we're already switching IT systems. I had just gotten used to all the reporting programs and data bases and now it's something new."

"No computers in my cab. Just an old fashioned two-way, plus KBOB music on the car radio."

"You still enjoy just driving around the park?"

"All I have to think about is who's my next fare going to be and where am I going to go for lunch."

"But now?"

"Hell, now I'm just trying to tell the good guys from the bad guys. Driving me crazy."

Howard made a few final taps on his keyboard and leaned back from his desk. "I've been encouraging my guys to keep their ears open twenty-four/seven around here. Rather than interrogate people, I asked them to hang out and just listen, ask a question now and again, but mainly just soak up the small talk and see what it yields."

"Pick up anything new?"

"I've learned that problems in the garage started about five months ago. The place is big, like a factory," he said. "There's obviously cooperative work among departments, but the body and frame shop employees are the most tight lipped and keep more to themselves. Rey's focusing on the body shop, isn't he?"

Lyle nodded in agreement, though he wasn't really sure.

"We've talked to mechanics and Rey's guys have been out here a lot doing the same thing. And nobody's talking. Some people have something to hide, but, all in all, I think many of the of guys—especially those working outside of the body and frame shop—say they don't know anything because they *don't*."

"And some are afraid to say anything," Lyle said. "I mean I would be after what happened to Don Perez. And I think the guys in maintenance—where Don used to work—are especially nervous."

"Afraid and/or uninformed. Either way we get nothing. So what I'm saying is, it's not a big conspiracy. Maybe a handful of guys responsible."

"I hope you're right," Lyle said. "So, you want to get a beer and mingle among the suspects?"

Howard got up and reached for his coat. When he stood, Lyle noticed he had a pistol clipped to his belt.

"You always wear that at the park?"

"Only since the Perez murder and the attempt on Kate's life."

"But we want to fit in tonight. Yeah lots of employees know us on sight, but you don't need to remind them you're security chief," Lyle said. "And why don't you leave your jacket behind, too. I'd say your tie was optional."

Howard slipped off his holster and carried it with him as they walked outside. "I'll leave it in the car."

In the parking lot, they found Howard's restored 1975 Ford sedan painted and equipped like a retro police cruiser. The car carried a radio set to the San Navarro County Sheriff's Department frequency. As Howard pulled out, Lyle listened to the radio's mundane chatter, one officer reporting his dinner break, another announcing a stop to help a stranded motorist. Lyle started to turn down the volume when he heard a familiar voice.

"This is Martinez in unit one-seven. I'm stopped near the corner of Mojave Drive and Ponderosa Street near a dirt side road. There's a light-colored pickup matching the description of the vehicle wanted in the Sorensen incident. I'm going to investigate. Request back up."

Chapter 43

Howard glanced at Lyle. The radio dispatcher's scratchy voice asked Martinez if the pickup was on the street. Lyle strained to listen.

"Negative. Vehicle is stopped in the brush near this location."

"Pondersoa Street," Lyle said, "That's mostly open desert. I know where it is."

Without saying anything, Howard flipped on his car's flashing lights and hit the gas. "You know the area better than I do," he said when they came to an intersection.

"Turn right here, then left, and go a few miles down."

Lyle and Howard arrived at the scene as a sheriff's car pulled up. A deputy with bright red hair jumped out. He had his flashlight in one hand; his other hand rested on the butt of his pistol. Dying light from the setting sun cast a hazy red glow over the desert.

Lyle got out and walked to Martinez's empty cruiser parked at the curb. He stared across the desert, hoping to see his friend. He didn't see Rey, nor could he see a pickup truck. Howard picked up a flashlight from his car, but the beam did little to brighten the shadowy, dry landscape. Lyle noticed Howard had also retrieved his semi-auto and clipped it to his waist band.

"Point the light over here," Lyle said to Howard, indicating a gravel road leading off into the brush. After only thirty feet, the road turned into a narrow rock-filled trail. Rey's sheriff's car couldn't have navigated over the rocks, but crushed chaparral and buckthorn bushes showed that some high-clearance vehicle drove through recently. Howard said something to the deputy, who recognized him, and the two advanced down the trail with Lyle close behind, pausing occasionally to listen.

After covering 400 feet, Lyle had heard nothing but the crunch of shoes on gravel and the cry of an early nighthawk. He looked ahead, watching for any movement in the stark countryside. Then Howard spoke.

"Rey, Rey Martinez. Can you hear me? This is Howard and deputy Nagel. We're here on the trail."

Lyle froze, listening for a response. He waited for a full minute. No voice answered back.

At a small clearing farther on it looked as if a truck might have turned around. Lyle asked the deputy to point his flashlight at a relatively smooth portion of sand. The beam showed distorted footprints in the loose soil. Hard to categorize but definitely footprints. The deputy drew his pistol. All three men paused to listen again. Silence.

"Looks like a truck stopped here," Howard said, pointing to gravel ruts, "and then headed out that way."

Lyle paced around the clearing, looking off in all directions before he realized he might be trampling evidence. Evidence of what? Did Rey take off after someone? Get a ride with someone he knew? Could he be bound up in the back of a four-wheel-drive pickup?

As Lyle fretted, Howard and Deputy Nagel spread out beyond the clearing, Howard going west, Nagel going east, their flashlight beams dancing through the murky air like giant fire flies among the desert plants.

"Shit," the deputy said from seventy five feet away.

"What?" Lyle heard Howard ask.

"Bumped into a cactus."

After a moment Lyle looked in the direction of Howard's voice and couldn't see his light. Seeing a clump of trees ahead—and something else—Lyle moved forward, but cautiously since he didn't have a light and his loafers were made for walking paved streets or sitting in his cab. Ahead another fifty feet, he reached the trees and saw the object he'd been focused on. Only an oddly shaped boulder.

"Here," Howard yelled. "Here he is."

Lyle turned and moved as quickly as he could, stubbing his toe on a rock.

In a minute, he knelt down next to Howard. Rey lay on the ground, his hair matted with fresh blood.

Lyle spun around half expecting to see the person or persons who did it. But even in the dim twilight, he could see nothing but rocks and desert scrub.

"He's breathing," Howard said. "Call an ambulance."

Martinez's uniform was sprinkled with dirt, his sleeve torn. Had he been knocked down, beaten up, run over? The only blood Lyle could see in the beam of Howard's light flowed along the side of Martinez's head. Lyle's rudimentary knowledge of first aid told him to check to make sure Rey's airway was open as Howard applied a handkerchief to the head wound. Martinez's breathing sounded labored. Lyle looked at Rey's arms and legs. Nothing *appeared* broken. His sidearm was missing.

Lyle stood up, again staring into the darkness, looking for anything.

"Ambulance is on the way," Deputy Nagel said, suddenly appearing at Lyle's side.

"Rey's pistol's missing," Lyle said to the deputy, "let's look for it."

Lyle and Nagel searched the area for the gun or anything else useful while Howard watched Rey. The deputy's light found impressions in the ground where the truck likely passed by, not deep enough to identify tire treads, but enough to show the truck's route out of the area. *Did they hit Rey with the truck?*

In a few minutes, Lyle heard sirens.

Chapter 44

Hours later, Kate, Lyle, Howard, and Sheriff Wisniewski stood in the hallway outside Rey's Flagstaff hospital, room talking with his wife.

"Doc says he's got a concussion," Wisniewski said, "cracked rib, and broken arm. His vitals are otherwise good—"

"But he's unconscious," Melissa Martinez said. "I want him to wake *up*."

"He'll come through," Howard said. "I've seen this before. He'll be okay."

He spoke with the sound of authority. Kate hoped he was right.

"You can sit with him," a nurse told Mrs. Martinez.

Kate moved to her side and gave her a hug before Rey's wife walked into his room. Kate glanced through the doorway and saw Rey, motionless on his bed, oxygen tubes in his nose and wires connecting him to electronic monitors. She said a silent prayer.

"What the *hell* is going on?" Wisniewski said almost to himself. Then his cell phone beeped and he pulled it out of his pocket. "Yeah, go ahead." He took several steps down the hall.

"Murders, drugs, now Rey," Lyle said, hardly moving his lips.

"How is he?" a voice behind Kate said.

She turned and saw Detective Smith walking up the hall. Kate explained Rey's condition.

"Is he going to be okay?" Smith asked.

"We think so," Howard said, either speaking from conviction or at least trying to boost the group's spirits.

"Did you find anything at the scene?" Lyle asked Detective Smith.

Kate watched as Smith nodded but motioned toward the sheriff. A young detective consults her boss first. Lyle wandered down the hall to an unoccupied waiting area where a dozen chairs formed a semicircle around a low table littered with magazines. He slumped down on the end chair. Kate sat next to him. Lyle's downcast expression mirrored Kate's feelings. After a moment, Howard joined them.

"Son of a bitch," the sheriff grumbled as he walked over and sat at the other end of the semicircle from Kate.

"Problem?" Kate asked.

"That was the chairman of the county board of supervisors. SOB has a scanner. Must be how he found out. Wants to know what I'm doing about the *crime wave*. Doesn't ask me about Rey's condition." Wisniewski, wearing jeans and a western shirt, glared at Kate and the men on either side of her. "Next I expect to hear from your boss, Maxwell, as soon as *he* finds out."

Kate heard footsteps and turned to see Smith and another man in shirtsleeves and wearing a gun—presumably another detective—walk past and sit next to the sheriff. Balding, with his hair cut to about a half an inch, the man leaned over and spoke to Wisniewski in low tones. Kate couldn't hear what he said, but the sheriff's loud response was, "Shit, what'd I expect? How about the dash cam?"

The detective spoke again and Kate could only pick up a few words. After another exchange with the sheriff, the man got up. He looked at his watch, said something to the sheriff and Smith, then walked down the hall to the elevators. Except for their little half circle in the waiting area, the floor was quiet. Kate could just see a nurse sitting a counter at the far end of the hall monitoring a computer screen.

"This has got to be connected to the guys who tried to run me down," Kate said, turning to Lyle. "You said Rey was investigating a pickup with a camper shell?"

"Yeah. That's what we heard on the radio," Lyle said.

"Rey said it could be the truck that went after you," Howard added.

"And all this comes down to drugs in the garage," Kate said.

"Howard and I were talking," Lyle said, "and we thin—"

"Okay, what do you guys know?" Wisniewski said in a voice loud enough to be heard across the table between them and perhaps in the next county.

"About what?" Lyle asked.

"About this whole shit mess. That's what."

"We have some theories," Howard said. "My guys have talked to a lot of employees, but—"

"C'mon over here and tell me, dammit. We gotta get this whole thing under control, and we need to do it now." The sheriff motioned for the NC trio to move closer.

When the three got up, Lyle pushed the table back and moved other chairs together so they could talk more easily with Wisniewski and Detective Smith. Kate could see the sheriff's expression reflected more than his usual gruff self. He leaned forward, looking directly at Howard and Lyle as he spoke. He introduced Smith to the park's security chief, then Howard explained their idea that most garage employees were nervous, but also ignorant of criminal activity. "The body and frame shop employees look like the most likely perps," he said, "but apparently no one has a record—or anything to speak of."

Smith leaned over and whispered something to the sheriff.

"That's interesting," he said. "Tell them."

"We ran checks on many of the body shop employees," she said as she glanced at a notepad. "One of them, Blake

Alston, has convictions for battery and drug offenses. He was pretty cool about it when we questioned him. Said he was framed—of course."

"Are you sure?" asked Howard seated opposite Smith

"I ran the check myself," Smith said, staring at Howard then glancing at the sheriff.

Howard glared. "Okay, because I looked at his personnel file and it was clean."

"What records are you looking at?" the sheriff asked.

"As chief of security, I have access to personnel files. We ran a routine background check when the park hired him, and it showed no criminal activity. No arrests. Nothing."

"Would he have been hired," Kate asked, "with felony convictions?"

"Hell, no," Howard said. "At least I wouldn't have approved it. Physical violence *and* drug convictions?"

"But here's the thing about Alston," Detective Smith said. She paused and looked at the sheriff. He nodded for her to continue. "Blake Alston has the strongest alibi of the group. He wasn't working the day the murder took place. His alibi stands up. Undersheriff Martinez interviewed people who were with him."

"Can I ask, sheriff," Lyle said, "did your people find anything at the scene tonight?"

"Yeah, you can ask. I'm asking questions, too. Everyone has to focus on this. Understand me?" He looked from Smith to Lyle, Kate, and Howard. "I need to know what everybody knows, even before you know it."

The sheriff's garbled syntax didn't faze Kate. Crisis time.

"Detective Gage who was just here says we got squat out there at the scene. The dash cam video doesn't help identify the suspect vehicle. It's a light-colored pickup with a camper shell. That's all. There was lots of brush in front of it, it was getting dark, and the truck was a long ways from Rey's car. After a few minutes, the truck drove out of the camera's view."

Sounds like the truck that chased me. Kate lamented, *her* description of the pickup was so sketchy as to be of little use, except for one thing. "Did it have a big, black bumper?"

Smith nodded, looked at the sheriff, then said, "They looked for that and they saw *something* on the front of the truck."

"Did you find Rey's gun?" Howard asked Smith.

"Negative," Smith said. "Deputies brought in a few lights—"

"But we don't know exactly what happened," the sheriff interrupted, "so we don't know how big the crime scene is." He paused, ran a hand through his shiny black hair, and stared at the group. "I think we all agree the murders and other crimes are connected."

"Except the Poole murder," Lyle said. "Yes, it could be drug related but evidence is not persuasive."

"You got other suspects, don't you?" Wisniewski asked Smith.

She hesitated.

"C'mon, we have to *solve* these damn cases. Rey's conked out. We're shorthanded. Get on with it."

"Yes, sir. Suspects. There's an ex-wife and some business connections of Poole's. We only discovered the murder yesterday, sir, and—"

"I know. It's been twenty-four hours."

"Yes, sir."

"Rey interviewed the ex-wife and her boyfriend in Glendale," Lyle said. "She's an alcoholic—a practicing alcoholic according to recent events at the park." When Lyle mentioned Nick Rafferty, Smith nodded her head. She'd kept up to date on reports.

"What are you doing next?" the sheriff asked Smith.

"A man named Creston Dealey," she said. "He's next on my interrogation list."

"Yes, and he should be," Kate said. "I'd like to question him myself. And don't forget Remo Bellard." She started to explain the competing marijuana propositions, but the sheriff interrupted.

"I know all about Consumer Cannabis and Poole's initiatives," he said. "And now we have a little more information from the ME on Poole. The time of death was likely not before nine thirty yesterday morning. Closest they could come was nine thirty to ten thirty. Cause of death was cranial impact, most likely on the edge of his kitchen table. The other side of his head suffered a wide abrasion caused by the impact, most likely, of a smooth object applied with great force. Detective Smith is working on the Poole murder," Wisniewski continued, "along with Rey who was also coordinating the Perez investigation. But it's mine now, too. Everything's on me."

Wisniewski's phone buzzed. He picked it up. "Yeah. No, don't do that. Listen, just you hold on. I'm on my way. Yeah, I know how long it'll take. But that new county road cuts off a lot of time." The sheriff put his phone back in his jean's back pocket and got up. "I gotta get back to Polk. My code three lights are getting a workout tonight. Listen, I know you guys all got vested interests, but we're all on the same side. Got it? I want to hear from anyone who knows anything—any time."

Competing thoughts filled Kate's head as she walked out to the parking lot with Lyle.

"So, we all stick together and we'll solve this," Lyle said without enthusiasm.

"Yes," said Kate. *And pray we don't lose Rey.*

Chapter 45

Kate didn't want to go to work on time the next morning and—she rolled over and looked at her alarm clock—obviously she hadn't. Trixie sat on the end of the bed. Apparently, she wasn't going to climb up on Kate's chest and rouse her either. She had other priorities, like grooming. *Joann is probably at her desk already wondering where I am and what is going on.*

"Trixie, get me a cup of coffee." That had about as much chance of happening as Maxwell calling her up to say everything at the park was beautiful and she should take the day off.

But the attack on Rey was sure to fan the steady stream of media attention the park received now. She needed to bring her staff up to date and strategize how they could spin—she hated that word, *characterize* sounded better—recent events and put them in perspective: Ten or twenty thousand people still enjoyed themselves every day at Nostalgia City. Would the media already know about Rey? No reporters had shown up at the hospital.

Maxwell. Kate rubbed sleep from her eyes and reached over to her nightstand. She picked up her cell phone. She'd clicked on the mute button as she'd fallen into bed the night before. *Check messages. Who called? Four messages.* She started to listen when the phone rang.

"Hey, Miss PR. Don't you listen to messages?"

"I was just—"

"Just getting up? I thought you'd be busy today."

"What do you want, Sheriff?"

"What I want is for you to keep quiet on last night's attack on Rey Martinez. Don't talk to the press. I want a media blackout on this. We don't know what Rey may have seen, and until we can talk to him, I don't want this to get out. In the meantime, I put a deputy on his hospital door."

"You think they'd come after him?"

"Maybe. We don't know what he saw. If he talked to the suspects or what. So we keep this quiet while we try to find that truck."

"Okay, Sheriff. I'll talk to my staff."

"I wish you wouldn't talk to anyone."

"Okay. I'll keep quiet."

As soon as she hung up, she punched up her messages. She could easily guess who the callers would be.

"Kate, this is Joann." *Knew it.* "The sheriff called. He insisted that I give him your cell number. I didn't think you'd mind. He called it an emergency. You also got a call from a Detective Tiffany Smith. She didn't leave a message. Are you coming in this morning?"

The last two messages were from the sheriff wanting to know where she was, and from Max wanting an update, now.

Kate sat on the edge of her bed. She pulled up one nightgown strap that had slipped off her shoulder. In a note-taking app on her phone she found where she's written the number of Consumer Cannabis. Eight-fifteen in the morning. They should be at work by now.

She identified herself and the person who answered the phone put her right though to Dealey.

As soon as Dealey picked up the phone, he offered condolences about Poole. Smart move. He even sounded sincere.

"Thanks very much," Kate said. "Since Arthur's death, I've talked to some of the other Safe Weed board members.

We're trying to decide what direction to take now. I was wondering, could I come over today, maybe this morning, to talk to you?"

"This is so tragic. Yes, of course. I would be happy to help in any way I can. As I said the other day, we have much in common. We can talk about anything you think might be mutually agreeable."

"Mutually agreeable," Kate repeated. "Yes, that's right. I can be there at...let's say, just before noon. Is that okay?"

Chapter 46

Dealey walked around his desk and extended his hand almost before Kate entered the spacious office. He offered coffee and directed Kate to a padded leather chair. As she walked past a half-height square bookcase, she noted the plaques and certificates on the wall. Still proud of his days on Wall Street, Dealey displayed framed notices of IPOs and brokerage credentials. A window behind Dealey looked out on a cactus garden courtyard and an arched doorway led off to the left.

Kate smoothed the skirt of her no-nonsense navy suit as she sat down. She started with something easy. "You must be about ready to submit your names to the secretary of state's office."

Dealey's smile was appropriately reserved. "Yes, probably by next week we will ask for authentication. I think it's important to do this in advance of the deadline. Candidly, it will give us more time to promote the campaign."

"You shift your attention from gathering signatures to persuading voters."

"Essentially correct." He offered his thin, teeth-baring smile. "We hope to get a campaign firm on board soon and get the ball rolling."

"So how do you think Arthur's death is going to affect the image of legal pot?"

"How do you mean?"

"Well, a murder does not give us a good name."

"Do the police think Mr. Poole was killed because he was promoting recreational marijuana?"

"The police? I don't know. Why do you—"

"The police would have talked to you," he said quickly then softened, "wouldn't they?" In a shirt and bright tie, without his suit coat, Dealey didn't look quite as aggressive as he had the week before.

"I don't have any idea why he was killed," Kate said.

"I guess there are more factors to influence this," Dealey said.

"This uncertainty..." Kate said, hoping he would finish her sentence.

"Yes, this uncertainty would be resolved if we worked together. Now that Arthur has passed away—"

"You mean that he's not an obstacle now?"

"No, of course not. We're all saddened."

"But life goes on and the ballot proposition must keep going?"

"Not like that." Dealey looked away. "Maybe I was overly harsh, but we have to realize that—"

"Did you try to get Remo to work for you?"

"What?" Dealey's gaze snapped back to Kate. "I don't want him to work for me. He works for Poole, for you."

"You wouldn't like to have a snitch in the other camp?"

A slit appeared between Dealey's lips, his teeth shone white. "I thought we were going to talk about cooperating."

Kate returned his stare.

He straightened his back, attempted a smile. "Now, Ms. Sorensen, I think we need to—"

Dealey stopped mid-sentence when Sheriff Jeb Wisniewski crashed through the office door followed closely by Dealey's assistant.

"I'm sorry, Mr. Dealey," she started to say.

Wisniewski waved her away and shut the door.

The sheriff advanced toward Dealey's desk. "What do mean by running away from my investigator?" As he moved, the sheriff's sports jacket flapped open exposing a chrome-plated revolver at his waist. "You can't dodge a *murder* investigation."

"What is this?" Dealey stood. "Who the hell—"

"Who the hell am I?" Wisniewski said. "I'm sheriff of San Navarro County. And you're in a load o' trouble."

"What are you talking about? What are you doing here?"

"You own that fancy blue sports car out front?"

"Yes, why—"

"Because when my investigator came to see you this morning, you ran out."

"I had a meeting this morning. I didn't know—"

"Bullcrap." Wisniewski waved at hand at the door. "She talked to your receptionist out there. And the next thing Detective Smith hears is that car of yours revving out of the parking lot. She saw you drive away at a high rate of speed." The sheriff was at his abrasive best. *Kate* felt intimidated, and the sheriff was yelling at *Dealey*.

"Well excuse me. Why didn't she call ahead? Why didn't she chase me? I know nothing about this." Dealey spoke in forceful tones. He'd wavered when the sheriff entered but now he tried to regain equilibrium. He gestured toward Kate. "This is Kate Sorensen, an executive from Nostalgia City. We're in the middle of a meeting. If you want to make an appointment."

Did Dealey think he could get rid of Sheriff Wisniewski that easily?

"I know Ms. Sorensen, thanks." Wisniewski touched the tip of his cowboy hat. "Now why don't you calm down, sit down, and tell me why you killed Arthur Poole."

"I'm a murder suspect? You're kidding. Why would I do that? Now really, Sheriff." Dealey sat down and clamped his mouth shut. He looked at Kate for a moment then focused on Wisniewski.

Kate enjoyed her front-row seat.

"Well?" Wisniewski said.

"Look, Sheriff, or whoever you are, rushing in here with

wild accusations is...well it's ludicrous."

Wisniewski took a step toward Dealey's desk. "Cut this bullcrap and tell me where you were Monday morning."

"I told you, you can't do this." Dealey's resolve weakened. Kate could hear it in his voice. Then a light colored his eyes. "You're a long way from San Navarro County, aren't you? Out of your jurisdiction. I should call the Scottsdale police and report this abuse."

"Why don't you do that, Dealey? I talked to Sergeant Zachery on my way down here, to let him know what I was going to do." The sheriff's gruff expression turned into a malevolent smile. He sat down on the other guest chair in front of Dealey's polished desk. "But I've got a better idea," Wisniewski said. "I'll just get a warrant. A judge in Polk is a poker buddy of mine. He'll issue a warrant on a phone call, and I'll drag your ass back to San Navarro County and hold you there until you answer everything. And maybe I'll alert the media that you're being questioned in connection with the murder. What would *that* do to your marijuana proposition?"

"Do that and I'll sue you."

"Go ahead. The city attorney needs work. Besides, how would *that* play in the media? Maybe Ms. Sorensen can tell us."

"Okay, Sheriff. Let's get this over with. I had nothing to do with the murder. I barely knew the man."

"Did you meet with him last week?"

"Yes. We talked about working together on communications."

The sheriff just glared at Dealey, his dark eyes staring out from under the brim of his hat.

"Look, I had no reason to kill him. No motive."

Wisniewski glanced to his right at Kate. She slowly shook her head.

"No motive? You have opposing pot ballot measures. Both of you are not going to get approved. I read the fine print. Poole's initiative sounds a little more customer friendly—if you call dope peddling friendly."

"It's different approaches," Dealey said. "Consumer Cannabis has the resources to create a smooth running market in Arizona. And we'll be contributing millions of dollars in taxes for education. That's the real winner, the schools." The smug expression Kate remembered from their last meeting tugged at the corners of his mouth.

"And with Poole out of the way—"

"Doesn't change anything," Dealey said "We're going to be on the ballot for sure."

"Ask him about calling Arthur on Sunday evening," Kate said.

Dealey flashed her a deadly glare.

"I'm getting there," Wisniewski said. "So why *did* you call Poole Sunday?"

"Call him? I wanted to ask him about some of the things we discussed last week."

"Why Sunday night? Were you setting up a meeting?"

"I called to offer him a medical marijuana dispensary. I thought that was his interest."

"You expect something in exchange for this?" Wisniewski said.

"Just goodwill. We really must work together."

"More bullcrap." Wisniewski leaned forward. "Trying to buy him off?"

"Look, I didn't know he was going to be killed." Dealey leaned on his elbows and rubbed his hands together. "It has nothing to do with our cannabis business."

Sheriff Wisniewski relaxed back in his chair. He pushed his hat back two inches off his forehead. "I'd like to know where you were Monday morning."

"Monday morning?" Dealey looked blankly at Kate for a moment. "Monday morning I was at a chamber of commerce meeting in Flagstaff."

"What time?"

"The meeting started at ten."

"How'd you get there?"

"I drove up from my home here in Scottsdale."

"And you got there at ten. When did you leave the meeting?"

"About noon I think. No, we finished up at twelve-thirty. I stopped at a café in Flagstaff for lunch before driving back."

"Can you prove you were in a restaurant?"

"Yes. I charged it. I can get a receipt. And call the chamber. Talk to Doug Reach. We talked about dispensaries in Flagstaff and about school issues." Dealey put his hands flat on his desk. He looked safe and satisfied. Maybe he knew when Arthur was killed from media reports. He was covered.

Wisniewski continued firing questions at him, but Dealey's renewed confidence didn't fade. When the sheriff finished by obtaining Dealey's home address and cell phone number, he got up to leave. Kate decided it would be a good time for her exit as well.

"Dealey probably knew when Arthur was killed," Kate said when she and the sheriff stood outside next to her car."

"Maybe. But we'll check his alibi. I'll talk to his wife. I'll go to Flagstaff if necessary. Maybe I'll ask a friend in the Scottsdale PD to cruise by his house a few times in a black and white. Make sure he sees him. Get him nervous. Maybe he'll make a mistake."

"Could you really get a warrant for Dealey that quickly?"

"Hell no. Yeah, I play poker with Judge Tanner, but we're not exactly on the best terms. He supported my opponent—under the table of course—in the last election. And sometimes he makes us jump through too many goddamned hoops to get a simple, damn warrant."

Kate smiled. "No matter. It worked."

"I'm kinda off my game. Was up most of the night."

"Yes. Anything new on Rey's condition?"

Wisniewski shook his head.

Chapter 47

Lyle walked into the detective bureau and found Detective Smith staring blankly at her computer screen. Her desk was one of five crowded into the room and the only one occupied. A beleaguered black ceiling fan stirred the stale air. In a corner sat a large white board on an easel with scribbled notes, the names *Perez* and *Poole* in large letters at the top. A watercooler supporting a five-gallon bottle, half empty, completed the ensemble.

Smith obviously didn't hear Lyle approach, nor see him when he stood at the front of her desk. When he said, "Detective Smith?" she jumped as if she'd received 110 volts. Her arm banged her desktop as she reached for something.

"Mr. Deming. Sorry, you startled me." She smiled at herself. "Obviously."

"That's a nice smile. You weren't smiling when I came in. No luck with the Poole case or Rey's?"

"No, sir. A disappointing morning."

"I know about disappointing mornings. I had weeks of them. Months. Running down clues, alibis, witnesses. Half the time, nothing panned out."

"Yes, sir."

"So formal. My dad used to want me to call him sir. I'm just an ex-cop cab driver."

"What can I do for you Mr.—"

Lyle held up a hand.

"Okay, Lyle. How can I help you?"

Lyle wanted to put Detective Smith at her ease, given what he planned to ask. But she seemed a hard case this morning. She had to be warm in her tailored suit. Maybe she was keeping up an image in the office, no doubt filled with nothing but men.

"Well, I'm sure what I have in mind will not make your day much better, but I just have a hunch about a suspect in the Perez murder."

"Why don't you sit down?" Smith said. Seeing no guest chair next to her desk, she started to get up.

"I'll get it," Lyle said and he took a few steps to retrieve a nicked wooden office chair. The chair looked retro, but the sheriff's office was not part of Nostalgia City. The furniture was probably *left over* from the 1970s. Or maybe '80s. "Things are kind of tight in here."

"Yeah, we're remodeling."

"Rey told me." Almost immediately Lyle felt guilty for not asking about Martinez's condition when he walked in the sheriff's office. "I called the hospital this morning, but they wouldn't tell me anything. I even had them put the deputy on guard on the phone but he didn't really know."

"No change," Smith said.

Lyle sat in the antique chair. "There's this guy, Cody Hooper. He's somebody who slipped through the cracks when Rey and the other officers were interviewing mechanics. He runs his own auto repair shop, but he also works at the park." Lyle explained that Hooper was a relatively new hire at the NC garage and that he was used as a jack-of-all-trades. "He worked all over the shop. I'm sure he would have known Don Perez. But when I asked him if he knew him, he said 'no.'"

"Why would he say that?"

"That's what I'd like to find out."

"Does he have any connection to the body shop?"

"Well, he probably worked there, too. Other than that, I don't know."

"Sounds like a lead. He should have been questioned."

"He's working in his garage today. I wonder if we could go over there. I tried to talk to him the other day and—"

"Mr. Deming, Lyle, I appreciate the tip. And I know Martinez and the sheriff trust you and Kate."

"But you'd rather question him yourself without a civilian tagging along."

"It would just be more efficient. I can go over there. I'm up to speed on the case notes."

But she's inexperienced. Is she going to intimidate that low-life Hooper or vice versa? "Your call, detective. Would you mind if I came back later to find out how it went?"

Smith paused before she answered and set her jaw. "Okay."

Lyle gave her Hooper's address and said he'd check back later. He walked out to his rejuvenated Mustang and called Howard Chaffee's cell phone. He knew the chief of security had a waiver to carry his phone at all times in the park.

"Where the hell are you, Howard? All I can hear is shouting."

"I'm at the Ferris wheel."

"You going to be there long?"

"Probably. We have an *issue*."

"Anybody hurt?"

"Nothing like that. What's up?"

"I need to ask you something, Can I come over?"

"Sure. I'm the guy in the blue blazer and tie."

Dressed as he usually did for work, Howard would stand out among the thrill seekers at the NC Fun Zone. As he drove back to the park, Lyle wondered what catastrophe had brought Howard out of his office. A string of violent crimes stained Polk, the park, and life in general. *And Howard was concerned about the Ferris wheel?*

Once in the park, Lyle used his ID to get into Fun Zone. He could see the arc of the Ferris wheel as he walked through the retro midway. The wheel didn't move.

He found Howard huddled with several employees. The Ferris wheel attendants wore powder blue slacks, powder blue shirts, and yellow hats. And as Lyle looked up at the motionless wheel, he realized the couple at the top of the ride wore nothing.

"Do I see what I think I see up there?" Lyle asked when Howard walked over.

Howard tried to suppress a smile. "That crazy young couple up there decided the wheel would be the best place to have sex."

"Really? They're just waving at the crowd."

"They just got into it when one of the attendants saw them as their gondola passed the low point and started ascending."

Lyle couldn't help smiling as he looked skyward to see the young woman and man naked, at least from the waist up, waiving and laughing.

"Let me guess," Lyle said. "Alcohol have something to do with this?"

"They were passing a bottle back and forth earlier. The ride supervisor stopped the wheel, stranding them more or less out of sight."

"Why don't you just lower the wheel and throw a wet towel or something over them?"

"That's what my Fun Zone security supervisor wanted to do, but the Fun Zone day manager wants to clear this whole area first."

"Limit the exposure—so to speak—just to the people still on the ride?"

"Something like that. I heard this on our two-way and had to see for myself."

"I see what you mean," Lyle said, gazing up at the young woman waving to the crowd below.

"That's not what I meant. Come to find out, this is not uncommon in theme parks. I think we need to standardize our response. Now, did you want to talk with me?"

"Okay. I can make it quick." Lyle explained the situation with Hooper. "I have a feeling he's involved somehow. I just wanted to ask you to look at his file and see if he has a record."

"Isn't this the guy who worked on your car?"

"Yeah, but it doesn't have anything to do with that. He's evasive and he lied. We need to check his record."

"If it's anything serious, he wouldn't be working here."

"Like Blake Alston."

"Not really. I rechecked our files this morning and I was right. They show a spotless background."

"Would you see what you can find out about Hooper, please?"

∽∾∽

Lyle didn't wait to watch the frisky couple off-loaded from the Ferris wheel.

When he walked back into the sheriff's detective bureau, Smith's expression hadn't changed. If anything she looked more unhappy.

"Mr. Deming, you didn't tell me you had a dispute with Hooper over car repairs."

Shit. "I thought about mentioning that after I left. But it's unrelated." Lyle sat next to Detective Smith's desk.

"Right away, he asked me if I came to talk to him because of you. He said he repaired your car and now you were trying to get your money back."

"That's not what happened." Lyle looked across the room then back at Smith. "I'm sorry. I should have told you, but the circumstances are the same. He was never interviewed, and he denied knowing Perez."

Smith picked up a small notepad from her desk and flipped it open. "He said he remembered your asking about Perez."

"He did?"

"He said you didn't ask him if he *knew* Perez, just if Perez worked for him."

Lyle's answer came out slowly. "Yeah."

Smith picked up a pen and tapped it slowly against the notepad as she spoke. "He said he assumed you *knew* he worked part-time in the NC garage and would *know* Perez."

"That sounds like doubletalk."

"Hooper stated that lots of people know he works at the park. That's how he gets park employees as customers—through word of mouth."

"Yeah, that's how I found him too, from another cab driver." Lyle stopped. *I sound like an idiot.* "But I didn't know he worked at the park."

"But you did have a dispute with him."

"Yes, I did, but it doesn't have anything to do with the murder. Did you ask Hooper anything else?"

"Yes. How well did he know Perez? Was he surprised at the murder? Where was he the night Perez was killed? Does he know anyone who would want to kill Perez? Why does he think Perez was killed? Has he ever seen drugs in the garage?" She threw her pen down on the desk and it tumbled into the base of her computer screen. "That about cover it?"

Chapter 48

The hands-free communication command center was the best part of Kate's new hybrid SUV. Coming back from Scottsdale, traveling north on Interstate 17, she checked messages and returned calls. The message from the alternative weekly reporter sounded the most intriguing—and important.

"Astoria?" Kate said.

"Two things, Kate. I filed my story about the pot propositions, but I'm working on something else and I'd like to get a comment from you. There's a rumor that if Arthur Poole's Safe Weed Project didn't make it to the ballot, that he'd, y'know, trash the Consumer Cannabis bill."

"Where did you hear that?" Kate said, knowing a reporter likely wouldn't divulge a source. She might even resent the question.

"I can't tell you my source, but I've heard this more than one place. Really, it's, like, what everybody believes."

Although Arthur never told her he would oppose the Legal Marijuana Control Initiative if Safe Weed faltered, the reporter's assertion came as no surprise. "You've written stories about Arthur before," Kate said. "You know how he thought marijuana should be marketed. Besides, who says Safe Weed is not going on the ballot?"

"So you're going ahead with the campaign?"

"We don't know. We're still working on signatures and

the board will be meeting to decide our direction. I promise to tell you exactly what happens."

Kate had only talked to two other board members since Poole's murder. She assigned Joann to talk to all of them and arrange a meeting.

"Thanks for that, anyway. Please get back to me on it. I tried Creston Dealey several times today and his office is giving me the runaround."

Kate almost bit her lip to keep from telling the reporter about the sheriff's visit with Dealey. "I will keep you up to date on Safe Weed. And you know you can reach me almost any time."

"One other thing," the reporter said. "Kinda weird. Have you heard of Reverend Nathaniel Jameson?"

"Uh huh," Kate grunted.

"He's goin' all over Phoenix dissing Arthur Poole. He's doing some big evangelist thing, like sermons, and he talks about weed. Says it's dangerous and so is everyone who is trying to make it legal. Evil, he says. And he calls Mr. Poole names. Says *he's* evil. Dealey too. What's up with that? Doesn't he have respect for the dead?"

Kate could hear Reverend Nathaniel's voice echoing in the Polk library building. *Slandering Arthur after he died?* "Are you sure? That's...that's disgusting."

"One of our reporters taped him, but it was on TV, too. You can probably find it on the Web. Aren't ministers supposed to be respectful? You know, pious?"

Kate gripped the steering wheel. "Astoria, thank you. I'll check up on Reverend Nathaniel and get back to you with a comment."

Kate drove for several miles trying to image the insensitivity that would drive someone—a minister, for God's sake—to condemn someone who was brutally murdered. Not just someone, *Arthur*. Stupid, irresponsible, sickening. Kate could think of many words for it.

What was Lyle doing today? They hadn't really talked about what their next steps would be. The attack on Rey, on top of everything else, left her dazed and restless, no doubt Lyle, too.

"What's going on, Lyle?" she said when he picked up. "You making any progress?"

"Not much. How about you?"

"Our sheriff is making the rounds of the suspects. I went to see Creston Dealey this morning and Wisniewski barged into his office and badgered him into talking. The sheriff was in high style, but he didn't get Dealey to confess. What are you doing today? You said you had a lead on Perez."

"Did I ever tell you about the productivity percentage in the average felony investigation?"

Was Lyle making a joke? She could hear something discouraging in his voice.

"Let's just say it wasn't a productive morning," he said.

"I never told you about the evangelist, Reverend Nathaniel Jameson, did I?"

"Reverend who?"

"He goes by Reverend Nathaniel. I saw him in Polk. He makes me mad. He's been saying—hey, have you had lunch? I'm hungry and I need to talk. I'm driving back from Scottsdale. I'm just about to where the interstate hits San Navarro Highway. I'm going to stop at the dinosaur place."

"The one with brontosaurus burgers?"

"Yeah."

"They make you eat in caves."

"I know. We'll have privacy. See you as soon as you can get there. And Lyle, bring your yellow pad."

Chapter 49

Lyle entered the prehistoric jungle restaurant and walked up to the host, a middle-aged man in a safari outfit. "I'm looking for a tall blonde," Lyle said.

"So am I," said the man.

Lyle was in no mood for jokes. "She's waiting for me." *Who is this guy, Henny Youngman?*

"Right this way, sir." The host led Lyle through a seating area filled with faux jungle plants and animal sounds. At the rear, a row of plaster caves, like homes for giant burrowing animals, formed booths.

Kate sat in a corner cave sipping coffee. Lyle had to duck under a row of blunt stalactites.

"How'd you squeeze in here?" he asked Kate as he slid into the booth.

"Cozy, isn't it? I think they remodeled this place after the park went in."

"Yeah."

"Okay, what's wrong?"

Before he could answer, a server appeared wearing an animal skin dress and leotard. "May I bring you a beverage?"

"Yeah a beer." He looked at Kate. "No. Make it an Arnold Palmer. Thanks."

Lyle felt Kate's hand on his arm. She touched the rubber band on his wrist then slid her arm behind him and drew him close. Her kiss almost blotted out everything else in the world.

"Hmm. That's better," he said.

"Your lead not pan out this morning?"

"You could say that. More like I jumped down the wrong rabbit hole."

"Now there's a metaphor."

"What happened to *you* today?"

"Everything's getting to be too much." She sighed. "Much too much. And I know we have to move fast. That's why I wanted to talk. I thought we'd nail Dealey today, but he denied everything and claimed he'd been at a meeting in Flagstaff at ten o'clock Monday morning."

Lyle's drink arrived. Kate got a refill on her coffee. After they ordered, Lyle pulled out his yellow pad. His notes comprised crimes, times, places, suspects, and hunches and amounted to very little. Dressed in a cream blouse and a sleeveless jacket of some sort, Kate managed to *look* composed. "We should get busy," he said.

"Yes." She put down her coffee cup. "Let's do what we know how to do. Follow your lists. Look at this analytically."

"One thing has been bugging me," Lyle said. "I made a note. We're assuming that the person who had coffee with Arthur, is the one who killed him."

"That's what it looked like."

"But what if he met with someone, and a little later a third person showed up. Or maybe the real killer followed the person who had coffee with Arthur."

"But we haven't found anyone who even admits to having *seen* Arthur on Monday."

"The way you say that makes the theory sound screwy."

Kate pointed to Lyle's yellow pad. "What else have we got?"

"Dealey is at the top of the list, but from what you said, maybe he has an alibi."

"The sheriff said he'd have the alibi checked out. Then

we'll see. In the meantime, I'm waiting for a call from a friend of mine in New York. I asked him to check out Dealey's Wall Street past. Could be useful."

"What about Bellard?"

"He says he was taking time off from the store at the time of the murder, but he can't prove where he was."

"We could ask the sheriff to get a warrant to look at Bellard's cell phone records. See where he really was at that time. But—"

"Can you do that?"

"Yes, cell phone companies keep records for months, years. We could find out the location of his cell phone during Monday. We used to do this in Phoenix."

"Using the location of cell towers?"

"Right, but come to think of it, there aren't many cell towers in the Polk area. Maybe we couldn't get any closer than a mile or more radius."

"That wouldn't do much good," Kate said, "would it? Polk's a small town."

"*And* we'd have to give the sheriff some idea of a motive for Bellard."

"Motive? How many do you want?"

"How many can we prove?"

"Jealousy. He wanted to be running the show. Money. He thought there was big money in growing and selling, but Arthur was more interested in medical applications. And, Remo's also got something going with Dealey. I just don't know what. We need to talk to him again."

When their food arrived, Kate poured dressing on her pterodactyl cobb salad and Lyle peered under the bun of his burger. "Mmm, T-rex sauce, my favorite."

After Kate had taken a bite, she said, "I talked with a writer from the *Phoenix Weekly*. She said there's a rumor that if the Safe Weed proposition didn't qualify for the ballot, Arthur would oppose *Dealey's* proposition."

"That sounds like a motive, for Dealey, not Bellard. Would Arthur's opposition be a big threat to Dealey?"

"Yes. If Arthur told all the pro-pot people—the ones who want marijuana to be home-grown—to boycott Consumer Cannabis, it would sink it. Or probably would. The latest polls show only a tiny lead for recreational marijuana. All Arthur would have to do is syphon away a few percentage points."

"Presumably Bellard wouldn't want that to happen either."

"No, that would kill his possibility for getting rich growing pot."

"Is this rumor true?"

"Could be. This writer's got a good journalistic sense. And—oh, yes, I should have told you this first off—she also told me that this minister, this televangelist, has been criticizing Arthur by name—even after his death. Makes me furious."

"You said you saw him in Polk?"

"Yes. You should have seen his diatribe, his anti-pot sermon." Kate waved a finger in the air. "'Anyone associated with it is doomed to perdition.' The crowd ate it up."

"Lots of people think pot is bad. But do they really get worked up over it?"

"They sure do. You didn't see the performance Saturday, a forum on legalizing marijuana. Arthur was there too, but he left early, after his talk. Many people in the audience were against him. They sounded angry. As Arthur left, it looked like one guy wanted to follow him. Then once the reverend got started, it was a good thing Arthur *wasn't* there."

"What, lynch mob mentality? Over pot?"

"Almost." Kate paused and put her fork down.

"And this was just this past Saturday, two days before Arthur's murder?"

"Yes." Kate looked out of their cave at customers seated amid rubber plants and bromeliads.

"But would someone really kill him because he wants to legalize pot?"

"I suppose, if they were mad enough or crazy."

"Or both," Lyle said. "Did you talk with Arthur after the meeting?"

"No," she sighed, "I didn't see him again. We were going to get together Monday for a meal."

"This Reverend Nathaniel sounds like he has a following."

"The people in that meeting sure knew who he was," Kate said.

"Maybe I'll talk to him. See if he's been getting any fan mail from local nut jobs."

"You think he'd tell you if he has contact from the mentally disturbed? Maybe he protects his flock."

"People like that always attract a few unbalanced fans they'd rather not have around."

"Why don't you let me handle it?" Kate said, "I think Reverend Nathaniel might be more susceptible to female persuasion."

"We could just give this to the sheriff. Vamping this guy may or may not work. Who knows if this is even a good lead."

"I'd like an excuse to talk to him and tell him what I think of his demeaning Arthur after he was killed. *Nobody* should do that, especially a minister. He's big and he presents himself as if he's this all-powerful spiritual presence. But when he speaks he reminds me of a bobble-head doll."

Kate wants to settle the score for Arthur every way she can. "Okay. But why not check with the sheriff? Maybe he'd be willing to send a deputy. You could be there at the same time."

"Somebody needs to set this hypocrite straight. I know where he is. The reporter told me. He's staying at some ritzy ranch in Carefree."

"From what you said, he deserves a scolding, but then he wouldn't help us identify any local crazies, would he?"

"I'll be circumspect."

"Likely this won't pan out, but we can eliminate possible suspects."

"You've told me. Eliminating suspects, even unlikely ones, lets the astute detective focus, with more assurance, on more probable ones." She took the notepad from Lyle and scribbled a name on the list. "Here's one more."

Lyle looked at his notepad. "Fapp?"

Chapter 50

"*Daniel* Fapp," Kate said as she finished her lunch. "He runs the Bohemian Coffee House next to Xanadu. He had a running disagreement with Arthur over signs and parking and incense."

"Incense?"

"Oh, the smell from Arthur's store. But it got settled, more or less. Fapp's just a touchy, grumpy...something."

"Suspect?"

"I thought so, but no. I put him on my list, but took him off. He's not a murderer. Tiff questioned him too, and she agrees. But what about Persis Poole? You talked to her, what do you think? What did Rey—oh, we need to call and find out about Rey." *How could we forget?*

Lyle pulled out his cell phone. He finished his conversation with, "Okay, thanks."

Kate looked at him.

"No change. Damn."

"Vitals?"

"Vital signs are still good," Lyle said. "He's healthy, he's just not awake."

Silence descended on their table for a minute. Kate absently twirled a strand of her hair and tried to think. *Two murders, a crazy person tries to run me down, Rey is knocked out, and drug dealing is on everyone's mind.* A different animal-skin-clad person appeared and cleared their plates, upsetting Kate's ruminations. Lyle ordered coffee.

"Let's get on with it," Kate said. "Arthur's ex-wife."

"She said lots of nasty things about Arthur, but I don't think she could get her shit together enough to plan a murder. *Maybe* spur of the moment. But as I said yesterday, she's scrawny and doesn't look like she could hurt anyone." Lyle looked at his notes. "You told Rey that Arthur had done nice things for Persis. But the ex's take is that Arthur was holier than thou, trying to show off, lording over her. I guess we should to talk to her *and* Nick Rafferty again. This time separate them."

"We've got too many people to talk to. We should see what Tiff is doing, who she's talking to."

"I don't think she's going to be too eager to help me anymore."

"Why?"

Lyle looked as if he were trying to find the right words. Their animal-skin server brought coffee and their bill.

"Okay, I got crazy again." Lyle recounted his exchanges with Smith, before and after the detective talked to Hooper.

Kate wagged a finger at Lyle "There's another reason why Tiff was short tempered today. Remember I told you the sheriff showed up at Consumer Cannabis? He barged in because Dealey wouldn't talk to Tiff. He snuck out and drove off while she waited in his outer office."

"So she had to tell Wisniewski she screwed up. That took guts. And then I show up and put her in the middle of a fight with Hooper. I get the picture."

"So what do you have in your journal there about Perez suspects—*other* Perez suspects?"

Lyle went over the guys in the shop he'd talked to and who had been investigated by Rey and deputies. "This guy Blake's criminal record would qualify him for a job with Pablo Escobar. That is, if you talk to Detective Smith. Remember what she said the other night? If you talk to Howard, the guy'd qualify for the Partridge Family. I don't know who the murderer is, but it's obvious the guy who tried to run you down *and* got Rey, either works in the garage or is connected to the Perez murder."

"Anyone else on the list? What about Mrs. Perez? Spouses are always suspect."

"I think we've overlooked her. I talked to her right after the murder and decided she was uninvolved. A grieving widow. But you know, she didn't seem surprised by any of it. Distressed, grieving yes, but almost like she expected something to happen. I made a note of that right then, but didn't see a motive. But that was before we knew about the drugs."

"She couldn't get into the garage and operate the lift."

"But she could get someone to do it for her."

"Mrs. Perez is back on my list. Maybe we should talk to her again, too."

"Quite a list," Kate said.

"I'll scan all my notes and send them to you. Maybe you can see something I missed."

"We need to get busy."

"Are you buying lunch today?"

"No, Max is."

On their way out to the parking lot, Kate said, "I'm going to see if I can talk to the reverend this afternoon. Get that out of the way."

"Agreed. Howard said he would check something for me, and I want to stick my nose in the garage again. I'm headed back to the park."

As she opened her SUV's door and sat down, Kate remembered another suspect.

Chapter 51

"Lyle honey, did anyone tell you that Luis was leaving?" Gayle LeBlanc said. "Y'know, Luis Nieto?"

"What do you mean *leaving*?" Lyle said over his cell phone as he pulled into the NC employee parking lot near the garage.

"He turned in his notice this morning. I thought you'd want to know. He's leaving today."

"For good?"

"Yeah. He took an early shift today. Gave me one day's notice. He dropped that little lagniappe on my desk this morning. So where'm I going to find another mechanic right away?

"Mechanics-R-Us?"

"You are funny, Lyle honey."

"Why's he leaving?"

"He was kinda vague. Said something about visiting family and getting a job somewheres else. I called security and asked them if I should call the sheriff, but they said they'd take care of it. Is he a suspect?"

"Could be."

"I don't think he did it. He was probably Don Perez's best friend in the garage. And he's so quiet."

"Maybe he didn't do it, but he knows more than he's saying."

"I think he's scared. Scared of something."

"You're right on there, Gayle. Where's Luis now?"

"I don't know. He went to the HR office then cleaned out his stuff."

Lyle got out of his car and saw Nieto in his blue mechanics uniform walk across the parking lot, carrying a heavy-looking gym bag. Lyle almost called out to him, then he stopped and ducked. He watched Nieto put his bag in his car and drive out of the lot.

Lyle fired up his Mustang and followed at a distance. He thought about calling the sheriff's office, but decided to see where Nieto led him.

Nieto drove into Polk, through the commercial district and out to a residential area on the west side of town. As they drove down an unevenly paved street, Lyle recognized the neighborhood. After a few blocks, Lyle braked and pulled to the curb when he saw Nieto turn into the Perez driveway. *Lydia Perez. What hasn't she told us?*

Mrs. Perez met Nieto at the door. After Nieto said something, Mrs. Perez shook her head. Nieto raised his arms as if he were pleading. After a moment, she motioned for him to come inside.

Lyle's head starting spinning possibilities. Lydia Perez grieved, but didn't seem surprised that something happened to her husband. Was she in some sort of partnership with Luis? That didn't sound logical. Most likely Nieto wanted something from Mrs. Perez, but what?

Judging by Nieto's expression when he left the Perez residence a few minutes later, he didn't get what he wanted. He looked up and down the street before he got back in his old Chevy compact and pulled out. Lyle followed from a block away as Nieto doubled back to the Polk business district and pulled into a bank parking lot. Lyle turned into the lot, but parked as far away as possible. Nieto knew what he looked like.

The former NC mechanic got out of his car carrying a plastic bag. He folded it and stuck it under his arm. Lyle had a pretty good idea Nieto didn't stop at the bank for a free toaster. *Did banks still do that? Yeah, probably twenty or thirty years ago.* Lyle waited until Nieto walked inside, then he slowly approached the bank's double glass doors. He saw Nieto at a teller window, so he went inside and busied himself at a brochure rack. The branch was big enough, with enough customers waiting in line, that Lyle remained inconspicuous, he hoped.

Soon a teller led Nieto across the lobby to an area partitioned with half-height walls. Beyond a partition, Lyle saw a vault door. Nieto wanted access to a safe deposit box. That was all Lyle needed to know, so he left the bank and sat back in his car.

Soon Nieto walked out with his plastic bag full of something. Probably not bank statements. When Nieto backed out of his parking space, he turned in Lyle's direction and accelerated. Caught off guard for a moment, Lyle turned his head. Did Nieto see him? He'd soon find out.

A steady flow of cars moved down four-lane Red Rock Avenue as Nieto pulled into traffic. Lyle let two cars get between him and Nieto as his quarry traveled south. After two blocks, Nieto's Chevy darted around a corner to the right and raced ahead, a light trail of exhaust streaming behind him. Was he leaving town right now? If Nieto already spotted him in the bank lot, Lyle didn't have anything to lose, so he asked his Mustang for more speed and jerked the wheel to the right. Where was Nieto?

Lyle knew Nieto's old Chevy was no match for his Mustang, so he must have turned quickly into one of several residential side streets. But which one? Lyle took a left, raced down a block, and looked both ways. Nothing. Sixty-year old homes crowded each other on small lots. Most had driveways. Reversing his route, he turned down another street and saw the tail end of Nieto's Chevy at the end of a long drive.

Lyle parked and walked down the street. He saw Nieto's car tucked in behind a house fronting the street and next to a second, smaller home at the end of the long driveway. Lyle knocked on the door and waited.

He heard noises inside and wondered if Nieto planned to duck out some back door or window. Then the door opened quickly making Lyle jump.

Chapter 52

The famous Reverend Nathaniel Jameson must have had upper crust supporters because the "ranch" where he was staying looked more like a trendy, gated community in the center of the trendy small town of Carefree, north of Phoenix. Kate had phoned the reverend's administrative assistant telling her she was an NC VP and headed a committee to establish the park's policies regarding *marijuana*. She emphasized the word as if she were talking about the park's policy on rat control. She said she wanted to get the reverend's input on several issues, and she stressed the urgency of talking with him. She thought it best if she explained the real reason for the visit in person. Kate drove down to Carefree with only the assurance she could talk with Mrs. Periwinkle, the administrative assistant.

Within the gated community, she was told to look for two homes enclosed by a low stucco wall. Two giant saguaros guarded the entrance, with the reverend ensconced in the home on the right. Before she got out of her car, Kate took off her tunic vest, removing one layer, the better to get the reverend's attention, if necessary. Mrs. Rhonda Periwinkle met her at the door. She looked like she should be working for a college professor or perhaps a real minister rather than the flashy televangelist. She led Kate toward a sitting room.

Mrs. Periwinkle's brown hair was turning gray and she wore a tweed skirt, not exactly suited to the desert. "The reverend is working on a sermon," she said, indicating a partially closed door.

Kate paused, pushed the door farther open, and saw Reverend Nathaniel sitting at a desk, staring at a laptop screen. She stood erect and flashed him a smile when he looked up. "Good afternoon, Reverend," Kate said.

"This is Kate Sorensen from Nostalgia City," Mrs. Periwinkle said. Trying to steer Kate past the door she said, "Reverend Jameson is very busy."

"No, no," he said. "Please, come in."

Kate brushed her hair away from the side of her face and held eye contact with the reverend as he came around the front of his desk. She felt obvious, and she fought the feeling of embarrassment. But she soon relaxed when she saw the silver-haired reverend smiling and taking her all in, his gaze resting on her boobs, then her legs. When they shook hands, he held her hand a moment too long.

"You're with the theme park," he said as Mrs. Periwinkle stepped out of the room.

"Yes, have you been there?"

"No, I haven't. Please have a seat."

Kate sat in one of the two overstuffed chairs in front of the desk and crossed her legs. Obviously he didn't remember her from the Polk library.

Reverend Jameson took the chair opposite her. He moved the bottom of his red tie so it lined up straight, over the buttons on his white shirt, then he gazed at Kate's legs before resuming eye contact.

"Thank you for seeing me," Kate said, not completely intending the double meaning.

"I think you spoke to Mrs. P. about marijuana." He said it like he was talking about the weather. Not quite the tone he used at his library talk or his TV tirades in the news clips Kate watched on her phone before she arrived.

"Marijuana, yes. But related to Arthur Poole. I'm helping the police try to find who murdered him."

Jameson's expression didn't change.

"You recognize that name?"

"Yes, I believe so," he said.

Believe so? "Yes?" Kate liked to create silence and let the other person fill it.

"He was involved in the legalization proposition," Reverend Jameson said, "and your park's plans for marijuana."

"The park has no official plans to be involved with marijuana." Again, she waited.

Reverend Jameson glanced at Kate's legs but then looked across the room. "He worked for the park and promoted marijuana." This time he added derision to the last word.

"He didn't work for the park. He operated a store separately. A concessionaire."

Kate wanted to let the reverend take another glance at her legs, then pop him one. But she needed information. "I'm hoping you can help us."

"I don't know how I could be of any help. If you're looking for spiritual guidance for his family, perhaps I could recommend—"

"No, we're not looking for that. But thank you."

"Then what do you want?" Did he seem unsteady?

"At your talk in Polk and later in Sun City, and other places, you've generated noisy crowds."

Reverend Jameson started nodding his agreement and approval. Kate saw a bobble head.

She leaned back in her chair and uncrossed her legs. "The sheriff's department thinks it's possible that someone who has been following your campaign could have…well, gone off the deep end." She asked him if he ever received mail from disturbed people. People who might have advocated violence against anyone who used marijuana or supported legalization.

Reverend Jameson looked at her with an eager expression. Was it her legs?

"Naturally," she said, "I'm not referring to the people genuinely devoted to your cause."

"Yes," he said, his head still moving in agreement.

"But the occasional kook who may or may not be dangerous."

"You know I preach nothing but peace and nonviolence."

Yes, like you did in Polk, you liar. You attacked Arthur simply to boost your own ratings. She said, "Of course. But you may have received mail or email—or maybe even phone calls—from disturbed persons, people who want to divert your noble cause for evil purposes."

He stopped nodding his head and frowned. "My personal mail?"

"Yes. Mail from the mentally ill sometimes helps solve cases. But I can understand your hesitation. I talked to the sheriff today and he or deputies can come over and explain the urgency of this. I think they may be on the way now."

"Of course I don't know of anyone specifically," he said. "I do get lots of mail, but Mrs. Periwinkle could help you. You see, she supervises my communications. We could ask her."

"That would be a big help. We can save the sheriff a trip then." She got up and took a step to the door. "Shall we speak to her?"

The reverend rose and moved toward the door. He stood as tall as Kate. He placed a hand on her shoulder and left it there briefly as they walked out.

Chapter 53

Luis Nieto held his front door open about two feet. "What'd you want?" He looked at Lyle then glanced over Lyle's shoulder.

"It's just me, Luis. I wanted to talk to you before you bail out on Nostalgia City."

His breathing elevated, Nieto looked like he might be ready to slam the door.

"I know what's going on in the garage," Lyle said. "I know why you went to see Don's widow. Running away is *not* going to make you safe."

Nieto seemed to waver.

"I can help. Just let me in for a minute to talk. No one followed me. When we're done you can take off if you want to."

Looking over Lyle's shoulder and down the drive one more time, Nieto opened the door.

Cardboard boxes filled with kitchen tools, a lamp, blanket, and other household items sat on the floor. Modest but new-looking chairs, tables and a low couch furnished the small living room.

Nieto moved uneasily across the floor.

"Sit down for a minute," Lyle said, taking a chair himself. Nieto sat on the edge of a cloth armchair. "People in the garage are running a drug trade. If you were part of that, you can't just change your mind and run away. They will find you."

Nieto sat alternately gripping the arms of his chair and rubbing his hands on his thighs. Lyle could see tiny spots of perspiration along the edge of his tightly cropped dark hair. "I'm no drug dealer," he said.

"Then what are you running away from?"

"They kill Don. Now they gonna kill me."

"Who is going to kill you?" Lyle listed off the names of a few prime suspects in the garage.

Nieto pursed his lips, lowered his head, and stared at the floor.

"Don was part of the drug cartel, one of the workers, wasn't he?"

"No. Don no push drugs either, he just—"

"If he wasn't involved in the drugs, why was he *killed*?" Lyle leaned forward, raising his voice. "You can tell me, Luis, and it will go no further. Or I can call the sheriff and he can ask you all about it—at the station." Lyle pulled out his cell phone.

Eventually, Luis Nieto told his story. A few months earlier, Don Perez had spotted mechanics unloading drugs from a junked car that arrived from Mexico. Instead of turning them in, Perez asked for a cut, just a little something every week to keep his mouth shut. Nieto emphasized how many thousands of dollars' worth of drugs were being delivered. Perez's blackmail amounted to peanuts.

At first, Nieto didn't know what was going on, except that his best friend at work suddenly had enough money for a down payment on a new car and other luxuries. One day Nieto saw Perez getting his payoff, and he figured out the rest. Perez got so much, wouldn't it be right for him to share a little with his friend? So Perez and Nieto shared the blackmail until one day Perez asked for more. The next day, Nieto found his body crushed under the car. As Nieto talked about finding Perez, he started to sob, then shake.

Lyle was surprised that Perez stayed alive as long as he did. He gave Nieto time to recover then encouraged him to finish his story. Of course, Nieto was sickened when he found the body. Then scared, panic-stricken. He knew that Perez didn't tell anyone he was sharing the blackmail with his friend. But he worried Perez might have kept some sort of record of the payments that might implicate him.

Lyle interrupted Nieto's story. "So you broke into the Perez residence looking for his records?" Lyle asked.

Nieto nodded.

"If you were scared, why didn't you run away two weeks ago?"

Nieto explained he was as scared to run as he was to stay. He hoped the drug dealers would either quit after the DEA raid or perhaps get arrested. When neither happened, he sent his wife and two kids away to stay with relatives in Phoenix and he held his breath every day he went to work. Then the day before, he overheard someone saying he thought there was *a leak* in the garage. That was all Nieto needed.

He tried to find out anything he could from Lydia Perez, then collected his blackmail money, and decided to take off.

"Luis, tell me who did this and they'll get arrested. You'll be safe. The sheriff will protect you." Lyle ran through his list of suspects again. Nieto raised his shoulders, his arms quaking." No, señor. They kill my family. They kill me."

The knock at the door sent Nieto leaping out of his chair with a sharp cry. Lyle got up to look through the peep hole. He stood beside the doorway and leaned over so he didn't present a bigger target if someone decided to shoot through the door.

A man stood right outside. Jeb Wisniewski.

"Come on in, Sheriff. Luis was just telling me all about the drug ring at the garage. Perez was killed because he was blackmailing the drug cartel. Can you imagine that?"

"Sounds like a good way to commit suicide," Wisniewski said. "So who are the bad guys. Who's running the show?"

"That's the part Luis is not eager to talk about."

Nieto stood at the other end of the room, next to the kitchen door, looking like he wanted to run somewhere. Lyle told the sheriff how Nieto got involved with the drug dealers and that he refused to name names.

"I must go," Nieto said. "I did not do anything wrong."

"We're kinda short on witnesses," the sheriff said. "I'd like to persuade you to stick around a while."

"No, no." Nieto trembled. "They know I'm talking to you."

"I guess I'd tend to be a little tight lipped, too," Lyle said, taking a step toward the sheriff and lowering voice, "if I saw my best buddy flattened like roadkill."

The sheriff glared at Nieto.

"I doubt you'll get anything more out of him," Lyle said. "He's in shock, terrified for his family. Maybe you can hold for a little while. He could turn out to be a good witness if we can find out who killed Perez. If you need an excuse to keep him in custody, ask him about the burglary at the Perez residence or the bag full of second-hand blackmail money he has around here somewhere."

"I think we can handle this, Mr. Deming. Don't you worry."

"How did you find us?"

"Good police work. When we heard that señor Nieto planned to leave, one of my detectives staked out the house. By the way, on your way out, would you ask her to come in here?"

Outside on the street, Lyle saw Detective Tiffany Smith leaning against an unmarked sheriff's car. She wore the same suit from earlier that day, the jacket unbuttoned. "The sheriff would like to see you," Lyle said. "I think you're going to be giving Luis a ride."

Smith just nodded her head slightly and started toward the house.

"Detective Smith, about this morning. I'm sorry. I know it looked like I was trying to use you to settle a score, but I wasn't. I *just* had a hunch."

Smith turned to Lyle. "Yes, I resented the hell out of it. But for what it's worth, I don't know if he's the garage killer or not, but I didn't like the guy."

Chapter 54

Kate walked out of Reverend Jameson's office into a large adjoining room, the reverend right behind her. Mrs. Periwinkle sat at a rectangular wooden table set up as a desk. She worked at a laptop computer surrounded by stacks of papers and file folders. A file cabinet on wheels sat next to the table.

"Do we ever get mail from people with strange ideas?" the reverend asked. "People who say things that are objectionable?"

"Hate mail?" Mrs. Periwinkle asked.

"No," Kate offered. "Mail from crazy people. Dangerous people. People who may agree with what the reverend says, but who carry it way too far."

"Yes, we have some strange ones," the reverend's administrative assistant said.

"Ms. Sorensen is working with the police," Jameson said. He explained what Kate was looking for.

Mrs. Periwinkle asked Kate to pull up a chair next to her and she showed her how she cataloged mail, email, and voice mail. As Kate listened, she looked up to see the reverend just standing across the table.

"I need to get back to work," he said. "I hope this is helpful to you. Please say good bye before you leave."

"Oh, yes, I'd like to talk to you some more," Kate said with a smile.

She spent a half hour going through the messages Mrs. Periwinkle considered strange, unusual, or downright vile. In the end, Kate came up with only one name worth considering. But this would eliminate a possibility and let them move on.

Kate would forward to the sheriff the name of one person in the area who had contacted Reverend Nathaniel twice since his appearance in Polk. The person wanted the reverend to know he could *deal* with the pot-smoking, drug-pushing assholes. And if Reverend Nathaniel would like him to *take care of* anyone bothering him at one of his sermons, let him know.

Kate thanked Mrs. Periwinkle who got up to accompany her to the door. "Remember, Reverend Nathaniel wanted you to tell him when you're leaving."

"Yes, of course."

Kate rapped lightly on the door before stepping in. Reverend Nathaniel was all smiles. He got up from his desk. Kate closed the door behind her.

"Would you care to sit down?"

Kate walked over to one of the overstuffed chairs and rather than sit, she stood next to it, placing a hand on the back. Reverend Jameson didn't seem to know whether to sit or stand. That was fine.

"Was Mrs. Periwinkle able to help you?"

"Yes. We only identified one person who might be a dangerous possibility. I will pass this along and the sheriff will have to decide. But let me ask you something about Arthur Poole. You called him a dope promoter at one of your sermons the other day. And that was the nicest thing you said."

Reverend Nathaniel's smile started to fade, but he still enjoyed the view.

"You called Arthur Poole a drug pusher and a threat to society," Kate said. "Tell me, do you always slander the dead? Someone who can't defend himself."

The reverend's head jerked back. His stylish coif swayed. "I never defame the departed. What are you saying?"

"Did you know that Arthur Poole was murdered Monday?"

Jameson's bobble head moved slightly.

"When did you find out about this?" Kate asked.

Seconds passed before he answered. "I don't know. Yesterday perhaps. Did you know Mr. Poole?"

"Yes, I knew him. Obviously, you didn't or you wouldn't have slandered him. Slandered him when he was dead."

"You don't need to use that tone of voice. I never intended to disparage his memory. This is unfortunate." He brought his hands together in front of his chest and gripped them tightly. Was he going to pray? "Please, I didn't know." He lowered his voice and his eyes.

Kate took it as a show of phony contrition. But could he have made an honest mistake?

"However," the reverend said, "he *was* in a dangerous business."

"And he deserved to be murdered?"

"Of course not. You're jumping to conclusions. My sermons point out the evil that drugs pose to our society. You see?"

"Okay. I'll share that with the county sheriff."

His laugh was meant to be dismissive. It sounded hollow.

"Well, I'm sorry, Reverend Jameson. I'm sorry for upsetting you." She *tried* to sound sincere. She could pour on contrition, too. She dipped her head slightly and started to reach out to shake hands. Then she drew her hand back when she thought of something. "Your online calendar says you gave a talk late Monday afternoon. What did you do Monday morning?"

"A meeting with clergy at—" He almost got through his answer when he realized Kate intended her question to suggest he could be a murder suspect.

Despite his scowl, Kate reached out to shake hands. He surprised her again by taking her hand in both of his. No problem. She had Purell in the car.

Before she had driven very far down the block, she had a wild idea and called Mrs. Periwinkle.

"Hi, this is Kate Sorensen. I was just talking to Reverend Nathaniel about his schedule this week. I thought I may have seen him Monday morning, but he said he had a meeting with clergy. Is that right?"

"Oh, he's so forgetful. That meeting was Tuesday. On Monday morning he took a drive to Sedona. He likes to get out in nature to find inspiration for his sermons."

Chapter 55

Lyle walked through the Casa Grande Beach Resort looking for Howard. As one of the higher end hotels in Nostalgia City, the resort attracted the more prosperous and often the oldest of the park's patrons. The hotel featured a sand beach and a lazy river swimming pool. Max copied the constantly flowing pool idea from one of his ex-competitors in Las Vegas.

Lyle caught up with Howard at a meeting room on the hotel's ground floor. Two hotel employees and a uniformed security officer crowded around, looking at a laptop display on a conference table. Howard stood on the other side of the table. When Lyle came in, he motioned for him to join him in the hallway.

"Did you straighten out the Ferris wheel lovers?" Lyle asked.

"Finally," Howard said. The security chief had loosened his tie and rolled up his sleeves.

"What happened?"

"It took too long. They didn't get the couple off the wheel until they'd had enough time to finish the bottle they'd brought along. The guy looked okay, but the woman was maybe one hundred pounds and the alcohol went right to her head. She was loopy when they got out. All in all, pretty much a disaster."

"And you waited around to see things through."

"You have a dirty mind, Deming. I had female officers there to help the young woman into her clothes. This *is* my job. Now I have a much better idea of how we're going to handle these things in future."

"Looks like you're into something else here, too. I hate to be a bother, but—"

"Yes, Okay. Quick. I checked Hooper's personnel file and saw that no one had ever run a background check."

Lyle rolled his eyes.

"No, I don't think it's suspicious. It wasn't skipped on purpose. I checked with HR and the garage was desperate for more mechanics when Hooper was hired. Preparing for the transition. So someone just forgot. Maybe the changes in the park's computer system kept this from being flagged. In any event, his *application* indicated no arrests, and he was approved.

"Did you run a check?"

"Didn't have time. I got this call and had to come right over. I asked someone to do it. I should have it soon."

Lyle's sighed.

"We're not letting up. This is just as important to me. I have two of my best guys working with sheriff's detectives on the Perez case, going back through evidence, interviews, looking through NC files. We're working damn hard on it. And now this hotel has a security problem."

"Something related?"

"No, a *different* problem. We have goddamned difficult crime in the park."

"That's okay. When I started here, I thought it would be Mayberry, too."

"I'll try to find out about that background check tonight," Howard said. He looked at his watch.

Lyle looked at his watch as he walked out of the hotel grounds. After six. What else could he do today? He wondered how Kate got on with the reverend. When he walked back to his car, he pulled out his phone and dialed a number. When he finished the call, he couldn't wait to dial Kate. She answered on the second ring.

"Not much luck with wacko suspects," Kate said. "I got one name that I passed on to the sheriff. And I told the reverend he was—"

"Kate, I have news, too," Lyle said interrupting. "Best of all. I just talked to the hospital. Rey regained consciousness."

"That's terrific," Kate said. "How's he doing?"

"I don't know. We can't visit him until tomorrow afternoon. They told me he was alert, but he couldn't remember everything."

Chapter 56

"Did I wake you up?" Kate said, sitting at her kitchen table, her cell phone on *speaker*.

"No," Lyle said, "but I'm on my first cup of coffee. I missed you last night."

"I know. I missed you, too." She visualized how he looked in the morning, unshaven and tousled. "But I was so wiped out I just had to crash."

"We covered a lot of ground yesterday."

"Uh huh. I was drained. As it turned out, I had a hard time getting to sleep. I kept trying to think how we could get Remo and Dealey to talk."

"At least we have Luis on ice—temporarily. But where do we go from here?"

"How about two suspects for the price of one?" Kate knew her words sounded flippant, but she was deadly serious.

"That could be a joke, but I don't think it is," Lyle said.

"I have a wild idea we might be able to catch Ree-mo and Dealey and prove they plotted against Arthur."

"To kill him?"

"Maybe not intentionally. I don't know exactly, but we *have* to try something. If we can catch them in the act, so to speak, they might break."

"Okay, what do you want to do?"

"Can you pick me up?"

An hour later Kate and Lyle sat in his Mustang in the parking lot of Remo Bellard's Polk apartment building.

"This may be a waste of a few hours," Kate said, "but if it works, we'll have a chance to rattle Remo and Dealey at the same time. See if we can shake the truth out of them. Just give me a couple of minutes."

Kate got out of the car, walked to Bellard's second-floor apartment, and knocked. When he opened the door, first surprise, then apprehension showed on his face. "Hello," was all he could manage.

"Remo," Kate began in a straightforward tone, "I know I was hard on you the other day, but I wanted to talk with you for a minute about the Safe Weed Project. We're going to be getting very busy." Kate put both hands in the pockets of her mid-length denim skirt and waited.

"Um, yes. Okay. Come in."

"I just have a couple of minutes," Kate said, stepping inside the door. "We have to work quickly and you know as much about the Safe Weed Project as anyone." She couldn't bring herself to smile, but she needed to hook him. She tried a hopeful look, meeting his eyes, then lowering her eyes to the *Xanadu* embroidered above the pocket of his button-down collar shirt.

"I, ah, what can I do? How can I be of help?" His dark eyes met hers once, but he seemed unsure where to look.

"I talked with the other board members and we're planning to hire signature gatherers or a signature firm to get us on the ballot in time."

"Really?" He paused. "Tactically, that's a positive choice, but the costs are—"

"That's not going to be a problem. Everyone involved sees that this is in our best interests."

"Yes, I see."

"So if you're willing to help, we'll set up a meeting soon. Maybe this weekend. Most of the board members are available. What's your schedule like?"

"I can be available this weekend."

"Good. And Remo, I wouldn't talk too much about this on the phone. That's why I came over instead of calling."

"What do you mean?"

"Because of the investigation, I think the sheriff is—"

"Listening on my phone?" Bellard's dark brows lowered.

"I wouldn't worry about it, though. Just don't talk about our plans. I don't want the sheriff's department to get in the way, if you know what I mean."

"I understand."

Kate hoped he did, because she didn't really. She'd made up the ploy early that morning. "And besides," she said, "the sheriff isn't exactly pro-pot, is he?" Kate could see Bellard's head working on the problem. "I'll call you tomorrow," she said, "and just tell you where the meeting will be. You'll know what I'm talking about."

Bellard nodded his head, his eyes glossing over momentarily as he thought. Kate held a serious expression briefly then tried her best to look positive, if not cordial. "I have to get back to the park," she said, "I'll call soon." She held her index finger vertically in front of her mouth to make sure he got the message.

Bellard took it all in. Would he panic, start scheming? She hoped so.

Back at the car, Kate got in and slouched down in the passenger seat.

"What's happening?" Lyle asked.

Kate explained what she'd told Bellard. "I'm hoping he will call Creston Dealey. If I scared him enough about his phone being tapped maybe, just maybe, he'll want to talk to Dealey in person."

"Hmm."

"Don't look so skeptical." Kate slapped Lyle's thigh. "I know, this could be a waste of time. But I checked to see that Dealey is in his office today. And, I called Paige Ellerbe and told her to collect information on signature gathering firms. So if Remo tries to check up on this, she'll back me up."

"So we wait?"

"Yes. I think," she crossed her fingers, "Remo will charge down to tell Dealey that Safe Weed will be on the ballot, after all. Remo has a shift scheduled in the shop later today, so if this works, he'll be leaving—"

"In the next hour or two?"

"Right. Did you bring coffee?"

"It's dangerous to drink too much coffee or anything on a stakeout."

Chapter 57

After about forty minutes, Bellard appeared on the walkway to the parking lot.

"That's him," Kate said, sliding down in her seat as far as she could. "Where's he going?"

"He's walking away from us. You can look. He's getting into a car."

Kate peered over the dashboard and felt an adrenalin rush, but she tried to minimize her expectations. "He could be going to the park, or shopping, but he changed out of his Xanadu shirt."

"We'll find out," Lyle said, starting up the Mustang. He let Bellard get a lead before he pulled out of the lot to follow.

Bellard drove a nondescript Nissan sedan, but Lyle had no trouble following at a safe distance. Kate gripped the armrest and looked at the rear of Bellard's car with anticipation.

After a few miles, they could see he was not heading for Nostalgia City. Eventually, he entered the freeway and drove south toward Phoenix.

"So far, so good," Lyle said. "He's headed in the direction of Dealey's office. Scottsdale, right?"

"Uh huh."

Only fifteen minutes had elapsed when Kate and Lyle watched Bellard signal and pull off the freeway at a small town. "Damn," Kate said. "He didn't fall for it. But where's he going?"

"Does he have a girlfriend?"

"I feel sorry for whoever *that* is."

Lyle slowed and pulled off the freeway. Up ahead Bellard's Nissan turned left; Kate and Lyle followed. As the traffic thinned out, Lyle eased off the gas and Kate strained to keep an eye on Bellard.

"I guess our option now," Kate said, "is to go back and grill Dealey and Remo again, separately."

"That we can do, but let's wait and see."

In less than a minute, Kate saw the Nissan pull into the parking lot of a commercial office complex. They approached, and she saw an optometrist, an insurance office—and a medical marijuana dispensary.

Green Leaves Marijuana Health said the sign above the office. In the sign's lower right corner Kate spotted the Consumer Cannabis logo. Bellard parked in front of the building. Lyle cruised by as they watched him go inside. Lyle pulled into the lot and parked a few spaces down.

"What's going on?" Lyle said. "Is he stressed so he needs a joint?"

"No," Kate said, countering Lyle's facetious tone. "That's a Consumer Cannabis store. Remo's reacting to our talk just now, but why this place? And where's Dealey?"

"We could go in and find out."

"Wait a minute. Let me see something."

Kate got out and looked over the top of Lyle's car down the row of parked vehicles. She quickly stuck her head back in the car. "I think Dealey's here. Let's give it a try."

Kate led Lyle toward the door but before they got there, he paused to look at a sports car.

"That's Creston Dealey's car," Kate said. "It's a McLaughlin or something. He's here."

Lyle took a step toward the low-slung vehicle. "It's a McLaren. I've read about them, but never seen one. They can go more than two hundred miles an hour. Probably cost more than my condo. This Dealey guy must be loaded."

"I don't think so," Kate said. "C'mon, let's go in."

"How do you want to work this?"

Kate shrugged. She felt energized. She wanted to get her hands on both men inside the office. "I'd like to split them up. Let's play it by ear."

Lyle held the door for her as she walked into an airy room with glass display cases. It could have been a retail store selling jewelry or cosmetics—except for the smell. Once you sniffed marijuana, you never forgot the aroma. Kate walked up to one of the two counters that ran across the side of the room. She could see bottles and jars of marijuana buds in the cases along with pipes, vape kits, and prepackaged pot.

Kate smiled at the man in his twenties behind the counter. He looked more like a stoner than a pharmacist, which he wasn't. Marijuana dispensaries were not drug stores. "I want to see Remo Bellard."

The man leaned on the counter with one hand and picked lint off his shirt sleeve with the other. Kate suspected he might have been sampling the products. He stared at Kate with an amused look.

"He just walked in a couple of minutes ago," Kate explained.

"Oh," the young man said, now seeming to recognize Kate's attractiveness—or simply her presence. He breathed in as if he were getting high solely from the room's atmosphere. He nodded toward a door at the opposite side of the room. "He's in with Mr. Dealey. He can't be disturbed. Can I help you?"

"We'll just say hi," Kate said, striding toward the door marked *Office.*

She opened the door and stepped in with Lyle right behind her. Creston Dealey looked up from a desk on the left side of the room. Bellard leaned against a long, waist-high cabinet piled with boxes, papers, and medicine containers. "Kate," he bawled.

Caught you. "Good morning, gentlemen," Kate said. "Remo, what a coincidence. You and I were just talking about the marijuana proposition and here you are an hour later discussing it with Mr. Dealey." She stepped to the middle of the room and turned to Dealey. "And Creston, I thought you told me and the sheriff that Remo didn't work for you. You said he worked for Arthur. Are you a little mixed up?"

"I don't like you barging in here," Dealey said, more surprised than angered. "Mr. Bellard and I were just discussing—well, it's none of your business. Please go away." He waved the back of his hand at her as if he were shooing a fly.

"No so fast," Kate said. She looked at Lyle. "I've always wanted to use that expression." Turning back to Dealey, she said, "Creston, you surprise me. I thought you'd be a little more discreet. Remo, you still expect to have a job at Xanadu—and work on the Safe Weed Project?"

"I know what you're thinking, Kate," Bellard blurted. "Really, it's just, I mean we need to work together. It's like...I can explain. Maybe we can talk—"

"Hold that thought," Kate said. "Right now I want to talk to your boss. Why don't you step outside for a minute? We'll talk later. I'm sure I'll understand your position." *You snake.* "You can explain everything to Mr. Deming. This is Lyle Deming. He used to be a Phoenix police detective sergeant. He's investigating Arthur Poole's murder."

"Yes," Lyle said, "We'd like to find out which one of you killed him."

Bellard stared at Lyle, wide-eyed. Dealey grimaced.

"Did you think we came here to discuss Remo's little corporate espionage?" Kate said.

"Ridiculous. I went over all this with the sheriff," Dealey said. "I had nothing to do with it. I'm completely exonerated. Completely. Now please get out and leave us alone."

Kate and Lyle didn't move.

"Mr. Bellard and I are just talking about business. It's private and there's nothing illegal here."

"No?" Kate said. "We'll see. Remo…" She gestured to the door.

"I have nothing to discuss with you, Ms. Sorensen," Dealey said. "So you two can let us get back to our conversation."

"Oh," Kate said, looking at Dealey's two-thousand-dollar suit. "I thought we'd talk about Bachand Securities."

"What?" Dealey said.

"The four of us can discuss this if you like. I received some information from New York recently and—"

"Shut up," Dealey said. After a few moments he looked at Bellard. "Remo, excuse us for just a minute, would you? I'm sorry, this woman is being irrational. We'll settle this in a moment." He shook his head then glanced down at the phone on his desk. "Okay. We can talk for five minutes. Then you'll leave. Agreed?"

Chapter 58

"Creston, I think you have *two* motives for killing Arthur," Kate said when they were alone, "and it all revolves around your need for cash. I talked to someone I know in New York, a financial writer. He did a little digging." She walked slowly across the room in front of Dealey's desk. "You used to work at Bachand Securities before you got the job at Consumer Cannabis. This made me wonder, why does someone leave a seven-figure job in New York to move to Arizona and sell marijuana? Was this the only job you could get?"

Dealey sat with his hands in his lap, his gray-green eyes glaring at Kate. His jaw muscles tightened.

"This person I know in New York said that, about the time you left the Bachand hedge fund, there were some *irregularities*. You left unexpectedly and I'm guessing your bank balance dropped unexpectedly, too. Did you have to make restitution to escape jail time? Were the court records sealed? That's the information I received." Kate walked over and sat in the chair in front of Dealey's desk. The metal, utilitarian furniture in the dispensary office contrasted with the luxury of Dealey's Scottsdale office.

Dealey spoke through clenched teeth. "What are you getting at? What do you want? This has *nothing* to do with Poole."

"Creston, you're a suspicious guy. I think you have a lot

to hide. Does the State of Arizona permit convicted felons to propose ballot propositions? Or is your corporation the legal entity behind it? I don't know. I didn't have time to check."

Dealey leaned back in his seat and crossed his arms on his chest.

"You're just filled with irregularities."

"You don't understand any of this."

"Here's what I understand. You left New York with a big lifestyle to keep up, but not a lot of money. So you'd do anything to get your initiative passed."

"You can't prove anything."

"I'm talking about getting rid of the competition."

"You know that's a lie. Besides, Arthur wasn't going to make it to the ballot anyway. He didn't have the financial backing."

"You didn't know that for sure. Even Remo didn't know everything. But I heard an interesting rumor. Tell me if you heard this. The word was that if the Safe Weed Project failed, Arthur would tell his supporters to vote against Consumer Cannabis. With the narrow margins of approval, that would just about sink you."

Dealey shook his head. "No, no."

"I know you didn't do it on purpose. It was an accident. You got in a fight. The sheriff's department will understand that."

Dealey swallowed before raising his voice. "You know I wasn't anywhere near Polk when Arthur Poole was murdered." He waved his hands in front of him, over his desk. "You can say whatever you want. Threaten me. But I had nothing to do with it."

"Okay. For a moment, let's pretend we believe your story. Let's talk about Remo. He's your Safe Weed inside man. Arthur makes a decision, and Remo runs to tattle on him. Great system."

Dealey leaned forward with a combination smile and sneer. "Just business. Ever heard of it? Apparently Poole shot down some of Remo's ideas so he offered me information about Safe Weed."

"Did he also tell you where Arthur Poole lived?"

"No. Stop it."

"So Remo told you everything that Arthur did and you paid him for it."

Dealey looked at Kate as if she were a child who just learned there was no Santa Claus.

"And he told you about Arthur's interest in the medicinal side of marijuana," Kate said. "That's why you tried to buy him off with a dispensary."

Dealey looked at his watch. "We're done here. Say what you want about conducting a campaign. This is the business world every day. No one will care." He started to get up.

"Wait a second. I'm not quite finished. Remo was mad at Arthur. And, let's face it, he's impulsive and selfish. That's how you got *him* to kill Arthur."

Dealey puffed air between his lips. "Remo? He wasn't going to benefit from this. He can work in one of the stores if he wants to, but that's it. He wasn't going to get rich."

"But you didn't tell him that. Maybe you told him you'd be partners. If you persuaded him that Arthur stood in the way of his rich life, it would have pushed him over the edge. It would have been easy for him to knock Arthur on the head when they were talking in his kitchen. Maybe he didn't mean to kill him. But he did. And you know what that makes you."

"Remo," Dealey said, looking apprehensive. "He's a jerk, a fool. I didn't make any deal with him."

"Maybe, maybe not. But if he killed Arthur, the sheriff will be explaining to you all about being an accessory to murder."

Kate could see cracks in Dealey's wall of separation as he stared across the room processing his culpability. "No, no," he said. "This is all lies. All shit. Get the hell out of here, now."

Kate stood. She held up a hand to Dealey. "No, don't bother to get up. I'll let myself out. I'll send Remo back in here, after I find where Lyle took him. I'm sure you'll have a meaningful conversation."

Chapter 59

Lyle sat facing Bellard at a metal table in front of an independent coffee place a few doors down from the dispensary. He knew well that Kate could take care of herself. Nevertheless, he looked up often toward the dispensary door.

When she walked out, he waved and got up. Without saying anything, he extended his arm straight at Bellard's face, his outstretched finger an inch from Bellard's nose. Bellard understood the message: don't move. Slouching in his seat, he hunched over his coffee.

Lyle walked down to meet Kate, out of Remo's hearing. "What happened?"

"Dealey still denies having anything to do with Arthur's death. Obviously, he was getting secret information from that rat over there." She gestured toward Bellard's back. "But that's just normal business practice to him. He says he knew Arthur would never make it to the ballot, so Safe Weed wasn't a threat. And of course, he claims he was in Flagstaff."

"His alibi checks out," Lyle said. "I just talked to the sheriff's department."

"Really?"

"He was at that meeting at ten o'clock and he *did* have lunch in Flagstaff."

"Damn, Dealey has all the answers. He also thinks Remo

is too stupid or unimaginative to kill Arthur, even accidentally."

They stood on the covered walkway in front of an insurance office, Lyle taking occasional glances at Bellard. "If Dealey didn't do it, maybe he pushed Bellard into it. Then he'd be an accessory."

"Yes, an accessory. I threw that bomb at Dealey too, without much result. Maybe that was a mistake. What's Remo's story?"

"He started off very uptight. Guess he wasn't paying attention back there in the office. He thought I was *still* a Phoenix cop. Maybe it was my sport coat and white shirt. He told me what a loss Arthur's death was and how he regretted *betraying* him, though he didn't use that word. He called it a bad business decision."

Kate glared down the walkway at Bellard. "He probably got that line from Dealey."

"He says Dealey blackmailed him into telling him all about the Safe Weed campaign. Dealey gave him money and told him if he didn't give him Arthur's secrets, he'd tell Arthur that Remo sold him out anyway."

"I think he's lying. Selling out Arthur for money was probably his idea. Dealey wouldn't need to blackmail him."

"And of course Remo had nothing to do with Arthur's death," Lyle said. "He says he told you and the sheriff everything."

"But he has no alibi," Kate said. "I'll take a shot at him. We'd have more ammunition if Dealey ratted him out."

"Remo doesn't know that."

"Oh, yeah," Kate said as she put her hands in her pockets and Lyle noticed her brighten up.

They turned and walked toward Bellard. Before they sat down, Lyle saw Dealey charge out of the dispensary office, jump in his car, and race off.

As everyone watched him go, Lyle pulled another chair over to the table and Kate sat next to Bellard. They were alone on the café sidewalk. Lyle watched Bellard's expression as the dark-haired back stabber tried to muster a smile for Kate's benefit. The smile disappeared quickly.

"It's all over," Kate said. "Lyle's going to call the sheriff. Dealey told me how you killed Arthur."

Bellard gripped the edge of the small table nearly toppling the coffee cups. "That bastard. That bastard. What did he say?"

Kate let Bellard fume. When he let go of the table, he had better control of his voice. "Kate," he said, his voice a whiney whisper, "I would never do something like that."

"Never? Like you'd never put your hands all over Paige Ellerbe? I know about you Remo. But you won't have to worry about sexual harassment charges. I think first degree murder will put you away long enough."

Lyle watched the performance. Kate sounded venomous.

"Okay, maybe it wasn't on purpose," Kate said. "You didn't mean to kill him. It was an accident. You met with him early that morning and had an argument. It just happened." She looked at Lyle. "We know how it is, don't we?"

"They'll go easy on you," Lyle said.

"No, Kate, why would I kill him? I admired him. He gave me my job."

"I know you argued over the indoor grow farm. Arthur said it was your idea. He wasn't interested in it. He wanted to focus on getting on the ballot."

"Creston Dealey says I killed him, huh? What about *Dealey*? He had the motive. I wondered if *he* killed Arthur. *He* had something to gain."

"So you thought Dealey killed Arthur, but you still ran to him after I visited you this morning? And you're telling me you had regard for poor Arthur?"

Bellard seemed to withdraw into himself, looking first at Kate, then down at the table. "What evidence is there? I was never at Arthur's home. He didn't do business there. He preferred his office. I slept in that morning then went to work."

Was Bellard persuading himself of his own innocence? Lyle had seen that before, but it didn't guarantee guilt, either.

"It appears," Bellard said, "that all you have is Creston Dealey's unsubstantiated accusation, an accusation from someone who really had something to gain by killing our Arthur."

༺༻

"Sorry, Kate," Lyle said as they drove back to Nostalgia City. "I know he deserved it, but you shouldn't have hit him. That kind of thing can complicate a prosecution."

"I just slapped him. I couldn't take it. He called him '*our* Arthur.' Arthur trusted that sleaze ball, and he tricked him, throwing in with Dealey. I should have hit him harder. One for Paige, too."

"I agree. But we have to get something more on him before the sheriff will act. Right now we can't *prove* he did it. If we could show that Arthur *knew* what Bellard was up to, that would be something to make Arthur confront him." Secretly, Lyle loved watching Kate smack the smoldering SOB. "And Dealey. He may have a sound alibi, but he still acts guilty, don't you think?"

"I don't think anything he does is on the up and up," Kate said. "A friend of mine checked his background. He embezzled or defrauded clients or something like that. But he managed to make a deal to get out of it. He's used to getting his own way, and when he doesn't, he cheats." Kate lapsed into silence. When they reached the park she said, "I'm beginning to understand what you usually say about police work."

"Do you mean the part about it being full of dead ends or the part about it being frustrating and soul killing?"

"Yes. And you took the frustrations much too hard."

"I know. And the Perez case is *two weeks old*."

Chapter 60

Rey Martinez grinned when Lyle walked into his hospital room.

He looked better than Lyle expected. Despite having an IV in his arm, electrode wires snaking across the bed, and a bandage on his head, his color seemed normal. Lyle looked at him and saw not drugged stupor, but Rey's quick mind reflected in his eyes.

"My head hurts, my arm hurts, but I'm back with the living," Rey said. "The arm break was a minor fracture. Should heal up quickly."

"You had a concussion," Lyle said. "You were out."

"Always master of the obvious."

"You *are* feeling better." Lyle smiled tentatively.

"I remember *almost* everything. And that's good, according to the doc."

"Yeah, your boss told me. Your memory is a good indication that you'll have a full recovery."

Rey held up his arm that wasn't attached to the IV and crossed his fingers. "They said you found me."

"I was there, but Howard found you first."

"Howard went looking for me?"

"Yes."

"Hmm. He did."

"What do you remember about last night?"

"I was coming back from a call that turned out to be

nothing when I saw a pickup like the one Kate described. I saw it cross a side street in front of me. It was a block and a half away so I couldn't be sure. I followed it. It sped up, jumped off the street onto a gravel road, and headed out into the desert. By the time I got there, it was way ahead of me. No way my black and white was going to go over the rocks, so I pulled over to go out on foot."

"That was when you called in, right?"

"Yes, I called in then went down this road to where the truck had stopped. I had my hand on my pistol as I approached. At first I couldn't tell if maybe someone was just four-wheeling and got stuck. Maybe I should have pulled the gun out. But I don't think it would have made a difference. I remember hearing the truck start up...and then nothing."

"Someone hit you over the head?"

Martinez shook his head slowly. "Oh, that hurts." He closed his eyes. "Next thing I knew, it was almost a day later and I'm here in the hospital. Sheriff says he thinks my arm broke when they hit me with the truck. The head injury could have come then." Martinez paused as if the few minutes of talking had tired him out. "Or maybe someone hit me first."

"I'm just glad you're back," Lyle said, touching Rey's good arm. He leaned back in the visitor chair and glanced at the monitor panel showing Rey's heart rate.

"No perps caught," Rey said.

"But I think we're on the edge."

"The edge of what?" Rey said, opening his eyes.

"Solving the cases. We know everything we need to know. We just need a break, inspiration, something." Lyle got up. "I'll let you rest."

"Wait a minute. Tell me what you've got so far."

"You don't want to sleep?"

"Yeah, but just tell me, first."

"Okay." Lyle settled back in his chair and gave Rey a quick review of the Poole case, the suspects they'd talked to, and the theories he and Kate had debated. Rey closed his eyes but motioned for Lyle to continue.

"All right, I may as well tell you the latest on the Perez case." Lyle told Rey about the confusion with background checks and how he'd helped the sheriff keep Luis Nieto from leaving town.

"Nieto didn't do it," Rey said. "When he saw the body, he freaked. Couldn't stay at work." Rey opened his eyes and looked at Lyle.

"I finally figured that out, too."

"I've been lying here thinking about the cases." Rey closed his eyes.

Lyle explained his theorizing with Howard and how they'd heard Rey's radio call for help when they were leaving the security office. Rey didn't respond, so Lyle continued, recounting, with only a modicum of embarrassment, told how he'd seen Cody Hooper's truck at the NC garage and wound up arguing with him. Then he explained the results of Tiffany Smith's interrogation of Hooper. "Pretty stupid, huh?"

Rey didn't say anything.

"Rey?"

He opened his eyes. He spoke three sentences.

"How did I miss that?" Lyle said. "Oh shit. Of course."

Rey offered a wan smile, indicating either he was tired out or that his conclusion from the evidence Lyle presented was elementary. "There ya go," he whispered.

"This is just like Nero Wolf," Lyle said. "Ever read him? Years ago a mystery writer named Rex Stout wrote these novels where Wolf would sit in his apartment all day tending to his orchids while his sidekick Archie did all the leg work. Archie would come back, explain the case, and Wolf would tell him whodunit. Just like that. See what I mean? Rey?"

Lyle got up and tiptoed out. Walking back to his car, he looked at his watch. Not yet five o'clock. He'd wait until dark to confirm Rey's suspicions.

Chapter 61

"So you really don't want any streakers?"

"No," Kate said.

"Curtis from advertising suggested it. It *is* period-authentic," Drenda said, "approximately. Although it's popularity peaked in 1974, streaking continued throughout the decade."

Kate sat behind her desk, toying with a brass paperweight in the shape of a basketball hoop. "Well then, let Bill Curtis streak *his* naked butt across the park. Maybe that'll give him his jollies."

"Okay then," said Drenda, seated opposite Kate.

"Sorry, I don't mean to be bitchy, but that's a stupid idea. I'm sure Max would *love* to encourage our over-sixty visitors to strip naked and run around."

After the disappointing questioning of Dealey and Bellard, Kate visited her office for the first time that day to spend a couple of hours catching up on park business. If she focused on PR work, it might permit her cognitive functions to realign, jell, or do *something*.

"I don't see how you can concentrate," Drenda said. "*One* murder, then Mr. Poole. It's difficult to comprehend. I know you must be preoccupied, and I hate to bring these issues to you—"

"Don't worry about it. This is what I need—something else besides *death* for a few minutes."

Drenda wore a bell-sleeve jacket over a snug sheath dress. Cute, but out of the question for Kate. Drenda shopped in the petite department.

"Then we will exclude streaking as an element of the transition," Drenda said. "I'll be content to deliver that message to advertising. I have just a few more fundamentals to go over. You know the transition begins in two weeks."

"Yes. Too soon."

"About disco music."

"It's unavoidable," Kate said, "mandatory, even if our favorite DJ refuses to play it."

"Two of the hotels will have disco dance parties with house bands. The Centerville Tavern has already installed a disco ball."

"How about the CB radios for the rental cars?"

"Sensitive topic. Another grand idea that hasn't reached fruition. The garage is overworked at present. Getting newer cars rehabilitated is all they can handle."

"Maybe later," Kate said. "I always wondered who our guests would talk to anyway."

"Ten-four, good buddy." Drenda smiled. "A little idiosyncratic jargon from the period."

"Keep your ears on?"

"Very good. You weren't around then, either. I had to research this."

"I did look at your outline last night, too. Very thorough. As it should be, our *transition*—" Kate started to make air quotes then stopped herself. She took a breath, and started again. "This will be gradual, like real life."

Kate's desk phone buzzed.

"Were you expecting Detective Smith?" her secretary said.

"No, but tell her to wait just a second."

"We're done," Drenda said, picking up her tablet computer from the edge of Kate's desk and slipping it into a large leather purse. "If you get ideas about signage or anything, call me."

❦❦❦

"I just have a few questions," Detective Smith said when she sat in front of Kate's desk. "And the sheriff said I could pass along some information to see if you might be able to add anything." She paused a moment as if remembering something. "You know that Undersheriff Martinez has regained consciousness."

"I know. That's fantastic. How is he doing?"

"Very well. Looks like he'll make a full recovery."

Kate breathed a sigh of relief.

"Just a couple of items then," Smith said, "regarding two individuals."

"Go ahead."

"First, Persis Poole, Arthur Poole's ex-wife. You provided some information about her, and Undersheriff Martinez questioned her the day after the murder. We did a background check and found out she has a record going back to when she lived in Oregon." Smith flipped pages of her notepad. "It's a strange case. She was drunk and drove her car off a bridge into the Willamette River in Portland—fifty feet down to the water. Her name was Persis Jameson at the time. This was before she was married. The car hit the water and didn't sink right away. Two Portland officers happened to see the crash. They jumped into the river and pulled her out. She was lucky. Amazingly, she escaped with just cuts and bruises. But when they got her to safety, she *hit* one of the officers. She was that drunk. They arrested her on multiple charges. They still remember this case at the Portland PD. The officer I spoke to goes, 'Is that crazy bridge jumper in trouble again?' She had another DUI before this," Smith said. "After the bridge incident, she lost her license and got a suspended sentence."

"I wonder if Arthur knew about this," Kate said.

"She could have cleaned up her act before they got married then slipped back into it."

"Could be. Or maybe Arthur knew about her alcoholism and thought he could save her. He was like that. Apparently, they tried rehab, but it didn't take. Sometime after that, they got divorced."

"She blames her ex-husband for her problems."

"Yes, I know," Kate said. *Sounds like this warrants a talk with Persis.*

"Well, I came out to the park to talk with Bellard. I called his home but got no answer."

"Did you find out something about him?"

"Affirmative."

"I can tell you a few things about him, too," Kate said.

"I just finished going through Poole's office laptop and found out he was having troubles with Bellard."

"I'm not surprised. But of course Remo said everything was fine."

"I found notes about conversations Poole had with Bellard—Remo—about an idea to grow marijuana in a warehouse here in the park."

"Yes, they told me all about it," Kate said. "I can give you more details."

"Well, Poole recently decided against the project but found out that Bellard had been working on it anyway, when he should have been putting in hours at the store. He also thought Bellard was a little too cozy with Creston Dealey. I found a reprimand letter Poole gave him. I think he was working up to fire Remo."

Chapter 62

As night started to take over the Arizona desert, Lyle checked the magazine of his 9mm pistol. He stuck the gun in his waist holster and put on a light windbreaker. Rey knew Lyle's ideas about the Perez murder weren't crazy. And now Lyle would prove it.

As he drove toward Polk, Lyle turned on the radio and heard the Cornelius Brothers and Sister Rose doing "Treat Her Like a Lady." The song's rhythm and repetitious lyrics matched the thudding of his Mustang's tires bumping over pavement joints. He cruised by Cody Hooper's repair shop. Doors were closed, no lights burned in the office, and Lyle saw no one around.

Hooper's Auto Repair and Towing comprised two buildings, the main garage fronting on Agave Street and a warehouse at the rear. An alley separated the garage from the storehouse that backed up to Wheeler Lane, a block to the east. Lyle drove around the block and parked on Wheeler Lane near the back of the warehouse. A standard door and a metal roll-up faced Wheeler.

Lyle got out and tried the doors. Locked. A passageway between the warehouse and an adjoining building ran along the south side of the warehouse all the way to the alley. Lyle heard only the sound of his feet on the asphalt as he moved down the walkway. Shielded by shadows, he approached, step by cautious step. Halfway down the passageway, the building next to the warehouse ended at a parking lot, empty except for Hooper's tow truck. Lyle saw a standard door on the side of the warehouse. He continued to the alley where a wide, vehicle-size roll-up provided access to the warehouse from the alley.

Having seen no signs of a burglar alarm, Lyle decided to concentrate on the side door. One of the skills he acquired during his nearly twenty years on the Phoenix Police Department was lock picking. He never got good at it, but the lock on the warehouse side door looked pretty basic. Lyle got the door open without leaving a trace of his work.

With only moonlight filtered through dirty skylights for illumination, Lyle could make out a line of three cars along the wall near him. Rows of tall, sturdy metal shelves took up the center of the building, each shelf lined with bins and small boxes, probably where Hooper stored auto parts. Chain link fence with a gate isolated a corner of the building. Lyle pulled out his flashlight. The beam showed a desk, chair, metal storage cabinet, and a stack of cardboard boxes behind the fence. A combination lock secured the chain-link gate.

Lyle shined his light along the row of cars: one recent model, others about twenty years old. Not what he was looking for. Keeping his flashlight beam pointed down, he walked around the high rows of shelving toward the chain-link corner. The air smelled of dust and motor oil.

The sound of a car moving down the alley made Lyle shut off his light. The car slowed as it passed the building, but its sound soon faded. Lyle turned his light back on and directed the beam down the far side of the building. Stacks of tires stood in the distant corner next to a pickup camper shell. Closer to him sat low mounds of assorted car body parts, some covered with tarps.

Lyle's heart started beating faster. He crept toward the auto body parts with his light in front of him, his head bent. He laughed at himself. Why was he ducking down? No one could see him. He straightened up and ran his light along the edge of the high ceiling. He'd forgotten to look for surveillance cameras.

Apparently no one was spying on him so he picked his way through the automotive junk. He stopped at the first tarp-covered pile and lifted the canvass. Under the tarp Lyle saw the hood, grill, and front fenders of an old, red Chevy Monte Carlo. He'd found the drug-laden car that Hooper used his tow truck to steal from the transport trailer in Camp Verde. Obviously Hooper was cutting up the car to disguise and ultimately remove the evidence. Time to call the sheriff and get the hell out of there.

Before he reached for his cell phone, Lyle lifted the grill to confirm the Monte Carlo's logo. When he did, a metal bracket fell off and landed loudly on one of the fenders. Lyle heard something else. The echo of the bracket he dropped? He listened for a moment. At first he heard nothing, then the sound of feet running toward him. Lyle turned off his light, stuffed it in his pocket, and reached for his semi-auto. He could hear someone coming, but couldn't see anything. He dashed for cover, running in between the aisles of shelving, gripping his pistol. Foolishly perhaps, he had not kept a round chambered. So as quietly as he could, he pulled the slide back and let it slip forward until it clicked into place. Then he heard the distinctive sound of a shell being cycled into a pump-action shotgun. *Oh shit.*

"That you, Hooper?" Lyle said into the silence with bravado coming from God-knows-where. "I found the Monte Carlo. The sheriff'll be here any minute." *If I'd had time to call him.*

Lyle listened again. Someone with harder soled shoes than Lyle's was walking up the next aisle over. Lyle estimated he was a couple of steps ahead of whoever it was. He planned to stop at the end of the aisle and surprise the person when he stepped out from behind the shelves. Just as Lyle reached the end of the aisle, his pistol in front of him, he heard a noise from the other side of the building. Then a light flashed from outside and the door slammed. Lyle glanced in the other direction for just a moment. But it was enough time for the man with the shotgun to lurch around the corner and bring the shotgun barrel down on Lyle's arm.

In one second, Lyle's gun flew out of his hand and clattered on the floor. When Lyle raised both arms defensively, his assailant drove the shotgun barrel into his stomach. Lyle doubled over. When he choked down a breath and stood up, fluorescent lights blazed from above. Lyle knew the man pointing the short-barreled shotgun at his chest. The guy had a thin moustache under a slightly hooked nose and a scar running down his cheek. Even though the man wasn't wearing wraparound shades, Lyle recognized the Mexican cartel thug who chased him from Agua Prieta. The man smiled. Next to him stood NC mechanic Blake Alston, the man who had just rushed into the building. As the Mexican steadied the shotgun at Lyle, Alston bent over and picked up Lyle's pistol. He seemed unsure of what do with it at first, then he tucked it into his waistband.

"You don't know when to stay out of trouble, do you, señor?" the Mexican told Lyle. "Now we going to have to kill you."

"Why don't we take him out to the desert and do it there?" Alston said.

"Because Hooper and the shipment going to be here in ten minutes."

"But I thought—"

"You don't need to know everything." The man looked at Lyle. "You, on your knees."

Lyle had an idea what was going to happen next. He knelt on the concrete floor, looking at his executioner.

"He said he called the sheriff," the Mexican said, "but he's lying. He didn't have time. I heard him. He didn't talk to anyone. The man with the shotgun lowered the weapon as he pulled a small caliber pistol from his pocket. "This is untraceable. You can dump the body in the desert later."

The Mexican stepped behind him, and Lyle waited to feel the gun barrel at the back of his head.

Chapter 63

After more than an hour at her desk trying to focus on media relations but frequently drifting back to Dealey, Bellard, and the whole mess, Kate gave up. She called the sheriff's department to find out if Remo Bellard had been brought in for questioning. That information would have to come from the sheriff, she was told, and he was in a meeting. *Did Remo come up with an alibi? Was the investigation shifting to Persis Poole?*

Kate decided *she* needed to talk to Arthur's ex. Did Persis kill him because she blamed him for everything bad that happened to her? Because she thought she might inherit something?"

Lyle didn't answer his cell phone so Kate decided to head south and talk to Persis by herself. She had her address and phone number from Lyle's notes. Before she left, she called to make sure Persis would be home. She concocted a strange-sounding story about wanting to tell Persis about the park's retirement plan and Arthur's estate. Kate felt foolish for not coming up with a better excuse, but from the sound of Persis's voice, she was already half tanked and eager to hear anything about money.

As Kate cruised south down the interstate heading for Glendale, she listened to a Phoenix radio station.

"As the deadline nears for submission of voter initiatives to the secretary of state's office," the news announcer said,

"Creston Dealey, vice president of Consumer Cannabis, said he's confident his marijuana ballot measure will qualify for the general election.

"Campaigns to legalize marijuana have drawn criticism from local community leaders," the announcer said, "and from a California televangelist. Reverend Nathaniel Jameson has been holding a series of public meetings as part of his crusade through area cities. Tonight he's speaking at seven o'clock at Terrace High School in Phoenix. He's been stepping up his criticism of legalization advocates. He spoke yesterday at Desert Glory Church."

The announcer paused, then Kate heard the now-familiar voice of Reverend Nathaniel. "Pot is *already* in high schools, my friends. Why should it be made legal? Why should it be available everywhere? Why? Parents, the answer is *money*. Companies stand to make millions. These organizations don't care about your children. They're drug dealing devils who want to cash in at the expense of your kids..."

The words crashed out of the radio, but Kate stopped listening. She didn't need to hear any more. *Of course.* She almost slammed on the brakes, then she recovered and floored it, racing down the interstate. She called Lyle again. No answer. Then she made another call. She didn't know if she'd need help or what kind of help she'd need. She looked at the clock on the dashboard. Already after seven. She entered a destination in her car's navigation system and set her course. She'd be late. She hoped not too late.

A large building at the front of the Terrace High School campus looked like a theater. People were already coming out the exits and walking to the parking lot when Kate arrived. She parked in the first spot she could find and hurried toward the closest entrance. Near the building she sidestepped the flow of students and parents. The program had obviously drawn a large crowd.

She maneuvered her way through the busy foyer—everyone going in the opposite direction—and walked into the theater. Rows of seats sat empty. The stage held a few chairs arranged around a lectern. Standing in front of the stage to the right, at audience level, stood Reverend Nathaniel Jameson. He wore a dark robe and solemn expression as he talked with a student. Three others waited in line to see him. Kate walked down the left aisle, stopping short of the stage. The reverend stood with his back to her, speaking to a young man.

"I appreciate your being here tonight," Reverend Nathaniel said, "and remember, just say 'no' to pot and tell your parents they need to vote against drugs in your school."

The student thanked the reverend and they shook hands. Kate waited until the final student had talked to Reverend Nathaniel. As the last of his audience headed for the door, he unfastened the top buttons to his robe and turned to start up the short stairs to the stage.

"Did you tell them about the drug dealing devils tonight, Reverend?" Kate said. "Bad people like Arthur Poole?"

Reverend Nathaniel Jameson stopped on the first step and turned around. Kate could see a silky red tie where his robe fell open. "Well, good evening," he said. He ran a hand along the back of his head, brushing his flowing silver hair. "Did you hear my sermon?" He stepped off the stairs and smiled.

"No, I got here a bit late. I missed your performance. I'm sure you killed them."

"Pity. You see I simply tried to explain how decent, honest people should reject the spreading of drugs all over this wonderful state. They expressed their appreciation. But you mentioned Mr. Poole. Have the authorities had any luck in finding out what happened to him? Was the information we gave you of any help?"

Kate admired his composure. He spoke with concern he might show a troubled parishioner. "No, reverend, it didn't help at all. But what *was* a big help was finding out your daughter's maiden name: Jameson. Persis Jameson. And you called your son-in-law a drug-dealing devil."

Chapter 64

Lyle cringed. But the gun didn't fire. He heard a grunt and turned to see his would-be assassin on the ground, unconscious. Blake stood over him holding Lyle's semi-auto by the barrel.

"Thanks," Lyle said. "Are *you* going kill me now, or—"

"I'm an agent, DEA."

"I was hoping." Lyle stood up. "Now what?"

"We've got to get rid of him. *Did* you call the Sheriff?"

"No."

"Good, okay. He could mess things up here. But I have to call this in."

"Are you planning something?"

"Yeah, we were, but we didn't know when the shipment would arrive."

"Did you kill him?" Lyle said, looking at the man on the floor.

"I dunno. I had to hit him hard enough to stop him from shooting you."

Lyle reached down and felt for the gunman's carotid artery. "He's alive."

Alston looked around the warehouse. "Shit, we gotta do something. Can you drag him out that side door? I have to call."

Alston reached for his cell phone, then he and Lyle heard at least two vehicles pull up in the alley. In a moment, someone banged on the metal roll-up door.

"Just a second," Alston yelled. Then to Lyle, "Can you get this guy out of here and call the agency for me? Remember this number." He rattled off a phone number and Lyle repeated it aloud as he dragged the slightly built Mexican toward the door.

"Hey in there," said a voice from the alley.

"Coming," Alston replied.

At the side door, Alston helped Lyle lift the inert body over his shoulder. Fortunately, the cartel thug didn't weigh too much. As Lyle stumbled outside, he heard the motor lifting the warehouse door.

Lyle hurried down the passageway, reciting the DEA number in his head. When he reached Wheeler Lane, he peered up and down the street looking for movement. He saw no one so he staggered to his Mustang under the motionless weight of his captive. With only a little trouble, Lyle placed the man in the trunk of his car. The only thing Lyle found to secure the man to prevent him from causing trouble if he regained consciousness—which he doubted given his slack jaw and shallow breathing—was roll of electrical tape. Lyle used the whole roll to wrap up the man's hands and feet. He put strips across his mouth for good measure, made sure the man could breathe, then latched the trunk lid.

As he got in the car, he had his cell phone in hand and recorded the DEA emergency number in his contacts list. Then he called the sheriff.

"How many of them are there?" Sheriff Wisniewski asked after Lyle had explained the situation.

"I don't know, but I can find out."

"Don't you do something stupid that will tip them off."

"I already got *that* out of my system. A cartel soldier almost put a bullet in the back of my head. Now he's in the back of my car."

"Okay, Deming, we'll pick him up later. Now go over the layout with me again then get the hell out of there."

Lyle reviewed the various entrances to the warehouse and reminded Wisniewski not to shoot Alston. The sheriff said he would respond with as many deputies as he could muster.

"What about calling DEA?" Lyle said. "I have a special number."

"I've got their numbers. Leave that to me." The sheriff hung up.

The sheriff's impromptu raid would be risky at best. Lyle wished he could tell the sheriff exactly what to expect. It would improve the odds for the deputies. He drove around the corner and stopped in the alley two blocks from the garage and storehouse. With his gun returned to its holster, he walked along the side of the alley, listening with every step. Light spilled into the alley from the wide roll-up door and three vehicles bunched up in front of the storehouse. Lyle could hear but a faint hum of voices. As he got closer, he saw someone guarding the entrance. A man carrying a gun with a long magazine stepped out the door and looked up and down the alley. Lyle froze against a wall. The man walked back inside.

Lyle hurried across the parking lot adjacent to the warehouse and approached the door he had opened before. Still unlocked. Lyle opened the door a crack and squinted through the opening. When he didn't see any movement, he pushed the door open and crept inside.

Voices came from the front corner of the building. As he moved forward, Lyle was shielded by the rows of industrial shelving. As he got closer, he could look between the containers and auto parts on an upper shelf. He saw five—no six—men gathered at the front of the warehouse. The gate to the area fenced-off with chain link stood open and two men sat inside. Stacks of plastic-wrapped packages—likely cocaine—covered the desktop. One man wearing a baseball cap on backward sat facing Lyle. Squinting, Lyle could make out an unusually shaped stain on the back of the hat. Below the hat Lyle saw the face of Cody Hooper. The other man, heavy set with light red hair, sat with his back to Lyle, counting the packages and placing them in cardboard boxes. Periodically Hooper, wearing a Batman T-shirt, paused to refer to a sheaf of papers. Two other men stood talking. Alston leaned against the edge of the open door to the alley, talking to the guard Lyle had seen. The guard carried some form of submachine gun.

Both of the two men standing had pistols tucked into their waistbands. Lyle moved closer—as close as he dared—to see if he could spot any more weapons. As he drew up behind the end of the row of shelving, his leg nudged a cardboard box that teetered and fell to the floor. Lyle held his breath.

"What was that?" said one of the men standing outside the fenced area.

"Probably Pedro," said another man, "he's guarding the back door."

"Or Julio," said another. "He was supposed to be here first. Where is he?"

Lyle now knew the name of the guy in his trunk. He also knew someone was guarding the rear door. He took a quick look at the scene in front of him and saw no other weapons. He started to back his way out of the building when the man packing the drugs with Hooper stood up and turned around. Niles "Dutch" DeGroot.

"What's happening," DeGroot said.

One of the other men waved him off and he went back to stacking drugs.

As soon as he was outside, Lyle headed down the passageway to Wheeler Street. The rear door to the storehouse was closed. Was Pedro waiting just inside with a gun? Lyle turned when he heard a car crossing a side street. The star on the door told Lyle the posse had arrived.

He trotted down to the cross street on the balls of his feet. When he turned the corner he ran right into a deputy holding a semi-auto.

"Whoa," Lyle said and immediately put up his hands. "I'm Lyle Deming. I called the sheriff about this."

"It's okay," said another deputy behind the first one. Lyle recognized Sergeant Keith Galton.

"I just came from the warehouse," Lyle said. "They're repacking the drugs. There's seven of them, including one guy at the back door on Wheeler Street." He pointed toward the corner. "If you give me a pad I can draw you a quick map."

Lyle sketched the layout of the warehouse, showing where he last saw everyone, including Alston. "Here's the alley," he said, pointing to his drawing. "If you put cars at each end, here and here, you can block them. Their cars are parked in the alley." As he explained the weapons he'd seen, more sheriff's cars rolled up.

"I thought I told you to stay the hell away," Sheriff Wisniewski said jumping out of his cruiser.

"He's showing us the layout and what weapons they have," Sergeant Galton said.

Wisniewski looked at Lyle's sketch. "This will help. Now where's this DEA agent?"

Lyle spoke to the sheriff and the deputies who had gathered around. "Alston is blond, about thirty—maybe younger—and about this tall." Lyle gestured. "He's wearing a light blue, short-sleeved shirt. No one else has a shirt that color." He explained where he'd last seen him and added, "He's expecting a raid, but from DEA, not you."

"We'll handle it," Wisniewski said. "Now you get the hell out of the way."

Lyle gave the sheriff a mock salute and turned to go. As he did, an SUV unit rolled up and more deputies piled out. They wore helmets, bullet-proof vests, and carried rifles.

Lyle looked back at the sheriff.

"Overwhelming force," Wisniewski said.

Chapter 65

Reverend Jameson stared at Kate. He lowered his heavy brows turning his benevolent expression into one of apprehension or was it malice? "What do you want?"

"You didn't tell the sheriff that Arthur was your ex-son-in-law," Kate said, "did you?"

"I never talked with the sheriff in your town." He smiled now, standing at the base of the high school stage stairs, but the look gave Kate chills. She took a half step back. "But I met with law enforcement here in the Phoenix area. We discussed the rampant use of marijuana and how it can be discouraged. And we all agree stricter enforcement is paramount." He straightened his clerical robe on his shoulders. "So you see, law enforcement knows me. We're working together. As for this unfortunate Poole situation, you should leave that to the authorities. That would be best, don't you agree?"

The reverend gave Kate one more look then stepped back on the stairs.

Before he could take two steps, a short young woman appeared behind him. She wore a white blouse and short skirt. "Reverend Nathaniel," she said in a squeaky voice, "your talk was, ah, so inspiring."

Reverend Nathaniel turned. "How kind of you," he said,

stepping off the stairs again. "Were your parents here with you tonight?"

"No, they couldn't make it," she said, looking up into the reverend's face, then staring down at her shoes. "I just, well, I wanted to tell you I will remember everything you said tonight."

"Thank you," he said, touching the girl's shoulder. "You don't have to be shy. I'm glad you liked my sermon and please be sure to tell you parents about how important their vote is."

The girl nodded.

"And tell your teachers, too."

"I will," she said as she backed up slowly, smiling up at the reverend.

As the girl stepped away, Reverend Nathaniel turned back toward the stage stairs and mounted them two at a time.

Kate followed.

"So, you know some Phoenix cops, Reverend. Maybe they'll come watch your murder trial."

Reverend Nathaniel picked up papers off the lectern and walked toward a row of side curtains that sheltered the theater wings. He stepped between two curtains then looked over his shoulder. "You still here? You ought to take your misguided ideas back to the theme park. It's make-believe too." He took determined steps away from her, apparently looking for something.

Kate steeled herself and followed him, stride for stride. He stopped at a table holding an old-style leather briefcase and a four-inch thick Bible covered with gold scrollwork. Turning his back to Kate, Reverend Jameson unbuttoned his robe and folded it on the table. "I need to leave now. We have nothing more to discuss."

"Yes, we do," Kate said. "I'd like to know why you killed my friend Arthur. Did you know that he did everything he could to help Persis? But Persis didn't want help. She just wanted money. And you blamed *Arthur* for her addiction? She had a problem long before she met Arthur. She got drunk and crashed into the river in Portland where you used to live."

Kate could see his reaction, the muscles tightening in his powerful shoulders. She continued talking to his back. "You moved down to southern California and somehow became this big TV preacher. Sanctimonious, self-righteous." Now confronting the horror that took her dear friend's life, Kate couldn't stop. "With those millions you made preaching the gospel did you get help for Persis? Did you care? Or did you just dole out a little money when she begged you so she'd go away?"

Reverend Jameson turned around, his face colored with anger. "You don't know my daughter. Arthur, my former son-in-law, abandoned her. She even came to this forsaken desert to be with him and he turned his back on her. He was supposed to be a male nurse. He violated his oath."

"*His* oath?" Kate stepped toward the reverend. "You got your start preaching in the Pacific Northwest where I met Arthur. My mother was hospitalized in Portland. This person you called a drug dealing devil looked after her for months when she was in and out of the hospital. He showed kindness, tenderness, and empathy. Are you familiar with those qualities?"

"How dare you speak to me that way? Arthur brought this on himself." He clenched his fist then jabbed a finger in the air at Kate. "Not only did he damage my daughter irreparably, he once called my campaign a sham. All he wanted was to spread his drug culture."

"So you killed him."

Reverend Jameson stared at Kate for a moment then turned and put his papers and his Bible in his case. "My cause is moral, Miss Sorensen," he said, latching the top of the case. He picked it up by the handle, then spun around—and swung the case at Kate's head.

She saw it coming and jerked backward but not in time to avoid a glancing blow. She staggered back, almost falling, then knelt on one knee, her head exploding with pain. Blood trickled down her cheek. But she didn't move. She breathed rapidly through her nose as the reverend loomed over her. "You killed him," she said.

"But you'll never prove it. It was an accident. I meant to get his attention. He wasn't listening, just like you." Reverend Jameson held the case in front of him, his arms shaking, his jaw tight. "I told him Persis was his responsibility. He got her into it. He made her unstable. You know that."

"You killed Arthur because he didn't *listen* to you?" Kate wiped the blood from her face with the back of her hand and touched the floor to steady herself. "If it was an accident, why did you wipe your fingerprints off everything and leave him to die?"

"I prayed for him," he said. "We can only hope he will find salvation." The reverend looked almost tranquil now as he raised the heavy case above his head—then froze.

The young woman he'd been talking with minutes earlier stepped from around a side curtain. She looked like an average high school student except for her penetrating stare and the Beretta pistol she pointed at Reverend Jameson.

"Reverend," Kate said. "Meet Detective Tiffany Smith."

Chapter 66

Lyle jogged around the block back to his car. He got in and saw a sheriff's cruiser parked diagonally across the alley, 200 feet in front of him. A deputy stood next to the car. Looking down the alley, he thought he saw another sheriff's car, similarly parked, on the other side of the warehouse. He hoped his directions for the sheriff would give the deputies an advantage.

The single burst of an automatic weapon's fire resounded down the alley. A volley of individual shots followed—then silence. Lyle sat in his car, gripping the steering wheel. Waiting. Minutes passed without a sound. Lyle hoped it meant the deputies had surprised the drug dealers. He could imagine the guard with the submachine gun lying on the floor with the rest of the gang standing with hands in the air, Sheriff Jeb Wisniewski barking orders.

Pulsing strobe lights on top of the vehicle speeding down the alley toward him broke his reverie. Blinding high beams kept Lyle from identifying the car. The flashing lights shone yellow. Not a sheriff's car.

The deputy next to the sheriff's car blocking the alley in front of Lyle fired two shots at the advancing vehicle then dived out of the way. The truck crashed in to the black and white's rear fender.

The sheriff's car slammed against a building and Cody Hooper's tow truck raced by. The truck turned onto the next street with a squeal of rubber and clang of metal as a loose chain banged the side of the wrecker.

Lyle fired up his engine and instead of trying to turn around in the alley, he jammed the Mustang into reverse and floored it. With a tire-burning screech, the car rocketed backward until it hit the street. Lyle swung the wheel to the left, then threw the floor shift into drive and raced after the tow truck.

Hooper's two-block lead evaporated in a half mile as Lyle's V-8 pushed his car to seventy miles per hour in seconds. *Hooper has no chance. He's desperate, dangerous.* Lyle anticipated Hooper's next move—almost too late. With Lyle closing on the truck's tail, Hooper slammed on his brakes.

Lyle saw the brake lights and knew he didn't have time to stop. He swerved to the right and crushed the brake pedal at the same time. His left front fender scraped the truck's tail with a high-pitched sound that made Lyle clench his teeth. As the wrecker accelerated away, Lyle wanted to pull out his pistol and fire. But they had entered a residential neighborhood, and Lyle didn't want a shot to go astray.

Hooper apparently had no such compunction because he reached out the window holding a gun and fired in the general direction of Lyle's car. While trying to control a careering tow truck, he had little chance of hitting the Mustang. The reckless shots, however, angered Lyle and he pulled up to the truck again.

Hooper stopped shooting and turned sharply right, light from his flashing amber beacons bouncing off mail boxes and homes, announcing his presence in the tree-lined street. Lyle stayed close—but not too close—and pondered what to do. After three blocks he saw red and blue lights in his rearview. A sheriff's car had joined the chase. Perhaps other deputies would be blocking the roads ahead.

In the next block, Hooper started to turn left, but his top-heavy vehicle couldn't remain upright at that speed. As the truck started to tip, Hooper over corrected. The tow truck wavered but remained upright, jumped a curb, and crashed through a fire hydrant at forty miles per hour. The truck raced across a lawn and dived into a double garage door. The door buckled backward as Hooper's truck compressed it into a car parked inside the garage. The sound of a thirty-foot-high tower of gushing water dampened the explosion of metal on metal as Hooper's wrecker came to a stop.

Lyle steered around the rushing fountain and pulled to the curb. He jumped out, reaching for his gun. The flying water obscured his view of the garage momentarily. At the same time, a sheriff's car screeched to a halt just before the water spray. A deputy got out, his weapon drawn, and took a position behind the front fender of his car. Surviving the crash, Hooper fired at the black and white from somewhere in the garage. A second sheriff's cruiser arrived and pulled up next to the first one. Two deputies now exchanged shots with Hooper.

The garage of the 1960s ranch house sat at the far end of the home from Lyle's position. Several mature trees grew in the front yard and a row of shrubs seemed to mark the property line to the right. Lyle dashed along the bushes and came to a wooden gate providing access to the back yard. It clicked open and Lyle ran across the back of the house to the garage. The crash hadn't penetrated the rear garage wall. A backyard door to the garage stood open. Lyle crouched and stepped in.

The front of the homeowner's sedan had been pushed into storage cabinets that kept it from knocking out the rear wall. Cabinet doors, broken shelves, and household goods covered the car's hood. The garage door covered the rest of the car. Hooper's truck sat halfway in and out of the garage, its pulsing amber beams flashing like macabre disco lights illuminating the scene of twisted metal.

A deputy fired a shot and Lyle saw Hooper duck behind his truck's bent driver's door. Lyle didn't have a clear shot at Hooper so he started to back out of the garage, the better to avoid being plugged by a deputy. At that moment, Hooper turned, looking for a way out. He saw Lyle, spun, and fired.

The shot hit the back of the garage.

Outside, Lyle dashed over to a low block wall that outlined a patio. Hooper followed. With seemingly no fear, Hooper advanced on Lyle. Blood, either from the crash or a sheriff's deputy's bullet, streamed down from under Cody Hooper's cap and his left arm hung loose at his side. He held his large-caliber revolver in his right. As Hooper stepped closer, Lyle squatted behind the wall and aimed at Hooper's chest. Hooper fired first.

Click.

Hooper swore and pulled the trigger again and again with the same result. He stood there firing his empty gun as Lyle got up and wrestled him to the ground then called in the deputies.

"I told you to stay the hell away," Sheriff Wisniewski said minutes later.

"You're welcome," Lyle said.

Across the front yard, Hooper sat on the tailgate of an ambulance while EMTs checked him. One deputy sat next to him, a hand clamped on Hooper's good arm. A second deputy stood watch, hand on holster.

"How'd he get away?" Lyle asked the sheriff

"He must have gone outside looking for something just before we rushed in. That agent, Alston, spotted him but he got away before we could grab him."

"How'd it go down? Anybody hurt?"

"Yeah, some guy with a KG-Nine. He only had time to rattle off one burst with that thing. Got our attention right away. We took him down quick and the rest of them were too surprised to do much."

"I didn't know you had a SWAT team."

"We don't. I called out every reserve officer I have and borrowed deputies from Yavapai County. We never needed to mount an attack like this before. Fortunately, none o' my guys got hurt."

"Alston okay?"

"Yeah, he knew someone was comin' so he was ready to get out of the way. He said DeGroot was the top dog here in Polk. Got hired on at the park so they could use the beat up cars you import from Mexico to run drugs. DeGroot shut up and just kept calling for an attorney."

"Did you know about the video," Lyle said, "of the guy in the hat coming out of the NC garage after the Perez murder?"

"I read about it in Rey's report. There's a picture in the file."

Lyle gestured toward the ambulance. "Hooper's cap. By killing Perez, Hooper ended the blackmail—"

"And," the sheriff said, "he made sure everyone on the garage floor was too scared to say anything—to anyone."

"Did you call the feds?"

"Yeah."

"Did you gloat?"

"I don't do gloat. We just did our jobs tonight. As it turned out, I think they were kinda grateful we were there to save their guy. They couldn't have put anything together tonight before the drugs were on their way to Phoenix, LA, or wherever. I'd say we picked up a haul worth maybe eight figures."

Jurisdictional peace reigns. Lyle wandered over to his car and examined the front fender. He ran his finger along a nine-inch scar scraped down to the bare metal. When he heard sounds coming from the trunk, he remembered his reluctant passenger.

"Sheriff," Lyle said walking back to the ambulance, "I forgot. You were supposed to relieve me of the guy in my trunk. The one who tried to kill me."

"Oh, yeah. Alston said something about that. Let's go take a look."

Before he followed the sheriff to his car, Lyle walked over to Hooper. His head and arm now bandaged, deputies were putting him in cuffs.

"Say, Cody," Lyle said. "My Mustang's a little scratched up. Can I bring it into your shop tomorrow?"

Chapter 67

Tent cards on the tables said, "Welcome to 1980." Plastic Pac Man tokens served as place-setting souvenirs. The disc jockey at the front of the banquet room played Olivia Newton-John's "Magic." Dinner dishes already cleared, some people lingered at their tables, others stood near the bar or the dance floor talking in small groups. Recent deaths and incidents of violence dampened the mood and transformed what had been intended as the Transition Celebration into a subdued gathering for park executives. In a few days, the public would see the TV commercials proclaiming Nostalgia City's transformation into a town from the eightieth year of the twentieth century.

"I believe the TV announcements overly concentrate on the modifications we've made to encompass 1980," Drenda said. She and Kate sat alone at a banquet table sipping their coffee. "For example, in 1980 the vast majority of cars on the road were from the early- or mid-1970s to the late 1960s—and older. In 1980, buildings in most small towns similar to ours dated back to the 1920s and thirties."

"The commercials *are* overblown," Kate said, "but your subtle changes in the park are just the right touch to move Nostalgia City's timeline up five years. Our baby boomers, our senior visitors will find lots of good memories here. But now slightly younger guests will find reminders of their youth."

"Sorry to be going on about this," said the senior vice president of history and culture. "You're the one who has been through the real emotional upheaval the past weeks."

Kate touched the bandage on her head. "Upheaval's a good word. I don't know how I let that reverend catch me off guard. Thankfully, Tiffany was there. She'll get credit for his arrest. It will help her career."

"Killing his own former son-in-law," Drenda said. "The hatred must have run deep."

"A mixed up, dysfunctional family, the Jamesons. Poor Arthur. He fell in love and must have thought he could help Persis change."

"He never mentioned to you that this Reverend Jameson was his ex-father in law?"

"No," Kate said. "It never came up. Arthur was a private person. He didn't burden you with complaints. And I never talked to him again after Reverend Jameson showed up at that Polk community meeting. I didn't even know about Arthur's ex-wife's problems until I heard her arguing with him at his Xanadu office one day."

"I'm so sorry you lost your friend," Drenda said. "Do you think you'll keep working on his marijuana proposition?"

"Arthur was the brains and heart behind the Safe Weed Project. In order to get on the ballot now, we'd have to hire campaign firms to collect signatures. No one is willing to put up the money. Max is ready to let it drop."

"Does that other pot proposition have a chance?"

"I doubt it. Arthur told several people in the pot community that if his ballot measure didn't make it, he would oppose Consumer Cannabis because the company wants to monopolize the pot market and restrict access. It's been in the news."

Kate toyed with one of the Pac Man tokens and stared across the room at Lyle. He stood next to an empty table, drink in hand, talking to Howard Chaffee.

Drenda followed Kate's gaze. "Are you and he, ah…"

"Lyle? Oh, you could say we're ah."

※ ※ ※

"Lots more paperwork and court filings ahead," Howard said, "but I'm glad to have the dark days behind us."

"I think the park will bounce back," Lyle said. "Kate'll see to that." He put his drink down on a nearby table so he could pick up his dessert plate and fork a bite of chocolate cake into his mouth.

"When you look back on everything, the evidence was there," Howard said. "The trail led from Perez to his wife, to Luis, to the stolen Chevy Monte Carlo, to Guerra in Mexico, and on to Hooper and DeGroot." He leaned over and picked up his coffee cup. "Wish I could have put it all together at the time."

Lyle started to talk, but had to pause to swallow a second forkful of cake. "But you figured out about the mole in the garage."

"Yes, but I could have looked at Alston harder, focused more on the conflicting information on his background. I thought it was maybe a data mistake instead of the DEA's plan."

"Yeah, Alston said his boss realized that someone in the cartel might be able to check his background. So the feds created his criminal record *after* he went to work at the NC garage, just in case."

"And the DEA didn't come back after the botched raid," Howard said taking a thoughtful sip of coffee, "even after the murder."

"Alston didn't know the cartel was going to kill Perez. He tried to find out who did it but without jeopardizing his cover because the DEA wanted to arrest as many members as possible—"

"And trace the drugs back to the source."

"Risky strategy the way they stretched it out," Lyle said,

"but it worked—with a little help from the sheriff."

"This way they were able to arrest the two other NC garage employees—in addition to Hooper and Dutch—who were also dirty."

"The futile DEA raid almost wrecked everything," Lyle said. "That Phoenix supervisor got a bad tip and obviously he was on his own crusade and wasn't coordinating with Alston's team."

"What about Mrs. Perez?"

"Of course she wasn't involved, but there was more to it. Her husband's death didn't completely surprise her. She suspected he was involved in *something*."

Howard finished his coffee. "I guess Luis finally decided to talk."

"Took him a long time. The sheriff had to prove to him that the drug gang was behind bars. They even needed the county's consulting shrink to talk to him. He still gets the shakes, but I think he'll decide to be a witness. It was Luis who put that note on the sheriff's deputy's car."

"I didn't know about that."

"Oh, right after the murder, a deputy on patrol in Polk found a note on his windshield that said Perez's death wasn't an accident."

"That was easy to figure."

Lyle grunted in agreement as he finished his cake.

"All in all, you get credit for solving this," Howard said, "for figuring out about Hooper, the tow truck, the stolen Monte Carlo, the load of dope. And at the same time, Kate figured out who killed Poole."

"Yes, she did," Lyle said looking across the room at Kate. "But I didn't solve the murder and drug case."

"No?"

"Sure, I went off half-cocked about Hooper. I thought he was a crook—because he f-ed up my car and charged me for it. It threw me at first when Gayle said that no one ever had a bad word to say about Hooper."

"That's because they were all scared shitless of him."

"Right, but it was Rey who put it all together."

"Rey?"

"Lying there in his hospital bed, his head jolted and jumbled from a collision with a truck, Rey sorted it out. Someone stole the old drug-loaded Monte Carlo off the transport. The car didn't run. Didn't even roll too well. Had to be someone with a tow truck to haul it out of there quickly. And Rey saw that Hooper had escaped the interrogations because he only worked part-time in the NC garage. When I saw him in the hospital, Rey told me all this and suggested I check out Hooper's facility, see what I could find."

Howard knotted his forehead. "Rey, huh?"

"Yup. He even guessed right that one of the mechanics started the divorce rumor after Perez's death to try to confuse the investigation."

"How's Rey doing now that he's out of the hospital?"

"He's going back to work next week. Except for a blank spot in his memory when he was clobbered—and a broken arm that's healing—he's doing well."

"For a while I thought he—"

"Was a lightweight? I told you."

"I know. I'll have to go see him, see how he's doing."

"I guess nobody ever found Tony Guerra," Lyle said.

"His family relocated. Maybe he escaped with them. The park hired another guy to scrounge cars." Howard set his coffee cup down and picked up his suit coat from the back of a chair. "This party's more like a wake. I'm going to find my wife and take her home."

As Howard left, Lyle wandered over to Kate's table and stood behind her. He smiled at Drenda then put his hands on Kate's shoulders and squeezed. She leaned her head back and looked up at him.

"You guys enjoying yourselves?" he said. "Or rehashing the insane preacher's secret life."

"More like the latter, I'm afraid," Kate said. "I thought he was a pretentious jerk, but I overlooked him as a suspect."

"Until you found out he was Persis's father, there's no way you could have known," Lyle said. "Who would suspect a preacher?"

"Sad but true, I guess. Even his secretary, who had been with him for a year, didn't know about Persis."

"The only thing he is going to be praying for now," Drenda said, "is a nonviolent cellmate."

Kate nodded at Drenda then looked back up at Lyle. "You ready to leave?"

"Almost," he said, squeezing Kate again. "Just give me a couple of minutes." He moved to Kate's side, leaned over, kissed her on the cheek, then strolled to the front of the room.

"How you doin' tonight, Earl."

"Y'know, mellow, baby." Earl Williams placed the tone arm on a record and Captain and Tennille started, "Do That To Me One More Time."

"Nice of you to provide the entertainment for the transition gala."

"Least I could do for what you guys been through."

"It's over."

"Did the park ever sue the feds for trashing that car they busted up looking for drugs?"

"No idea. Maybe they'll forget it. A lawsuit would just remind everyone about the drugs."

"How you and your girlfriend doin'?"

"She's the reason I got in here tonight. The senior management list doesn't include cab drivers. I'm her date."

"That's not 'zactly what I meant." He pointed to Kate's table. "I saw you two over there. I thought you didn't want anyone to know."

"We really don't. Is it obvious?"

"You're looking good, Mr. Deming."

"And you, my friend, played a couple of disco songs tonight. I thought you refused."

"Oh, well. Some o' that stuff's not too bad. Barry White, Village People, some others."

"Abba?"

"Maybe."

"Kate and I are leaving, but I should tell you that it doesn't look good for the pot propositions. You may have to stick with your supplier."

"No problem, bro," Earl said.

"So *that's* why you're mellow tonight."

ACKNOWLEDGEMENTS

Many thanks to Lauri Wellington, Faith, and the entire team at Black Opal Books for helping make this book a reality.

In addition, many other people helped make this book possible. I'm indebted to the members of my critique group: Barbara Ristine, Christine Smith, Lynda Bailey, and Barbara J. Smith who spotted difficulties, prodded, and helped polish this along the way. Beta readers contributed much and kept me on my toes during revisions. Thanks to Michael Thomas, Les Cohen, Jane Gorby, Craig Holland, Mary Piper, and Peggy Ezidro. Christel Hall's editing skills were invaluable, as usual. And thanks to Carol Coleman for proofing help.

For technical help with law enforcement and automotive subjects, I thank Joe Toft, Detective Dustin Dodd, and Bill Fogel. Any errors are mine, not theirs.

I'd also like to acknowledge my late friend, artist and writer James McCormick, who let me borrow the character name Creston Dealey from one of his flash fiction stories. Thanks Jim.

I salute my writer friends, some of whom belong to the Sacramento Chapter of Sisters in Crime, for their encouragement and support. And, as always, I thank my wife for her love and for putting up with me.

Note from the author

Thanks for reading my book. If you enjoyed this, please consider writing a short review on any book website you like to use. Reviews help writers many ways, ultimately allowing us to write more for you. If you would like to contact me or find out more about my other books, please visit my website: https://baconsmysteries.com

About the Author

Mark S. Bacon began his career as a Southern California newspaper police reporter, one of his crime stories becoming key evidence in a murder case that spanned decades. After working for two newspapers, he moved to advertising and marketing when he became a copywriter for Knott's Berry Farm, the large theme park down the road from Disneyland. Experience working at Knott's formed part of the inspiration for his creation of Nostalgia City theme park.

Before turning to fiction, Bacon wrote business books including *Do-It-yourself Direct Marketing*, printed in three editions, four languages, named best business book of the year by *Library Journal*, and selected by the Book of the Month Club and two other book clubs. His articles have appeared in the *Washington Post*, *Cleveland Plain Dealer*, *San Antonio Express News*, *The Denver Post*, *Orange Coast*, and many other publications. Most recently he was a correspondent for the *San Francisco Chronicle*.

The Marijuana Murders is the third book in the Nostalgia City Mystery series that began with *Death in Nostalgia City*. The first book introduced ex-cop-turned-cab-driver Lyle Deming and PR executive Kate Sorensen, a former college basketball star. *Death in Nostalgia City* was recommended for book clubs in 2019 by the American Library Association, and *Desert Kill Switch*, the second book in the series, was the top fiction entry in the 2018 Great Southwest Book Festival. Bacon is working on mystery number four.

He is also the author of flash fiction mystery books including, *Cops, Crooks and Other Stories in 100 Words*. He and his wife, Anne, live in Reno with their golden retriever, Willow.